The Dark Chronicles

An erotic telling of the Arthurian myth

A. A. Cain

Copyright © 2019 by A. A. Cain

Published by: A.A.Cain, PO Box 117, Campbelltown, South Australia, 5074.

Email: writingbyaacain.gmail.com

First Edition: 2019

ISBN:

epub   978-0-9876330-0-2

pdf   978-0-9876330-4-0

print   978-0-9876330-2-6

Cover art by Michelle Tocilj   www.tociljdesigns.de

Contents

The Dragen Awakens

I was there.

The day the earth roared louder than thunder, and ash and floating rock fell into the sea all around the ship, and the sea rose and dropped five huge times, I was there.

The voyage had been long, south down the long coast of Shi, aboard a tall ship made by the Emperor, three galleys high and two sails wide, his gift for my voyage. I made the Emperor a map when I returned from the mountain gone from the sea, and that was my gift in return and my thanks.

"I did not know other kings' lands lay beyond the frozen mountains and long deserts; these are not my people," he said, as he marvelled upon the map. "How many years did you say, travelling here?"

Two hundred men rowed when the air was still and the ship made head to the south. I had heard tell of the smoking island; captains and commanders sailing up from the south, from Banteen and Baatuwara, landed and told stories in the ports, and they were always the same, these stories.

"High from the sea," they told. "The mountain grows high from the sea, the height of two tall men each year."

The stories made me curious and I thought upon brother Plinius and his boat, and the cloud rolling down the high mountain that he saw, swift as water and dreadful, both cities gone and the earth all alive.

This was a bigger dragen coiled in rock and fire, molten rock in its blood and smoken ash in its breath. I was curious and made my way south.

"We will stay on the water," the captain said, "and not make landfall there. The craft will be safe, but the shore is not safe."

The commander I found to discover the place was the sixth seaman in a long line and his greatest scare was to sail close to the land.

"I'll not do it," he said. "I'll sail off the shore the distance where the mountains are small and far away." He was certain. "My grandfather taught me this, and his grandfather before him." I trusted him, and the ship turned once around the mountain, so I could see with mine own eyes that the stories were true.

The mountain was tall, perfectly shaped like the high Fuuj near the castle of Prince Shotogku in Japon, but the top was rock and rubble, not snow, and I could see with my eyes that no bush or grass or tree grew there. Smoke rose, a straight long column climbed high into the sky until the wind and the clouds tore it apart.

"You see it, sire, and I wish it behind us."

The captain's nervousness crept upon me, and I am used to rooks and ravens and tall stones and do not get nerves. But even I could feel the low breath upon the air, beneath our hearing all a giant throb upon the water, strange ripples shimmering in circles on the surface of the sea.

"See it, sire, and we shall make our way off. There are no birds here and the fish are gone too. Let us not stay long."

The captain was nervous, and I shared it, so we made our way off, until the top of the mountain only could be seen, the horizon a long darkness against the westering sun, and the cap smoking there, its long thread climbing highest to the sky, and lingering up high, threading smoke through the finest clouds like sand in a stream.

That night, a storming rain surrounded the ship and the clouds dropped low. The captain kept small sails aloft so the ship could still make head, but its movement in the water was slow, just enough to steer. The captain kept towards morning, and the sea shuddered and pulsed beneath the hull, and far off from the land we could hear low groans and echoes. Nobody knew the meaning of the sound, it was uncertain and unregular.

"Look toward the west, sire, I think the dragen awakens and we might see it roar."

In the galley and on the poop, the men were hushed and low songs began. These men had no words on their fingers, no pens, but with their songs and stories the remembering began, and the tells would pass down from father to son. Just like in my home land, but the longest trails there sing from mother to daughter. It is different here; I am not so familiar with it.

"Look, sire, the sky is strange."

It was low dawn and the cloud was lifted. To the east, the sun was just shimmering on the horizon, and in the opposite place the coiling high smoking column threaded red and twisting black, so we knew that it moved and spun from the ground, reaching higher for the air than before, thrust upwards in a massive force. The column was thicker, too, pulsed red with coiling veins standing thick and twisting.

The captain looked at me, a wry smile on his face. "Where is the dragen's woman, sire, that he stands so hard?"

I laughed, and looked to the sky, but there was no Goddess there, not that night.

"He is waking on his own, then, this dragen. The earth is no different from us mortal men, it seems, standing hard in the morn."

Our light comedy betrayed a fear that was in us both, and the words were repeated by the men to ease their waiting dread. There was laughter from the fore deck and jealous jesting, as one of the young sailors stood high on the rigging and jetted a long golden arc to the sea, his prick thick and hard in his hand, making proof of our observation.

"That boy will please his maiden, when we next make port," I smiled, my own morning glory a softer thing now, for I am old already.

"Or a man, to be fucked by that," mused the captain. "Indeed, a man too would enjoy that length."

"No different than a mortal woman, then," I replied.

"Or your Goddess," said the captain, for I had shared with him some of the hidden beliefs of my distant isle, slumbering since the centurions came and their long walls built.

I thought to return there soon, but my curiosity always kept me wandering. Always under the same stars though, always under the same stars and the light of the moon. This night, the moon was full and glowed high in the brightening morning sky.

Our low words between us were but waiting. The captain and I both knew, and all the men too, that we would go from this day with a tale of a thousand tellings. Witness the distant land and the thick water beneath our ship, keeping us safe above the rock and ground. Some last instinctive nervousness moved upon the captain, and he called for twenty oars to turn the head of the ship to face the mountain and its breath, coiling thicker now and pluming up like a giant mushroom top widening the sky. The world panted, a low grumbling through the air and it was like distant thunder but constant, a moan, a groan.

"Your ears men, keep your hands over your ears as best you can," the captain called, and his leftenants repeated his warning to all the men. And now the sound was louder still and we could not hear our voices.

"Sire," I could see the captain's lips move. And he pointed.

Of a sudden, I saw the base of the horizon where the sky touched the sea and the land and where the smoke was a single column; I saw the blackness and grumbling smoke suddenly grow wide and huge, twice as wide, four times, ten. An enormous fist of smoke and glowering rock and flame bloomed like some huge sun, red, thick red, like some monstrous dome that grew and grew and touched the sky, so high our necks bent back. The jet of black and red, thick

5

coiling and roiling, twisted upwards like some monstrous gush and it was everything in front of us, and the black punch exploded higher.

A strange shimmer took the air, and we watched terrified as across the water ran a massive fierce circle of light, steaming water and smoke as if it rushed before a furious breath, like every forge of hell opening at once and Lucif's terrible angels running from the bowels of the earth, flaring banners on the air behind them. Then the strange fast thing in the air was upon us, and blasted past us, rocking the ship in one huge surge, and sucked the air from our mouths. My ears thickened and were painful, and I swallowed and swallowed until my ears eased and then…

…the sound, oh the noise and fire and thunder of the sound. A monstrous massive noise so huge, so loud, my guts shook and my head was pummelled and crushed. I looked to the captain and his mouth was a grimace, his hands pressing hard against his ears pressing to stop the explosion, the thunderous loudest thing. I fell to the deck and he did too, writhing in agony and pain and my ears hurting, hurting, I'm screaming. The thunder was right inside my head and then it was gone, a strange ringing, then silence, a silence so black and vast and huge. My mouth was wide and screaming but there was no sound but a giant loud ringing like a million bells in the towers on high. My ears filled with that sound and there was a terrible pulsing thing throbbing within the sound, and it was fast and terrified and I knew my blood was screaming and my heart, all I could hear was my heart. Thumping, thumping, thumping.

I felt a grip on my arm. The captain clenched my wrist with one hand and pointed with the other. His ears were bleeding and the corners of his eyes too, but the horror in his eyes made me look where he pointed. The captain let me go, and he wrapt his arms around a post from the deck and gripped his hands on his forearms, locking himself there. From the place of the explosion I saw, and it came across the sea faster than a fleeing horse, faster than the speeding cheetah as it coursed upon its prey in long away Ethiop, a mounding rise of water, foam flying from its top. It was smooth and unbroken, but huge and swelling grey and black and it sped upon the ship.

The prow of the ship dipped once as the water rose, then the ship angled upwards as the huge unbreaking surge of the sea lifted us up and up, the sea swelling like a massive thing and the ship rose so high that I could see the distant land and a long surging white band where the wave hit the land and covered it, racing over the trees and swirling there. Then the ship fell and fell and we pressed down between the walls of sea. Behind us the height of the water raced away from us, curious eddies and trails and whirlpools following behind. In front of the ship, another wall of water reared above us and again the ship ran up highest and again I saw the thundering white gash upon the land. This time trees were torn and tumbled as the water surged into the land and plashed upon the mountains high.

Three times more the ship rocked up onto the black and churning sea, then the water stopped its movement up and down and the ship was thrown and tossed into a swift current that pulled us towards the centre of this maelstrom. Giant whirlpools and running rivers in the sea channelled us onwards and inwards towards the belching place.

The captain gestured to men to mass their strength onto the steering oar, all movements commanded in dumb show because we were all in deafness to the world, and he commanded every oar to the stroke to slow the hellish slide towards the swirling watery centre. Slowly the strength of the men beat the run of the sea, or the sea slowed, I do not know which, but soon we were able to stand off the same distance everywhere, and to circle the hellish spinning hole, water tumbling into the pit, steaming and churning like a thousand thunderous falls, gone into hell.

For I could see that's what it was. Where once was a mountain high and from its top the belching column of smoke, now the land was utterly gone. The smoke and exploding gush was still happening, a steady flow still a thick plume into the air two miles wide I thought, judging as best I could for we stood miles off, reaching to the top of the sky.

Like the world's highest thunder anvil, grey clouds riven by lightning, the smoke rose into the sky. I could see cracks of lightning flickering within the cloud and it was a new storm up in there. But the gush was from under the water and steam was in the smoke, swirling and mixing white and black and grey, and all through the middle of it was orange and flowing up pushing red, like a forge made by a thousand smiths. I could feel the heat of it, all upon my face and arms.

Another hell began. Ash and black rain began to spot the deck and soon every man above the decks had his mouth wrapped in cloth to breathe. The captain ordered the ship to turn, to head from that place. Two hundred oars pushed against the sea, and we were all a silence still, not a man hearing his brother, no drums for they were pointless. Those of us who did not row brought clean water to those who did row, and where a man fell exhausted on his oar, another man dragged him away and took his stroke. For every man one of us knew this was a dreadful place, and our curiosity was done now.

Slowly we made a safer place in the ocean. We were gone from sight of the land, but not from the sight of the earth's spew as it still rose. The captain kept us on for a whole day, and the next time the sun rose it was red, blood red. And the moon too, that night and the next and the next, as she waned, she was red, blood red.

Half through the next day our ears came back and our voices and sounds were dull and muffled. A constant ringing began in mine own ears. Some of the men were deaf completely and gestured and moved their hands in dumb show, and they could not hear. The captain moved among them with his leftenants, and knew the men to be fearful but still brave. This shudder of the world would mark them, and they would remember the mad man that was in my head, for bringing them here.

But man is a curious beast and still some wanted to know more. The captain set the ship's boat to the sea and he took the ten strongest men to the oars, just in case, but the wind ran high and we sailed fast towards the mountain gone, and still erupting up to the sky. Black dust fell about us everywhere, and soon all of us could have grinned like a black man from Ethiop where the cheetahs are, our eyes peering mad upon the sea.

And the boat stopped, prevented on its way.

"These rocks, they float on the water and are as light as fluff," marvelled the captain, and so it was.

I remembered Plinius, and he too wrote of floating stones, and so the guts of the earth were the same, even in distant places. I took small pieces of those miracle rocks and placed them in my travelling box.

"Have you seen enough now, sire, can we make our way to the ship and north from this place?"

"Yes. Even my curiosity, which is much, is held happy to be gone from this place, well gone at that." I looked one last time at the monstrous thrust of gas and rock and smoke and steam, thoughtful as to what it meant. "The dragen, then, is riding from this place and is awoken. He rides upon the air."

The captain laughed and remembered our nervous conversation. "Perhaps the dragen awakes in the morning every thousand years and fucks the world with his glorious seed, and jets upon the sky." He looked at me. "Can your Goddess take that fuck, do you ponder? Spreading her legs wide?"

"Ah, that I don't know," I replied. "Perhaps she sleeps. But this noise and roar, I think, will have been heard a thousand miles from this confounding centre and will awaken most anything."

I looked towards the sea and pondered something of the geography of this place.

"Those high waves, how fast do you think they ran, those five high waves running from this explosion? How fast? Surely they must reach every place where there is a beach and a tide. The waves, so much taller than a tide, surely they will find every dry stone and make it wet, on a beach and by the shore?"

"Aye, sire, I think you right. My grandpere taught me of strange tides between tides, when the water rose when it shouldn't. He always taught me that it was a dragen stomping somewhere, making its way on the world, a drinkin' and a dancin'." He looked at me, man to man, and grinned. "Just like us mortal men, then, a looking for his mate."

We sailed away from that place and passed through the straits of Malac as we made our way north, and could see the dreadful path of the waves on the land as we passed. Ten men high or twenty, we could not imagine the destruction as those waves thundered, but we could see the torn and tangled trees, the whole floating shore a mess of bodies and floating things, the trail that was left by the waves and the furious sea. Later, in port, and months after, before I left that eastern land, I heard stories of cities and places ripped asunder, all men and women and children lost, countless they were, and beyond number.

After six months I left that country, thanking the Emperor for indulging my curiosity and sharing with him the dreaming smoke, pipes each night and a favourite wench, slit eyes and sleepy; and made my way west over the land and by boat, following the red clouds. Every day and every night, the skies were red and people were afraid. Long winters were beginning, those with the longest memories and the best songs said, for they could remember their stories of the earth down through long ages from the times of the thick ice and the melting, singing their songs and remembering.

My name is Maerlyn, and when the mountain of Krachoa exploded that morning, I was there.

It is a long way home, and I am called by the dragen. There is work to be done. I hope I am not too old.

Five Waves

"Mother, why is the moon red?"

Nymue was always curious and knew the cycles of the moon like the counting of her heart, constant, regular and well understood. She knew the moon's phases, from full to sickle, then nothing at all but always returning. This moon was a count of ten days after the full, a crescent high against the sharp, brilliant stars. Nymue had never seen the moon blood red before, not this deep red straight from hell, nor the rising and setting sun scarlet as it rose and fell. Like blood, the sky shimmered with colour, even the high clouds in the middle of the day glowed brilliant pink, shifting on the wind.

"Why is the sky bleeding? Mother, tell me!"

The girl was insistent and Vivyane knew this was good, because it spoke of a spirit in her daughter that was strong, but sometimes the questions, the endless questions, they were too much; and the girl not ready to be taught, not yet.

"Child, I do not know it, but I fear it is a sign. Something is coming, I can feel it my bones, coming huge."

Vivyane shivered and held her arms to her own body for strength and comfort. I must gather in my Sisters, she thought to herself, I will need them around me. And the child too, but she is not ready, not yet.

"Child, go, don't bother me. I don't know why."

"Mother, your bones! Why do you read the guts of birds if your bones already know?"

"Hush child, away with you. Go to the sea while the tide is low, and bring back some cockles."

Vivyane gave the girl a leather bag with a thick strap for her slim shoulders.

"Don't forget to watch the sand. As soon as the tide turns, walk ahead of it quickly. Don't get caught."

She knew Nymue would watch the water closely. Every child around the estuary learned the huge extremes of the tide from when they were very small, and all learned to swim instinctively. Their lives depended on it, down by the water. The tides were huge, as high as seven men standing on another man's shoulders, and rushed into the estuary. Where the sea narrowed, further north and east, the water made a breaking wave, every day. Boats could only cross when the high tide turned and the water flattened.

Nymue set off, the satchel bumping against her side. She was small for her age, not yet fourteen, but her limbs were strong and quick. She would climb trees and fearlessly find the highest nests. At first she stole the eggs, but then her mother showed her how to cradle fallen birds in the cup of her hands and to feel the tiny spirits there, and Nymue learned the strength of every life, and how it was vital to keep it.

Nymue kept to the south side of the river, for she knew the sands were widest there, where the river met the sea; she would see the flood of the tide as it broke over the bar and wouldn't need to run. As she reached the shore, Nymue looked high to the sun and judged the

14

length of the shadows, knowing she must wait a short time for the tide to reach its lowest ebb.

The girl had an instinctive, immediate grasp of numbers and angles, and remembered the shadows of the sun, from solstice to solstice. It pleased her, this endless round, and she took confidence from its constancy and predictability. Her mother might use the guts of birds for her auguries, but the daughter already knew deeper, longer rhythms.

Satisfied that she had the most use of her time with the tide at its lowest ebb, Nymue set off over the hard sand, her footsteps a straight trail behind her to the dunes. After a count of a hundred breaths she stopped and turned, and her track went straight back and blurred into a single line, and she was surrounded by damp sand. Behind her and to the south Nymue could see the far curve of land. To the west where the sun set she could see the distant shimmer of water, not yet breaking the bar. She had plenty of time before the tide turned, and she began to dig.

Slowly Nymue filled her satchel with the small cockle shells, dreamily looking forward to their salty taste and the soft flesh boiled open in an iron kettle on the fire, picked up with a precious fork found in an abandoned villa.

Nymue often day-dreamed, her mind in a hundred places, none of them where she actually was; and the open expanse of sand echoed the spaces in her mind, vast and wide, looking always outwards. She wriggled her toes in the sand, feeling the water just below the surface, warm in the sun. Nymue felt luxurious, stretching her young body under the high, hot sun.

Something caught her eye and she was aware of a strange silence. Off towards the sea, she saw a flock of wading birds rising from the sand, then another and another, a myriad of shapes rising against the sky. *What has startled them?* thought Nymue, *why are the birds rising?* Usually, the birds stayed down on the wide sands, probing with their long beaks for worms and slithering things that lived in the mud.

On edge now, Nymue turned to face the distant estuary, straining her eyes to see what had alarmed the birds. With a thump of her heart, she saw, far off but nothing should be there, she saw a shimmering edge of white, moving fast upon the sands. She looked around her, instinctively checking where the land was. Something was not right, what was that shimmer, that running line?

With a surge of horror, Nymue saw it was water, a band of water moving fast across the sand. *But the tide is down,* she whispered to herself, not believing this impossible thing. She heard a distant rush and it was the sound of waves in a storm pushed high upon the beach and breaking. Nymue knew this was not right. The wave was an unnatural thing, and she began to run. As she ran she tied the satchel with its strap and held it close to her breast to keep it there. She ran, her breath heaving, but the sound of the rushing water was faster behind her. Nymue knew she could not turn around, that would stop her flight, so she did not see the rising wave pushing up, following her faster than a horse runs, following her faster than she could run.

The front of the wave caught Nymue and knocked her feet from under her, and she was tumbling, tumbling, thrown forward by the force and speed of the wave, which smashed into her back and rushed past her. She made herself as small as she could, folding herself into the smallest ball of a girl, a tiny thing like a rock or a pebble, to fall down to the sand and let the water rush over her. The tumult of the wave sped on towards the land, and she rose to the surface, gasping for air, but in a still water behind the roaring spume and the breaking peak.

Quickly, Nymue oriented herself to the land, *oh but it's so far away.* The water rushed and swirled around her, and she knew this was no tide, for as sudden as the wave had broken up around her, then with a mighty huge suck, the water shot back towards the sea, a fast moving sheet of rippling, awful water, brown with mud and sand, until the sand was bare.

Nymue sobbed for breath and pulled her shift around her. Her hands still grabbed the satchel, clutching it so tight her fingers were white. Shakily she got to her feet and tried to make sense of what had happened. She squeezed water from her long hair, heavy to her waist with water and sand. She did not understand what this was. How could the tide rise and fall so fast? Never before had she seen a breaking wave cover these sands. Twice, when she was younger, she had gone farther out than was wise; but those times, why, she could steadily walk before the water and it would follow her like a puppy, catching her ankles but only inches deep. A skip and a jump would leave the tide behind.

But this, this was wrong, so wrong. A wave couldn't come and go like that, mother earth didn't move that way. The tide came in and the tide went out, and it was predictable and a perfect thing. This was very wrong. Nymue looked to the sky. It was wrong, too, the baleful red of the high sun. Where was the perfect white light of the daily sun? Wrongness surged around the girl, and she was scared.

And her guts; Mother, what was this sudden sharp pain in the depths of her belly? What hand gripped her right inside? Nymue bent double with cramps, and remembered her sisters when the curse first came upon them. She fell to the sand, winded by the sudden pain, and rocked there, holding herself tight. The girl fought tears brought by the pain, but she cried out without knowing, her cry soaring up like a frightened bird. Lying on the wet sand, shivering with cold, Nymue clutched herself until slowly the pain eased. Shaking, she crawled for a short while, then pushed herself to her feet.

Nymue limped towards the distant shore, the satchel heavy about her neck. The dunes were so far away, she hurt from the cramps, and she hurt from the pounding she had received from the malignant wave. Then horror, once again horror, she heard again the rushing of water rising behind her. She turned to face the wave and stood terrified as she saw it rush towards her, a wall of water higher than her head. This time, though, she was better prepared. Just before the water took her, Nymue took in the biggest, deepest breath she could, and threw herself in the same direction as the rushing, roaring wave, letting it carry her towards the shore.

The girl remembered how quickly the previous wave had turned and sucked back to sea, and knew she must grip the sand like a limpet to stop herself being dragged back out. So Nymue used the malevolence of the wrongness against itself, and let herself be swept and tumbled towards the shore, terror still in her limbs, but carried by this force, not fighting it. Gulping for air, she was swept along, and the wave took her in. Some sense in the girl told her the moment of the back surge, and she dived down and plunged her hands into the grip of the sand and held herself there as the water rushed back out. As she did so, Nymue felt the satchel rip from her body and it was lost to the sea.

But she survived. For a second time, Nymue struggled to her feet as the hateful waters withdrew. She wasted no time making for the dunes, but they were still so far away. So far. Without the bag, she just had to move herself, and she did, with shuffling steps. Her body was bruised and bashed, and again she felt the awful cramp deep in her belly. Sobbing with pain, she lurched forward, and slowly the dunes came into view. She struggled on, weak with exhaustion, not knowing if the nightmare world was over or if it was just beginning.

With a third horrible rush, another wave smashed into her, but even in her dread Nymue sensed a regularity to them. Again she was spun and tumbled and thrust towards the shore. She was weaker now, and when the wave sucked back it pulled her feet from under her and dragged her back the same distance she had tumbled, and she was no closer to the shore. This time too, the furious sea ripped and tore the girl's garments from her body, and she was naked and small, a tired hurt animal, but with an animal's instinct for survival. She pulled herself to her feet and limped towards the dunes, counting this time, counting, counting, and was warned.

When the fourth wave struck, Nymue stood firm, neither going with the wave nor surrendering to it, but stood still and anchored, pushing her feet into the sand. Mother earth gave her strength, and so Nymue stood against the fourth wave, and it was smaller than the other waves, and she let it pass.

Knowing now the horrible, inevitable intervals between the dreadful surges, this time she made herself run, driving her thin naked limbs as fast as she had ever run. Ignoring the sharp stabbing pains in her belly she kept on, and struggled in the softer sand and up the slope. Nymue realised she had left the long breadth of the sand and was in the foot of the dunes. She stopped and looked down, and saw that the wrongness that was the water between the tides, even now the waves had reached this high.

Nymue struggled on, and saw that she had finally reached the line of the highest tide and must now be safe. Turning towards the sea, the dreadful sea, she held her arms around her smallness and waited. She did not wait long, but the fifth wave was small and weak, as if it too had tired in its rush upon the sand. By the time it reached her, its force was spent and the water didn't reach her knees. The muddy flow slopped and shifted around Nymue, but it was sluggish and slow.

As she stood there, small and naked and alone, Nymue felt a curious pulse in the base of her belly and a long, loose feeling there, not as fierce as the cramps before, but new to her and heavy. She felt a wetness on her legs, and as the foul wave retreated, Nymue watched it take swirls of red blood away from her, pulling and threading thin trails of rich red blood. And she bled, her first course given up to the horrible surge of the fifth wave, and she didn't know what it meant. She looked up at the sky, and the harsh red clouds flowed there, echoing her young womanhood as the foul water washed her first blood away.

Nymue shook, her body exhausted and shocked, weakened with the terror of the water, weakened by her blood. Somehow she knew that the fifth wave was the last, that the proper tide would walk across the sand like it always did, and the world would turn as it always turned.

Her animal instinct was still strong, and she made herself climb to the height of the dune, some final safe place where the sand was dry. She found a small hollow and crept near to a thicket of small trees, and collapsed, small and huddled, turning within herself. With a long shudder, her exhausted body slumped into unconsciousness, and she felt nothing, no pain, no fear, just nothing.

Then, in her nothingness, Nymue felt herself rising, light and buoyant, her spirit rising. She felt herself turn, rolling once, and her eyes opened. She looked down and saw a small huddled thing curled small on itself, curled on the ground, and it grew smaller. The child lay sleeping, and at first Nymue wondered who she was, this bleeding and scratched girl; then realised the girl was herself. Then her body didn't matter, as she felt herself rise and rise, high to the sky. She felt a small tug in her belly, and looked at herself and saw a streaming silver chord, no thicker than a hair, but shimmering white light and silver brightness, streaming down to the small pale thing on the ground.

Eyes wide with wonder now, Nymue was high above the earth, and saw off to the east, where the morning sun rises, far off in the shimmering distance, the conical rise of the sacred hill surrounded by water. She knew she would go there soon, to the Isle of Glas. Her spirit rushed on and higher, and far below her, Nymue saw the estuary as it narrowed between the rising hills on either side, like a woman's thighs parting and the rolling hills beyond. Nymue saw the Goddess below her sleeping, her lush curves sinuous and fertile, waiting.

And look, down there in the sea, Nymue saw five curving lines beating and running against the shore and some mysterious male force was in them, some huge force pushed them on, surging up into the Goddess and stirring her with some new awakening.

Then, with a snap and a jolt, Nymue's vision ended and her world went black. She felt a rush and a surge and the clutching of cold flesh, and blackness descended over her. She felt nothing more.

"Child, my poor child, what has happened here?"

Vivyane was frantic, her mother's senses fully alert, searching as soon as she realised the girl should have returned. Vivyane knew the water well. She had not seen the five waves, but she could tell from the twisting and spiralling drags of water on the far sands, and the rivulets and rushing paths made high in the dunes, that something strange and fierce had passed through here.

Vivyane wrapped the girl in a coarse woollen cloth to cover her nakedness and to make her warm. She stood, and cradling her small daughter close to her body, Vivyane made her way back to their home. In the courtyard, serving girls rushed to find soft bindings and fresh water and to fan the fire in the hearth. Vivyane cleansed her daughter, and she was covered in bruises and scratches.

"I'm bleeding, Mother, my blood is upon me." Nymue's voice was small, barely a whisper. "I flew, mother, and saw the Goddess, our holy mother."

Vivyane didn't doubt, but there were more than two mysteries here. "Why are you naked, child? Where are your clothes?"

"I lost the cockles, the sea took everything from me. I couldn't run, I tried, Mama, but I couldn't run fast enough. I flew, Mama, so high. I'm so tired, let me sleep." Nymue opened her eyes. "Five waves, Mother, but the last one was small. I was scared, Mama, so scared. I flew up into the sky. The waves tumbled me around and round. I lost the cockles, Mother."

Her eyes flickered and closed, and Vivyane sat by her little daughter all through the night.

"Little sparrow," she sang, "little sparrow…"

Nymue slept, and Vivyane wondered why the Goddess had called upon the girl. Her auguries had not foretold this; they were silent and told her nothing.

Above them, the sickle moon was a baleful red; and in the morning the sun rose in its own blood and the world turned and turned. The sun rose and the sun fell, and the moon turned too, always red.

In her long delirium, Nymue whispered, "There's a dragen coming, Mother, he's coming soon with his hot breath and sharp claws. There's a dragen coming soon."

Long Paths and Stone Circles

For five years Nymue lived in the Isle of Glas and was taught by the sisterhood there. They taught her mysteries of the Goddess and the long lines of song down through the ages, the lines and curves of her country, the sacred places, her holy wells.

Nymue, who was blooded in water risen wrong and foul, grasped immediately the cleansing power of tumbling waters and fast streams, high mountains and clean rain. Her favourite art was learned from the fish and the bird, the creatures with scales slipped in silver and wings that soared.

She especially loved the little egret with its wings of purity and white, for it was the first rising of those birds that warned her of the terrible sea. When the trance was upon her from smoke and mushroom and song, Nymue soared high with the birds, and they were her totem, feathers and white.

The shock of the five waves and the bringing of her blood had drained the colour from Nymue's hair, and ever after it was white, the longest whitest white.

"She is marked," said her mother, "forever marked." Her whiteness marked her, and Nymue was different now.

The women from Glas also taught Nymue the new Christ and the Holy Mother, that she might know shifts in allegiance led by priests from Rome, ascetics and monks who grew afraid of women and their magick. Some were hermits and holy, not so lost to the older ways, who still knew the cry of the fox and the creak of the tree and the old stone rings.

Other men were less wise, wrapping themselves in purple cloth and red wine, calling it blood, building crosses and chapels from new stone. Nymue, who knew blood, quickly learned this falseness. She watched the way the holy men looked at her, and she turned from them, full knowing where her power lay. She walked away, dragging their eyes behind her, holding her head high; and her hips swayed.

Nyneve, Vivyane's elder sister and Nymue's aunt, watched the girl as she grew from a child into a young woman, and saw her solitude and inner strength.

"She will be a powerful one, the spirit moves within her and she has seen the Goddess," Nyneve counselled, and the two older women wondered how best to guide the girl. "She is young, only nineteen years, but nearly ready, I think, for the ceremony of the midsummer sun."

Vivyane looked closely at her sister. "Do you think so, truly? So soon?"

"Nymue is different, she knows songs from our Mother and also from the ancient fathers. She walks in circles and straight lines. She is fire and water both; tree and stone. I've not seen it before." Nyneve paused, deep in thought. "Her moon curse was unusual, blooded by water under a burning sky, and her hair is bled white. And remember what she said in her trance: the dragen comes? The girl is different, Sister, she will go beyond us."

Vivyane was torn. She was priestess and mother both, and remembered the tiny babe at her breast, all those years ago. "She's my little girl." Vivyane gazed into the fire in front of them. "She's still my little girl."

Nyneve was silent for a moment. "Maybe we wait. Maybe we do that. Another year."

"Another year, yes." Vivyane was thankful for her older sister. "She can wait."

Nymue did not want to wait. "Mother, I am marked white. I am near twenty years old, nineteen turns of the midsummer sun and the midwinter solstice. I know the world turns, seasons wake and die. This doesn't change, I count the turns. I stand in the stones and see the longer cycles turning there." She was impatient. "I know the rounds, Mother, my mind sees them and I understand them. The ancient ones who left the stones, they knew them too."

Nymue looked at her mother fiercely, challenging Vivyane with her stronger knowledge. Nymue respected the song memories and the long poems of her mother and Nyneve, but she understood deeper truths, permanence recorded in stone and ditch, post and hole.

"Mother, let me do this."

Nymue thought her plan sound and set her mind to convince Vivyane. "Let me do this. For a year, let me wander to the ends of this isle, south where the land joins the Atlant ocean; and north to the mountains and cold hills. I will follow the curves of our Goddess and the hidden ways. Let me find more circles of stone and understand their counting, sun and moon and the evening star and the blood red star. My mind remembers it all, Mother, and I can learn it."

She reached the core of her argument. "Only then, when I truly understand the ancient wisdom, only then will I submit to the ceremony of the sun." Her argument was cunning: "The Goddess rides with the moon, Mother, I need to know how the moon turns before I know the sun."

Vivyane gazed upon the girl and was silent. She looked into the heart of the fire and watched the heating embers crackle and spit. Slowly, she reached to a bag on the hearth and pulled a handful of seeds from it. Vivyane turned the seeds over in her hand, looking down at the different shapes and sizes there, like tiny stones; then threw them into the fire. With a sizzle the seeds burst in the heat and a spicy aroma spread through the room. The three women breathed deeply, and their sight sharpened.

Suddenly, a heated seed shot from the fire and landed on Nymue's leg. She flicked away the hot shell and soothed the hot place with a tongue wetted fingertip.

Nyneve nodded once. "The fire talks, and marks the girl. She will do this, for twelve moons, as she says."

"Thank you, wise mother, my aunt. I will do it right."

Nymue smiled to herself. Her stubbornness had prevailed.

The stones were in a high place. Leading up to the height of the hill, parallel lines of stones crossed the country, ending paths and starting paths. Sight lines led the eye to notches on the horizon, or tall trees; and there were messages here, left from long ago.

Nymue dropped her travelling bag from her shoulders, stretching her spine to give herself relief from the weight of it. She was a small figure in the landscape, almost hidden within her cloak of deerskin leather, worked soft and light and carefully stitched. Her white token feathers were sewn around the collar, setting a crown behind her hair, all white. Nymue was travelling, walking miles each day, and coiled her hair high to keep it hidden. It would fall later around her body and pale skin, when she danced.

She sat cross legged and unravelled the woven string laces from her boots, hard leather and waxed with animal fat to protect against cold water. Nymue carefully checked the seams and the condition of the soles, noting she would need to thicken them before she moved north for the winter. Good enough for now. She unwrapped bread from a parcel of leaves and ate for a full belly. This night would be long.

To the west, the sun lowered its last light, casting long shadows from the line of stones up the hill. Behind Nymue the moon was already high, its blood finally fading after five long years. The moon was full and the Goddess would strengthen her this night. Around the girl, shadows from the sun ran long and black, and shadows from the moon grew shorter.

Nymue waited until it was time.

Nymue had studied the geometry of the hill as she walked towards it that afternoon. She understood most of it, but the final mystery lay ahead, higher on the hill where she could not see. She did not know the final shape of it, its centre, but had discovered over time that not knowing was best. The alertness that came with discovery tuned her intuition, she found a deep place in the base of her belly that was instinctive, animal, ancient. It was that knowledge Nymue sought, and the primal energy with it. This was her magick now.

She ate three small seeds and a dried husk to sharpen her vision, to hear like a cat, to smell like a fox and to taste like the adder, the snake. The moon spread silver on the grass. Nymue's tongue flickered and her senses grew hot. She stood, and dropped her cloak to the ground, spreading it wide. She would need it later, to hide within.

Nymue undid the buttons on her jerkin, bone and loop, and cast it from her body, together with her woven woollen vest. Her pale breasts were tight and hard already, a low ache behind her throbbed nipples. She released her hair from its tie, and it fell around her, an unnatural cloak of snow uncut to her waist. She unlaced the tied straps from her leggings and pulled them down.

Nymue placed her garments in neat piles around the edge of her cloak, carefully spaced and a hex. She traced them together with her finger on the ground and it was a hiding mark. Spirits might wake and follow her, but her belongings were material things and would be left alone now. High in a tree an owl waited, keeping watch over her camp. Birds followed Nymue, always and constant.

Nymue stood, her naked body glowing pale in the moonlight, a small white triangle at the base of her belly. Her eyes were black and wide, and she began to turn. Slowly at first, her bare feet sliding over the short grass, making slow weaves in and around the lines of stones, tracing spirals as she moved up the hill. Nymue looked to the ground and saw the lines and leys, then quickly looked to the sky to mark the planets and stars. Her mind instantly mapped the patterns of this place, and she saw it lined to the dog and the crab and the goat. This was a place of the moon, an ancient place.

Knowing this, Nymue changed the pattern of her dance in tiny, subtle ways, shifting the patterns she made so that older spirits could see her, hear her feet, and wake. She moved higher up the hill and spun faster, heating her body and igniting the first small flames of ecstasy. Her nipples thickened and her breasts ached, and deep in the depths of her belly her sex stirred and slipped, thickening with blood pumping hot. Nymue's breath quickened and now she ran, turning faster until she fell, falling dizzy on the grass, her lithe frame writhing. Her back arched, and she cupped her cunt in the palm of her hand, gripping it closed with her thighs. She was pale and small under the bright light of the moon, and the spell was upon her, spiralling high from the potions she had taken and her frantic dance.

Crying out to the moon, Nymue dipped her fingers into her sliding cunt, pressing her palm hard on her clitoris and circling there, driving hot pleasure into her body. Panting, she crawled to the long stone in the centre of the array and writhed upon it like a snake. The stone was worn smooth with cups and hollows, and her body slid into a place that was made a thousand years ago and visited by a thousand spirits since. Nymue's vision was upon her now, and her fingers sank into the fabric of the stone and she felt the primal rock. She called out, and in her own voice she answered, and she was in her body and outside it too.

Her eyes blinked, and she spiralled and turned and looked down. Nymue saw the girl with fingers sliding in her cunt and knew it was herself. She flew, propelled upwards by the force of her rising, circling energy, sex magick thickening between her legs. Below her, Nymue's body orgasmed, and in the sky she felt a jolt in her gut, and the silver thread pulsed. Energy flowed into her from the ancient rock and Nymue felt its power, its sacral heart, and she soared higher.

Below her, the Mother Goddess lay upon the land and she awoke, her turns and curves smooth and remembering, her limbs spreading valleys and pinions of rock. Springs burst as the earth turned, new waters flowing to quench the coming dragen.

Below her, the body of Nymue was small upon the stone. Her eyes rolled back in her head and she could not see, but still she ran her fingers over her clitoris, shuddering her body with little shocks and her pulse stayed fast. After some time her mind twisted and Nymue felt a tug in her belly. She rolled again and felt a hot heat envelope her. Her hands pressed against the stone and it was hard now, growing cold beneath her, and her body lay on the rock. Nymue dipped her fingers between the lips of her sex a last time and felt her hot heat. She anointed her brow with her silvery wet, and locked the spell of this place into her mind.

Slowly, tired now with the spell cooling in her bones and blood, Nymue made her way back down between the paths of stone and rock. She slid her feet over the cool grass and it was soothing after her earlier spinning dance. Finding her cloak on the ground, Nymue dragged it to a sheltering dip beside a row of low bushes. She bundled all of her belongings around her, and curled herself small like an animal. Nymue pulled the cloak completely about herself and was hidden from the world.

She fell into a dreamless sleep, curled tiny and warm like a beast. Deep in her mind, Nymue added this array of stones, more complex than most, to a growing catalogue of places she had danced within. She remembered the conjurings deep in her muscles, and her magickal weave grew stronger.

Above her, the owl flew off and hunted. Five minutes later it returned, hovering with a weightless drop of its wings over the bundle on the ground. The owl dropped a small dead body of a mouse, that the girl might feed in the morning.

So Nymue travelled the length and breadth of Albion over the course of that year and found a hundred circles of ancient stone. She studied their rounds and spirals, saw how they aligned to the moon or the sun or the stars. Nymue tapped into their ancient and pure sex magick, sucking the energy of the land deep into her womb. She discovered an extraordinary surge of energy when one night she drew blood from her sickle moon cunt and anointed the stone with it. Her fuck on the stone was made more powerful as her own blood surge aligned with the spin of the circle, and so Nymue learned that special conjuring must wait for her own bleed each month.

Nymue stored her growing knowledge deep in the depths of her mind. Her dreams worked on the patterns and shapes she could not consciously see, and her dream weaves combined with the mazes and meanders she walked upon, and slowly her natural power grew and became unnatural.

The witch Nymue became so receptive of places in the country of the Goddess, spiralling in towards pivots and curving around copses, that she would walk upon a path and feel a tingle in her nipples and a throb in her clitoris and she would know. A conjure would fall upon her and a spell, and over time she learned to do without seed and trance and smoke. Nymue learned to channel the pure voice of her crying cunt and her weeping blood and she grew strong.

Songs began, and the men of Christ heard of white Nymue and were afraid, wringing their hands in their purple sleeves and trying to find faith in their filthy water. They began to chant of her. This woman, they said, was seduced by the snake and was evil and wrong.

Nymue laughed, for the villagers looked for a crone, white haired and bent; whereas she walked the land young and pale, her mane of hair beautiful and pure. So she hid in plain sight, and became an angel. Young priests were seduced by the stories of Nymue carried on whispers and rumours. In years to come they blurred the idea of her with that of the Holy Mother, and became confused. But not yet.

Conjuring was ahead of her now, spells to be woven across the land and remembered. In the south, men grew restless and tribal armies massed. The land began to shake.

Nymue turned her head towards home and the Isle of Glas, to her mother. She was ready now, for the ceremony of the sun. She returned home.

"Mother, I am returned."

Vivyane looked upon her daughter and saw her new, quiet confidence and her silent strength. "Nymue, my daughter, let me look upon you."

The girl's mother knew her daughter's stubbornness from when she was small, but what might once have been petulance was now pride, and deserved; and what was once ignorance, by the Goddess, was now wisdom. How could a girl so young, just twenty now, be so wise? What deep learning had she found, this woman?

"Nymue, I look at you and I see someone I don't know, not anymore."

Vivyane sensed the young woman before her, standing quietly by her hearth, was no longer of this home. She looked again, and wasn't sure.

"Oh Mother, I am always your daughter; the babe you suckled, the child who grew. I'm just a little older now, Mama, that's all. But I still have the little scar on my knee from when I fell on the sharp shell, down on the beach, when I was ten." Nymue remembered everything. "And the long scars on my side, from when the wave tumbled me and dragged me along." That was an elemental thing and Nymue remembered. "You carried me home in your arms, Mama, when I was naked and broken."

Nymue went to her mother and held her arms around her. "I'm the same daughter, Mother. I've learned new songs, but I don't forget the old ones."

Vivyane welcomed the girl's love, but even so, she felt like the child now. Nymue had a new spirit in her, and Vivyane was uncertain, afraid.

"Do not fear, sister," Nyneve saw the uncertainty in her sister's eyes. "Nymue is still with the Goddess, and does not desert us."

Nyneve knew something of stones and blood, but sensed the girl knew more. She would speak with Nymue later, to glean something of her stronger magick.

"But Nymue, we have not told you. He returns. The Maerlyn walks the land of Albion once more. You need to be ready."

The Ceremony of the Sun

I was there.

When the witch Nymue met the Sun King, and took in his heat, I was there. The Goddess help me, for I am old and she is young, yet I am still bewitched.

I arrived back in Albion after a long pass of years from when I left the land of the Eastern Emperor. He of course named himself Emperor of the Central Kingdom, for he knew no other. In my mind he was Emperor of an eastern kingdom, one of several like Japon or Kor. The centre of the world was a different place altogether, more desert now than kingdom, but caliphates nevertheless. And camels. Snorting, lecherous beasts, hundreds of 'em.

As I travelled towards the setting sun, always the setting sun, each day I heard tell of a monstrous noise heard from afar, from the east and south. I counted the days and the miles each day, so I knew that the noise they heard was the monstrous explosion of Krachoa that day when I saw the mountain disappear and the monstrous sea rise five times. I was astonished at the distance the noise went. A Hindi man in Delhee heard it, an Arab in the depths of Pirsia of the two rivers heard it, but duller. No wonder then, that on the ship we were all deaf for days and my ears still ring. A thousand miles, more, even a Roman could not measure it. Surely the most monstrous noise the world has ever heard!

And by the ocean's edge, all around Indee and up into Araby where the dhows sail with their triangle sails, I could see with mine own eyes the blasted coast and destructed places. Five huge waves it was, every man counted five, and the waves taller than fifty men or more, roaring from the sea, sweeping all before. I made a map and plotted on it what I knew, all of my geography, and marked the days the waves swept up hell from the oceans. And so I understood the speed of it and the distance. I talked with wise men and holy men and men who fought with gods, and the wisest of us all knew this: surely the world was unhinged on its rounds of the sun by the cataclysm, and was made all wrong.

The blood red skies lasted for years and more years, and every farmer told the crops grew bad, and the winters grew longer, and tiny babies all died, their mothers could not feed them. And so the world groaned and suffered, and the dragen was awakened. Men began to fight, for they were afraid, and fight is what scared men do. And through it all I travelled west, ever west, Albi calling to my bones, to my blood, summoning me back home.

So I came, eventually, to Gaul where once the Romans were, and summonsed a small ship to sail at my command to the Isle of Albion my Mother, my Goddess. When I landed under the high white cliffs, I made send a fast message ahead of me to the Sisters, that they might welcome me and hear my long songs, for I sing of many things. The minstrel Maerlyn!

I jest, my voice is weak and I cannot sing. But my tell, by the Goddess, you cannot quieten an old fool, my tell goes on forever.

Yet I heard back soonest, before I departed. Nyneve wrote me and I read her scroll, ink on linen, on a rolled scroll.

'We are come upon you half way,' she wrote, 'do not come to Glas, for we will meet you. My sister Vivyane and her blood kin, we come half way. Remember the babe, Nymue of Vivyane born? She is grown, and surpasses us, a mighty witch and Daughter of the Goddess now. She is upon us, truly, the girl Nymue is born of bird and sea, and five cruel waves brought on her moon and blood. Meet us half way, Maer Maerlyn, for it is soon half summer.'

Little Nymue, who I dandled on my knee when she was just small! Little Nymue grown? By the Goddess, have I been away that long? Ah me, that child! Grown? I could not credit it, yet the Sisters said half way and half summer, and the little one there.

And five waves, how could that be, at the end of the long Atlant? I did not know the oceans joined, but five waves? I knew I must discover when, and make another mark on my map, and guess upon the joining up of waters. I knew the days and distance in the one big ocean all around Indee, and it was a constant speed the waves moved there, and fast. Once I knew what days passed in the ocean Atlant, I would guess what distances there were between. Was the world so small? And the dragen so quick?

But Nymue grown? Her palest blue eyes, like ice on cold water, and her rich red hair! Ah me, I'm grown too old. That little pale girl, all grown!

So I made my way to the great plain where the trees stand far off and are distant, far over the horizon. On the day before half summer I camped down where the old wooden circle lay, made of great trunks of trees but all fallen and gone now, beside the river Avyn where it makes a great loop. A gathering was there, tents and fires made in rows where dogs ran and children too, until they were hushed by their mothers and made to turn away in respect. But the smallest children were cheeky and quick, and their bright eyes peered at me from behind their mothers' legs. I winked at some of them as I passed by, and heard their laughing chatter as I walked on. "The Maerlyn is here, look, there, dressed in white."

More a dirty grey, I think, for the dust collects and my cloak drags upon the path. Perhaps I should be more ceremonial, with a high head piece or some such to suit the part, but the priests of Rome do that. I don't wish to be stained like their souls, the stupid fools. The Christ of an only god and his mother with a cunt for an ear? Where's the sense in that? But the rolling back of the rock from the grave, that was good theatre, a clever touch. I wonder if I shall remember that, when it's time for me to go? We'll see. But hush, here we are.

Before me laid out was a large tent, with four high poles at the entrance, smoke curling from its thatched roof. I was made welcome by a sloe eyed girl, dark and small, with hair twisted around all black and thick, and she was the second daughter of some distant lord upon a pilgrimage. Her father tried to impress, but he was a thickun from the north by the wall, and kept on about four black horses. I could not make out what he meant, but he was good natured and had a barrel of honey mead wine, so a good fellow too.

I did not tarry long with him, because I had to be at the henge before dawn and wanted sleep before the breaking of day. The girl was sent to warm my back, and she curled behind me snug and sweet. I was tired from the day, and did not touch her even though she offered, with her small hands and high breasts. She was warm against me, and her breath sighed in her throat like a tiny wind as she fell into sleep.

"Tell your father I thank him, he's a generous man," I smiled at her and whispered on. "Just make it all up in the morning, you're a good daughter, tell him what you will."

My old staff still stiffens in my hand and in a tight girl's place, yet it's a slower thing now. Sometimes it's enough just to feel the hot young heat of life by my side, and know that it goes on forever. She warmed my back as I slept, and was peaceful like a sleeping cat by the hearth. A sweet young maid.

"Maer, it is time. The moon is high and full and lightens our way. It is mid of the night and we need our procession."

Ah good, I had around me a small group of acolytes who knew the ancient ways, and would do justice as we moved along the old paths. I envied those who first made the ceremonial way, a thousand years gone but still sung in the song. They would have seen the wide way cut white, the chalk piled high against green grass, straight and white, glowing under the moon. Now, time and rain have softened these ancient places and their marks are fading lost. But we know, and walk the ways.

The land sloped up away from the river. We the small group of us made our way up the long slope, mayhap half a mile as a man walks, then turned our eyes to the west and saw in the long distance the stones made high and in a ring, capped and round. Under the high white moon the henge stood grey and silver, and we proceeded towards it, a silence upon us, for this was a sacred place. It is best to hear a sacred place in silence, the better to hear it talk. We made our way, and I led.

Our ceremonial way was a steady pace, and behind us to the morning came that first wash of a cooler breeze, as the sun far off began to warm the land, to caress the sleeping Goddess in his hands. This day was the single day, the half summer, when the day was longest, aye, but would grow shorter still. The great wheel turned and with it our fortune, always on. Sometimes I ponder it, a thousand years more, a thousand thousand, but even my imagination fails that.

This day I was to be outside the circle, watching in. The sun expected new magick, an initiation, a christening. This old fool was long ago dunked in the water of the stream, and my tokens had long forgotten who they served. Mine own skin was left, and it my strength, and my bones. And my memories. They leak from my eyes, sometimes, and trace my skin. But no matter, it's not my day today.

I stood by the leaning stone that shadowed the first sun's glimpse and pointed into the greater place, cunningly aligned and grey in the high moonlight. This was a foretell, the moon full on the half summer's rise. A portent then, and a pivot in time and place. I greeted the stone, old friend, and touched my fingertips to its skin.

Comfortable cold, my hand was warm. The young maid's heat lingered, and my old belly throbbed warm. Ahh, so it's that magick? I had forgotten that, my first ceremony, so long ago. Yeay in truth mine old cock didn't forget; a singular mind, tight focussed for a tight, hot place.

Looking on, the sky lightened a fraction, with a glimmer pink like the first bud of a nipple. The soft mistral dropped and the grass was still, a faint shimmer of morning dew spread light upon the tops. A mist of tiny spider webs was gossamer fine all around and the land lay veiled with the finest sheen, all a ready to vanish and disappear with the light.

"Maer, look, they come." My young leftenant pointed back, and my eyes sharpened, an old trick, and I saw.

"Go to your place," I said, and he did.

I watched the new ceremony begin, and it was slow walking. My Sisters knew their times, better ever than I did. So I waited, knowing that they knew their perfect pace. Ah Goddess, is that third one there the little Nymue, grown? Oh, the sweet thing. Even then, far off, I was struck blind and could not rightly see, but could not strip my eyes from her. But her hair, where is her rich red hair? She shines pure white, she dazzles me.

The line of women followed the same path down the centre of the cursus that we men had walked. At the front of the line I could see the tall figure of Nyn Nyneve, honoured by her age, the eldest of the Sisters. Viv Vivyane followed her, and her honour was the motherhood of the sorceress, the new witch. Both the older women were garbed in the green and brown of the field and earth, in symbol of that which grew and that which buried.

In the third place, sheathed in long white and a virtuous gown, walked the young woman, Nym Nymue of the five waves, as I knew her now to be. Her feet were bare that she could feel the skin of the Goddess beneath her, and she walked and was white against the slowly rising dawn. The collar of her gown was threaded with the long feathers and the short feathers of all her tokens and animates. I saw that she had flown with birds of white and grey and black and brown, small and large. The feathers circled the back of her long white hair like a high crowned crest, and she was initiate and commander, the same both at once, the white Nymue as I knew her now to be.

Nymue was no longer the young girl I knew before my long departure. Now she was strong and a woman, but still young with it. She walked confidently down into the high stones of the first carved circle, that was circled around with high curved lintels. Some were fallen and broken, for the henge was an ancient place, mysterious in how it was made, but ancient stones still standing.

It counted clever. Some holes were for the moon and all its rises and retrogrades, its backward moves; and the stones knew where the sun rose and fell. This day the sun would rise behind me, and the long shadow of the leaning stone point straight towards the gap between the highest stones, massive high. The half summer sun would rise straight and true, fair between the high rocks.

The procession paused, and a low chant began and a ringing of small bells. The chimes echoed around the stones and answered the first notes with their second sound. Cleverly the chanting voices and other ringing bells weaved sound around the place and a slow rhythm started, liken to a dream but in the waking time. Nymue began a small dancing movement, and she began to turn and weave around the Prescel ring of stones all blue and grey, brought from a far mountain. I knew the distant quarry place, and the spirits in the stone walked them here, I am sure. There could be no other way.

Nymue danced on, and I saw a spirit in her, a trancement and a spell. As I watched I slowly understand the hex she made, to trap the bright Sun Lord to her will. I wondered how one yet twenty turns could know this spell. Where had she learned this maze? I thought I knew the land's paths and ways, but I could see from her clever patterns that Nymue knew them too. I had learned fifty years or more for my know, yet here she was, Nymue of the thousand ways, and barely grown. I wondered if I had anything to teach her, or if she knew it better already, and might teach me.

As I gazed upon Nymue, the sky shifted from a silver grey to a brightening light, and between me and the standing stones, the leaning stone cast the first shadow, and the bright Lord Sun was coming. Between the narrowest, tallest stones, the mightiest ones, Nymue's dance halted still, and she stood with her arms stretched wide that she felt both rocks. She paused just for a moment, and I saw her heaving breasts as she fast breathed from her dance. I came down closer, but am a man, so could not enter the ring, not this day.

45

The high Lord Sun would come this half summer day and want a woman, not some old man, so I stayed beyond the circling stones.

Nymue stepped back three paces from between the stones, and two small maids, carefully instructed, dragged in from the other side a wide fur, huge it was, from a stag. They made it straight, and had small pillows too, and made an open bed. They ran away and were gone.

Vivyane her mother went to the daughter and they kissed, full hard on their lips, and small blood was bit on Nymue's lip by her mother there and it was an anointment. Nymue stood, yet her mother was taller, so I knew the girl might stand by me and look at my chest. I am tall and thin. Her wide, high fan of tokens and long feathers disguised her height. Nymue was not so tall, but stood it so, and her spirit made her tallest of all. Next to her, I would always crawl on my knees.

Vivyane reached for Nymue's throat and undid a clasp there. The white gown slid like snow from a mountain and pooled to Nymue's feet and the girl stood naked. She faced away from me, so I saw the smallness of her waist and the spread of her curved hips, and her back. Nymue's beautiful hair was tied in three places, long white snow down her body. She stood there, and the shape of her was a pleasure for this old man. Pah, I am too old, she needs a much younger man.

But this day, she was to bed the Sun Lord, spread her thighs wide for his fuck of the morning light, right up between her legs and into her sweet cunt that I could only imagine in my dreaming ways. But fuck, that imagining was enough, I felt a throb in my loins. My old prick began to thicken and stretch, and the Sun Lord's not even here yet with his strength.

I waited. The shadow from the stone moved along the grass, the Sun soon to shine above the portal stone and knock there, for entrance.

Nymue lay on the skin, and from the outside of the circle I watched as she caressed herself with her own hands, pressing her hands down hard onto her nipples, and they stood tight. Her hands were slow, but I could see they knew the shape of her body and I saw a dip of her fingers between her legs and a first slide there, her hair a thick white fur against her pale flesh. There was a trance upon her, and she lay between the stones. Nymue cried out, and her voice was like a bird, a wailing cry.

The sound of her voice lurched into me, and my prick grew harder. Around me, I sensed my leftenants too were wanting to fuck, and in the circle, the women a fucked upon their fingers, urging Nymue on with their own magick entanglement. The stones watched, and the Sun rose above the portal stone. The land shimmered, waiting for the moment when the Sun King rose up from the distance of the far horizon. I looked back upon the east and there he was, rising red and round; the thick long rod of the portal rock become his shaft, all illumined veined and red, rising high up from the earth and the Sun rose hard.

His huge roundness was perfectly aligned, and the shaft of his half summer glory was long and straight and true and glowed all upon the place. He the Sun Lord moved and shone between the tall stones that were made to receive him and this bright morning fuck of powerful light.

From between the stones I heard the crooning cry of a woman, "Ahh Lord, mine own cunt widens for your heat, fuck into me," and it was Nymue on her back, her cunt arched up between her legs thrusted high, her legs wide to welcome in the light. Her body shuddered golden in the morning beams of the rising Sun, and his golden shining rod thrust down into her with all the heat and shafting fuck of the Sun Lord morning risen.

Nymue was blazed gold and crying out in his hands hot in her flesh and skin, and her fingers spread apart the folds of her cunt so the Lord Sun could fuck into her this half summer's day. With a keen that echoed into the stones, Nymue collapsed weak on the ground and twitched and writhed there, a glowing in the light, and her body grew still.

"Do not touch her, she soars!" Nyneve's shout warned the truth, and Nymue lay there, her eyes agone from her face and rolled back white. I could not see her fly, but knew that she did, her sex magick undaunted by the strength of this place. By the Goddess, Nymue now the strongest witch of all the Sisters and some of them very strong indeed; that she dared to take the Lord on his day and live, where others had bellies cut red and a sacrifice and died, in earlier years, when not a one was ready.

I leaned against the rock, my cheek against the old stone there, and spread my fingers wide to embrace the warming heat. Around me, the air shimmered and a strange crackling sound came upon the world and an odd scent like air around a waterfall, a crispness. I stood away from the stone and took some paces back. Looking away from the henge, but near it and wide, I saw down upon the grass a strange veil, some strangeness along the ground, a hazing light. Within the light I could see whole bands of taller grass bend and snap, shaping a strange pattern all amongst the grass.

I knew of circles and hexes made on these wide plains, seeing them with their spirals and mazes, and wondered on them, but did not know how they were made. But the grass would bend, corn especially, and patterns made that only a bird could see. Ah, a bird, Nymue on high, soaring. Of course, she will know and might tell, when the trancement stops.

The morning sun rose away and up from the shafted rock, and his prick was gone, Nym Nymue well fucked and a high priestess now, for the Goddess and the Sun Lord both. The sun arose and it was the longest day, all to shorten and shrink and grow cold and midwinter. I wondered then if white Nymue would return to this place when covered in snow, or was this day high magick enough, and she so strong?

Inside the circle, Nymue was fallen still between the tallest stones, her body not moving, completely still. Nyneve bade the small maids to take skins and cover the priestess and quickly come away, so not to disturb her flight.

I stole away to the place where the grass shimmered and hazed, and was astonished to see great curves in the grass made there, great circles and small, huge spirals made in the grass. The stalks were all bent, laid in patterns interwoven, laid this way and that. I looked to the sky, but it was cloudless blue. Up highest high, where my sharpest eyes could just see, I saw a soaring white bird and knew that Nymue still flew, her trancement thick and the Sun's golden seed still in her, high above all the Goddess to see. I would speak with her later, when Nymue was all recovered.

Meanwhile, my curiosity was first in my mind, and I bade to me good leftenants and made them to measure and map, to draw this strange geography that I might know it like a bird does. All above and looking down, spinning around this sacred place. I pondered on it and wondered if the ancient makers, dragging stone and standing rock all ringed around, had they made their stones to remember twisted patterns in the grass? This whole place is circles and circles, marked in stone and dug upon the ground. Did another Maer like me, long ago, make a geometry when the high ice melted back and this land lay smooth and new like a baby? I imagined soft smooth skin, and thought that he might have, when the Goddess first woke from the cold.

Later, back away in the tents and camps along the river Avyn, I went to the Sister's tent and was greeted there by Nyneve and Vivyane. They looked upon the girl with the white hair who still lay curled and sleeping, out of her trance now but tired.

"Maer, she is mighty now and powerful, an elemental thing. Do you know it, and why?"

"Nyn," I replied, respectful of her wisdom, and I wondering too, "I do not know it, but see it like you do. Know this, there is some work upon the land, and methinks we might all be called upon." I sat and wondered, and look upon the small shape of the white priestess sleeping there. "Nymue, I think, might have much magick to make, and mysteries too. She is powerful." I looked upon the girl, and there must have been something in my eyes when I looked.

"Care upon you, Maer Maerlyn, take care upon yourself. Do not become seduced by her."

Nyneve looked upon me, and was solemn, and her words were wise. Vivyane looked up and nodded, and they both were warning me, for they both knew the girl and I did not. But I feared it was too late.

I was there.

When the white witch Nymue met the Sun King and took in his heat, I Maer Maerlyn was there. The Goddess help me, for I am old and she is young, yet I fear I am bewitched.

The Mask in the Mist

I was there.

When magick made a bridge of mist and a prince's seed made an unborn king, I Maer Maerlyn was there, a petty dabbling sorcerer stealing love like a thief.

After the solstice and ceremony of the Sun, when Nym Nymue was made consort and queen, the Lady went her way and I the Maerlyn went mine. Both our paths ran through the land, spiralled and straight, hers and mine, collecting legiances and curses. We did not happen upon each other many times, she serving the Goddess her way and me doing service mine. The Sisters in the Isle of Glas learned both our songs and collected news, so we knew what each the other did, but our paths seldom crossed.

In truth, Nymue's white purity frightened me yet bewitched me too. I might wish the forty years between us gone, but the Goddess never wheels the stars backwards, only forwards. I looked upon Nym Nymue when I saw her and had to turn away in torment and despair. Even I cannot sorcer a new face for these old bones, it cannot be done; and besides, who would do it?

I lie. I would be the very first to reverse my time if I could, if I could lie every night with Nymue, with a face that pleased her. I would do it, if I could. By the Goddess, there is something about the girl that reaches right into my guts and grips me there, twisting my belly like a silly boy seeing a sweet girl the first ever time. I turn stupid when I see her, so make sure I keep away as best I can. The land does not need another dolt, there are plenty enough of those in chapels and monasteries as it is.

In time, I found myself useful in making stratagems and plans down on the long peninsula, where Moors come up from Iber and Afriq, sailing their ocean ships bringing silks and spices brought across the long Atlant. Their trade made the tribes and kings down south grow strong, and their new wealth struck jealousy into olden reigns further north, living poor on turnips.

So fights and battles began, camps in high places became forts with embankments, ancient harbours were dug deeper for larger vessels. Warriors and fools circled around the land, legiances grew strong, fell weak, scattered, and rose again. Daughters and sons made dynasties and disasters, barren brides and fecund sons, bastards became princes and kings begat kings. I became Maerlyn the engineer, building fortresses impregnable made of stone and rock instead of thatch and wood. I made defences with a rare skill, and none so great as the fortress by the sea they called Tyntangel. The Gorloys Duke lived there and his Lady Ygraine, by the sea. They hearkened both to me and took my wisdom and advice.

And my diplomacy! Yeay by the Goddess I had a smooth tongue, layering bedazzlement and charm by equal measure, convincing this court and that to combine their armies, choose their arms and legiances together. I even convinced some fool bishop or other, I cannot remember his credulous name, to twice tithe his church monies to Gorloys, and he to grow stronger for it. So I, Maer

Maerlyn, embedded mine self in Gorloys' court and knew the people there.

Midwives came and delivered of Ygraine a daughter, Morgayse who was first born and Gorloys' first daughter. And ten years on, a second child Morgayne did fret and cry upon the tit, who was the second daughter, but no son born.

Morgayse was a daughter like unto her mother, tall and fair even as a maid. Morgayne was contrary, small and dark and fey, a tiny child sitting with darkness in her eyes, watching, watching, watching all the time. Of this time I now tell, she crawled along in her swaddling clothes and still could not speak. But watching, oh yes, those little black eyes; hell's mouth might have spawned the imp. I was nervous around the child and no friends with her. Her little black eyes, they saw too much. Morgayne of the night, born in the darkest dark of the moon when the candle guttered and the midwife wiped the caul away that nobody might see.

Ygraine now, oh yes, she was a woman worth keeping away from other men in the high halls of Tyntangel's keep, circled nearly all around by sea and high cliffs. Ygraine now, yes. A strapping tall woman, with a great mane of waved golden hair and splendid thighs, long and firm. I imagined her grip and her strongness. Yeay, she was a beauty, truly. Gorloys was ever jealous and tried always to hide his wife away, but the Lady Ygraine would not comply and did not obey him.

Princes came to the court to make treat with the Duke and to pledge legiance and horse for his campaigns, for Gorloys made excellent command. With the assist of my devious strategy, more forces joined the Duke's legions and made win upon northern and eastern losers and knaves, and his kingdom was made. But no sons for the kingdom to keep.

The princes looked upon Ygraine secretly and lusted. She made no shame and would dance with them, flagrantly. She was Gorloys' cursed wife, but ah, her sweet blue eyes kept such false innocence. Ygraine thought she was not barren of boys. Her belief it was the Duke who made bed with her and brought only girls. Ygraine looked with delight at the young princes and scoundrels who came to her husband's court, and thought upon her loins she could get a man to fuck who made men, not girls.

Gorloys knew this and bade her locked away. She fought upon and rattled the door, but was well guarded by his trusted legion, true aye to the Duke. Ygraine and her women, the Duke and his men. 'Twould be a brave man to step between, or foolish.

There soon came to the Duke's court a powerful prince, Uthur by birth, pen Dragen by standard and flag, a great commander and captain of men. I was intrigued by his standard, and remembered back to the dragen let loose from the mountain afar to the east and the cataclysm on the earth. I wondered at the man arrogant enough to fly that flag, and made to watch upon him. I made a pledge too, to discover Uthur's advisor, for any man so audacious would indeed be well advised. I wondered how I did not know of this man before now, for common enough, I Maer Maerlyn should be that advice.

55

This Uthur took one look at the fair Ygraine and was smitten, that I could see. He wanted her plain, and his look was more than politick, it was lust, straight and simple. Her to wrap those legs and firm thighs about his waist, for to fuck the Lady Ygraine? He would make battle, I thought, and fight Gorloys even as he supped with the Duke and drank his cup. Love's traitor then, the ancient game. I would look upon it only, 'twould be a foolish man to step between, or brave.

"Maerlyn, do you skulk and watch from behind the kitchen door, like a servant child or some malodorous cook, making unto men poisons and soporifics?"

By the Goddess, what? What jest is this, who speaks to me with a contempt, but so familiar yet?

"Oh Maerlyn, have you forgot, your favourite sister's daughter's voice? I'm sad, that I am forgot so soon." Her voice was light and lyrical, a gentle teasing croon.

Oh Goddess, I was not prepared for this, not her. I turned slowly and looked upon the Lady, the white Nym Nymue, and even then was smit. She looked up at me, fond indulgence in her eyes, and she knew. She knew this old man was bewitched by her and could not get away, did not want to run, could not even if he tried.

"What witchery, Nymue, what witchery do you bring?" My mind, though struck by surprise, was seldom slow to grip and grasp at truths and lies; and I saw before me the pen Dragen's advice, that by superior strategy would assist. This man Uthur, then, must truly be a new and huge force upon the land, that Nymue would cleave to him and give him words. The Lady did not dabble foolish, so it followed she sought me here, deliberately.

"I am found for your strategy then?" I asked.

"Ah, Maer, yeay, I have thought upon it true, these last years, and this man Uthur is important to us; but he will be surpassed, we make it so."

We make it so? Nym Nymue not strong enough to do her magick solely?

"What conjuring do you propose, Lady, that we make it so?"

"Maer, you may be old, but you grasp quick the entire board, you see it whole already!" Nymue looked at me and the crease in her eyes was friendly. "It will not be so hard then, not so hard as I thought."

She paused, and ran her hand through her hair, still white like snow, but cut short and cropped about her skull. "I have talked it with the Sisters, my mother and Nyn Nyneve, and we think it possible." She touched my arm, and blood thundered through me and bumps on the goose took to my arms. "We will make it so, you and me, Maer Maerlyn, you and me."

So the Sisters knew it and plotted, for the Goddess? Powerful then, the magick proposed, but needing man and woman both to sorcer, the most powerful magickians in the land? She and me? What audacity is this, that I do not know it? I looked upon Nymue and knew I was but an apprentice now. The Goddess is well served then, that she finds Maer Maerlyn and Nym Nymue to do her will.

"And Uthur, what is he in this?"

"Ah, yeay, the powerful prince. See, who does he gaze upon, so full of lust?"

I looked to where Uthur sat and followed his gaze. Ygraine then, fucked by his eyes, as clearly as two follows one, and three follows two.

"Come, Maerlyn. I will explain, and then we conjure. My sickle moon is upon me, mine own power is strongest in me this night and it is time." Nymue looked across to the high table.

"See, the Duke and the prince make ready to ride. My plan unfolds tonight." Nymue looked up at me. "Do you feel strong tonight, Maer, or do I make it so?" She teased, and I was taunted.

Goddess, what do you have for me, planned and determined, that Nymue knows and I do not?

"Come away, Maer, to Uthur's camp. I have a travelling tent there, safe and remote. Uthur's troops dare not disturb me where I sleep, and we shall have peace to do our work." She smiled and her eyes laughed. "They fear the white one and it suits me, mostly."

Nymue went from the room and bade me follow. I did not know her idea of peace and thought I understood the guards' fear. I feared my bones and my body might find her presence not so peaceful, and her talk of her sickle moon power unsettled me, as I knew from tales of Glas something of Nymue's conjure.

I also knew her singular focus and the heights she might soar, her tokens dropped from shoulders and rising up. My mind remembered Nymue's gold kissed nakedness at the ceremony of the half summer sun, and the precious curves of her delicate waist and the patch of white at the base of her belly. I remembered, yeay, and wanted. How could I not? I was always ever becharmed by the girl, and she knew it. Nymue looked upon me, and knew it.

The shock of the five high waves - I knew now her terrified tale - was a permanent mark all upon her. Nymue's cropped white hair now hid her age, and she flickered between young woman and old crone in a flash, but was artful and mysteried her years, that no-one could tell. I knew, of course, having counted the years since she was a babe on Vivyane's breast, and did not ponder her disguise.

Uthur's camp was pitched on the meadows before Tyntangel, his tents made in rows and his horse saddled up. Nym Nymue and I watched as the war horses thudded by, their big hooves plashing on the mud, their riders full rigged. The pen Dragen standard fluttered at the lead, and the colours of Gorloys Duke beside.

As the prince Dragen passed by my Lady, Uthur pulled up the reins on his horse and leaned low to Nymue's ear. He glanced up and saw Gorloys ride on.

"Is it this night, Lady, that I shall have Ygraine and betray the Duke?"

Ah, so that is the plot, but I knew not the working of it.

"Yes, Lord. Keep to the side of any skirmish this night, that you might withdraw suddenly, when my messenger comes. Then obey all, every voice you hear, even if the sense of it makes no sense."

Nymue looked up at Uthur's high frame on his huge horse, and by any measure, she should be the smaller one. But when I looked upon them both, Nymue seemed to stand taller than he, and I wondered on at the plot, knowing it hers and not his.

Her words echoed: I have talked it with the Sisters and we think it possible. But only with me to aid and participate, yet still I knew it not.

Nymue whispered to mine ear, "Yeay, his lust falls to my plan and will focus him strong. His belief and desire will speed his feet, Maer, and we will not have to concentrate long. Uthur's want is our help, and will feed the spell."

The witch looked up to mine eyes and we were a tall thin man and a woman delicate and small. I wondered at her strength. And doubted mine.

"But you are uncertain, Maer. I must explain it, and so doing, begin our sorcery that must combine the man with a mask to claim entry to the keep, that Uthur may go there." Nymue turned on her toe and made way to her tent. "I need your geography of the place, Maer, to know the hidden doors and escapes, and to guide the man when he returns from battle. The entrance is hardest by. You know it."

Indeed I know it, for I made it. I did not see how it could be done, to gain entry, if Uthur did not know the watch and the word.

I followed Nymue to her tent and she spoke true. It was distant from the rest of the camp, and from within it I could look down over my fortified entrance to Tyntangel. There I saw the watch. Uthur unknowing of the word, how could he pass?

"Maer, as we make it, so will it be. For the Goddess, who needs a new king."

Nymue poured wine from a goblet and we both supped from the same cup. The palms of her hands covered the backs of my long fingers and again my heart a thumped and beat faster. I felt old and young both, and did not know what I should do.

"Follow, Maerlyn, come within."

Ah, my familiar name then, and I am beckoned. I knew not what was to happen, but guessed her conjure was begun with the sip from the cup, some calming thing. Nymue led me into a second chamber of the tent.

"Wait," she commanded, as she herself went behind a screen and was hid. The screen was high, and Nymue was hidden from mine sight. I heard the squeal of a hinge, ungreased it must have been, and the flutter of cloth. Nymue came from behind the screen and she was all in her white, symbolic. Her hair was bare and uncovered, short against her skull, and the whiteness of it captured my eye like new snow. Her pale blue eyes gazed upon me, forthright but friendly, yet a concentration on her face. Her spell was started.

Nymue came towards me and took my grizzled grey head in the palms of her hands, and she kissed me.

"Maerlyn, you and I this night must work up our strengths and powers, as the Hindi Maithuna teaches us, ancient wise. As I love you, so shall it be."

Love? The woman talks to me of love?

"What lie is this, Nymue, that you talk of love?"

My voice cracked. I could not keep my head straight through this nonsense. Even if I might want it so every time I looked at her, I knew it false.

"Do you doubt, Maerlyn?" Her voice sunk low, like honey and smooth. "Oh Maerlyn, doubt me not, yet true."

Nymue began a small flowing dance, weaving her hands up and about my body, touching me not but I felt her presence there. Her arms made a sinuous rhythm and her palms caressed the air around me, a floating from my skin. Candles flickered in the tent and burned whiter, as if a new fuel was in the air. I stood still in the place and felt a surge through my old bones and muscles. In the base of my belly a heat began and my root began a swell.

"What heat is this, Nymue, that you bring?"

"The fire is always lit, dearest one, I have seen it in your eyes. I've always known it and could fan it when I like. But tonight is not frivolous, Maerlyn, it is a sacrifice, our love used for something else." Her voice was a low croon, a low song around me as she wandered, and sweet honey to mine ears.

"We make it so, yet when our Mother commands, only then. There is a greater will." Nymue stopped her spin in front of me and looked up at me. "Care not, Maerlyn. If the Mother wants it, we make it so." She smiled, and it was a softness. "You and me."

The witch reached to her throat where there was a simple clasp and dropped her gown away.

Nymue stood before me naked, her pale flesh flickering and shadowed in the candle light. She stood still and unmoving, the top of her sweet head barely reaching level my lips, for I am tall and she is not. Nymue looked up at me and the blacks of her eyes were jet and wide, else the rest of her was pale and white. Her breasts were pleasing round, a gentle swell most firm and nipples dark and hard. I looked down, I could not look away. Her belly was flat and smooth, a white triangle of fur at the base of it, soft looking like a white pole cat. Ah, Nymue. My own flesh stirred at the sight.

"Maerlyn, we must make ourselves hot with each other, to call up lust magick and drive Uthur to Ygraine to rut in our stead." Her eyes looked glazed, and she dipped her fingers between her legs and then to my lips, scenting me with her perfume, musky and dark. "Wait."

And she ran to the curtains of the tent that was the entry way, and her body was curving and sweet, her little waist just a span of my hands if I touched her. She called to her maid.

"Send message to pen Dragen, a quickness in the feet who take it. Tell him, return from the battle soonest, time is a running now under the sickle moon. My strength, it is rising strong. Quick."

Nymue returned her whiteness to me, and her fingers clasped unto the cord about my throat and loosened it. My cloak fell away.

"You do it Maerlyn, be naked too, with me in the flesh."

I unravelled my clothes, my britches and my tunic vest, casting them to the ground in heaps, and soonest stood naked as the day I came crying into the world. I sensed now the way of it, our high magick to conjure visions and delusions that Uthur might pass. To do it Nym Nymue and Maer Maerlyn both needs place our own lustingness on each other, but nay to consummate. Our flow of energy must be powerful strong to combine, the witch and magickian together.

"Your wood, Maerlyn, ist made thick for me?"

Even in her magick, I saw a sweet smile in Nymue's eyes, making this old man hard like I was young again and her the cause. She gripped me in her hands and held me tight, then placed my length to her belly and her breasts, feeling my hot heat there.

"Ah, Maerlyn, your rod makes heat on my flesh and burns me against my skin."

Nymue's hands were warm and started a slow caress. Pleasing thick, my cock was long in her hands and she stroked me up, faster and slower. She sank to her knees afore me and crooned her lips around my plum, humming a low song on my flesh, suckling up on me, sending heat and thrills up my spine. So the witch made me rise, and I grew strong.

Her tune changed and one hand dropped away between her legs and she dropped to the ground like a dog on all fours. Displaying her cunt for my eyes, she played apart her purple and red lips, and her cunt was a bright split in her white flesh. I feasted my eyes on her ass cheeks and fresh cunt, seen for the first time and I hoped not the last.

"Do your eyes like this sight, Maerlyn, my wet cunt opening to your tongue?"

I needed no directions, but sucked Nymue's honeyed cunt to my mouth and tasted her to my tongue and to my lips. I reached under her body, finding her swaying tits and cupping them. So I found the witch Nymue and tasted her, and her blood was metallic on my tongue. Her sickle moon was upon her, her tide drawing out and turning, and her sex opening up.

Nymue started up a low chant in her throat, her moans a rhythmic sound, and I supped upon her cup and she started up a high ecstasy but never peaked. Her body was flushing all pink as her strength rose, yet she surged and stopped, surged and stopped; and so did I. Between us the air began to coil and shift, a smoking thing pulling sacral energy from within her cunt and all along my cock, and the air crackled and glowed.

She moved again, and Nymue made me sit. She sat upon my lap, her legs wrapped around my waist. My cock never went into Nymue, we did not fuck, but her cunt was wet on my rising balls and all along the base of my shaft and she slid. Her blood painted my cock all red and we breathed in and out each other's breath, spiralling up and both soaring outside ourselves. Twisting into the sky we spun about each other, our silver chords twisting together and we merged as one magickian, male and female under the sky and the sickle moon. We made our conjure and our spirits rose up over the world.

Looking down onto the earth away a distance we could see a tumult and dark movement of horse and men, pyres and flame. Of a sudden I looked with her eyes and she with mine, and saw a great horse break from the mass and gallop.

With a jerk and a rapid plummet I sank back to my warm flesh and Nymue's arms were around me and mine around her. Our bodies shuddered and our white heat was high up in our brains, streaming from between our eyes. Our streaming sex energy was thick and strong, but no fluids jetting or erupting as we weaved our flows together.

Nymue rolled from me, her fingers thick in her cunt to drip up more magick, my passion feeding hers, and she remembering all the spiralling stones in her brain and surging strong circles.

"Go, Maer, you lead him."

She moaned at the loss of me. Oh sweet thing, I to leave you?

"I to conjure false faces, Maer, it will drain me and collapse me and you will find me curled and sleeping."

Nymue gazed her lovely eyes to my face and I saw her all there; the smallest girl and my heart ached, but the strongest woman too and my cock throbbed.

Outside the tent I heard the clop of hooves and the horse's pant. "Go, he is here."

I wrapped my travelling cloak twice around me and grabbed a belt and my leathern boots, stumbling by the curtained entrance to pull them onto my feet. My cock still thick and long, a high heat in my balls, I left the tent.

Ahead of me Uthur sat on his huge high horse, his breath panting fast from his ride. As I watched, I saw the strangest shimmer, a whole shift in the air about his face, and I knew the magick Nymue made, a new disguise and shifting mask for the man. She could not do it for my lust, but she could make it for this Lord; cursed witch, yet I loved her too.

I walked down to the horse and took up its bridle. "Come sire, look straight ahead, do not shift thy gaze from above the horse's head." I led the horse along. "Do not startle if you hear the Duke's name. He does not ride beside you."

"I betray the Duke, is all?"

"Yes, sire. A betrayal. But must be done."

For the Goddess, I thought to myself, and now understood the plot. The shimmer and mist in the air made strange light around Uthur's head, and Gorloys' face became his, a new mask.

"Ride on, sire, look straight. Pass the watch and they will see only the Duke. Never speak, or they will know 'tis not he on this horse." I passed Uthur the bridle rein. "Remember sire, no words, just thy wrong visage. I will walk besides, they know me."

The plot was done and Nymue's magick held. Uthur the betrayer passed over the draw and into the mist, and all alike Gorloys he looked, in the eyes of the watch. Nymue's spell was wide and in the minds of many, for to convince. I saw the way of her sacrifice and mine, and thought this night's purpose an important thing, a turning pivot on the world, and the Goddess made it so.

"Duke Gorloys returns," a soldier cried, "let him pass, ride by." Uthur spurred on his horse and entered the fort. "Maer Maerlyn too, on the Duke's business."

So the watch was passed and fooled, and the garrison thought the Duke rode amongst them. But it was a false man, a mask, a traitor. Led on by a man seduced by a witch's magick, ha. Man is ever human and his lusts determine everything, I'm no different. I pretend my task is for the Goddess but it's mine own lust for the white Lady that she commanded here.

But the plot. "Walk on sire, along the path to Ygraine's dwell, past the last few of Gorloys' men."

I hoped Nymue's magical vision would hold, for I saw cracks and shadows on the false face, the true Uthur flickering in and out. The witch Nymue must be past tired now, reaching for too many minds to change all their senses.

I passed my hand within my cloak and loose britches, and felt my hot thickness there, hanging softer now but still full thick from the heat of her. The stickiness from Nymue's blooding cunt slicked my hand and I imagined her there, a fallen in the bed, one hand fingered between her legs, the other pressed against her thick long teat, cupping her own breast where my hand should be. My cock rose to my hand, a last thrust of sacral light to fake their minds. The distant Nymue must have sensed my rise, for Gorloys' face sharpened over Uthur's, and hid the true visage.

"Pass by, Duke. The Lady is within."

The last of Gorloys' men all fooled, and Uthur now in the women's compound. I saw his true face clear and knew that Nymue fell from consciousness into a long swoon, the dear girl done and this old man still work to do.

"This way sire, to the Lady's room, that she might know you and be delighted in your man. 'Till the cock cries, Lord, whence we escape by boat."

"Wizard, you have made magick for my filthy lust and I betray a good man. Is this what women do to us?"

"No sire, it is what men will do for women. Don't think they manipulate you, when 'tis you that wants, that simple. You wished into Ygraine to fuck and we made it so." His high moral stance sickened me, but there was a bargain here. "You owe us payment on, Uthur Lord, and it will be ours, whatever it may. The Goddess is in us all, sire, and demanding." I preached to him. "Don't falter now."

My small speech was urgent and made to convince. This man could not turn feeble on us, not from our sacrifice, Nymue and mine and no consummation.

"Go sire, to Ygraine for to fuck her and make her yours." I grew tired of his dilly dally. "Uthur Lord, are you a man or a tiny mouse? D'ost thou fear a strapping woman, who flirted you with her eyes."

"Curse you, wizard, don't mock me. I do it."

"Till the cockerel crows, Lord, no more. Go, rise your cock between your legs and greet Ygraine."

And the plot now, I fully understood it all and warned. "And sire, yeay even so Ygraine has wondrous breasts and a round belly, spill no seed outside on them. Fuck up into her, Lord, as if a babe to make."

Thus goaded on, I trusted to Uthur's massive opinion of himself to prove this night, to shaft the Lady Ygraine long and sweet, several times as he could, to fuck her all night.

Uthur passed down a thin corridor, shuffling sideways his shoulders were so broad, and brushed aside a curtain. I heard a startled yelp and a shushed quietness, then a low murmuring made and light laughs. I knew it Ygraine with a happiness in her and a new cock soon.

I heard Ygraine's low call to her woman, "Caitlyyn, come for the child, take her to sleep with her sister, her to be warm in another bed."

I stepped back into a darkness to hide as a girl came for the child. It was the small dark thing, the little Morgayne, sleepy tousled with her thick black hair. As Caitlyyn carried the babe on her shoulder down along the passage, I swear I saw the glint of the child's eye spy me in the alcove there. I shuddered, for her look was unblinking and a scaring thing, even for a man who does not fright easy. I did not like the imp and she not me either, in her darkness.

Soon from the end of the corridor I heard the sounds of Uthur and Ygraine together, their low murmurs and rustles on a bed. Her low moans soon, and Uthur's groans. Fuck them, they took the lust that was mine and my white witch, and they had it for themselves, all on the back of our spell. Fuck the Goddess too, always making it duty and not mine own pleasure.

Yet the low calling of the woman Ygraine, urging tenderly up the fuck into her higher and deeper, sweet crooning in her throat; I could not stay soft, my own thick syrup still settled in my balls. Hearing any woman cry out for a man would make a man rise, unless he only liked boys. Yet this old man always loved women, and Ygraine's calling, although not for me, sang in my ears.

I imagined the white Nymue in my head all mine, but the vision was not enough, she was not there. So I crept along the corridor to nearer see Ygraine and Uthur make the two backed beast, and found another alcove there against an ancient rock. I felt the stone with my hand and knew it to be an old one, stolen from its place in a ringed circle to make a new corner on this house. I could watch and see and hear, and through a gap I saw the arch of Ygraine's throat as she reached her head back. Her body was arched back and I could see she was fucked into swift and sure, for her full tits bounced and shuddered and her mouth was open, a silent cry fucked out of her on every panting breath.

I couldn't not. I Maer Maerlyn reached into my britches and dropped them to the ground and wrapped my cloak around me and wrapped my hand around my cock, thick and heated hard. All the long night of my spell making with Nymue thickened in my hand and my spine arched too, to Ygraine's moan. I supported my weight standing 'gainst the ancient stone with one palm wide and felt it warm beneath my skin; and with my other hand began a silent stroke.

Nymue behind my closed eyes, her smiling lips, her long red hair when she was young, her white long hair when she was fucked by the Sun, her short white hair from this night when we made false fuck for magick and all I wanted was her. Sweet girl, her honey sweet cunt and her high firm tits, and I imagined her bouncing on me, her body arched with my length long inside her. That was not enough either, and my mind ran back over women I'd known until they all blurred and merged in my head. My cock was thick and pleasing hard in my hand, and soon I just fell into the sense of my own pleasure, slipping my hand all along.

"Maer, let me, you should not be alone when the Lord and Lady rouse us with their fuck."

A young voice whispered up to my ear and a small warm hand crept around my shaft. It was Caitlyyn, come to find me. "Away. We do not need their sounds, we make our own. Their fuck has made me wet, and you're a man." She took me by the hand, the pretty little wench, and took me to a servant's room. "You might be old, but your wood is hard and will satisfy me, make me smile."

I saw a glint in Caitlyyn's eye in the candle light, and she was cheerful and honest and kind to me, old Maerlyn. I was thankful, and taught her a thing or two. We played together and I drank from Caitlyyn's slippery cunny, her cup, and diddled her asshole with my finger and my tongue because she wanted it so. She gobbled on my prick and thrust her finger up my bum, clever girl, and finally, when my balls had had enough and were full from all the long sex and lust, sweet kisses and moans in the night.

"Don't make a baby, Maer Maerlyn, in mine cunny." She was a sensible girl and of the earth and no pretending she was grand, just a lusty girl well made and wet on my tongue. "Just spill your cream on my tits, Maer, and I be your serving girl and rub it all in like a creamy mess and lick it from my finger, see."

And she held her finger up and sucked it into her mouth, her eyes all laughing with her fun and play. And sometimes, like once I said sweet warmth was enough, sometimes it's not. So I did, I spilled all my full balls all over her bouncing tits and left her skin with my creamy white sauce. Caitlyyn laughed and rubbed it all in, all around her nips and sucked it from her fingers and smiled.

"Silly man, there. Isn't that better than a spurt on the floor, all jealous and cross?"

"Lovely girl, yes, you do me kind, you're so much better than my hand."

"And you know it, Maer?"

"What do I know?"

"That I be here, whenever you might want; for the dark child might have a sible tonight, from the way I heard my mistress' lusty cries; and children need a caring for."

She was right, the clever girl, and might be a sweet, regular thing if I stayed with Gorloys in his service. But the magick made by Nymue was clearly aiming at child by Ygraine, fathered by Uthur, and would surely change the politick of the court. Changeable winds were blowing and I feared a storm. Mine advice might shift and swing where the wind was strongest.

Hark, the cockerel called. I must to Uthur and be departed, before Gorloys returned. I kissed the sweet Caitlyyn goodnight on her lips. She was a fine girl and good, and I bade her well. No promises. I left her small servant's room and snuck back to Ygraine's chambers to call Lord Uthur away.

I crept to the corridor like a thief, and stopped short of the door, nearly treading on a small scuttling thing sliding upon the floor. It was Morgayne, the smallest child, 'scaped from her sister's room to find her mother. As I say, I nearly trodden on the child, yet stopped my foot in time. The imp stared at me with her malevolent eyes and I felt accused. In truth, the tiny creature was right. My deeds this night did not favour her.

Morgayne gripped mine ankle with her fierce little hands and dug her tiny nails into my skin. I bit my lip to not cry out, but then I yelped. The cursed child had bit mine ankle, her sharp new teeth pulling blood from my flesh. Like as to a small cringing dog, I shook my foot and the child was flung away from me, sliding till she crashed against the wall. Morgayne started a loud mewling, a hideous cry, enough to waken devils from the pit.

Ygraine her mother rushed out. "What do you do, Maer Maerlyn, that she cries?"

"Nothing, I swear, my Lady; but the child did bite and tastes blood."

My defence sounded feeble, for what grown man could not stop a child?

"What do you, wizard, that cruels the child and makes her cry?" Uthur too, and his lust the ultimate cause, for Ygraine discarded the babe for Uthur to grapple himself onto her tit.

"Don't preach at me, sire. Your voice is not without stain now, for you fucked the varmint's mother in your lust. Don't pretend to love this child, this loveless thing." I stood against his will. "You do not. I lovest the child more, and I do not love it."

Uthur glared at me, filth in his eyes yet silence made, for I spoke truth against him, and he knew it

"Bid the Lady gone with her babe, to quieten it." I turned from the chamber. "We need to be gone, sire, your life depends on it."

I spoke some truth, for Uthur was still hidden. Gorloys' troops thought the Duke was in the fort and in his wife's chamber. They did not know Uthur wandered there.

"Skulk, sire, scuttle like a lowly cur." I was shaming him, who doubted my defence and I shamed too. "We must away to a small boat and oars, to quickly scape the island, yet we be found here."

Uthur saw my reason and followed on down a steep path to a beach where small boats always placed. We pushed a boat out to the waves and careful climbed aboard, making sure not to tip and rock. Luck was upon us, for a thick mist quickly hid us, and we were quiet upon the oars. We need not long to make another beach a distance from Tyntangel's defences, running the boat ashore upon the pebbles.

"Lord, you must take another horse from your troop and ride back to the fake friendship. You are never friends now but an enemy, if he discovers you between Ygraine's legs."

I wondered at the politick needed if indeed Ygraine were fucked with child and it a boy. Gorloys was not stupid. He see a babe's head and know it not his, he might wonder which prince or stable boy had fucked the Lady. Yet I was not sure how Uthur could vantage this, first thing.

But all that later. "Go now, Lord. Tarry not. Find a horse and ride circuitous paths back to the skirmish, so it looks like you made other business and chopped heads distant."

"Yes, I see it, the subterfuge I needs make." Uthur looked on me, and I could not truly judge his face. "You and the witch, you have used my lust for your own reasons, I fear, and I know it not." Uthur pondered on it a moment. "Can I trust you, Maer Maerlyn?"

"Trust, Lord? I think not. I do not trust mine self, so any other person does, is a fool."

Uthur laughed, "Good answer, Maer, good wisdom indeed!" He chuckled on. "I like you wizard, even tho you call me a cur and a mouse." He slapped me on the back and I fare near snapped, his hand so strong. "A cur, wizard? I like it!"

"Not a poodle sire, on a lady's lap. More a snuffling hound, under her skirts."

Uthur looked on at me, scarce believing my words, then his face lit with a wry smile. "Ah, wizard, you know me well already, a mangy dog sniffing for cunt, well practised." He looked about and saw that the sun was climbing and a clearing the mist. "Best on, then."

"And Maer," he was thoughtful now, "when a low prince gets assist from the white Lady the sorceress, and she recruits the land's best mage to her aid, that prince be a fool if he not pay attention, yeay? D'ost I need worry my back?"

"Your back, Lord? Need not worry, sire. I've seen it, crooked and bent. You have no Brutus with a knife, unlike that Roman, Caesar.

"That far, you seest that far?"

"Yes, Lord. But cannot see tomorrow. Go now, sire, we can talk all day. You must ride."

76

Too late. That very moment we heard on the distance the high call of a horn and the far sound of galloping horse, and all shouting. We hurried to the top of a high place and saw rising dust and thundering horse, and Gorloys' pennant at the van. But it was turned on its head, the colours upturned, all the symbol of death and it streamed behind, the rider so quick.

We heard the leftenant's cry. "Death on the battle! The Duke Gorloys dead. Undone!"

"What curse is this?" spat Uthur. "I should hast defended him, our flags side by side against the northern threat."

"False loyalty, Lord, too late. You betrayed him when first you saw Ygraine."

And Uthur's lust betrayed him first, I thought, when Nymue saw it. I understood it now, the Sister's long plot all unravelled, waiting for the right man and the wrong, and the timing of the moon. Ordained and fateful running, all puppets. Vivyane's favourite entrails could not have seen it, but Nyn Nyneve and Nym Nymue with their older know of ancient paths. What genius, to see the longer spirals! Truly I am the apprentice.

But a quick and sudden one, my mind spinning to an instant plan, and Uthur next to me its means.

"Take horse, Lord Uthur, and five of your fastest men. Make chase and hunt down the attacker, venge the dead Duke. Return with a head on a pike, declare yourself king in this court."

Uthur saw the quickness of it too. I saw the glint in his eye as he calculated fast his moves and winnings; the Duke's men, his court, his queen, pen Dragen flying fast in the wind.

"A fortuitous fuck then, Maer, that gives me good fortune."

"Don't gloat on it sire, remember the payment. We will call on it when ready, the witch and I."

"Payment fair made, even if I know it not, if I can make myself king." Uthur looked me direct in the eye and we understood each other well.

"Make vengeance, Lord, and it is your crown. Go!"

I turned from him and went. I had woman's work to do.

I was there.

When magick made a bridge of mist and a prince's seed made an unborn king, I was there, a petty dabbling sorcerer stealing love like a thief.

The Young Commander

Uthur pen Dragen returned from the field with the head of a northern prince, a pretender, skewered on his lance. Thus Duke Gorloys was revenged, and the small mystery of his passing of the watch, that very same night, was forgotten. Or at least, only dimly remembered except by those intimately involved. I was able to recover Uthur's horse before the unusual saddle pommel was recognised. The horse, sensible beast, knew its own way back to the meadow, so I only had to sneak it out in the dark of night, bags of straw over its hooves to stop its clop, and slap it on its rump. It made its own way home.

The guard and watch, convinced they had seen Duke Gorloys return to the fort for to fuck his wife and make her squeal, then contrive to get himself killed the very same night; they were harder to confuse. My solution, and it cost me a sore head over several nights, was to join the men and make merry with good wine and honey mead. I made them so legless and my stupid head too, that by the end of it they were convinced a man lived upon the moon, or the moon was made of cheese, one of the two. Any suggestion that the Duke entered Tyntangel that night, other than on a hearse the next morning, became no more than a stupid drunken story.

I think it must have been cheese, for I've heard that theory told more recently. I don't have the heart to tell those believers I made it all up. Some people are like priests, they're so credulous they will believe anything told with conviction.

Uthur might have pondered for a moment the diplomacy and the nicety of entering Tyntangel fortress so soon after the death of Gorloys. If he did think ont, it was only a tiny moment, possibly no longer than the pause in which to catch his breath as he dismounted the horse he rode in on. He mayhap decided that the triumphant entry of a vengeful prince, satisfied with the head of another man's foe, made good theatre; and it naturally followed that a declaration of a kingdom, made by uniting his own realm with that of the Duke, was good practice.

Suffice it said, Uthur King, pen Dragen, was crowned that next night. Nym Nymue, being his advice and counsel and the land's high witch besides, blessed a crown and placed it on his head. Nymue held a secret smile on her face for the plan, her pivot for a turning world, was speedy beyond all expectation.

Nymue. I shall return to her, as I always want to do.

The little doxy Caitlyyn, the practical maid, became ever more practical and pleasing with me. It seems she liked my height but more the proportionate length of me; and liked it to fill her asshole up, her womb being out of bounds for sensibility's sake, and because she liked it. I did not mind it, not at all. Her squeeze was tight and reminded me of Greek boys from my youth with their thin cocks, more seed than sense. It was an easy change to reach under a firm young body and find soft, warm breasts instead of a flat chest and a hard prod. Mayhap as I get older my tastes change, or mayhap I just can't make my mind up. I don't know it.

The vantage too, of keeping Caitlyyn the maid favoured and friendly, her ass upfucked, was her access to the Lady Ygraine's moods and thoughts. My, they changed upon change promptly after Gorloys' death, I could barely keep up.

Ygraine wore the widow's black for almost a respectable time, but then her belly began to show and it became a matter of what was tasteful in terms of a new marriage to a new king. Uthur, knowing the Lady's belly was his in truth, encouraged the suggestion that the old Duke, in the nights before his unfortunate battle, had mustered a final fuck.

"Let's hope the child looks like its mother," Uthur said. "Whatever sex it be."

"Yeay, Lord, we wait. Time will tell whether we need another tale to make. A child strapping fair like its mother would be no shame. You could pamper your own babe, and folk will credit you. 'Look yon King, he loves the child like 'twas his own.' It will not harm thy good name."

All seemed well, then, with the pivot and the plot. All well, except the child Morgayne. Too young to reason with, too young to make drunk and forget, the dark child became even more silent and ever more watchful. Morgayne never cried, not once, not since she slid against the wall with my ankle blood on her lips. She had the taste of me, and I feared her like a bat.

Morgayne hated me, I knew it. As years passed on I could see her little black mind connected me with the loss of her father and the removal of her mother to the new king's bed. I could not veil the truth with lies, not with the child Morgayne. She grew uneasy on me, and I kept caution with her. I felt a deep foreboding come with Morgayne, but conjure as I might, I could not tell it. Just a blackness in my mind. Like poison, she would fill a dark cup. The dark Morgayne was only a child, but I did not doubt her malice.

Nymue? Nay, not yet. Suffice to say this old fool, besotten, is besotted. Having been naked with her, for the command of sex magick and its quick force in the minds of men, made it worse for me, and better. She torments me, and I crave witch and woman both.

About half way through the time just told, about the time when Ygraine knew a child was coming but before the world saw, she summonsed me.

"Maer Maerlyn, what knowledge you of this woman Nym Nymue, who has the ear of Uthur?" Ygraine gazed upon me forthright, and hearkened for my truth.

So I lied. "I have heard tell of her, Lady, a powerful Sister of Glas, but I know not whence she came, nor how Uthur found her."

I could not tell the good Lady that Nymue found Uthur, and Ygraine too, with their human frailties of lust and desire, perfect fodder for her longer plan. And my place in Ygraine's seduction by Uthur? Best a secret kept, truth untold, the better to dissemble when required.

"Why ask, Lady?" A little knowledge of motive travels far and is always useful.

"I know not. Some feeling, something in my bones, I don't know it."

Ygraine struggled with her presentiment, to articulate some hidden knowledge clumsily arrived at, for she was no witch. She was unskilled and untutored in those arts, and best that it was so. Meddling was bad enough when one knew what to do and when to stop; so if the woman didn't know it, she couldn't influence it.

My problem is not knowing when to stop. I just keep on and on at it and fall into trouble often. Or perhaps it's mischief, which is a lighter handed thing.

It was a shame in a small way that Ygraine had a nervousness about her unborn child, for I liked the Lady. Whilst she yearned a lusty cock between her legs and did not reliably get one with the old Duke, she was artfully woman enough to wile the new Uthur and to be his match. The Lady Ygraine would sit well beside pen Dragen's throne and would, methought, be reliable as his consort. Her elder daughter Morgayse was Ygraine in miniature, whilst Morgayne was not. Ygraine had at least one marrying daughter, but I wasn't sure of two.

"How to cope with your little one, Lady, if she has a sister or a brother?"

Even though I did not warm to Morgayne, she was but a toddle and I should try to be kinder.

"I don't know it, Maerlyn, she is so quiet and observes us too well, she uneases me." Ygraine looked at me and didn't judge, I hoped, for my careless reaction in the corridor. Ygraine carried her guilt too for her daughter, sending the little babe from her breast that night. "I don't know it. Mayhap when the new babe suckles, I bring Morgayne back to my tit, in penance." She sat thoughtful, and whispered, "Morgayne is a difficult child to love, but I must, I'm her mother."

I looked upon Ygraine and for once in my prattling life was silent. Morgayne, then, uncertain with her mother, yet so small. It was a wrongness, but I wasn't certain it could ever be made right. Cursed, just for being the dark Morgayne.

"Sire, what thoughts you on the timing of a marriage?"

Having something of Ygraine's ear, I thought it wise to secure the new king's too. I'm turning into a meddling old woman, I'll be at my thimble next.

"The respectful time, I think," replied Uthur. "When my Lady shows, I'm content to let folk think the old Duke did well just before he died, and bring the child up as his."

We looked at each other straight. "I guess, Maer, that the child itself be the payment demanded by Nym Nymue and yourself for services that night." A wry smile curled Uthur's lip. "It suits me, therefore, to be one distant from the child, to say it not mine, if I do not know its destiny and do not control it." He studied me close. "You do not want the child to die, you want its life, I sense that."

"Yeay, Uthur, I know not all the white Lady's plot; but life, yes, is central to it. I swear on my unreliable soul, sire, that I shall look to the child with care whilst I can, and watch over it."

"Swear, Maerlyn? Thou commit that much of your soul to my child? I scarce believe that. Are you doting as you get older?"

"As unreliable as always, Lord, you know it."

Uthur laughed. "So it's a promise then, Maer?"

"Yeay, sire. Yet unclear in my head whom I promise it to."

Perfectly clear, but not to be said. Nymue commands me, she always did.

"The marriage then, sire. One year and one day, to the night, and the babe be born a year's three-quarter done."

"We plan on it, Maer."

"Just the checking of it, sire. Never questioned, always planned."

"I knew it. Is there anything you don't know, Maer Maerlyn?"

Yes in truth. The white Lady and the dark child. Both were veiled and hidden from my eyes, and only one heart known. A dangerous sentiment, mine own.

"I know this, Lord: I know nothing."

Thus it happened. A boy was born, fair unto his mother. Artur named and on his mother's tit; and as Ygraine thought it best, his part sister Morgayne beside him.

I looked upon them, and wondered.

"D'ost wonder, Maer, what you see?" Nymue stood beside me, silently, and linked her arm through mine. Like proud parents, we watched upon the little pair and saw the future sleeping there.

"Do you know it, Nymue, have you seen it all?" I was intrigued as to the Lady's prescience, mine being covered by darkness and cloaks, blind even in the brightest light.

"I know the most of it from pen Dragen's blood and the boy, least ways the first of it. But Gorloys' blood, I cannot see it. Morgayne is dark to me, I cannot see her at all."

Morgayne then, unknown to us both and veiled.

"The future lies uncertain, but is always near." No question, but deeds undetermined and both of us blind. For a pair of seers, they say the best in the land, we bumbled worse than clumsy bees, hmmm, hmmm.

"Nym Nymue, now, what you?"

"To find iron and silver, copper and gold, and a hot fire to cook it in and an anvil to make it sharp. The boy will need proof, I must arrange it. You will hear rumours when the time is come, and know it for what it is."

Nymue stood beside me, her arm resting inside mine. I looked down on her cropped white head and wondered at her will, and the absence of mine own. We were silent for a long pass of time, lost in our own thoughts. Then she stirred, and shifted away. As Nymue silently faded into the night, her fingers trailed loosely along my skin, down my arm, trailed down to my finger tips as light as a feather and finally drifted away, as if she'd never been there at all.

So Uthur married the Lady Ygraine and the knowledge of Artur their son held secret from the court. Artur became known as the heir of

Gorloys, and was like unto his mother, Ygraine. Over time he grew tall and fair like a brother to Morgayse, most unlike his half sister the little Morgayne.

Yet by age there was not much between the dark imp Morgayne and the boy, and to my surprise, the little girl took unto her brother without objection. As they grew and weaned from Ygraine's tit, they became inseparable. The little girl would pull the boy around Tyntangel by his tiny hand. The court became used to the quick shadow of her blackness and his golden sunnyness. They would cuddle together and sleep like wild creatures warm in the night, making small nests of bedding in this room and that.

Even when Ygraine bore two daughters to Uthur proper in quick succession, Claryyne and Arcyfleur, the two older children played on their games and stayed together, growing older, growing up.

Time passed and Gorloys' eldest, the sweet Morgayse, was betrothed to King Lot of Orkney and sent far north. Uthur decided, for reasons I mostly understood but could not properly question, that Artur too would go north with the older girl.

Morgayne was torn asunder from her half brother, and glowered all around her and fell silent again. They were both too young. I could not fathom it, but could not defend it either. It fair broke my heart to see their tears, but Uthur would not be persuaded. It was his punishment on us, Nymue and me, the price of his debt and his silence.

To the north I went, my soul foolishly promised to Uthur, King; dragging Artur away from his mother and his sisters and most of all from the little dark Morgayne. I became Uthur's scape and Uthur's goat, and my ankle ached when it was cold.

Time passed and now, aye, the core of it. All else before is preparatory. I must remain with my wits about me, to tell it. The tell is lonely and on my shoulders only. They are all gone, quite gone. This tree, little sparrow, little sparrow. I might be mad, quite mad, tweet, tweet.

Artur was five when sent from Tyntangel to the distant Orkney Isles, leaving behind his half sister, Morgayne. The boy did not know who his true father was, so listened to stories from Morgayse about Gorloys and thought them true, when she spoke of their father. In the far north of the land the boy began to know his oldest sister better, and they clung to each other for comfort, the warmth of family strong between them. He became known as Artur son of Gorloys, brother to the Orkney queen.

At first, Morgayse curled warm around him in her bed, but over time King Lot brought her to his chamber, and Morgayse left the boy for her man. She bore three boys over a period of five years, and mothering them meant a stop to sistering Artur. So he was thrown onto his own resources, and became solitary and alone. He wasn't resentful, loved his sister still, and respected Lot. He began to learn the duties of a decent courtier, to become a loyal man. Memories of distant Tyntangel grew dim and Artur knew not his true father nor mother. Only the scattered memory of his sister Morgayne stayed with him, but even she faded into dreams.

On occasion the mage Maerlyn travelled to the islands, and once the Lady Nymue, as if to check on him. But neither of them stayed long, and slowly Artur's world settled into a routine of fishing boats and long trips by sea. Each year as he grew, Morgayse would knit for him a corded woollen jumper of unwashed sheep's wool. The greased wool shed water almost like a duck and kept him dry, even in a storm. The pattern was always the same, so if he was found drowned, he would be known. Every wife and mother marked her man and sons that way, elaborate patterns artfully knit, defence against the sea's anonymity.

The sea journeys Artur took became longer, north and west to the island hot with volcanoes and cold with ice, the island edged with high cliffs and few low passages to the sea. There he learned runes and a different speech; and it was there too, near his sixteenth birthday, that he discovered the delights of a girl his own age.

Morgayne returned to Artur in his dreams, and she was older too. Her hands moved slowly.

Older now, Artur commanded boats to the east, making landfall in long fjords and sailing along coasts with high mountains. He began to understand the value of trade and barter, the importance of good will and good trust, and became a fair man. A leader of men, commanding ships carrying trade.

Time passed.

In the south, a dying king lay dying, and had no sons, only daughters. Word travelled slowly. Princes gathered in circles, whispering, wondering what lineage mattered. Birds flew out of season, white birds soared high and circling, rising on high currents, strange cries catching on the wind.

Rumours grew of a new spring burst forth, a sacred place for the Goddess; and beside it a rock, a clefted rock. It was a strange place, full of half truths.

Rumours ran: rocks weeping, stones dancing, tears in the rain, feathers twisting in the air.

The Knife in the Rock

I was there.

When a solitary boy, just breaking man, pulled a knife from a tight rock and found himself king, I was there.

I wasn't the only one of course, as one might expect for a coronation. Both fate and conjure meant there was quite the cavalcade of characters, even if some of them were uncertain of their true roles and their place in the affairs of men. I trust that I keep my wits about me to tell it all in roughly the right order. Somewhat right, at least, or the essence of it, barely. They've left me to tell it, the Sisters, for they have gone. But I get ahead of myself.

The problem with passing time is the waiting. I grow easily bored and want to meddle, to prod my finger like a boy with a stick into a wasps' nest. I grow lazy too, and find others to do my work. I'm for the main event, I think, to lie and truth the biggest things, not the dull parts in between. But still, the waiting around had its vantages. I had a pair of new boots made, and boots are made for walking, so I walked.

It's a long way to the north, and time was running now. To get there and back before Uthur the dying king died, or at least to return before it got complicated by a pretender and a topple from the throne. So I acquired a donkey to carry my ass somewhat quicker. Some would say it the other way round, but I don't like carrots. My legs are long, and the donkey's legs shorter, so we scooted along like some six legged beast, my legs doing some of the work like an overgrown child on a toy wooden horse. Snot nosed children ran along beside me, laughing and fooling and urging me on, any old fool but a serious one. Well hidden in plain sight, I've found, is the best way to skulk.

"Why not get a high horse, old man?"

"Less far to fall and break my own neck. When I want to get off, I just stand." I demonstrated, "Walk on, donkey!" Laughter followed me and good jest, and thus I made my way north.

Coming to a harbour, where I needs find plank and sails to carry me on, I remembered a return a long time ago when I also found the sea a barrier, and on the other side processions and the sun rising.

I remembered the first see of Nymue's white - her hair had been so russetty red - and the sight of her standing naked between the stones. The view of the cleft between her legs as the Sun fucked his shafting rays into her cunt, that is in my mind obviously; but it's the memory of her little waist and the sweet curve of her hips that I remember best, as Nymue stood looking away, her arms stretched wide to the stones. And standing beside me watching over the two babes, blond and black, her fingers on my arm like a ghost.

Had it finally come to this, a turning of a page with the book started so long ago? In that moment I understood something of the writing monks in their tiny stone cells, quills and ink and an old story barely remembered and the rest made up; and felt kindred to them. My tell is just as daft as theirs. My embroidery is better, I hope, although I do like their blues and gold. The quill on my pen is white, yeay, one of hers. A spot is on my page; is that rain, blowing in? I meander when I should remember.

The sea was calm as I crossed to the islands, and by comparison my mind flashed back to the heaving oceans and giant waves surged up by the explosion of the earth, so long ago; yet yesterday in the long haul of the shifting world. The dragen stirred then and thundered across the sea. Nymue's blood started and magick was ending and starting now. There was a destiny starting to unravel, yet the destined did not know it. No wonder it was calm, it always is when a storm is coming.

A last subterfuge was needed, but a simple one. King Lot to go south, perhaps a wider kingdom to make, and the young Artur besides to carry his flag. I would accompany them south, on a horse this time, my donkey done. And respect given to Maer Maerlyn properly this time, not by gaggling children.

People sometimes wonder why I am always in the right place when matters of the land unfold. It helps, I suppose, when I write much of it, Nym Nymue too and the Sisters. By staying one page ahead in the book, we might call it prescience. Do it often enough and it becomes hindsight. But then I spied Artur's blond head, he was tall and slender awaiting on the shore. I remembered back to the black hair of his half sister Morgayne, and realised I knew nothing at all. Blackness in a bottomless cup, Artur like as not to fall in and drown.

I wondered if Nymue had mastered the girl, or whether she too was stumbling in the dark. And here I was, about to lead young Artur south. I shuddered, and my ankle throbbed. The dark Morgayne would be twenty now, the same age Nymue was when she discovered the sun. I pondered the coincidence of that. But the boat was running in fast on a brisk breeze, and I could see a welcome party on the shore. Darkness and dreaming would have to wait.

"Artur, hail," I shouted across the narrowing gap between the boat I sailed in on and the dock he stood upon. "You have grown or I have shrunk, these years. Fellow, how is your sister?" In truth I could ask him this, as Morgayse and Artur shared their mother, Ygraine. The tangle of fathers could wait.

"She is well, Maer, practised at mothering now, three lads to satisfy her and the old Lot a fourth." Artur laughed, as the not so old Lot standing beside him grinned and slapped his arm.

"Have you come to teach the boy respect, Maer? See how he regards me simple because his sister would marry me? In truth, Maer, I tire of his impudence." Lot's arm around the youth's shoulders confirmed the lie and the fondness of the king. "Truth is, Maerlyn, young Artur is a good man. 'Tis a shame I have three boys, for he would make a good heir."

I would that Lot gave less of his truth. He made everything I say doubly false and a pretence. This idle talk of kings unnerved me, for I had not yet given my message. Later, in a high hall and before a roaring hearth, would be best. A hot fire stops many a shiver, and a flickering flame can be used to say many sooths. And to roast chestnuts, harvested from the last wood before the sea. I proffered a bag as a simple gift.

"Welcome round my fire then. Come down to the long hall and put your boots up on a bench." Lot turned and swing his cloak behind him. "You can tell us news from the south when we've fed. I've heard rumblings that pen Dragen lies dying. Is there truth in it?"

"Aye, there is truth in that. We must sort out his kingdom, and propose a parly of men round a table to do it."

Nym Nymue and I had been busy, scurrying from realm to courtyard to cottage, urging kings and princes to set aside differences and meet on a great field near the Monnow mouth, on the border lands. Lot was respected for his wisdom and would wield good legiance. He was an essential friend and Morgayse a useful marriage. The pivot needed to turn, else the plan fail.

Artur stood by, listening. A wise man, he said nothing and used his ears instead. Whereas I prattle on in my ignorance yet people still consider me wise. I cannot fathom it, but there it is. I fool everyone except myself, yet call me a fool and I'll bow. Jingle, jingle, bells on my cap.

A number of days later we set back onto the sea, to return to the mainland the quicker way. Lot suggested we take his best small ship, Artur to command, to sail to the west and all down the long coast, past the Hebrydes and into the Seas of Malin and Eire. And to continue all around the bulge of Wales and past the hills from where the sacred stones walked, from Prescel high down across the dales. Ten days and nights it took, sailing on; and I to know Artur better and what the Lord Lot said of him, standing by the steering oar or leaning our backs back against the mast.

As we sailed up into the long Syvern channel we passed far off the dreadful beach where Nymue ran from the terrible waves and began her witchery. I swear I saw a high flying white bird on the wing, yet it might have just been me, wistful and longing for her. I glanced to Artur, but he just gazed straight on past the mast, waiting for his destination and guiding Lot's ship with a sure hand.

Lot beside me, I turned to him and asked, "The youth is strong and steady, what think you of him and men, can he command?"

"What say you, Maer? Do you know what I might guess? Is the boy of different blood, under my roof like a cuckoo all these years?" Lot looked me straight in the eye, and for once my lies kept their silence and truth passed my lips, a rare thing.

"Yeay, Lord. Sent by Uthur with his sister to you, to hide from the daily mess of pen Dragen's court, sanctioned and silenced by Nym Nymue and the Sisters." I looked back to Artur. "Does he guess, thinkst you?"

Lot pondered it, and scratched his head. "Guess, guess not. I don't know it." He too watched Artur, watching the sea. "The Sisters, you say? Hmmm, they've not stirred for a long while, Maer, not for many a long year's passing." Lot shook his head. "Is it a big turn in the world? I don't wonder it."

I always wonder on it, but can never grasp it fully.

We ran up against a small pier and cast ropes ashore. Lot commanded his troop to take up their arms and to make square behind us, and we marched on like half a legion of old; a small force but a reminder to those who watched. Any king that walked with me,

Maer Maerlyn, would be known as mostly wise, despite what I say about mine own wisdom. I watched the crowds as they saw Artur and wondered about the tall, slender youth.

"Whose is the boy that Maerlyn brings?"

I saw too the way maids of the villages watched Artur, puffing up their pretty breasts and touching their hair as he passed by. Whispers followed, and as whispers do, spread on ahead of us; so by the time we came upon the Monnow fields an entourage encouraged us on, well met. Curiosity followed on soft paws like a cat. Artur stood tall amongst it all, and seemed not disappointed by the fuss.

Ahead of us I saw the flag of pen Dragen fluttering above a travelling tent, and wondered if it meant the man or the message. Behind and a way off, I saw a smaller tent, and flying from its centre a taller totem, feathers of birds unimaginable flickering in a grey coil of smoke circling up. My old heart thumped at the promise of the white Nymue. She was here. Culmination, surely, of her weave and spell, and still the innocent all unknowing. I watched for Artur, but he was well accustomed as a sailor to rest when the sea heaved and the winds roared, and was sitting with his back to a tree, a dozing there, all unperturbed.

I looked to Lot and said, "I'll go see the Dragen's tent, confirm who it is within, and ponder what next." I looked him fair on. "What see you to wander also amongst good men, to judge their mood and motive, influence it where needs."

"Yeay, Maer, that I will." Lot moved off. "We'll sup tonight with some brother made most welcome to us, and peaceful." He looked over to the tall oak under which Artur sat, all a sleeping propped against the tree. "Yon Artur, he's not easy to excite. I envy that, his steadiness."

"Aye, a good habit in truth. Let him sleep, while he may."

I made my way to the pen Dragen's tent and bowed obedience at its entrance, for even if it was not the king inside, his pennant flew above and was the symbol of Uthur the king. I did not expect to see him within, as even the last time I spoke to him, Uthur was frail and slightly mad in his words, unlikely to travel. And indeed, no king was there; but Ygraine his nearly widowed wife, Uthur's queen instead of the man. "Lady, d'ost travel without your Lord?" I went to her with a gracious bow, for she was a good woman and had served the king well. And without her, Nymue's weave would be barren and my part in it pointless too. Ygraine's belly suited us.

"Greetings, Maer, well met." She looked at me with fondness, her favourite fool. "Yeay, he king is old and feeble made. We travel on, and he stays at Tyntangel." Y gazed at me, with a small, tired smile. Her hair was silver now, the gold of her youth all gone. A fine woman still and doubtless, not alone. "Have you my son, Maerlyn, have you brought me my boy?"

"Aye, Lady. Up yonder field by the spreading oak, he rests himself, his back against the trunk of it. I will find him when he wakes and bring him here to you, to his mother."

"Thank you, Maer. I've not seen my son grown. He'll be a stranger to me."

"He is your son, Lady. A boy never forgets his mother."

"Nor his sister."

I turned at her voice, so soft, no more than a whisper, and gripped the staff in my hand for balance and strength. To see her, the peril to the plan, was to be afraid. I so rarely was afraid. "My brother then, to greet his sister?

Morgayne stepped from a dark shadow and darkness seemed to follow her, blackening the light like some flickering unholy candle. Her movement into the light was penumbral and dark, the hem of her long gown making a coil of black cloth as she turned. Morgayne was tall, near as tall as me, but I could get no sense of her frame. She was clad in a swirling black gown and a cloak, clinging and falling as she moved, shifting the eye from the darkest black to a shimmering midnight blue. Morgayne's hair was the blackest black that I always remembered and always wanted to forget, the longest hair.

"Lady." No speech, I didn't know what to say. Could I run? No, I'd just fall and foolish be.

"Maer Maerlyn," and my back shivered in a strange seduction that I knew was utterly false. This woman had no love for me, I knew it; yet the way her tongue curled around my name was melodious and a thrill deep in my gut.

"Maerlyn, hast brought my brother, to see his mother and his sister?"

Morgayne's hand appeared from the depths of the gown with such a curious slowness, and I watched with a chill as she touched my arm, such familiarity yet she controlled it. The heat from her touch! I expected coldness. My old cock roused at her, betraying me, stirring at the animal heat of her. I did not expect it, nor want it either.

"What a shame my brother cannot see his father, all alive, yet nearly dead." I doubted somewhat, that she truly thought it. "I cared for the king so long, so carefully, all a sitting by his bed." Her voice continued in a low whisper, slightly husky, ever so vaguely a low song as if she were remembering. "He sipped from my cup, Maerlyn, mine own silver cup, all filled up with juniper berries and sweet honey."

Morgayne's eyes were black.

"What a shame I cannot see my father, Maerlyn. I was such a little girl when my father was taken away, all dead, a funeral pyre." She raised her eyes to me in a slow movement, not blinking, like an owl turning its head. "Sweet honey, Maerlyn, it hides so many tastes."

I looked to Ygraine as her daughter spoke and saw her shrink away, a fearful look and helpless. I remembered her words: Morgayne is a difficult child to love, yet I must. I'm her mother. Not easy then, the daughter; rarely loved.

"Oh Maerlyn, do you wonder my sweet love for you, my honey in a cup?"

Morgayne's voice remained low, teasing me and a torment.

"I see it in your eyes. You doubt my love. Don't doubt, my Lord...." Her words were poison, sweet as syrup; her cup too, I would not drink from it.

"Oh Maerlyn, why do you look at me so?" She laughed, a low laugh, and my guts churned and swam.

"How is your ankle, Maer? Does it make you sore?"

The horror. Morgayne looked right at me, and swirled the tip of her tongue, blood red, over a long finger and with her little white teeth, pearl white, nipped at her own flesh. She looked aside at me from under the fall of her hair, and if she were a golden maid it would have been a flirt; but she was Morgayne, and it was malice black. Her smile was innocent and sweet, yet corrupted most foul. Mine ankle twinged and she laughed, low in her throat. How did she remember that? She was less than two years old, still swaddled, yet she remembered the worst of me.

"Go from me, magician, leave my mother too."

Morgayne's look at me was obsidian black and full of scorn, her toying no longer pretty. I retired from the tent with the best grace I could, and knew it wise to keep quick caution around the black Morgayne.

"Go find your little white feather, dabbler, and sup at her dried up tit. I don't need you here." The venom in her voice was worse, because it was still seductive and low. "You're worse to me than a blathering priest and his sanctimonious eyes."

I scurried away, shocked at her black malice. My ankle throbbed, yet my cock a throbbing too. Hangst your head in shame, little brother, her honey is black like tar, bitter sweet. Don't taste it.

I shuffled around the rows of tents for a time to clear my mind of Morgayne's malevolence and to settle my wits, and in truth to lose the heat from my cock and uprising balls. The truth of her was terrible lust, as if she could draw it from me like a poultice does a wound, sucking up my own poison and dandling it in her slow, delicate hands. Morgayne's fingers on my arm were hot like fire when I expected cold, yet left a wantingness all through me. Was it me, I wondered, that made it so, or could she find weakness in every man and turn it so?

Feeling shamed and mortal, and lost from my certainties, I slowly made my way to Nymue's tent and a purer place, already seeking penance and a higher grace. But a warning too. If Morgayne could reduce me to a stupid cock high wreck with just a single touch, and I supposedly wise, what might she do with a weaker, stupid man? I laughed at mine own feeble thoughts. Morgayne's danger, and I saw it now - what might she do with a stronger man? I was uncertain and uneasy. Morgayne danced me widdershins and her spirals unspiralled, yet there she was, right at the very centre of things.

I found the entrance way to Nymue's small tent and stuck my head within. A small fire burned in the centre of the floor, and over it a small cauldron hung, beaten and patterned with a pair of opposite heads. They looked apart like Janus the old Roman, coming and going, both ways at once. So I knew the white Lady considered this place to be a centre of time and an axle around which round wheels would turn, and the turning upon us, so soon.

Her favourite stone circles told of centres and spirals and all things undone. Look the other way and things tightened and spun. Ah me, I should know by now not to breath in her air, Nymue's smokes and scents always do this to my poor brain, spinning it so quickly I was giddy and stumbled. Or was I just too tired now for all of this, wanting sleep like a baby and my head on a sweet breast, a heartbeat soft under my ear?

"Maerlyn, dear heart, wither thou? D'ost travel well and bring the boy?"

Oh Nymue, to hear her voice and her soft endearments, she always calmed me, and calms me now. I turned to her, and there she was, gazing up at me with her certain look, her lovely eyes.

"Ah, Maerlyn, something disturbs you, I can tell it." Nymue took my hand, and I could not help it, I trembled and shook. "Maer?"

"Artur's part blood sister, Morgayne, she is midnight and black. She is a peril to us, Nym Nymue, she is a future we cannot anticipate."

I needs make Nymue understand this, for a white witch might know black, and a woman might better know her own sex. I was no good for sensibility when it came to the matter of woman, for I had two heads and their use was interchangeable. I could never function clearly with the both of us, being a man it was one turn or t'other, never mind my age. Never both at once. I only had enough blood in my veins for one organ at a time, and Morgayne drew my blood to my prick like the moon drags the sea to the sand.

"Nymue, you must know it. She is peril, and powerful with it." I squeezed her hands to entrust her with my concern. "I fear her, the dark Morgayne."

Yet she thrilled me, and thrills me now.

Nymue sat and pondered, lines drawing in around her mouth. "Fear her, Maerlyn?" She shook her head, and reached for a pouch of seeds on a shelf. "You do not fear, Maerlyn, never once have I known that."

Nymue poured a handful of seeds into her palm, and the excuse of sorting them gave her more time to ponder it, shifting patterns in the grain in her hand. She made the seeds into a spiral and I sensed an absence in the tent as Nymue disappeared into a place inside her head, her finger still a rhythmic turn. She fell into a trancement, all inwards, her finger still a circling. Her eyes rolled back, yet still her finger spun and spiralled. I marvelled how fast she made the spell and dared not almost breath, to wake her from it, mindless.

The turn of her finger grew still. I waited. Outside, a patter of rain blew against the wall of the tent, and her flying cloth flappered above us in a small wind. I wondered if Nymue summonsed it, 'twould not surprise me if she did; or mayhap it was just the weather, blowing cold. I could encourage animals to howl and crawl, but I'd never mastered the wind, not quite. The white Nymue found great power in the old stones, and knew the mazes too, and all inside her head. I would fail at that skill, I know it. Time is like a sieve and my memories fall through it like sand.

Nymue shuddered, then shook her head as if to clear her way through mist, and the air breathed.

"I have seen it, Maer, as far ahead as the Goddess does grant me. The dark Morgayne is inevitable, but not yet."

Nymue reached out to me and touched the tips of her fingers to my wrist, and then to her lips as a little bless, a tiny caress.

"She is young, Maerlyn, as I was her age once. Dread her yes, but she is not into her power, not yet."

Nymue threw half the seeds to the fire where they crackled and spat, and dropped the rest into her pot where the bubbles rose up and pulled them floating all in. Another of her trancing scents rose to the air and thickened it, yet this once it soothed and settled me.

"Maer, we are near the end of it and the beginning. I know Uthur cannot last many more days, and we will hear a messenger soon. We will have princes and pretenders, thugs and theatricals before we can anoint the new king. Many will think it them, but the Goddess will mark but one. Come see."

She turned to a travelling box and lifted the lid. The hinges scraped like they did once before, such a long time ago. My old mind unravelled it quick and remembered the sight of her, her white gown falling. This storage place for the most precious things was always by her side, kept safe. Idle hands could never figure it, a cunning latch hidden most cleverly. I'd had it made for my old maps by a Chinee carpenter, but gifted it to Nymue one night in May, one year. I can't remember which, nor why. It was so long ago, just yesterday.

Nymue reached within and carefully pulled up a bound leather wrap. It was made from the softest leather, a pale pink like unto a little piglet. Mayhap as long as my fore arm, but thicker.

"Remember when the boy was made into his mother's womb, I departed for to find precious silver and metals and gold?" She laid the parcel on a small bench, un-knotting the tied up straps. "I knew to make a sign, a symbolic thing nobody must doubt, and only one might use." She unfolded the last fold of softest leather, and Nymue stroked it smooth. "Here 'tis, mined and beaten, emblazoned with proper jewels and a pommel dropped from the sky in flame."

I looked upon the object, and indeed knew it would be proof enough, when held up by a king. 'Twas a bright dagger, all silver through its blade, lines and spirals artfully made, curling about and around. At its quillion tips two dark rubies were embedded, and a polished sky stone in each side. I looked to Nymue, and knew it crafted with love and reverence by her hands, all magick woven in by fire.

"Scalibet, I named it, Maer. It waits for a king. But first, we must yield it to the Goddess, to be gripped so tight and only given up to the right man, as proof for all who see."

Nymue looked to me.

"It needs the two of us, Maer, a magicking between us, to make this work. My sickle moon is on me soon and I am strongest then. You know it." She smiled a little smile. "I know it too, dear heart, and all alike to conjure. We make it so."

Ah, I see it. Another conjure, and we to make a special place to bury a dagger deep. We make it so.

Some several days later Nymue moved her travelling tent to a small level field aside a steep chasm of bare rock. We moved up to it, she and I, following a narrow path beside a slow trickling stream that was all new, still cutting clean soil. I remembered a rumour heard of

106

a new spring risen in rocks, strange mists and birds out of season, and knew that Nymue had found a place where the Goddess lay close by, with caves all unusual all around.

A place of new natural power that suited her conjure, and mystery sufficient that the chaplet builders with their little stones all east west and their crisses and crosses and stagnant water, they would all keep away. That's always best, foolish priests the lot of them, best they stay away. They make me seem clever by comparison, even if I might look fine in their splendid robes.

No, even I could not put up with the nonsense that spills from their tongues. I might even start to believe it myself, then where would I be? Dribbling in my beard, most like. But I wander away from my purpose. I wonder it why? I'm forgetting to remember, or I'm remembering to forget. I'm never sure which. Truth seeps from my brain like melting snow, her hair was so white, and sooner or later I'll forget all of it. Cursed rain, it blows again through the window and spots my page. How does it do that, when the sky is blue? Pale blue, Nymue's eyes, looking up at me.

Nymue looked up at me and asked, "Ready Maer, that we make it so?" She placed the tips of her fingers to my forehead, and I was blessed. "Come, we be ready this night."

"Nym Nymue," and the formality dried my tongue; all I wanted was her sweet name on it, Nymue, just her, just me. "The Goddess commands, we make it so. Let it begin, this gyre."

Was that a little look of longing on her face as she looked up at me, or just my wistfulness, wishing it so? Our duty to the land lost us our intimacy, priests to a higher calling with too much ceremony. Yet ceremony must, for powerful things to be.

Nymue threw seeds and a powder upon the burning logs, and the air sizzled and crackled with a soporific and tangent smell, blue smoke rising and swirling lazily around. Her whiteness flickered in and out of the lowering dusk as she slowly circled round me. I stood central to the tent, unmoving so yet stirring, the base of my gut filling warmly. An image of an earlier rise flashed into my mind, a dark black shadow and black treacle in that voice, and two seductions were upon me. Both to rise me, the blackness and the white, and I the grey between. Ah fuck, they would both be the death of me.

"Yeay, Maerlyn, you respond too quick. I not the only one?"

Nymue knew it, my seduction came too easy as I wanted it so. Yet she continued her circling weave; my corruption inevitable then, and I bring the consequence. But our conjure must be done regardless, else all everything lost.

"You make my work harder, Maer Maerlyn, too many women here, yet the work is a two sexed thing. Concentrate on one, at least, if that bring your essence."

Her voice hardened against me and her eyes flashed warning. "Choose, my fool, don't unravel it now."

Nymue was right, yet she was challenged in mine own head. Inevitable then, the black Morgayne in the pit of it through me.

"You falter, Maer. Too much, too many." She stopped her movement around me. "But I too serious too."

Nymue looked upon me with a different look, and a softening in her eyes.

"Mayhap the bigger conjure wait."

She came up to me and placed her little hand on my chest, against my heart. Her hand was warm; and she pressed her fingers to the cloth, like does a cat on wool, one two three.

"Let me try a smaller spell, and gentler be."

Nymue turned and found another bag. A different balm, and sweeter, rose from the fire; and the seeds made a smaller poppling on the flame.

"Come to me, sweet wizard. The land can wait another moment, yeay?"

She was friendly to me. There was a small bed behind another dropping cloth, and Nymue took me to it, her hand reaching behind and I took it as she led. Oh Nymue.

She was slow and calm now, and deliberately undid hooks and belts and straps from mine garments, and they dropped one by one in heaps on the floor, her hands folding each thing as if putting it away. I too did the same with her clothes, and soon her shift and white gown were gone. We were both older than before, and our bodies lived in and comfortable. Nymue smiled to me, and the feet of crows were beside her eyes, and creased with a small laugh.

"Maerlyn," she said softly, and my name fell from her lips, just me. "My lovely man, come to my breast and lie."

Nymue was slight beside me, her breasts still firm as when she was younger. Perhaps a lower curve, maybe softer than before. She was older now, yet I was older too and my memory all distracted. But I felt young and forgot about mine age. My prick rose and pressed against her, and Nymue pushed her hip back against it. My fingers wandered to her lips, and she took my other hand in hers, turning it and placing my palm against her breast. Her nipple hardened under my rub. My cock bounced and again she pushed nicely back.

"Dost my olding body stir you, heart, and make you moan?"

She teased, my evidence beside her stiff and hard, no question needed but the answer given.

"Always, Nymue. I become a doltish boy and want to wrap you small, all up."

"Let's be slow and gentle then. We must make bigger magick later, and will need our breath and circling trance."

Nymue turned and nestled her haunches back to my groin. She reached between her legs and placed my cock up between them. Not moving, Nymue held me there, my heat flowing into her body.

"But now, just us. The Goddess can wait a few moments more."

So we lay, content and still. My mind pondered the white Nymue and marvelled that she loved me. We never say it, never did, yet something moved between us that was just a woman and a man. I can think no other reason, unless her back was cold and my belly hot, and she wanted warmth. Even that's enough, sometimes.

Nymue may have been the strongest priestess, but she was a woman too.

"Don't say it, Maerlyn. I know it."

Her low whisper was soft, barely heard. A woman, yet a priestess too, she reads my mind. Perhaps that's what women do, regardless. I'll never properly understand it.

A wash of light rain and a wind blew against the tent, and Nymue stirred.

"I am summonsed," she whispered. "I am begun."

She moved away and pushed me to my back, and my cock lay hard against my belly. Nymue climbed on to me and rested the wet cleft of her cunt along my shaft, and slid. The dark anoint of her blood left a trail along me, and she slipped and squirmed. Clenching tight onto me, my prick between her thighs, she arched up her back and lifted her arms straight above her head, as if reaching for the sky. The wall of the tent rattled, and a tension went through her body, all rigid. Nymue's nipples jutted hard. It was not just my heat on her sex that did it, she was responding now to spirits and rifts in the air.

She brought her arms back down and supported the little light weight of her against my chest, her palms against my nipples and her fingers all outspread. Nymue crouched above me like some animal, white and pure all along me, a pure snow fox or a white wolf. Her features grew pale and Nymue glimmered with a white light as she channelled energy down from the sky and into us both. My cock hardened like iron with the rich magick of it, and a seep of my spirit beaded from the tiny lips on my head. Nymue tipped that tiny clear bead to the end of her finger and touched it to her lips, and she was serious now.

Reaching to her own cleft, she twisted her little red nub and an ecstasy shuddered through her. Our ceremony was upon us, our sex magick tightening and throbbing in the air. Nymue shimmered above me, flickering in and out of focus, her voice a low growl from the back of her throat. Small moans rose up and I could not say if they were hers or mine.

"Unh, huh, huh." Regular and deep, we began to breath in and out each other's breath, as we clung and twisted on the bed. Writhing like snakes, we twisted and curved around each other, our arms wrapping around our bodies and gripping so tight. Our heat grew up around us, yet my cock never slid in and her cunt never opened around me, but we rubbed and twisted and grew red. My shaft thick and hard, Nymue's cunt wet and slick, yet we could not fuck into each other, no matter how we wanted it. Our sex and lust just a channel for the Goddess to enter our world through her mage and witch.

"Soonest, Maer, soon."

Nymue frantically scrabbled on the floor for our purpose. She rolled away from me and crawled like a lusting cat, her red sex clefted up high before mine eyes, oh fuck to suck upon it and taste her blood. She crawled on the floor and found the leather bundle with the sword all in it. Nymue's musky scent was in my nose and on my lips and I licked her and sucked between her legs and she pushed back against me, all opening up. Wet, so wet, yet duty to be done. My cock beat, and I was huge and hard, all a fuck ready to happen, but not into her, not her.

"Nym Nymue, get it, quick."

Our ceremony meant our names and titles, servants for the land, but still my tongue inside her cunt! The metal taste of her blood tangled my lips and my cock stretched hard to reach her. Nymue twisted away and quickly unravelled the pink leather sheath from the dagger Scalibet. She stood, and took the dagger's handle into her two hands. I lay panting on the floor beneath, my cock thick and red, veins threaded around the shaft, my balls ridden high and tight.

Nymue slowed, and caressed the handle of the dagger up between her legs, the blade pointing down towards my centre. Her eyes went black, and with an unblinking gaze Nymue slowly pushed the handle of the dagger up into her, fucking this symbol of a man deep into her cunt and holding it there. Fuck, the dagger of a king instead of my cock, and my sacrifice made. Nymue thrust the handle shaft into herself and moaned a long moan, oh fuck, not me.

She clenched it there within her cunt, then carefully lowered herself over me so the sharp point of the sword just touched the plum red head of my cock. Nymue paused above me, and spread open wide the lips of her cunt, the shafting dagger prick up in her, and showed me the bright red tip of her pleasure. With a single twirl of her pale fingers, Nymue teased up herself with a long cry, her bird beginning to take wing. The tip of the sword was a sharp point right on the centre of my shaft. With a curious twitch, the sword tip flickered and drew up a bead of my blood. I felt nothing, no pain, just saw the blood of it.

With a sensuous slide Nymue slid the dagger from her body, and presented it to me, the slick of her cunt and blood and sweet honey juice all over it.

"Take it, Maer Maerlyn, quick, to the rock."

I took the dagger, and tall and naked, my risen cock ahead of me, I walked to the rock. I was man, and in my hand was the symbol of men, all male, thrust up and hard. Beside me, all wet and open, was woman, white woman, the land's highest witch and servant, a good priestess, spread wide.

Our ceremony begun, our ceremony ending, Nym Nymue and I, Maer Maerlyn, stood before the rock in the glade of the Goddess. We took the dagger into our four hands, and found a cleft in the rock, and pressed it there, and pressed it there, and fucked it on home in the joy we never had, this woman, this man, she and me. From around the tight cleft the dagger made, clear water from a rising spring began to flow, as the Goddess received into herself this symbolic thing, this future king.

Nymue and I fell to our knees, my erection gone and my cock all soft, her breasts sagged and soft, our bodies drained. Above our heads the dagger was bedded into the rock, held by the Goddess, held tight. Our job done and our bodies surrendered, Nymue and I, Maerlyn, feeling ancient and old, turned from that place. Holding each other for comfort and to keep ourselves moving, we crept back to the tent.

Nymue threw some calming seeds to the fire, and we fell upon the bed. I lay curled all behind her, her small pale body in front of me, my hands held tight in hers. Covered in warm pelts of fur we soon both lapsed into animal dreams, twitching then dropping like cats. We slept, dead gone, all done.

On the morrow we stirred, and with a final conjure Nymue hid away her tent from eyes that see, a fine mist constantly in front of them. Yet we could sit and watch, seeing all that might pass in front of us, and observe the rock. At first there was small curiosity, but slowly over several days a greater word spread and was connected to earlier rumours, and a right procession of lords and pretenders wandered up the valley to see. None figured it, and not a single soul touched the shaft of the dagger. The obvious was understood then, a sacred place and the dagger somewhat special, awaiting a momentous thing.

I would wander down regular to the wider field and be seen by the princes all there and the various assembled kings, and my name was not connected to the mystery. Which meant I could play it to my own dice if I wanted, if I chose. Yet Nym Nymue had a final dramatic touch in mind which would make any subterfuge or artifice unnecessary.

"Just wait, Maer, your impatience is not a virtuous thing. When news comes of the death of Uthur, even the most wooden brained fool will understand it all." She stirred her fire with a short stick. "And bow down, as is appropriate."

I looked at Nymue, my eyebrow raised in a wry question, for I am her favourite fool yet she compares others to me?

"I be insulted by you, witch, that you compare the sawdust in my brain to the dull thoughts of ordinary men."

She laughed and her eyes sparkled.

"You jest, Maerlyn. You know it as well as I, there is only one who can pull the dagger from its place, and we put him there, so be it."

Nymue patterned the stick into a circle, and embers glowed brightly.

"Does the boy have a clue, Maerlyn?"

"I cannot say it, Nym. The Lord Lot is no fool, he guessed Artur was a cuckoo in his nest, but he remains discreet always."

I pondered the nature of the youth and his natural command.

"Artur always places his ears ahead of his mouth, and uses the brain between them well, I think."

"Your opposite then, heart?" Nymue laughed again, oh I love her delicate tease.

"Indeed. I may teach priests their foolishness yet." I paused, and thought about that. "No, they are excellent at it without tutelage, they do not need me."

"You need to tolerate them, Maer. They spread through the land, even if we do not like it." She stirred her stick in the fire once more, and of a sudden, an ember spat. Nymue brushed it from her leg.

"Ha. The spitting fire reminds me of the bargain I made with my mother and Nyn Nyneve, when I set out to learn the way of the witch."

She poked the embers once again. "Give me a year, Mother, I said."

Nymue looked up at me. "It's been many years, Maerlyn. I grow tired. I need to go from here, once this is done."

"Go, Nymue? Where to go, and do you leave me?" This was the first that I heard her mission done. I am a dullard, I had thought it just begun.

"Yeay, Maerlyn. I have conjured up a future, but once it begins to run, it runs on alone. I cannot see it beyond the next king crowned. Beyond that, too much is set in motion for me to command or steer."

She sat silent for a long while, slowly turning her stick in the fire back and forth, back and forth. Another ember spat. "I will go back to the Isle of Glas and greet my mother again, and the Sisters."

I did not know what to make of it. She never did answer my question's second part, and mayhap never will. So I dabble on alone. My quill shakes, and I curse the rain again, a spotting on my page. I thought I had pulled the shutters shut. The damn wind, it keeps blowing them open.

My head hurts. I didn't think it would end like this, a slow ache. Or is it my heart? Beat, beat, I'll go mad if I listen, go mad if I don't.

I'm not good at waiting, my fingers start to itch.

The itch didn't get so far as a scratch. Some days later we heard up from the distant field a carry on of trumpets and warnings made, all manner of horses moving in steady troops. I went down and found Lot, for his advice.

"It's pen Dragen, Maer. News has come, he is dead." Lot looked about the field, and pointed to the Lady Ygraine's tent. "See, his pennant flies half down and reversed. Ygraine wears black. Her veil hides her tears."

So, the wheel turned.

I looked to Lot. "Send Artur to his mother, who still remains queen, that she may find solace in her son returned." I scratched my beard, thoughtfully. "There needs be theatre first, before those assembled here see proof of the new king. Ygraine can set the time, as it suits her mood, and send him up the valley, best dressed."

I returned up the valley myself, and saw Nymue's charm on the water. Blood red it flowed, down from the rift in the rock, down the stream until it cut through the field. All it took was a whisper from behind a bush, "See, the blood of the Dragen flows, to mark the death of the king," and rumour flowed down the valley with the stream, and soon enough a number of princes and pretenders made their way to the dagger and tried pull it from the rock. Of course none succeeded, and merely got their boots wet.

"How long the pretence, Nymue, before the young king walks by?"

"Oh, let the failures fail some more, that they understand their eventual place in the court of the king. A little obedience hurt none, Maer." Nymue looked at me, and was that a brow quietly raised?

"Obedience, Nym? From me?" I laughed. "Now there's a doubtful thing."

118

"I know it, Maer. Maybe one day." She gently touched my arm. "Maybe one day."

Was it a portent, or just a woman speaking? I never could tell the difference.

"But look, who comes?"

A big man, solid like the trunk of a tree and tall, taller than most men, stood in the glade and looked upon the rock and the knife fixed firm. de Grance, a Breton prince, keen to claim a kingdom. Ah yes, a big man, all strength and sinews. And politick too, wise with it, or so he mostly thought. His fail would be worth to witness and would suit the plot well. Lesser kinglets and princedoms would see his poor work and line up behind him in order, like unto chickens, and know their place.

"He is a big man, Nymue. Some sport before the final act, it seems."

I was already thinking of the second place, and whether de Grance might fit it, with reluctant grace perhaps. Like Lot, a good ally, and a little daughter too. A handy thing when making courts, to have a dowry prize all growing up and pretty. Boys become men and look about themselves for comfort and a wife. Little arrangements, all lovely like flowers, can oft suit a table nicely. But I get ahead of myself. We haven't made the king, not yet.

de Grance moved silently around the soft grassed place, a muddied path worn to the face of the rock where the dagger's hilt stood proud. The bloodened water flow around its shaft and stained the stone, running in strands to the stream through the grass. He studied the place, and saw our mist to one side and his small court behind, a taggle of men and messengers fast of foot. He didn't know they would sit and save their feet, with nothing but a slow walk back.

But not knowing doesn't mean not trying. To his credit, de Grance properly knew his stage, and kenned that it was a meeting with the Goddess here. Clothes and trapments unnecessary and would not work. He knew it. A naked man against a naked rock, and a shaft in it like a fuck. To tease apart her delicate legs and ease the shaft from its place then, that was the task in front of him.

So he to one side and shucked off his clothes; and a prancing mince came down and took them away with a coy glance at his master as he scurried off. Ha, a stolen vest no doubt, and a spilling into cloth that night from a slender stroking cock. A worthy look, for de Grance turned a final circle once, a deliberate thing to impress upon the watchers his size and strength. His meat hung thick from a black haired place, and the muscles on his thighs and chest and gut were impressive big and firm.

I glanced across at Nymue and saw her eyes sparkle at her contemplation of the size of this big man. Her finger tapped once on the arm of her chair, as if keeping a score. I looked down to my own thin pins and wondered if I should take up rowing in a little boat. I could catch fish with a string and a hook, splish splash. Or cast about with a whirling feathery fly over my head, wish wash.

de Grance strode to the rock, and clenched and tightened the perfect muscles of his ass and his wide back, curling his toes to anchor himself in the mud. He laid up one hand onto the rock, two fingers on one side of the blade and two fingers the other, as if to feel its warmth and the wetness there. His other hand gripped the dagger's haft. I could see him flex his fingers and stretch his thumb, to test his own grip. And he gripped the handle, and all over his body every muscle tightened as he applied every part of his strength, great cords and sinews bulging from his skin. Yet it was never enough.

de Grance shook his head, to clear sweat from his eyes. He summonsed the mince for a dry cloth, and dried off the palms of his hands. The lucky little court, two nights! And again de Grance applied his force, and again his muscles thickened most memorably. Even Nymue let forth a little gasp of amazement and astonishment, and her fingers gripped the arm of her chair. Certain an impressive sight, but no good, not once did the knife even move.

He let go the dagger's handle. de Grance knew his defeat but knew too he was well defeated and his place in the queue assured. He went from there all a shaking his head and muttering, and I've never seen such a big man look so small. Best get your cloak around you, de Grance, I thought, before some other man sees you're not as strong as you think you are.

"It is good, Maer. Courts and princes will remember this stage and know the biggest man knows his place. I could not have writ it better, but man's vanity makes it so."

Nymue looked across at me. "de Grance is useful, Maer, his little princess too, when she comes of age. Look, remember her face."

She pointed aside, and there by a big horse a little girl stood, ten years maybe, or twelve at most, all awash with waves of fair golden hair. She looked shy and peeped at her father as he walked back to his place, wrapping his long cloak around him, all a hiding his nakedness. She saw it, and blushed.

de Grance stood with his huge hand on her little shoulder, and beside him she likened to a delicate doll. Miryamme, then, his princess watching on. Good, she will see the main act.

I turned to Nymue and wondered, "A last look, Nym Nymue? The little girl?"

"I think it so, Maer Maerlyn, but a shadow too." She was still. "A blackness in my mind, something moving slow behind it." Nymue shook her head to clear it. "I cannot see it, yet it's upon us, it's in this place."

I looked about yet the sun was bright. I knew the blackness, yet if the white Nymue did not see it and powerless? Mine ankle ached, and I felt the darkness. A battle on, but the white witch to Glas in retreat and the black witch already strong and stronger yet to be? Best not linger in the middle of that. My heart beat a double flutter which comes when I'm nervous and afraid.

"Ah, Maerlyn, 'tis nearly over. Our first circle done."

Up the path a small procession came, Lot with the Queen Ygraine by his side, a black veil covering her face. Artur walked with them and Ygraine his mother, her arm was linked with his. Artur walked tall, and passed by de Grance and seemed taller. Yet Artur was slender by compare, but nevertheless a bigger man, and seeming made it so. Of the black Morgayne I saw nothing, but mine ankle ached. The little Miryamme hid behind her father's leg, her tiny hand in his, so sweet a daughter fair.

Nymue leaned forward in her chair, and her shift fell loose about her body and I spied a dark nipple tighten. Her legs slipped apart and the long falls of her gown fell between. Her ankle was delicate and small. I looked to Nymue's throat, and a long faint blush was rising. She looked back at me, and gave a little sad smile, some last longing. Nymue reached behind and found a small bag. Her fingers shook as she cast seeds on the hot embers of her fire. The seeds crackled and spat, and a sweet scent reached up upon the air.

A last conjure then, for the Goddess, and I wondered at it, and Nymue's place. The long curving walks and spiralling stones, her witching tokens rising with white feathers on the wing, her songs and seasons short and long. And then done for long long turns of the sun and the moon, a resting place to get her energy back? In the Isle of Glas with the Sisters and her mother, a little girl returned.

This work hard then, and her white hair a sacrifice so young. The Goddess a fierce mistress; and Nymue's mother to sing, "Little sparrow, little sparrow," and comfort her where I could not. But where will I lay my head? Oh Nymue, my heart.

The three stopped in the glade. Artur turned to his mother, and lifted the black veil from her face. Ygraine reached both her hands to her son's face, and held Artur's cheeks as one does a precious gift, then reached her lips to his and kissed him. Artur's hands went upon her waist and she was precious too, I could see it in the softness of his touch. He took one finger tip to his own lips and blessed a kiss, and touched it to her lips, the last kiss of a prince; the next the kiss of a king. Artur turned to Lot, and rested his hands on the other man's shoulders, who had been a father to him and a teacher.

Artur then looked direct towards us and his eyes were focused far beyond where we sat, Nym Nymue and I, all hidden behind our mist. I suspect he knew what was behind it, for how could a mist survive the midday sun?

He stood astride the red flowing stream, and curious it was. The blood red flow stopped at his feet, and the water flowed clear beyond down the valley, all bubbling and swirling but clear. A whisper went through the people watching, "See, see how pen Dragen's blood stops at his feet, this Artur!"

Behind him, de Grance took a step forward as if to better see, and the look on his face was puzzled and strange, as if to say, what youth is this who dares better me?

Beside me, Nym Nymue was moving into her trance, her fingers and thumb idly teasing up a nipple, and her other hand gathering up cloth on her thigh. My blood thumped at the sight of her, and I too shuffled my legs about to cater for my thickening. My senses sharpened, and I scented the sharp metallic tang that was Nymue, her cunt scent rising, and my nostrils flared. A fainter scent troubled me, distant yet drifting in the air.

A wind shuddered the sides of our tent. Nymue's breath quickened, and I felt a pulsing throb in my belly. My cock grew hard, and my ankle pulsed with my heartbeat, quickening too. Ah fuck, the Goddess wanting our presence, the heating woman beside me; sweet fuck I wanted her, to gaze into her eyes, just us. But she was away and rising, her trancement upon her. She dipped a finger between her legs. That fainter scent?

In the glade, Artur looked down and saw the blood red river before, and looked behind him and saw it stop. He slowly undid a clasp around his neck and let the cloak fall to the ground, where it fell into the stream and stayed. Artur undid buttons of bone and straps of leather, and cast away the doublet and jerkin that covered his chest. They fell further behind him, but no man nor woman moved to get them. He knelt to one knee and undid the straps and ties that tightened his boot, and threw it aside; and the other one too.

He stood, his chest bare and broad, his back a ripple of muscle, a slender youth but tall. By compare to de Grance, a finer man, yet bigger in this place. Beside me, Nymue gasped, and her scent was high in my nose. I breathed her in deep, her honeyed sweetness a taste I knew on my tongue. And behind it, another sweeter taste, a cloying thing. My nostrils flared, and the scent was like liquorice, dark and musk. Mine ankle pulsed, and my cock thick and hard throbbed too. Behind my nipples, my chest stabbed with tight centres. My cock was hard, yet my hands gripped the arms of my chair. Darkness shuttered my mind and my ankle hurt. Two women digging into my head, and I helpless and stupid, a man with a cock. More blood than sense, and I knew it.

Afore us, Artur stripped away his leggings and britches and stood naked before the rock and the dagger. His was a tall slenderness, his shoulders wide and his hips narrow, the cheeks of his ass taut and finely curved. I saw the essence of old pen Dragen in his stance, the same strength and pride. Artur did not care for a parade, his purpose the rock and the blade afront of him, and he walked slowly towards the cliff. As he walked, the red of the water moved up the stream with him, the dragen's blood staying at his feet.

He reached unto the rock, and his hand went straight to the handle of the knife and gripped it. Beside me, Nymue gasped, a quick intake of her breath. I remembered her tell of the making of this blade, starting back when this man was born. And of course, her own cunt had gripped the handle where Artur's hand now gripped, and her sex was on it. The man's hand enveloped it and was man and woman both, as the Goddess needed for the land. Artur looked around as if perhaps he heard her cry, and it were possible, Nymue's magick flowing into the rock and lifting the mist.

As he turned, I saw Artur's rising prick thickening and hardening against his gut, and it was a beautiful shaft, firm and straight. A healthy thing, long and wonderfully proportioned. Nymue sighed, and her fingers were slippering wet between her legs. Artur gripped the dagger's haft, and he tensed his hand against the rock. He pulled upon the dagger with an exploratory force but no movement there. He stroked the rock with a delicate touch and a little whimper scaped from Nymue's throat as she connected with the stone and the Goddess all in her head.

From afar came a strange crawling rumble, as if a beast slithered on the land, and the earth gave a single shake. Artur eased his weight down onto the rock, and I saw his muscles tighten as he strengthened his grip. Again he pulled on the knife, and I heard a crackling sound and the blade moved. Nymue gasped out loud, and the scent of her cunt rose fragrant and filled my nose. I licked my lips and could almost taste her, and she channelled the Goddess through her body, kicking a leg out against the floor in her spasming heat. A second rocking rumble shook the place, and Artur eased again the blade and the rock yielded up some more. But the Goddess held it tight and made him pant and give it up.

Nym Nymue's rising pleasure spiralled to her stone and spring, and the tightness slowly yielded and gave up the shaft. A third surge thundered down the valley, and Artur's muscles bulged and tightened as he stood and gripped the sword, but still the rock gripped it tight and would not give it up.

And I shuddered, for looking up above Artur's head I saw a black shadow, swift and fast, crawl down from the top of the cliff and find a ledge, mayhap twice Artur's head from the ground. Morgayne was like some swift and climbing thing, clinging to the rock. Her long black hair was coiled tight around her naked waist, and her lean body was white flesh against her black hair, coiled round. She stopped above Artur's head, and her limbs moved strange and slow.

"Artur, brother mine from our mother! Look up and see your sister. I'm the fuck, not this foul sorcery."

Artur looked up, and above his head the black Morgayne crouched upon the rock and spread her legs apart. Up between her thighs her hair was thick and black and she spread her lips apart and dipped two fingers between, and Morgayne showed her brother her sex.

Artur gripped the sword once more and slid it from the rock, and a fourth shudder shook the place. Beside me Nymue fell in swoon upon the floor, her hands cupping her white sex. She cried out as she shuddered, and thick magick trammelled her body and shook it and the earth shook one more time.

Artur turned from the rock, the dagger Scalibet held high in his hands, both hands thrust high to the sky. His splendid shaft was hard and long against his gut, and as I watched I saw a thick jet of seed spurt from Artur's cock, and more and more again, and fall white against the earth, and he became King on the Goddess's soil, for the land.

His sister Morgayne dropped from the rock to Artur's feet, and scooped his seed to her fingers and spread it on her naked belly, streaked brown with mud and white with his cream, and her swirling hair all black and shining like some malignant, splendid wolf.

At the sight of her beautiful, black coiled hair and her pale, seductive nakedness my own cock surged, and my seed too spilled upon the ground, despite myself and because of my own fucking weakest self. Morgayne darted through the thinning mist and scooped up my spill. Whereas she spread Artur's seed all white around her belly, she crouched and wiped all mine around her asshole, and that was what she thought of me.

"Maer Maerlyn, you want my cunt, I know it. I can smell your lust, and taste it." She looked up at me from her crawling on the ground. "Maybe one day, Maerlyn." Her voice was sweet venom. "Maybe one day."

And her low voice, just a whisper, made it worse, and so much better too. I am enslaved between the black and the white, and I hate it and love it. I would not have it any other way.

I was there.

When a solitary boy, just breaking man, pulled a knife from a tight rock and found himself king, I was there.

Ties that Bind

"Follow me, Artur, follow me!"

Morgayne's high laughing cry echoed in the long stone corridor as her pattering feet ran ahead, faster than he could run. Artur never could catch her, the room would always be still when he reached the doorway.

"'Gayne, Gayne, stop hiding," Artur called into the dark room. He heard a rustle of straw, and a sweep of cloth along the floor. "Where are you, Gayne?"

"Here I am, Artur, you know I'm always here."

And his sister would jump up and wrap her arms around his back and pull him down to the floor. The straw would prickle his back as she pulled the linen shirt over his head. Morgayne would slowly stroke Artur's untidy blond hair from his eyes as she held her brother close to her breast. Her skin was always so warm and soft, so soft.

"I'm always here, Artur...."

Artur shuddered from sleep. His arm, thrown out from under the bed clothes, knocked against a low wooden shelf, rocking little carved statues standing there all in a row. He sat up, rubbing his forearm where it had banged against the wood, shaking his head to clear it from the dream. The dream.

He remembered the first time his sister appeared in his head, years before. He'd returned from one of his long sea voyages to the round island where the ice ran into the sea and volcanoes spat smoke and rock into the sky. The island where his first girl lived, the one who showed him both hunger and laughter with her legs spread wide and her arms wrapped tight around his back. The one who stole into his snug sleeping sack every night and risked the wrath of her father. His first girl.

But she wasn't his first girl. Back on his own island, the dark black eyes of his sister gazed at him every time he woke from the dream. Every time was waking twice, and as he grew older Morgayne's hands were always slow, so slow.

Artur hauled himself up from the bed, and pulled the long pelts of wolf and marten around his naked limbs for warmth. His morning cock was hard, harder still from the dream as it always was. He shuffled from the sleeping chamber, his head still echoing, and made his way outside to the stone gutter. Artur leaned his head against the wall, and with one arm held back the heavy pelts. He gripped the hard length of his cock and pushed it down away from his gut as best he could, it stood so high and hard. After some settling breaths, he let go a long piss, a hard jet driving against the wall, and his cock slowly eased and let him run the stream down the wall.

"Ahh, fuck, that's better." He shook the last drops, and looked down at his prick, still thick and long. "She haunts me, that is certain."

In his mind's eye, Artur replayed the vision of Morgayne as she crouched above him on the rock, displaying the dark lips of her cunt right above his head. He'd felt a curious power flowing from the stone and through the mist as he pulled loose the dagger Scalibet and felt its force. But he knew without doubt it was the thick coiled hair of his own sister, her naked cunt there in front of him real and raw, that surged up the first throb of seed from the base of his spine.

"I'm the fuck, not this foul sorcery!"

Morgayne's words still rang in his ears, now and at night when he stroked white cream high onto his chest. A king without a whore, his own sister there instead. Artur smiled a wry smile to himself. It's a strange way to start a kingdom. He shook his head to clear the fog.

Artur knotted belts about his waist and wandered slow and thoughtful across to the main hall, greeting the pig boy and the five girls who kept the goats and chickens, and knew the best herbs in the gardens.

"Lord, the morning greet you, sire."

Their voices were quiet in a respectful harmony, but the youngest girl was kicked in the shin by her older sister to make her bob down faster. Artur smiled as he saw it, winking at the little one in a conspiracy. Her little smile delighted him.

"And it greet you." He paused for a moment. "Emmelyne, the oldest mothering goat. Is she birthed yet, her belly so big?"

"No sire, it must be soon."

Emmelyne replied with a shyness and a pretty blush. The king remembered her name and the state of her goat. She would run to tell her mother.

"Ah good. Her cheese will sweeter be, if kids sup from her teat and we share a bit of her milk." Artur moved on, his easy charm a natural thing. "Rednock, your pig is too loud on the mornings, I cannot hear the crow of the cockerel."

"Sire, yes Lord, I'll…." Rednock stopped, seeing the king's grin and his laughing eyes.

"Don't worry it, lad. Methinks we need a new cockerel that knows a proper voice, not a new pig."

His diplomacy done for the day, Artur entered the main hall and found fresh bread there. He asked the cook for eggs, and sat with his back to the fire while they were cooked. By the time his meal was ready, the last vestiges of the dream had cleared from his mind, and Artur could think clearly. He was a practical man - he dreamed, his prick throbbed and jetted as a consequence, he awoke and was alone. All in his head then, these dreams, no matter, nor anyone to see. Morgayne's darkness spilled around him and was gone into the night, hidden there and silent.

"Ah, Maerlyn, I see you back from Tyntangel. How does my mother?"

"The Lady is well, Lord. The travel was tiring, as you know it from the distance, but your mother is content, I think."

"And my sisters?"

"They are both well, sire. Mourning the king, as you might expect. They tend the grave each day with flowers."

"Both, Maer? I have three sisters with my mother at Tyntangel, yet you only mention two." Artur looked directly at Maerlyn and saw the discomfort in his eyes. "Morgayne unsettles you, Maerlyn, I know it, yet she is my sister too. Don't forget it."

"Sire, I do not forget the Lady Morgayne." Maerlyn looked up to the distance as if he heard a far off call. "Beg forgiveness, Lord, if I accidentally offended thee."

"You make no accidents, Maer." Artur spoke casually, as if it was a passing observation, lightly said. "Best treat my sister thoughtfully. I take no offence, but the Lady might."

Artur rinsed his plate in a pot hanging over the hearth, and placed it back on a shelf for the next man. He dismissed the matter of his sister, and turned to practical things.

"Come, Maerlyn, I show you the work done on the defences whilst you were away south."

The Camlann fort took natural advantage of a high, flat topped hill carved and shaped in ancient times. The Romans favoured flatter places and defensive walls for their garrisons, but they were all crumbling now. Princes and kingdoms spread wide across the land, and high places made good sense with their long sight lines and wide vistas. Roads and pathways followed the curves of the ridges and the rivers, forests and woods filled the plains between. The goddess and her people softened the land, and Artur made Uthur's kingdom his own.

The Camlann defences comprised a series of banks and ditches, each higher than the last. The entrance way zigged and zagged between the banks, the first turn to the left, "So that we see the newcomers' sword hand," noted Artur, "and their shields made useless."

"Good practice, Lord, like unto a maze. The priestess Nym Nymue would favour it well, it is liken to her favourite spirals."

"Ah, the white priestess, yes." Artur studied the mage. "She has returned to the Isle of Glas, I've heard tell. Is that her truth, Maer?"

"Yeay, Lord, it is no lie." Maerlyn fell silent and his eyes focussed on a far distance for a long moment. He looked back at the young king. "Yet I know not her truth. She is a woman, sire."

"Aye. A woman. Creatures we men can never rightly understand." Artur pondered the older man. "And if you don't understand them, Maer, what chance have I?"

"Any man is wiser than I, Lord, don't doubt it. I would lose my feet if they were not joined to mine own legs."

Maerlyn diminished himself as he always did, yet Artur knew him wise with good cunning.

A good engineer, too. They wandered to the centre of the circled hill where a new great hall was being built to Maerlyn's design. Artur was building places for his court, mixing stone and wood together. The rock gave solid foundations, while the tree opened up galleries and high spaces. Soaring arches of strong oak were well braced to support a thick and heavy thatch, while smaller buildings were roofed with wooden shingles, easily made and speedily applied. A blacksmith made nails and sharp axes, and sawyers slid great blades back and forth, forth and back. Artur's court was a village, and in every place, large and small, he had blessed a round table so that every man and woman might sit and be heard, and no-one the head of it.

"And the postern, sire, has it been cut?" Maerlyn was referring to a narrow passage and a steep stair away from the entrance of the fort, to be used for hidden movements in and out of the place.

"Aye, it has. I will gate it and make it secure. Any hidden passage from the fort is also a passage back inside it." Artur again showed his practical nature. "I don't much care for secret ways, but I see there might be a use for it. The opening, 'tis well hid, and I will set a copse nearby to further disguise it."

"Best to hide in plain sight, sire. It is where I do it."

"I thought mist, Maer, is where you hid."

"Mist, sire? I could never master mist. Mist requires true sorcery. I can only manage puddles."

"Yet I felt the touch of a man in the magick, when I pulled Scalibet from the rock."

"Man and woman both, sire, but a woman guide it."

"Ah, I see," the young king replied. "Is that what they do?"

"Believe it, Lord. You can't deny them. Women get what they want, in all their ways."

"Yeay, I think it true. Politicking is the easier thing. Men I can predict and know." Artur turned on his heel. "Come, we could prattle on like this all day and still be no wiser." He smiled, content with his wisdom, or lack of it, this day. "You mentioned steam in a pipe some time ago. Did that speriment run?"

"Follow me, Artur, follow me."

Her voice was low, with a slight huskiness, almost lost in the long depths of the corridor. Artur heard the slide of cloth brushing over stone ahead of him, but when he reached the doorway it was quiet.

"Morgayne, are you there?"

His voice was a whisper as he entered the room, which was dark, unlit. Artur crept forward, until he felt a hand on his leg and higher, on his thigh. She pulled him down to the floor, and the straw was rough against his back as Morgayne pulled the linen shirt over his head.

"I'm always here, Artur."

She held his untidy blond head to her breast, and slowly stroked his forehead and hair with her long fingers. The flesh of her breast was warm and soft, so soft, and the beat of Morgayne's heart was steady and slow. Artur tilted his head up so his lips touched her throat and felt a pulse there. His hand moved down from her cheek, sliding languorously down her throat until it found a hard nipple on a tight breast. Artur pressed the palm of his hand against her breast and Morgayne sighed.

"Ah, brother, do you love me?" Morgayne whispered low. She held his hand to her breast with her own. Her fingers curled over the back of his hand and held his heat against hers, and her movements were considered and slow.

"Sister, you know it." Artur's voice was barely heard. "I do."

"Show me, then, my king."

Morgayne's hand slid down Artur's body, but before she reached his cock he throbbed and pulsed, and woke, panting. His cream was hot and sticky against his gut, and she was gone, dark and gone in the night.

Fuck. Again, she haunts me again. Artur lay still, as his breath slowed and his heart beat settled. His cock was still rock hard as it always was from the dream, but he left it untouched. Before sleep, his hand was enough, but following the dream, never enough. Morgayne's hands in the night were always so slow. His fingers were never enough, not when she was gone in the night.

Artur stirred, and moved to sit up. His hands felt a slight resistance, as if something was loosely strapped around his wrists, then it was gone, something broken, something snapped. He sat up, and looked down at his cock, still thick and hard. Shaking his head slowly, he circled his hand around the wetness on his gut, then smoothed the cream into his skin.

Artur hauled himself up from the bed and wrapped himself in his animal skins, the warmth of the dark wolf around his shoulders. He shuffled to the door, and pushed it aside. The drift of his breath on the cold air was like smoke as he moved outside. The stone was cold as he leaned against it, and steam rose from his piss as he patterned his flow down the wall.

Ah mother, the cold is upon us now, Artur thought, as he finished the piss. He looked up, and for a moment was distracted by shadows on the snow that looked like a trail of footprints. No, some trick of the moonlight, nobody would wander here, not by the king's quarters.

As he returned to his chamber, Artur blew on his hands to warm them. The sudden movement caused some long, fine strands of blackness to drift away from his wrists and fall slowly to the snow, where they lay like the finest cracks, darkest black, the thinnest threads against the whiteness of the snow. They melted away, and could be seen no more.

Artur returned to his sleeping chamber, restless and unsettled, as he so often was when the dream set itself in his mind so solidly. His mind flickered back to his first memories, when just a small boy; and his sister Gayne pulling him around the fortress by his little hand. She would chatter and laugh with him, but lock her lips against all sound whenever an adult passed by.

And the look of black filth she would give the tall thin man whenever he was near. Even as a child Artur knew well not to question that hatred. As a young man, wiser in the ways of passion and power, he sensed it wiser still never to come between two individuals with such an inextricable, inexplicable bond, an unbreakable thing. And yet, he loved them both. The fool Maerlyn who was no fool, and his dark sister Morgayne, forbidden to him through their mother, who crouched above him on the rock on his coronation day.

Artur's mind drifted and wandered, until finally he awoke to the feeble sun, its pale light slowly clearing the morning mist, creeping over the flagstones of his hearth. He crouched by the fire and blew life into its dull embers. Flames flickered and caught on the dry sticks and a carefully positioned log, and the night chill in the air slowly lifted.

He called for a maid to go to the main hall and the kitchen there, and bring back a break fast, and bring back normality too. Artur sought practical and plain people around him, as a foil for the politicking and pretence that went on between kingdoms.

After he had eaten, Artur dressed in warm robes, and set about to the hall. On his way, he saw again the cluster of children leading their animals out of the stables, on their meandering way down to the ponds and meadows below the fort.

"Emmelyne, has that mother goat birthed yet?"

"Triplets, sire, two does and a buck. They are back in the stables. It is a strange birth, out of season, so I keep them warm."

"Ah, that is well. You must show me later this day, when I return from my ride."

"It will please me, Lord, as it please you."

Emmelyne would run again to tell her mother, a bright shine in her eyes for the king's favour. Artur was not much older than the girl, and she sometimes day-dreamed - what would it be like to bed a king? But she was a practical girl, and shook her head, no. Far better to talk to the king about the things she knew, like goats. Every king should know about goats.

And horses. "Rednock. Your pig. Can it grow four long legs and a mane and a tail, and shod itself with shoes and nails?"

"No, sire. It's just a pig." Rednock was encouraged by the king's smile, his laughing eyes. "It snuffles a lot and rolls in mud, but it can't be rid."

"Well then, if I can't ride on your muddy pig, you'd best to the stables, lad, and stir that lazy groom for me. Pray tell him, the king requires a horse, saddled and fed."

Rednock turned to run.

"Down by the postern gate. Have the groom bring the horse there. Good man."

Artur reined in the horse, and the great beast stamped its hoof in the snow. Its breath rose in clouds of vapour which mingled and spiralled into the cold air. Artur's face and bare hands were chill from his swift ride. He pulled the collar of his cloak up to shield his face from the wind, and then tucked his hands in under his armpits to warm them.

"Walk on, tch, tch," he called to the horse, and it moved on slowly down the narrow path. All around the snow was limpid white, laying a soft carpet silent on the land. The smooth expanse was broken in places by narrow runs of animal tracks, massed and single, no creature to be seen. That was strange, usually Artur would spy some creature moving. On the horizon a stand of bare trees ran along a ridge, their branches thick with the massed nests of rooks. Empty nests now, in the colds of winter, nearing the shortest day.

Suddenly there was a rising burst of movement, and a shock of rooks took flight, their blackness stark against the white snow and the grey sky. What strangeness this, a parly of rooks this cold season? Artur wondered at the birds, normally gone in winter. He reined in the horse with one hand, the other still tucked close to his body for warmth. He watched the twisting spiral of birds as it rose high then circled, before dropping back to the branches. Artur heard their raucous cries from the distance, and looked for the disturbance.

There. A black figure moving slowly along the ridge, a solitary walker. Ah, gone below the line of trees. Artur was puzzled, he was some distance from the nearest village, and did not expect to see anyone around here. He flicked the reins, and the horse walked on, one ear forward and one ear back, alert with some animal sense. Artur sensed a tension in the horse, and leaned forward to calm it, speaking softly and patting its neck. He rode on, alert for something but he knew not what.

The horse kept moving, firm footed on the path which followed the contour of the slope, worn no doubt by sheep making their easy way. As they moved in under the line of trees Artur ducked his head to avoid low branches and cold dripping snow. After a short time he found it easier to dismount and walk ahead of the horse. The trees grew closer and the snow thinned, and the paths split and meandered and finally disappeared completely.

Artur crested the ridge, and below him, some distance away, he saw the black shape of the person walking. Too far off to make out any detail, the figure seemed almost to glide upon the snow, moving ahead at a faster pace. A long straight line of footprints stretched out behind, marking the person's path across the snow. Ahead, at the centre of a long valley through which a small, swift stream flowed, Artur saw a simple stone dwelling. Its roof of thatch was still carrying snow on its northern side, while the southern aspect was brighter in the struggling winter sun, water dripping from the high sloped roof.

Artur did not know the place, and was curious. He thought he knew the ways around Camlann well, but this was a valley and stream he was not familiar with, nor the dweller here. He remounted the horse, tch, tch, walk on. The horse trembled, its eyes wide, and again Artur leaned forward to settle its way. The movement of the figure ahead of him was somehow familiar, but he could not place it.

Slowly they moved up the floor of the valley, the tall, black figure never looking back, the king on his horse always looking forward and drawing closer. The woman ahead of him (she must be a woman, no man so tall would have such a slender build) was dressed in black so midnight dark that the light falling on her cloak was swallowed up, thick and velvet. Her long, jet black hair fell near as long as the cloak to her feet. It was tied in a single band level with her waist, so it billowed like black smoke about her back, and fell like black rain to her feet.

"Morgayne, is it you, dear sister?"

Artur called to her as he rode. She stopped, and turned to him, the hem of her cloak and the veil of her hair swirling as she turned. The horse reared its head high, the whites of its eyes rolling back.

"Artur..." Her voice was low, "Did you think it not?"

Morgayne reached her hand up to the horse's head with a strange, hypnotic movement, and the beast was calmed, its previous fear gone in an instant.

"I did not think at all, sister. What is it you do here?" Artur looked down at her, puzzled by her presence in this place. "Why do you not come to Camlann? You are the king's sister, and welcome there."

"Not so, Artur. There are those who doubt me." She looked at her brother intensely. "And I them."

"Ah, Morgayne, I know it so and fear it." He dismounted from the horse and moved towards her. "But I don't understand it. The Maerlyn is a good man."

Morgayne stayed her look on her brother's eyes, and the fingers of one hand opened slowly and spread, her fingers opening wide and then closing in like a claw gripping some invisible thing. Her eyes widened black, and any other man would have stepped back.

"He is filth, Artur, he is not worthy of me and runs to his white whore." Her voice was near a whisper, its malevolence made worse by her quietness. "You are their play thing, cursed by their games.

"But you are my brother too, and we ran together and you took my hand, and I pulled you along. Gayne, Gayne, is that you, where have you gone? You'd cry out my name and chase after me and I'd hide, and all I wanted was you my brother to play with and love." Morgayne's voice cracked like her heart. "But they took you from me, and I hated them. Maerlyn and your father and the monster in white, they took you from me and I hated them for it."

Her passion ached and tore at Artur's throat, and all the time Morgayne's voice was soft and low, her hatred a whisper blown away by the wind, but fierce, so utterly fierce. Any other man would have been afraid, but Artur was her brother and did not fear her.

His own ache was without words. Artur opened his arms and stepped forward to embrace his sister. Morgayne went to him. His arms went around her back and he held her close, and she was his sister and her hands were slow. She splayed her fingers over his heart, pressing like a cat does before it turns to sleep.

"Ah, Morgayne, it is not right that you dwell in hiding, deep in this valley with your solitary hut. Do you not beg for comforts?"

"Comforts, my Lord? I do not lack for any. Come look."

Morgayne caressed the hair on the back of Artur's head, her long fingers running through the wind knotted tangle of his hair. She turned away from him and walked to the door of the hut. It was curiously carved with spirals and circles, ancient patterns made in new wood. In the centre of the door, blazoned as warning and a curse, was the long oval slit of a danu na gig, freshly carved.

Artur saw it, and the hot image of his sister's cunt above him, Morgayne crouching on the rock on his celebrant day, raced through his mind. He felt a tightening deep in his gut, and she turned her head as if she felt it too. Her fingers spread, long and pale.

"Care for your horse, Artur. There is a shelter from the wind, on the lee." She touched her finger tips to the fresh cut wood. "Be quick. The clouds drop." Morgayne pushed open the door, and it scraped upon the stone. "A storm comes. I feel it."

It is in her eyes, I see it, thought Artur, as he tied up the horse and gave it feed. What is she here, my sister? What portent do I follow? Artur, a captain used to the sea, knew that caution in the face of elemental forces was a pointless art. The elements would prevail no matter the acts of a man. Morgayne was connected to the world through her witchery and magick, yet she was his sister too, and a woman. Artur brushed dusted snow from his cloak and stepped across her threshold. He was invited in, but entered as was his right. King in his land, and certain of his dominion.

Morgayne in hers, and certain of it too.

Inside the hut its dimensions were elusive. Morgayne circled the first room and lit several rushlights mounted in metal brackets on the walls. Their light sputtered and shifted on currents of air as she moved, then settled steady, casting circles of light on each wall and low penumbras on the floor. Small window openings high on the walls let the darkening daylight cast dull shadows. Morgayne placed cut logs onto the dark embers of the fire in the stone hearth, and slowly warmth crept into the room, red heat crackling open from the black coals.

"Brother, drop your cloak and stand before me, that I know my king."

"Sister, tie back your hair and stand before me, that I know my place."

"Ah, sweet brother, you know it." Morgayne's eyes widened as she heard his promise and his fealty.

"I've always known it, since you came to me in my dreams."

"Hmmm, yes, I remember you calling in the night, after you knew the girl from the round island under the volcanoes." Morgayne caressed Artur's neck, and he closed his eyes. "She woke your heart, didn't she, love?" Her fingers were warm and slow on his skin. "I heard you calling, how could I not?" Her voice just a whisper. "We're blood through our mother." Her lips touched his neck. "And you're my little brother." She kissed his lips. "Who I took by the hand into our favourite places." Her hand touched his skin. "Where nobody knew but me."

Artur stood in the centre of the room, motionless, as Morgayne circled around him once. She moved behind him, slid her arms around his body and held both hands to his chest. She was tall, the top of her head nearly level with Artur's, and her body long and lean. She pressed up against his back, holding him close. He shivered, but it wasn't cold in the room. The fire crackled and spat.

Morgayne reached for the broach and clip at his throat and undid the loops and straps. Artur's furs dropped to the floor. She slid around in front of him, and took his face in her hands, studying him. Artur's face was tanned brown from the wind and the elements, and his tangled hair a dirty blond. By contrast, Morgayne's skin was pale as the dropped snow outside, her hair black as night. She held him for a moment with a steady look in her eyes, then ran her fingers through his hair to the back of his head, pulling his mouth to hers.

Their kiss was long, a mutual delicate taste at first, then they were hungry for each other. Passion swept over them and their hands fought with buttons and straps, getting in each other's way as they tried to pull garments away from their bodies. Artur pushed Morgayne's hands from him, ah her touch is gone, so he could concentrate on the long row of buttons running from her throat, down between her slight breasts, to the base of her belly. He gripped the cloth in both hands and pushed it off her shoulders, down her arms. Some buttons popped away with his force and spun, spiralling and spinning on the floor.

The top half of her gown fell behind her, and Morgayne quickly tugged the fabric down from her waist and dropped it to the floor, a pool of blackness at her feet. She stood before him in a sheath of white linen, ties down one side. Artur reached for one of the ties, to pull it undone, but she stepped back, ah she is gone.

"Wait, brother, pull off your boots, your leggings and straps. 'Tis quicker, you do it!"

"Hungry for me, Gayne?" Artur looked up at her as knelt and loosened the straps.

At the sound of his oldest name for her, the strangest look came into her eyes. Morgayne's face flickered with quick shifting emotions.

"You know it, Artur. But we cannot, brother. Our mother is one, we come from same womb."

"Yet two fathers made us, and they are both dead." Artur stood before her, and touched his fingers to Morgayne's lips. "So we are blood, but only half blood."

"Artur, are you sure of it?" She scrutinised him. "Every man has to be born from his mother, but his father's a less certain thing."

"I am, sister, I am sure of it. How else did I pull Scalibet from the rock, else to be the dead king's son?"

"A symbol is not all of it, Artur." Morgayne gazed at him, pondering. "What proof you, that Uthur's blood is in your veins? The Lord Uthur let the rumour grow that my father, Gorloys, bedded our mother before he rode to his death. That might be the truth, little brother." She stopped talking and closed her eyes, deep in thought.

"I know it, brother, I know the proof. Uthur King, I nursed him on his dying bed. On his side, there was a dark bruise, a permanent thing on his flesh, just to the side of his hip. Like a spilt cup of wine, his flesh was bruised red." Morgayne looked at Artur closely. "Uthur marked it a thing from his youth, and his father before him was marked too, so he said."

Her argument rose to its conclusion. "The king's mark, Artur. Do you have it?" She challenged him, her brother a man, but was he a king? "Without Uthur's mark, you are not king, but ordinary flesh." Morgayne scrutinised him, her eyes blazing, seeking truth. "I don't remember seeing a mark on your skin."

"Ah sister, you think it ordinary flesh?"

Artur dropped away all of the garments from his limbs, and pealed the rough shirt over his head and stood before her naked.

"I am marked, and I thought it most curious. It grew darker as I grew older, and always most cleverly hidden. But I am marked, yes."

Morgayne's eyes widened at the sight of Artur naked before her, and her tongue darted red on her lips. Her gaze narrowed and she studied his flesh, looking this way and that on his body. She reached out her hand to touch his skin, and ran a single finger down his side, feather light. His cock twitched, a thickening started. Morgayne slowly moved around him, her finger tips trailing on his skin, across his back, and to his other side.

"You lie, Artur. You are not marked. I don't see it." Her voice was low, and her fingers lower.

"Cleverly hidden, my doubting sister, I said it was cleverly hidden." He smiled. "Your fingers keep their delicate stroke, you'll find it soon enough."

Artur shifted his feet apart, and his cock thickened some more, lengthening down his thigh. Morgayne licked her lips again, and her fingers wandered down.

Artur reached for a tie on the side of her shift and tugged, and the whole cord ran through the eyelets and loops all up and down the cloth. It opened away to reveal Morgayne's nakedness. She was tall and thin, her slight breasts with dark nipples standing hard already. Artur caressed her side with the fingers that undid the string, and reached inside the cloth to circle her waist. He pulled her to his own body, flesh against flesh, her breasts to his chest, her belly against his hard gut. Artur flicked the drape of cloth from his sister's shoulders and it fell to the floor.

Morgayne was an inch or two shorter than her brother, but her legs longer than his, so the thick black gloss of hair at the base of her belly rested over the root of his cock. She ground against him and felt his heat thicken. He wasn't yet hard, but growing harder.

Morgayne pressed again and her clit pushed to his flesh. She moaned, and the sound was deep in her throat, almost a growl.

She eased her legs apart to let the length of Artur's cock rise up between her thighs till it touched the lips of her cunt and she felt his heat. Morgayne rocked back and forth on him, spreading her gliding slide on Artur's flesh, at the same time gripping the firm curves of his ass in both hands. They swayed and ground against each other, Artur's arms wrapped tight around her, claiming her slender frame as his, her body captive. Morgayne did not fight him. She fucked upon his mouth with her tongue, thrusting it between his teeth and savouring the taste of him.

"Hidden where, brother, how can a blaze be hid?"

Artur chuckled. "You want to see the mark of the king upon me? What will I be then, sister, a brother or a king?"

He broke away from her grasp and stepped back. Finding a pool of light, dimming now as the rushes burned down, he stood before her, confident in himself, king. The flames flickered and dipped, and shadows shifted in the room. Artur's prick, released from the delicious grip of her thighs, stood long and hard up against his gut. Its head was a beautiful red, the deep colour of plums. The tip of him just touched the bottom of his navel, a good size. Morgayne's eyes lit up at the sight of him, and her hand reached out, her fingers stretching wide as if to measure his length.

"Brother, that's a fine cock your father gave you. I was so fleeting fast when you pulled the dagger from the rock, I did not properly see."

"Ah yes, and I looked up and saw your precious cunt, dark above me on the rock. I saw you well enough, your hand all covered in mud, your belly glistening with my seed."

Artur closed his eyes, remembering. He opened his eyes and saw her, gazing on him. He reached out one hand and took hers, and with his other hand splayed his fingers along his cock.

"See now the blaze, all on the base of my shaft. As I say, a curious thing, 'twas never there as a small boy. 'Tis why you never saw it, with your slow hands stroking."

Morgayne dropped to her knees before him, her great length of hair coiling on the floor. There, as Artur promised, his blaze was like an uneven bruise on the underside of his cock shaft, darker than the flesh of the rest of him, like a leaf wrapped around.

"A hidden thing, until my cock makes big to discover it."

Morgayne took the length of him in one hand and held it still for a moment, studying the birth mark on his cock. She looked up at Artur, a wry smile on her face.

"Who would have thought it, my little brother, the king!" She stroked, just once. "As you say, most cleverly hid."

Morgayne stroked him again, ever so slowly, her finger tips gliding lightly along his flesh. She dipped her hand between her legs and splayed her lips apart, anointing her finger tips with her own wetness, and trailed one sliding finger along the shaft.

"My sweet boy, grown to be king."

Morgayne stood, her hand holding him still. "Come, brother, I have a lying place within. A fit place to bed a king, I think."

Leading him by the cock, she walked through a low door into a second room. Artur followed, and this time was led across her threshold into Morgayne's dominion. Outside, a beat of rain blew against the door, and in the distance, thunder called. A storm was rising.

Inside the bed chamber a round iron stove radiated heat, a cleverly built thing. Artur recognised it as a device of Maerlyn's design, and wondered on it here. Not for long his wondering, as Morgayne, still leading him by the cock, turned down coverlets on a low bed. She pushed him down onto it, one hand splayed on Artur's chest, the other still gripping his length, her fingers a slow twist and a stroke, commanding the brother her king to her will.

"Hush, brother, I'm here. You're safe with me, you're always safe in the night with me."

Morgayne's whisper was close to his ear, and her lips dropped hot to his throat. Artur moaned with a starting lust, and reached up for her.

She pulled back, denying him. "Ah brother, slowly, slowly, my love. Let Gayne do it."

At the sound of her oldest name, whispered by her woman's lips, Artur twitched and his cock bounced. His fingers gripped the covers on the bed, and he waited for her fingers slow. His eyes closed, and he lay perfect on the bed, his body hard and muscled, his cock beautiful, long. His nipples rose in tight points. Morgayne looked down on him, and she dipped her fingers to her cunt again, anointing herself. Her nipples were dark and thick.

She crawled up his body and scented herself to Artur's breath, and blessed herself on his lips. Her eyes widened black and her own lust smell rose in the room, pungent and rich. Morgayne quivered, and slid along his body. Her cunt swelled, hot blood, her pulse beating steady and firm. The scent of sex swirled thick and heavy on the air.

She knelt up, and slowly separated long strands of her hair between her fingers. She tugged five strands from her head and coiled them all in a loop. Reaching for one of Artur's hands , Morgayne turned the hairs around his wrist and pulled them through. Four hairs pulled loose, yet one remained. She pulled it tight, and looped the black strand of hair, barely visible and dark as midnight, to a far bedpost.

"I bind you, brother, with mine hair, that no man has cut, no woman neither."

Morgayne repeated the ceremony at his wrist and ankles, and bound the man to her bed with the finest trancement and the thinnest web. Artur lay still, his cock rigid against his gut, a tiny shine glistening on its tip.

"Don't move, Artur, don't make a noise." She took his cock in her hand, and delicately held it high from his belly. She wound and wound the final strand of the hair from her head round and around Artur's cock, and her shadow was upon his tightness and bound him there.

Morgayne dipped her tongue to his tip, a delicate taste, and the opening of his prick widened. She probed her tongue, just once. His cock reared up.

"Oh Artur, does my taste taunt you?"

Low, so low, her voice just a breath in the room, but he knew her words so well from the dream.

"You know it, sister, you've always known it." Artur's whisper was barely spoken, she knew his words so well from the dream.

"Slowly, little brother, wait for Gayne now."

Morgayne lowered her body until she lay upon his, pushing his legs apart so her thighs were between his thighs, her cunt and dark hair pushing hard against his high, tight balls. Artur's hot, hard shaft lay long between her belly and his muscled gut, her nipples pressed to his chest, her tight breasts flattened. She outstretched her arms and laced her fingers through her brother's fingers, and it was a crucifixion on the bed. But there was no dead god here, it was life, thick lust and lost love, her brother the king and dark Morgayne in her domain.

She slid upon him, her pale body arching up like a snake, her midnight black hair coiled all around. Morgayne pressed her hot cunt to his core, and slid herself upwards until her thick dark hair glistened with her juice, and she sat upon his hard heat. Artur, his limbs trapped and spread wide by the binding of her hair, Morgayne's magick holding firm, could only moan and rock his head from side to side. She slid her red centre along his shaft but did not take him in.

Artur's eyes closed with the pleasure of her slow fuck, her slide on his shaft. Morgayne released her fingers from his, and brought her hands onto his chest. She crouched over him, and moved up higher, higher, until her ripe sex smothered his mouth and nose. Morgayne mewled and cried out like some animal, some rising bird, as Artur fucked up into his sister's cunt with his tongue, his legs thrashing and quivering but always held firm by the silken charm of her binding hair.

With a crump of thunder the storm outside thrust its force up against the house, rain smashing against the outside wall. A frightened cry was heard from Artur's horse, and was echoed by a primal cry from Morgayne, "Ahh brother, fuck, oh my king." She stretched her arms high in the air, her tight, heaving breasts glistening with the heat of her passion.

Morgayne lifted her cunt from her brother's face, and she turned so she faced his high, throbbing cock, beads glistening from its crack like tiny diamonds, clear and bright. She lowered her cunt to him again, and was pleasured by a long lick, a deep probe, and the king's tongue along her luscious slit. She reached behind and splayed herself wider with both hands, opening up her dark asshole to Artur's eyes. "Sister!" he cried, and thrust the point of his tongue into her sweet asshole, fucking her there, tasting her dark musk.

Morgayne pushed back. Artur forced his tongue deeper, pushing, fucking, a deeper fuck all up into her dark swollen core. With a guttural moan deep in her throat, "Unnh huh, more," she fell forward and took Artur's cock into her mouth, and they were coupled and circled onto each other. The rich, cloyed smell of their arousal filled the room, Morgayne's ass licked deep and her cunt spread wide, and her juice slick and shining on Artur's lips and nose and sucked hard into his mouth. Artur the king ate from his sister's cunt and ass, and Morgayne his sister suckled and spat and thrust her mouth to his cock.

Little brother, I've always got you.

Gayne, Gayne, I know I know it's always us us us.

Quick, quick, fly away. Don't go, uhh, uhh, sweet brother, I'll….

Artur's cock lurched and thrust twice without warning. Morgayne moved her head back till just the end of her brother's cock was in her mouth, his cream pumping, spurting. She drank his seed down and thrust her swollen cunt hard to Artur's face and came, hard; five times she shuddered upon his lips and tongue and face. She drank him down, squeezing up the last surge with her hand gripped round his cock, slowly, slowly. The mess of him was all around her mouth. Morgayne licked her lips and savoured his taste.

"My brother, my sweetness, my king."

She sat back, her fecund sex hot and swollen, trapping his sucking mouth and probing tongue. Morgayne looked down upon her brother's long cock. The heat and the blood of her suckling hunger had engorged Artur's cock so full, so thick and hard, his cock was still high and proud. The blazed birth mark was clear now, a vivid stain on the shaft.

"Ah yes, the king's mark on the king's rod. I am convinced, dear brother, 'tis true." She let him breath, but remained crouching over him, her thick black haired cunt for Artur's eyes to see.

"The queen's cup too, sucked up into mine mouth, drunk deep."

"The queen's cup, Artur? I'm not your queen, oh brother, not your queen."

She circled her hand in a slow, writhing movement around, releasing the hex on his binds. The gossamer lines on Artur's wrists and ankles crackled and broke, a tiny snap as the spell shattered. Artur rubbed a wrist and looked up at his sister, a memory on his face, a realisation that he had been bound before, in the night. Around his cock, the last coil of her hair vanished, a shimmering haze rising from his heat.

"I bind the king to me, Artur, when thick and hard and a lord's work doing."

Morgayne stroked a long, slow finger all down his body, over the tip of his cock and along his shaft.

"Yet I release my brother. I cannot sit by you as queen, Artur. I am your sister first, not queen. Don't think it."

The heat in the room swirled and dropped, and they curled around each other with the innocence of stolen children, Morgayne's hair all around in a circle protecting them from the storm. As she had so often, Morgayne held Artur's sleeping head to her breast and crooned a low, soothing song, stroking the soft skin of his cheek.

"You be their dangling puppet, little brother, the white bitch and her spawning fool; but Gayne's here, I'm always here."

Her long fingers stroked and stroked all upon his sleeping skin. Artur slept, and twitched in his dream like a dog. Morgayne stroked slowly, circling round, her fingers curled, her pale flesh inside her silken web of midnight hair.

Artur saddled up the horse and rode away from the valley, breaking a solitary path in the snow that fell overnight. Reaching the high ridge with its line of skeletal trees, the round masses of the rook nests heavy on their spreading boughs, he looked back. The long trail ran straight back down into the valley and was lost in a far mist. Of the stone dwelling with its carved wooden door, he could see nothing. It might never have been there. Artur leaned forward to horse's ear, murmuring settling words. They could have been murmured to himself.

He rubbed his wrists, and held them both up before his eyes. The finest line of red was marked upon his skin, on both wrists. No dream then, or I'm dreaming still. The horse was solid and steady beneath him, and he thought it not a dream. As Artur rode nearer the Camlann hill the beast's pace quickened, keen to be home, warm and sheltered.

The night remained a blurred thing, Morgayne vanished in the morning, all gone. Some food was there, and dropping heat from the hearth and stove, but Artur did not tarry. As he rode, his mind flickered back and all he could see was the dark swell of his sister's cunt, all he could taste was the spicy tang of her asshole, puckered and tight on his tongue.

Artur stopped the horse, sitting quite still until he felt the pulse of his heart in his chest. He shook his head as if saying no, then spurred the horse on. He rode fast and made a swift gallop, thundering on 'till he saw the fort ahead of him, smooth white embankments circling it all around.

"Artur king returns," shouted the watch. "Make way for the king."

Artur rode up the zig and zag of the entry path, the horse's hooves in a high prancing trot.

"Artur, hail. We did not expect you gone. Art' well? No harm?"

"No harm, Maer. We found shelter for the night. You know it, the long clear valley down Rhyadder way."

"Rhyadder, Lord? There's no clear valleys there, sire. 'Tis wooded, wooded all round." Maerlyn looked askance at the young king. "Are you sure of it, sire?"

Artur pondered a moment, then replied, "No. Not sure of it at all. No matter."

Only later did Artur realise that Maerlyn had not asked with whom he sheltered. He thought it curious, but not surprising. Maybe I am a puppet truly, and can do no thing unbidden. He shook his head, smiling to himself in wry amusement. It be what it be, dingle dangle.

"Rednock, how be that pig of yours? Has it been saddled and ridden yet?"

Artur walked into his usual life. No matter.

"Wake, Artur, be awake."

Her voice was a low caress, lost silences whispering in his head, all time lost, moments long yet fleeting still. His fingers gripped the heavy covers, and again he threw them from his body, away from the bed. Artur sat up against the carved wooden headpiece and steadied his breath. He looked down, and again his erection was hard like iron, a dull ache deep in his balls. He didn't touch himself.

"Gayne," he whispered, "you lied. You said you'd always be here."

He touched himself. Quick strokes would satisfy the urge and ease the ache, but would not silence Morgayne's voice in his head. A longer time, urging up deeper visions from deep within, would bring back the taste of her slick sex, the scent of her musky asshole. But he couldn't mimic her slow hands.

"Ah fuck, I need to solve this."

Artur spoke out loud to the silent room. He let go his cock, and pulled the coverlets up to warm himself. Mayhap I should take one of the girls from the village, he thought to himself. Young Emmelyne is pleasing fair with her round apple breasts and her long thighs. She's looked up at me with a certain look, when she thinks I do not see.

Artur pictured the girl and imagined his fingers undoing the ties on her blouse, pulling the coarse woollen skirt from her hips; and the girl crouching down on his upright cock, a questioning look of eager surprise in her eyes as she took him all in. Artur smiled at the thought of her freshness, the pretty Emmelyne with her hair all curled up in a bonnet, closing her eyes in her pleasure.

She's a pretty thing, brother mine, with her softest fluff, but she never compares to this. And in his mind the curling darkness of Morgayne's lush cunt and the thick petals of her lips splayed in front of his eyes, before covering his face with their wetness and her earthy scent. Artur gripped his shaft and started a slow slide, long and slow, along his cock, along his cock, and the darkness of his sister engulfed him.

In the morning, a raven's feather lay on the snow, just outside his door. Trailing from it, impossibly long, were several fine black hairs. Artur looked down at his wrists, but they were smooth and unmarked. Pausing a moment, he turned back to the door, and flicked the locking lever up and down a number of times. Ah yes, he thought, I need to invite her in. This is my domain, not hers.

Several nights later, at the height of the moon, silent midnight settled over the silver snow, a deadened hush all around, something drawing near. On a distant wind a wolf howled, and another, and one more, their song coming closer, heralding a journey made in the night. In a line of trees low against the horizon a rise of rooks, unnaturally awake at night, startled and flew, arcing across the eye of the moon, then dropped and settled.

Artur stirred from his chair, moved to the door and lifted its long wooden latch. He pushed the door an inch open, and the golden flicker of a single candle inside shadowed and flickered on the snow outside. Afar, he heard the dull click of the iron latch on the postern gate. She comes, he thought to himself, and I invite her in. This is my dominion, and this night she will wonder the dream, not I. He silently

162

moved behind a long falling tapestry, and was hid. Deep in his gut, muscles tightened and blood thickened, and his cock began to rise.

Silence ushered at the door, and it swung slowly into the room, its hinges greased with the fat of a lamb, making no noise. A hard shadow cast by the light of the moon fell on the stone floor and was broken up and shimmered by the low glow of the candle. Morgayne silently entered the room, the long black swirl of her cloak, all of black feathers, swallowing up the light. The candle fluttered, dipped, and the flame flickered then steadied. She pushed the door behind her, and the latch fell. The cloak settled around her like wings after flight.

"Artur, are you here?" Her voice was a soft whisper. "Brother?"

Artur stood silent, wondering what she would do. Always as a child, and always in his dreams, it was he who stood by the door and she who would hide inside; Gayne playing her games, but always holding him close. She stood unmoving, but was that uncertainty in her voice?

He changed his mind. She needed comfort. "Sister, you come to me this night, and I welcome you in." He stepped forward and held his palm to her cheek. He stroked his thumb down onto her lips and held it there, a gentle touch. "Gayne, you're cold. Shed your cloak and come within. A fire burns and mead warms, honey sweet as you favour it." He took her hand, and Morgayne, unaccustomed to courtesy, followed on. "Sister, how you, this cold night? Come, the fire will comfort you."

In a second chamber, walls covered with long draped cloth all finely embroidered, and a great bed carved and high, Artur lead his sister to a wooden settle in the nook of a fireplace and made her sit. He took her hands in his.

"Morgayne, so cold. You come a long distance cold and lonely." It wasn't a question, but a statement. "Alone no longer, heart. I'm here, now."

Artur's natural, practical command took over. He didn't question why his sister made her long journey, nor how. Her presence was sufficient, and she was cold. He poured for her a goblet of mead, warmed in a jug on the hearth. Morgayne wrapped both hands around it, and slowly the gentle heat eased the chill from her hands, and a faint flush of pink rose to her cheeks. She looked younger, of a sudden, as if their ages were reversed. Artur stood by her side, a companionable silence, and he watched a tension fall from her shoulders, a subtle shift. Morgayne looked up at him, and was that a lost quietness in her eyes?

"Why did they pull us apart, Artur? You should have been just a brother, my brother, our Morgayse's brother. But they tore us all apart." She spoke the words and her voice cracked. "And now I'm painted witch, and I do it all alone."

"The goddess calls us to our fates, Gayne. We can't fight nor question it. I am king, but did not ask it." He placed another log on the fire, and pondered her. "And you do it alone because there is no man your match." He placed his hand on her shoulder, and held her there. "Besides, Gayne, you scare men."

Morgayne looked up at him. "Do I scare you, Artur?"

"No. But then, I'm no ordinary man."

He dropped the cloak from his shoulders and stood before her naked, his cock thick between his thighs, dropping long. "Remember?"

"By the goddess, yes. I remember." Morgayne's fingers went to her throat, and the faint blush was deeper there, a tell-tale red. "Who could forget you, brother?"

"And king, sister, don't forget. King, here." Artur spoke lightly, but there was no doubting his intent.

"D'ost command thy sister, sire, all naked there and strong?" Morgayne's words were but a whisper, as she heard the intent.

Artur's cock thickened at the sound of her words, and her cunt bloomed. King and high priestess then, duty bound and duty called. A ceremony was about to begin.

"Which hex, brother, that you command it?"

His cock thickened more and began to rise, and Morgayne saw the king's mark dark against his flesh. His movement was untouched, stirred only by the call and response of their words. Her black pupils dilated and the flicker of her tongue passed her dark lips.

"You know it, sister. You've always known it."

"Ah king, I give it, I give it to your will."

Morgayne stood, and her feathered cloak spread wide as she turned. She was tall before him, the black shimmer of her cloak contrasting black to Artur's pale flesh. With her eyes fixed on his, the high king's shaft a certainty now, rigid and hard against his gut and no need for slow hands, she deftly unclipped a catch from about her neck. Morgayne cast the garment onto the bed, where it spread wide, the feathers fanning like some bird's huge wing.

Morgayne was clad in a clinging black, velvet black gown which hugged every part of her tall thin body. She kept her gaze high on Artur's face, holding his eyes with hers, her intensity matching his command. With a single high movement of her arm reaching up, she swiftly pulled a single cord from the front of the dress, and the whole black sheath split like some fantastic cocoon and her white skin shone and the black dress fell. Morgayne stood naked before him, nipples hard and dark on her small breasts. Her ribs shadowed and she was tall and gaunt before him, the long fall of her hair coiling all around, twisting and turning like a live thing.

She pulled five long hairs from the top of her head and gave them to her brother, the king. "Your will, brother, and you know it." Morgayne fell backwards onto the bed, all within the circle of her feathered cloak, and her limbs spread wide upon the bed. The dark place of her sex widened before Artur's watching eyes, and his cock lurched at the promise.

"My blood is upon me, brother, my magick is strong with the high moon. Be careful what you wish."

"Best not fuck then, sister, if your blood is rising strong. No matter, the king can mix his seed with his sister's blood and make a strong anointment, flesh on flesh. The goddess' will be done, yet we not see it and must wait."

Artur stepped towards Morgayne, and coiled one long hair from her head about and around one ankle and tied it to the bed. She moaned, deep in her throat. Artur moved to her other foot, and bound it too, coiling the hair all around. She sighed, soft like the wind. A bead of bright fluid shone on the tiny lips of his cock, the conjure rising up his essence. Artur moved to the head of the bed and pulled Morgayne's wrists up high, circling the third hair and the fourth about in a single twist, and bound her to the bed. All in her cloak of feathers, Morgayne quivered on the bed and moaned with her caught up lust.

Artur returned to the base of the bed and studied his work, looping the fifth hair between his fingers.

"Ah, Gayne, it's always you and me, and now I bind us."

He spun the silken fine length of the last hair five times around his shaft and looped it around his tight balls, tying him to the spell. Morgayne's hair was so long, Artur still had a long length to turn and loop and bind. He looked down upon his sister tied in her magick weave to the bed, then fell between her legs, his fingers opening up her dark haired cunt and spreading her lips gently wide before sucking up her whole cunt into his open mouth, sealing her lips with his.

Morgayne shuddered, and thrust up her centre to his mouth, her fingers helplessly twisting and stretching above her head, tied tight.

"Aah, fuck, eat me, drink me in, sweet fuck of mine, my king, my brother."

167

Her body rippled and twisted, the pleasure from her heated cunt spreading through her limbs like silver from a forge, hot and dangerous. Her finger tips tingled with wild energy, stretching and gripping on the air. A shimmer of blue heat flickered in her aura and Morgayne's spirit spun within a vortex of flickering colour.

Artur's mouth and tongue sucked and thrust in her sex, the tang of her blood like metal, and his colours too spiralled up from the pit of his spine and looped like a corona to the base of his neck. The air shimmered and a faint susurrus, a crackle of ether, could be heard, humming soft and low. Some elemental thing was being made from their blood and lust, their love and life.

Artur lifted his head from her dark centre, and crawled up beside his sister, his mouth a smear of her redness. He placed his finger on his lips and drew a dark line of blood and smear up around his cheek, around his eye in a circle, until the mark faded on his brow. He dropped his finger to his mouth again, and licked the tip of it wet. Artur dipped the finger to Morgayne's sex and again anointed it with blood and lust, then spiralled it the other way on his cheek and down around his chin. His look was serious, for he painted old sigils found on rock and stone, and made long connections. They would awaken spirits, take care in what you ask for.

Morgayne gazed up at him, her eyes black lust and narrowing to sharpen her sight and to see him clear.

"Tie us, brother, bind us in a circle. My hair, my single strand of hair."

Artur looked to his groin, and his cock stood thick and hard, deep red with his own blood and its head rich purple like a bruise. The thin dark circle of her hair looping around was a shadow line at the base of his shaft. He found the loose tail and stretched it out between his fingers to find the furthest end. Morgayne's nipples were hard and long, and Artur looped turns first about one nipple and then the other. The nubs darkened, and Morgayne gasped as her senses connected with his, tied through the long fine line between them.

Artur leaned down to his sister, and kissed her hot and warm upon the mouth, tasting her there. She returned the kiss, deep and hard, sucking on his tongue and biting on his lips. Above her head, the fingers of one hand entwined the fingers of the other, and she laced her hands together.

Artur lifted his head from the kiss, and moved down her body, sucking up one nipple and its spin of hair to his mouth, then the other, pulling up her shallow breasts in a hot suck so hard she gasped. Tight pain. More, my other hard tit. Morgayne pushed her body up to his mouth, to ease the pain and to make him bruise her again with his mouth. Artur trailed his tongue down the dark seam of her belly, following a thread of soft hair from her navel to the tip of her cunt, where he peeled apart her thick lips, throbbing with heat and her lust. He sucked up her clitoris deep into his mouth, swirling his tongue all around. Morgayne shuddered and writhed, jerking her core up from the bed, thrusting her pleasure into his heated mouth, meaningless sounds crooning from her throat.

He pulled his head away from her sex, a last lick and flick of his tongue. Finding the final length of the binding hair, Artur pushed back the folds of flesh from around her high clitoris, and spun the hair around. They were linked together, the ties that bind, from his thick long cock to her hard little clitoris, and through the heat of her nipples. Their auras merged and spun together in one single spinning thing. The conjure bloomed around them, and they were no longer king and high priestess, far beyond sister and brother, much more than a man and a woman. High magick, and the goddess called.

Morgayne was still spread wide on the bed, her legs wide and her hands tied high above her head. Energy spun between her tied together places and rippled to the ends of her limbs, crackling into the ether. Artur lay above her, his rod a burning heat along her belly, the root of it hard against the tip of her cunt. He wrapped one arm around her neck and pulled her face to his. Artur's heated balls were hard up against the open wetness of her cunt, and his cock along her belly, a sliding fuck, a sliding fuck.

He slid above her, their bellies slick with their sweat, and Inside them both long pleasure began, churning and building from deep within their centres. His churning seed and her blood on the high moon began its count to her beginning days. Morgayne's time was not here, not yet, so no magick wasted but her body a promise and her mind left behind. Artur mindless as he fucked upon her flesh, the thick hard slide of his cock up and down, up and down, until with a massive gasp he arched his back and, pressing his swollen balls deep to the wet slide of her cunt, shot a great stream up between her breasts right to her throat.

With a massive surge, her climax came, and with one huge thrust of her body Morgayne snapped the links and ties of her hair. She pulled her legs up to Artur and wrapped them around his back, and both hands cradled the back of his head. Morgayne's kisses devoured his mouth, and she gripped his body to hers, tight and tighter. No goddess, no priestess, no king; just the hot embrace of her brother, the only man she knew, the only man she loved.

"Call me Gayne, so it's just me."

Her whisper and sob was on his throat, and Artur held her body against his, and gently turned her so she lay beside him, their bellies still held firm and his beautiful cock between them, its heat a long sticky place and her breasts held close to his. He cradled her head against his chest, stroking over and over the top of her head. Her hands pressed against his chest like a cat's, and slowly the tension drained away from her body and she slept. Artur pulled the feathered cloak around them for warmth, and later in the night reached for a thick animal pelt and made it all around them.

Later still in the night Morgayne woke, and she was on her back, Artur's head nestled into her shoulder, his hand resting softly, cupping her breast. Morgayne stroked his tangled hair slowly, and ran her finger around the dried spirals on his face, silently. He stirred, murmured something in his sleep then settled again. She could feel the heat of his cock, soft now but still hot, against her thigh. She shifted slightly on the bed and, still cradling his head to her breast, cupped her hot sex in the palm of her other hand, letting the weight of her thighs trap her hand there. And she comforted herself, her sex untouched by man nor woman but only her brother's mouth and her own fingers. Morgayne held Artur's head to her chest, so if he awoke again in the depths of the night, he would hear her heart beat.

"I'm here, Artur," she whispered, "I'm always here."

On the morrow, Artur made it clear to Maerlyn that Morgayne was a part of his court.

"Maer, you will respect her. If you cannot, stay away. I play no favourites."

"With the lady's grace, sire, I will be kind; even if she be not kind to me."

"Politick, Maer?" Artur looked upon the mage with an eyebrow raised, a wry smile on his face. "Take care. You might believe it."

"Believe it sire? I say it, and what truth in words?"

"Try at least, Maer. My sister might surprise you." Artur turned as his sister drew near. "She might not, too."

"Maerlyn, do you doubt me?"

Morgayne's voice was honey smooth, sending a shiver up the old man's spine. She touched his arm with her fingers, and they were warm. "Oh, Maerlyn, don't fear me. I'm just a girl, unformed." Her eyebrow rose, the same as her brother's, teasing the man.

"Not a girl, lady, not unformed either, as I believe my eyes."

"Maerlyn, you tease. You flatter me."

Her laugh was high and light, and Maerlyn knew he was bewitched. He knew too, that she toyed with him.

"Stop, the both of you," said Artur. "Such sweetness, bees will fly from your mouths."

"Buzz, buzz," replied Maerlyn.

"Oh, my flower," added Morgayne. "I shall wear yellow, and live in a hive."

Artur looked at them both, and shook his head. "Well it is I love you both, and will walk between you. Yet you battle on, and surely 'tis sport?"

"'Tis not love, sire, that I know." Maerlyn looked at the priestess Morgayne. "And your sister knows it too."

"Ah, no matter. I'll walk the middle and take good counsel from you both."

Artur dismissed the feud between his sister and the magister from his business. "I speak of counsel. Sister, I bid you travel with me to Breton, to parley the Lord de Grance and plan our kingdom's trade. This next week. You do it?"

"My pleasure, brother, by your side."

Morgayne glanced across at Maerlyn, who was watching them both closely in a way she had seen before, his eyes cast down as if he saw nothing but his feet. But Morgayne knew the magician well, and thought he missed nothing, nothing at all. Maerlyn caught her glance and pondered it. His ankle itched, but he did not scratch it until after she was gone.

A week later a small ship sailed from the port where Artur, Maerlyn and Lot landed in the days before the rock and the dagger pulled from it, and Artur's crowning as king. Artur in command, the vessel made its way down the Syverne channel and south west past the long foot of the country, off into the deep Atlant where warm waters streamed up from the south. The ship made good way, a steady wind at its sails, and the thrusting peninsula of Breton was soon ahead of them. The Lady Morgayne sat regal before the mast, imperious and proud. Sailors scurried on the deck and in the ropes, and were in awe of her.

"What is the intent with de Grance, Artur?" Morgayne asked. " What trade you seek?"

"Tin and lead, sensible metals but dull. They can be worked and beaten for gutters and pipes, buildings to be made and fancily fitted. Tall trees, too. Cut and floated in huge rafts across the sea." Artur thought back to his trading runs to the cold countries east of Lot's islands, and the books and ledgers that recorded it all.

"And in return? What do we buy these tall trees and metals all with?"

"This moment I am not sure of it. Maerlyn thinks wool from the sheep's back, all spun and woven; I think it knowledge and craft might be best. Smaller ships can run a man fast, and he sell his cleverness. People need clever hands and will buy them. We'll see. de Grance is a fair man, and will offer us well."

"His little daughter, Miryamme. Is he offering a bride?" Morgayne looked at her brother, wondering if he sought a queen yet, or was content with his sister beside him.

"I had not thought it," replied Artur. "Besides, she is still just a girl, too young for a king. A pretty poppet to be sure, but no, I had not thought it."

Morgayne said no more. She would inspect the child for her own mind, knowing that a longer look was sometimes worth it. She knew Artur would need a suitable girl eventually, and some legiances grew slowly. If Miryamme was a poppet still, then a dowry set aside now would do de Grance no harm. Morgayne smiled wryly to herself. A dowager princess already, at my tender age, playing courts for my brother. If I meddle and grow old with it… I should prentice myself to the old meddler himself, and make sport at the same time. She shook her head and laughed quietly.

Artur glanced at his sister and saw there was a plot being made. He also saw a wildness in her hair from the wind, and colour high in her cheeks, for it was cold. An image of the strange house in the treeless valley, and the solitary line of footsteps to it, flashed into his mind; and he gazed upon his sister in her dark beauty. Ahh Gayne….

Morgayne looked up at her brother from where she sat, as if hearing a call from a distance. Their eyes met, and held for a long moment and a moment longer. Her eyes were as black as cold water on a moonless night, Artur's shading to a deep blue grey, changeable with the sky and cloud, and the shifting colour of the sea. They held a mutual gaze, and neither looked away until a shiver of wind caught and rattled the sails. Artur looked up to judge the wind, and leaned into the steering oar. The sail filled, and the small ship surged ahead on the sea, a small chop rising as the land drew near.

Sometime later they steered up a small inlet to a protected space in the lower reaches of a river. On one shore there were long timbered quays with a number of ships and other craft tied up. On the far shore, defensive timber palisades marked the boundaries of de Grance's fort. It was an impressive structure, a series of single and two storey buildings climbing the slope up away from the water's edge, and a short jetty jutting into the inlet. Artur turned the steering oar hard over and brought their ship in a long circle, turning it around and bringing it alongside the jetty.

Artur, dressed in his travelling furs and a long ceremonial cloak, strode down the gang plank of the ship, his head high and strides long. He was still a young king, yet he walked tall, reminding the older Duke who had drawn the dagger from the rock and made king. It was a simple gesture, needing no words, but a quiet reminder of the power of the king.

Morgayne, too, imposed her presence on the place, her black cloak all feathers falling, swirled around her in a curious slow motion, her jet black hair plaited in a long rope down her back and all looped back up and braided. The sailors were superstitious, and marked with their fingers the crescent of a watching eye on their foreheads, to keep them safe. Morgayne saw the men mutter, and a tiny smile creased the corners of her mouth. She might call up mermaids from the deep, to torment and drive them mad, or perhaps rats and spiders in the hold.

"Morgayne, don't think it. We return by sea and need the crew." Artur warned his sister and bade her stop, knowing her look.

"Ha, Artur, you spoil my games. I get bored. How to jape and jest, when my own brother sticks in the mud and wears clod's feet? Who can I play with tonight?"

"Oh Gayne, you always played with me when you got bored and restless."

Artur caught himself and quickly looked around. His use of her private name slipped out before he caught it, a not thinking thing. Morgayne looked at her brother carefully, no emotion in her eyes but a stillness there. She reached out slowly to touch his hand, just the tip of her fingers in a slow caress.

"I did, didn't I, brother." Her voice was a whisper, half talking to herself. Her forefinger moved down the side of his hand, and slipped away. "Go brother, be the king and make ceremony with the lord here. Treat and trade. I will to my own business make, and not bother you."

"What business, Morgayne? Make care with your conjure, or use it not at all, if it pleases thee."

"Fear it not, Artur, I will be innocent. I'll see the poppet, and be like her older sister, all sweet. She can show me her dolls."

Morgayne turned away, and walked ahead down the gang plank. On the quay, de Grance greeted her as a priestess, honour given. He took Morgayne's hand in his, brushing it to his lips. They made small chat for a moment, and then she turned to Miryamme, who stood shyly behind her father.

"Come, sister, show me around your father's kingdom. We don't need to hear these foolish men."

Miryamme's eyes opened wide, hearing the priestess dismiss her father in such a bold way, and the king too; and being called sister. She could never be that brave, not even once, and would never speak to her father like that. And never the king. Miryamme was astonished at Morgayne's words, and looked up to the older woman in wonder. She wanted to wear black feathers, but knew she never would. Morgayne looked back at Artur with a steady gaze, then turned to the young girl, bending down to hear her words.

"Show me your places, Miryamme. Every girl has her favourite places."

Artur went with de Grance to the main hall of the fortress and parlayed trade, metals and gold, timber and wool, and the payment for it. They bartered it mostly, carefully judging the surpluses and needs of each their own province, and served it well.

At the end of the long evening Artur withdrew to the main guest quarters, several rooms connected by a private corridor running high on the outer wall, facing inland to the forest. He sat on a low bench, his back against the wall, legs stretched out in front, his heels resting on a small stool. He wrapped his cape about him, protection from the cold, and dozed.

In the trees beyond, owls called, hoo hoo, and a distant wolf howled and was answered by its mate. As he dozed, Artur shed the king and became the man, distant from his crown and duty. No matter, nothing mattered, and he was at peace with himself, a mortal man. In his falling dream, he ran and came to a door. "Gayne," he whispered, "are you there?"

"Yes Artur, you know it, I'm here." Morgayne's low voice broke through his doze, and her fingers lingered on the back of his hand. "Come in from the cold, brother, we make our bed."

In a daze, not knowing if he was sleeping or awake - his sister's voice low, whispering like his dreams whispered in the night, he moved into the chamber. Morgayne stood in the middle of the open space between the door and the bed, holding out her hands to him. Her eyes, normally jet black with a piercing gaze, were softer, a hint of a smile at her temples.

"What is it sister, that gentles your mood?"

Artur stepped towards her, and placed his hands on her hips, a quiet possession and his own mood settling like still water in a sheltered lake.

"The little poppet, Miryamme, with her innocent prattle and bright eyes."

Morgayne reached to her brother's collar, pulling loose a knotted cord. "She's sweet and young, and made me forget my politick and sorcery. We chattered about nothing and she was a sweet little sister." Morgayne peeled back Artur's shirt from his shoulders and dropped it to the floor. "She will suit you, brother, when she comes to age."

Artur lifted his hand from Morgayne's waist and pulled upon the spiralling ribbon that held his sister's shift in place, slowly pulling it through the loops until it dropped to the ground in a spiral.

"What of you, sister, who cares for your future?"

He moved his hands inside the fall of the shift, moving the cloth aside from her torso and stroking up her sides to cup Morgayne's slight breasts. She took in a breath and her fingers shook, and she pressed them to his chest.

"Do not worry it, Artur, it's always you. The little one can wait for her king. You're my brother now, uncrowned."

"How long can we do this, Gayne?"

"Long enough, Artur. You are king, and can bid it; even if reluctant priests forbid it."

Morgayne knelt before her brother, unbuckled a wide leather belt from about his waist, and dropped it to the floor. She eased both hands inside the cloth, and eased the breaches down his firm thighs, and they dropped. Artur stood naked before his sister and she was on her knees. With both hands she held his thick erection for a short time, then, placing one palm gently under his heavy balls, and, holding his shaft in her other hand, she lowered her lips to the head of his cock, and took him in her mouth, holding him there, so still. Artur closed his eyes, and rested both hands at the back of her head. Morgayne held him in her mouth and her eyes closed. Neither moved, and then Morgayne began a slow stroke of his shaft. Artur's eyes closed, and the room was quiet.

Morgayne caressed the soft head of her brother's prick, and she wasn't a priestess, he wasn't a king, just brother and sister, separated so young. Their innocent comfort ripped from them, and adults now, they made a safe place in de Grance's fortress, a loyal place to the king.

In a tiny alcove above the room, Miryamme watched them and saw the naked man and Morgayne, who was like an older sister to the younger girl.

In the room, Artur touched his sister's hair and moved her from his heat. "Stand, Gayne, you kneel before a king, but you stand beside your brother."

He reached for her hands and she stood before him, his high shaft pressing up against her belly, she stood so close. Artur place his hands upon the bones of her hips, she was too thin, and then he found a cord, and her skirt fell away, leaving her naked before him, her long dark hair falling a long fall down her back.

In the tiny alcove above the room, Miryamme gasped, knowing now it was Morgayne from the rock. Miryamme had not realised it before. In her father's place, the lady was regal, tall and proud. At Artur's coronation, his strong hands upon the dagger and Miryamme couldn't look, there had been a quick black shadow, Morgayne some skuttling, spiderous thing, dropping to the earth and smearing sticky mud all over her belly. Miryamme didn't understand it, she was too young, an unformed girl, but Morgayne who played her sister, what manner of badness was this?

Miryamme crept away silently, her eyes never leaving the bodies of the two below.

In the room, brother and sister held each other, and Morgayne shifted wide her thighs. Artur placed his cock between her legs, and his hot heat rose and was cradled by her sex. Her lips were swollen and wet, her sliding juice was viscous and thick, for her eggs were upon her and she was calling, calling. Artur's cock throbbed, and a silver bead rose up his shaft and glistened at the tip.

"Come to bed sister, come curl before me, and I keep you warm."

Artur looked at the thin body of his sister Morgayne, and remembered how she held him on the straw floor of a room in Tyntangel, his head resting on her breastless chest.

"Artur, is it you?" Morgayne's voice was small, all befuddled, and he held her.

"It's all right, Gayne, I'm stronger now, it's always me."

"Artur?"

"Yes, sweet sister, what is it?"

"I don't know men, they fear me and run frightened from me."

"You scare them, Gayne, but you've never frightened me."

Artur took her by the hand, and led her to the bed. He placed her on her back and gently spread her thighs apart. Dark curls of hair shadowed her cleft, and hid it from his eyes. But Artur didn't look upon her sex. His eyes held hers as he climbed upon the bed, and placed himself over her. Artur took his shaft in his hand, and nestled it between the lips of her shadowed cunt. He looked down upon her face, and held her eyes, unblinking.

Artur sunk himself into his sister as if he'd been there one hundred times before, but they were always dreams. Morgayne's eyes darkened to black and opened wide as he slid inside her in one long, soft movement. When the base of his shaft pressed up hard against her sex, Morgayne's mouth opened in a silent O. She shuddered, a little orgasm rippling through her, and her eyes rolled back.

Morgayne brought her thighs up around her brother's waist and opened herself beneath him, her only trusted man. Artur began to move within her, and soon she writhed beneath him, her breath coming in fast pants as he thrust deep into her. He gripped her hands above her head, stretching out her long body as he lay his whole length upon her, fucking her slowly and then faster, faster then slower, sliding into her sacred flesh. Morgayne shuddered beneath him and another orgasm rippled through. With a high cry she shuddered again, and began to thrust back against him, urging him higher on the bed, deeper into her panting flesh. She came again, and this time the clench of her cunt began to suck upon his heat, pulling his flesh higher to her womb. Artur fucked up high into his sister's womb.

"Gayne, look."

Artur's voice was a command. She opened her eyes and saw only his face above her, a slight smile as he concentrated his flesh in her. Morgayne held his gaze as long as she could, but even with her witching ways she couldn't compete with her brother's simple love, and he overwhelmed her. With small sobs in the back of her throat,

Morgayne came again, and the clenching pulse of her body was stronger this time, drawing her brother's seed from deep within, and with a single cry of her special name…

"Gayne!"

… his cock throbbed and spurted hot thick seed deep into his sister's womb, leaving it thick and fertile there. Artur surged again and thrust.

"Yes," she cried, a simple word, and they shuddered around each other, limbs wrapping tight around and she hugged Artur's broad back, and he collapsed on to her, still breathing hard from his exertion. She held his head close against her shoulder, stroking his tangled hair as she always did, kissing him on his forehead.

"Hush, what sound was that?" Morgayne held a finger to Artur's lips, "Sssh."

Artur rolled to his side, his cock sliding from his sister, and looked around, propping his body up on one arm. By the door, a small figure shuffled in, clad in a sleeping gown. It was Miryamme, walking slowly, uncertainly, her eyes a wide stare. Morgayne moved quickly from the bed, and knelt before the girl, but did not touch her.

"Artur, the poppet. I think she dreams and walks, but does not see." She turned to her brother. "Come, carry the girl, we take her to her bed."

Artur bent to pick her up, and Miryamme was small in his arms. Morgayne threw a cloak around his shoulders, and circled herself with her cloak of black feathers. Artur carried the little Miryamme down the corridor to a smaller room, and placed her on a little bed. Morgayne took the girl's hand in her own, feeling for a pulse.

"She seems to be sleeping proper now. Take you to our bed, Artur, I shall sit with the little one 'til I'm sure."

"She's so small, Gayne. Only a little girl. I wonder how long she stood watching, and did her eyes see?"

"I don't know it. I stay with her tonight, and we watch her in the morning. We quiz de Grance, to know if it happened before. Or is a first thing." Morgayne pulled blankets around the child, and again felt her pulse. "Her heart is slower, I think she sleeps proper now." Morgayne touched her fingers to Artur's lips. "Go, I come to our bed when I am sure the girl sleeps true."

Artur left his sister with the girl, and made his way back to the chamber. He picked up the dropped clothes from the floor, and folded them to a chair. He stripped himself naked again and climbed to the bed.

His sleep that night was dreamless. In the other room, Morgayne sat silently and completely still. The little girl's fingers twitched in the woman's hand. Later, Morgayne slept. When she awoke, her hand was flat against her belly, low against her belly. The child lay asleep until the new day dawned, and didn't remember anything at all.

The next morning, Artur king awoke, and the sun rose.

The Screaming Blood

I was there.

When the witch Morgayne's belly was torn open and a child dragged screaming from her, I was there.

That day was eight moons off when Artur and Morgayne, sister and brother born to the same mother, descended the plank from their boat. Returned from de Grance, fealty done and good trade besides.

"A good mission, lord?"

"Yeay, Maer, 'twas well done, and a resting time too. All well here?"

"All well, the grand hall near built. And you an uncle, now. Your sister, the Lady Claryyne, has birthed a boy. A message come from Tyntangel, five days gone. Lancilet, first prince of Uthur's blood." Maerlyn paused. "Your heir, sire, until you father blood of your own."

"Aye, Claryyne was a good size the last time I saw her. Her birthing wife, who was that?"

"Caitlyyn, sire, who supped you when the Lady Ygraine grew tired. A good woman, the best child-wife I know." A fine bottom too, where oft I lodged my rod, she liking it there and me all undecided.

"And I, brother, I was the first child birthed by her skill."

My skin bumped up like the skin of a goose, hearing that dread low voice pouring honey into mine ear so smooth. The honey of a wasp could be no worse, yet her voice thrilled me so. My rod thickened, betraying my mind but obeying my soul, forsaking me. I turned, and my cursed ankle twisted.

Morgayne's slow stretching fingers crept through the air all slow, a landing on the back of my hand, leaving a little stroke there, tormenting me. Her fingers were warm when they should have been cold. When I turned and saw her look, her black eyes were like cold ice at midnight. Her lips smiled at me but her eyes did not.

"Maerlyn," black honey, drip drip in mine ear, "did you miss me, wizard, did you dream of me every night?" Morgayne sowed seeds, knowing it so and not caring, and I the cursed farmer; grow, grow. "Your ankle, Maer, is't better, or does the cold affect it?" She opened her mouth in a pouting kiss, showing the sharp little teeth that nipped and bit me when she was small.

"Morgayne, don't play. Enough. You tire me." Artur said it plain but no favours. None given her and none me. "Fight battles if you must, but not around me."

"I harmless be, brother, I just make jest."

At my expense, and I'm not the court jester. But I was surprised to see her let it go so quick, wondering if something ailed her head, that usually niggled at me. As Morgayne walked on, I saw the Lady's hand against her belly. Queasy from the sea perhaps? She did not look sea-rocking pale to me. She looked back at me over her shoulder, colour high on her cheeks, but I could not read her.

Artur followed her with his eyes, and of a sudden I saw the love in his eyes for his sister was something deeper. His eyes were black with lust, and his eyes undressed Morgayne as she walked away. I

187

made a note in my head of last night's moon, for to start a counting, if I guessed right. I might play the fool, but I seldom guessed wrong. Not when it mattered.

I quickly looked to my feet, to hide my curious glance. Even so, I was too slow.

"New boots, Maer, that you look at them and admire your toes?" Artur's comment was wry and I knew I was discovered in my speculation. "I can depend on you, Maerlyn. I won't doubt it."

"Never doubt me, sire."

I will do that for the both of us, I had no doubt of that, in the years ahead. I resolved at some time to visit the Sisters in the Isle of Glas, to see if their auguries knew of this turn. Or was it just a stumble, a tumble, just a man and a woman with a cock and a cunt and nothing in between?

Sure enough, Morgayne fell sick in the mornings and it wasn't food that made her so. I suggested to Artur that the young Emmelyne was a good, reliable girl who would shut her mouth when told, but practical too. The king agreed and the girl was appointed. To my surprise and probably hers, Morgayne accepted the interference and made Emmelyne welcome. Perhaps it was the girl's acceptance that being made big with babes was as natural as the world turning; perhaps it was her knowledge of primal beasts and their instincts, but whatever it was, Morgayne let her stay.

"She treats me like one of her goats, no different," Morgayne complained to her brother, but in good nature, a laugh in her voice.

Artur told me of it, and I glanced askance at him, scarce believing my ears and my good chance. I collected nettles and took them to Morgayne, hoping she would accept the jest.

"Maerlyn, do you bring me flowers from the fields? Heart, I never thought it true." She looked at me, and her face was pale and her smile was weak. And of a sudden she was human and in the strangest, strangest way that little smile touched me, and despite myself, I looked upon her differently.

"Aye, Lady, I picked each prickle away with my very own fingers."

I lied, of course, every prick and prickle was still on every stalk, and I handled them as gingerly as I handled my own words with Morgayne.

"How far can I throw you, Maerlyn?"

"You can't, Lady. I fly less than an inch."

"Ah, good, it is still as I thought, between us. You don't believe a word you say, and I don't either. So we understand each other still."

"I think, Lady, we always did understand each other, too well."

Morgayne smiled at me, and her teeth were white and small, and her lips were berry red. My cock beat with my heart and my ankle hurt. Her long, slow fingers grasped at the air between us, and I pulled myself back from her call.

I pondered Artur's admission of his love for his sister, and considered the timing of her moons. Were her breasts bigger, fuller already? She wore a loose gown, I could not truly tell. I know I cannot tell truthfully, but some things eventually cannot hide.

"Tis remarkable, how a woman's body changes, don't you think, Maerlyn, when she grows big with child?"

I forgot. Morgayne finds minds the easiest things to read, and mine befuddled like rocks on a beach just makes a loud clatter, and I am transparent. Shine the sun through me in the mornings and I could be a window in a chapel built by stupid priests. I looked at her and did not know how to answer.

Morgayne had the slightest smile on her lips, and did I see the slightest crease in the corners of her eyes?

"Come by again, Maer. I tire of the prattle of goat maids, my brother entertains state and makes treaty and cannot attend me. You at least amuse me, and you amuse yourself, so perhaps we can play chess and talk about the weather."

She called me by my title, Maer. That's not like her. "Am I your knight, Lady, or your priest?"

Her laugh was joyous, delighted in my jest. "Oh, Maerlyn, you know the smallest pawn always stands before the king!"

And the queen. This can't go on too much longer, Artur cannot keep this pretence of his sister by his side.

Morgayne glanced at me. "You're right, Maerlyn. Clever pawn. I have it managed. de Grance's girl, Miryamme, she will suffice."

I grasped it immediately. "Good fealty also, Lady, binding the south to Artur." My thoughts rattled on, oblivious of Morgayne in my head listening close. "But she is young. How to convince the king to wait?"

Morgayne looked at me with her black eyes, and ran fingers through her hair.

"Oh, I think my brother will listen to me. Don't you?"

I didn't doubt it, and resolved to ride to Glas on the morrow. How much of her was predictable, and how much predicted? I didn't know.

"Go, Maerlyn. I'm tired."

I looked at her, and Morgayne was pale, her hand moving in a settling motion on her belly. On the way out, I found Emmelyne and asked her to take broth to the Lady.

So it went. I was foolish, and Morgayne charmed and flattered me, she let me think she enjoyed my company or at least tolerated it. Maybe she did, an intelligent woman who grasped the power of the Goddess and turned it to her own ends, and I a circling, dancing fool who knew nothing.

But there was more that kept me close to the witch Morgayne. The auguries, entrails and other predictive things used by the wise Sisters of Glas, priestesses to the Goddess - all those predictions and portents had failed utterly to predict the simple love between a brother and a lost sister, two lost children torn apart, all tiny and small; and our plan the unmaking of them.

Vivyane, Nymue, and I, Maer Maerlyn. Fools and simpletons, all of us. Unpredicted by all, contemplated by none; the most powerful man in the land, conjured up in a bad plan years ago, had contrived with his half sister to make an heir before he even had a queen.

"Maerlyn, Artur at least trusts you. His sister Morgayne trusts no-one, but we cannot allow harm to her." Vivyane voiced the collective view. "We will need to watch closely in order to know all events, and hopefully guide them. Or at least, not be unravelled by them." She turned to me. "Maer Maerlyn, you will need to hold her close…"

"… as an enemy holds a man closer, Maerlyn?" Morgayne knew, of course, that she was unknown, and therefore an agent of chance. "Tis a pretty pickle, Maerlyn, is it not?" She laughed, with a genuine glee. "I can do what I please, since nobody knows it. Come, we will play the gammon board. We can practice dice." She shook two dice in a cup. "Oh look, two sixes! Here, you shake."

Predictably, two ones was the best I could do. Morgayne was delighted, and her fingers as she took the dice were warm against mine. Her eyes even smiled. I wasn't used to that, not at all, and it unnerved me. It still does, and I fall for it every time. Curse this wind rattling the window. It makes me look up and I lose my concentration.

Where was I?

Yes. The black Morgayne, slowly filling with child and not enjoying the mornings of it. Emmelyne would take her a hot cloth, boiled up in a hanging cauldron over the kitchen fire, and bathe the Lady Morgayne to ease her discomfort. I'd pass Emmelyne in the corridor and receive a warning of the Lady's temper for the day; and prepare myself to be her toy, her plaything when she was capricious. Or she would be kinder and greet me well, and Morgayne would be

192

content. I dared not call myself a friend to her, but I might have been. As always with a friend, I'm my own worst enemy. I can't predict myself, not any more. I certainly couldn't predict the Lady.

On occasion, Artur would visit, and for several days after Morgayne would be gentle with me; but then her mood would return, and I could settle myself for the more familiar world where I was her cruel whim one minute, her confidant the next. Hers was a creeping fear, I think.

One morning I arrived early. Emmelyne was still with the Lady, and I heard low voices. For some reason that was more than curiosity, more than idleness, I quietly edged down the corridor, keeping to the shadowed wall until I reached a dark alcove opposite the door to Morgayne's chamber. I skulked back into the shadow, and saw the Lady sitting on a bench, her head over a bucket, her legs spread wide. The folds of her simple linen gown fell between her legs and I saw nothing there. But the folds of cloth fell open about her body, and I saw the hang of her pale breasts like drops, long dark nipples rich and firm at their tips. And all around, Morgayne's long, black hair was coiled all around.

Emmelyne with her steaming cloth was wiping Morgayne's white face, then rubbed the cloth around the Lady's neck, and down between those breasts, lifting them up towards her body. Whilst it was practical and the motion of a maid washing her mistress, there was a firm caress in the way Emmelyne curved her hands over those breasts that was both intimate and allowed. I saw Morgayne's eyes close, and saw her lean forward just a fraction, dropping the fuller weight of her breasts into Emmelyne's cupped palms. As I watched, my old prick thickened and my nipples jabbed behind my chest. And as I watched, I saw Morgayne's eyes slowly open and look in my direction. I thought I was in shadow, but couldn't properly tell if she saw me.

A tiny smile curved on her mouth, and I thought I was probably seen.

"There's a draft, Emmelyne. Pull the curtain across the door."

I knew then that I was found, spying my eyes upon the Lady. She mentioned nothing of it later, when I called upon her properly. Her gaze was just as steady, her dark eyes penetrating my old mind and me all defenceless, and she could do with me what she wanted. Morgayne turned away from me, and her fingers dallied on my arm, dragging off my flesh slowly, trailing two fingers down over the back of my hand and away into the air. It was all I could do to bunch my hands into fists, or I would have foolishly reached after her fingers with my own.

"Come, Maerlyn, come sit by me at the window and we'll watch the world go by." Was it just mine ears, or did I hear a teasing emphasis on the word 'watch'?

"Are you feeling better, Lady, your sickness in the mornings?" I could not help myself, my words might just as well have been my legs, walking me forth into the light to make it obvious I had watched.

Morgayne looked directly into my eyes, and her brow crept up so I might know I was her game. "Aye, Maerlyn, it is near on three moons, and Emmelyne assures me that the sickness usually does not make four." She turned away and looked out the window, her hand resting on the swell of her belly. "Especially if it's a boy, Emmelyne says."

"I have heard that, Lady. I remember Caitlyyn saying it once. Your mother was long sick with you, yet stopped the sickness sooner with your brother."

"My brother. Little Artur. He did not torment his mother, then?"

"Not as Caitlyyn says it, Lady."

"Did I torment my mother, Maerlyn, do you think?"

I'm not your mother, Morgayne, yet you torment me.

Her eyes did not leave mine, but she was impenetrable, and it was I who looked away.

The next morning, I did not look away, and Morgayne did not want me to. She bade Emmelyne stand behind her as she bathed her Lady with the cloth, and again I was treated to the drop of Morgayne's breasts into the cup of the maid's hands. It was a treat for mine eyes, and my prick rose hard but I did not touch it. This time, Morgayne commanded Emmelyne to help with her chemise.

"Slip it over my head, Emmy, and wash down my back."

Morgayne stretched her arms high in the air, and showed me her naked torso, her swelling breasts, and the bones of her ribs. The pits of her arms were dark and haired, and the hollows were like two tight cunts before my eyes. Morgayne's eyes were closed, but she knew I was there, watching. I could see her nipples tight, and it might have been Emmelyne's fingers tugging or it might have been the knowledge of me. Emmelyne's eyes were closed as she washed her Lady's breasts and back, her lips slightly open, shiny with the lick of her tongue. My prick throbbed hard at the watching, but I did not touch it. And all around, Morgayne's hair coiled and fell all around.

Yet when I went away and came back all a proper visiting later on, with my hey derry down, all merry ding dong in the dell, all good cheer, all that balls of the dog and we both knew it; despite all that pretence, we pretended nothing happened in the morning light either. And Emmelyne was part of the secret and we all kept pretending nothing happened, but kept on doing it. All three of us doing nothing at all; and in that strange way the Lady and I kept a curious distance between us, as if we both of us dared not get too close, for fear of what it might mean. The black Morgayne and the grey Maerlyn; the land did not want such a combination and we both knew it, so this looking was how we channelled our lust.

Over time young Emmelyne became a shared messenger between us, because the morning bath slowly revealed more of the Lady Morgayne. Each day she would shed another article of clothing there before the bath, and Emmelyne would lasciviously wash the Lady down over her ripening belly and her bigging tits. And one day the long shift fell completely from Morgayne's waist and Emmelyne ran her hot cloth high up between the Lady's thighs and over her lush, dark haired cunt, and Morgayne spread wide her legs and I saw the same purple red crease of her that I saw that day she crawled down the rock at Artur's pulling of the sword. Morgayne was that same black witch who spat and crept like a spider, and scooped the spill of my cock and smeared it to the dark cloy of her anus, that dark sacred place, and anointed herself there with my juice.

Emmelyne came away from that bathing ritual with her fingers a sliding dip into the Lady's cunt all sticky and wet. Morgayne whispered in her maid's ear, all the time looking straight at me; and Emmelyne came to me and proffered those fingers to my lips and bade me suck. She whispered in my ear, "From the Lady." My prod reared and Emmelyne took it and stroked me into the palm of her hand until I spilt seed there, and she took it back to the Lady who spread it on her belly, and I don't know why Morgayne did it but she did.

So it went on. As the weather warmed and the pattern of the morning adjusted with the rising sun turning higher with the spring, Morgayne's childing body grew and her belly got bigger. Her morning bath with Emmelyne was no longer to sooth the Lady after sickness, for her vomit stopped and her food stayed down. It was clear now that Morgayne had truly accepted Emmelyne as her birthing maid, and the girl likewise saw the Lady as a physical, breeding creature all her very own, to kiss and caress, to stick her tongue and fingers into, all unashamed.

They let me watch, and Morgayne was content to let Emmelyne suck on my prick with her mouth that not long before had suckled on the Lady's cunt; and for me to suck on the girl's cunt that had not long since sat on Morgayne's face, for they supped upon each other. I sat and watched but never entered the room, and Morgayne stared and stared at me with her black, black eyes. Her berry red lips opened and she darted her tongue; and her fingers spread apart all the colours of her cunt, heavy red and pink and brown, for my eyes, my eyes, my staring eyes. An owl could not have been more wide eyed.

And her fingers, so warm on my arm when I greeted her at the midday day bell, all properly clothed and the earlier sights forgotten; her fingers in the morning would peal back her folds, clefted dark in her black haired cave, and flutter her red flesh slowly, so slowly. And my rod always rose.

"Lean over Maer's shoulder, Emmy, with your tight tits dropped in his hands, and grip his prick and make him spill, while I watch and diddle my own best place."

And Emmelyne would neatly toss and twist my prick and take the spill cupped in her hands to the Lady, and Morgayne would cream her silvering stretching belly or her heavy breasts with my juice, and rub it all in. But never did my hands touch her naked flesh, nor hers mine; just Emmelyne our willing emissary, for we both would please her, taking turns a lapping at her cunt.

The closest we ever got to each other, Morgayne and I, was one hot day around her sixth month when she lay on her back, her legs spread wide and her belly big and heavy, with Emmelyne's mouth on the Lady's cunt and my tongue in Emmy's forbidden hole, pushing her into the Lady. When off a sudden, Morgayne stopped her writhing and placed both hands on her belly, and she cried out in a massive wail.

"Get dressed, Emmy. Maerlyn, get thee gone. The baby's kicked, by the Goddess, kicked, and hard inside. I've felt a swimming before, but never a kick. Ohh, Goddess, there again. Unnhh."

I dressed, and to Artur went.

"The Lady, sire, she reports the child's kick. It thrives. I think your sister is startled by the movement and is afraid."

"Is it time to summon Caitlyyn, Maer; or to send my sister to our mother?" Artur gazed centrally at me and was certain. "I want the best for her, as she enters her last triangle." His eyes were sharp, and his lips set. "The child is wrong, Maer, unnatural and I know it; but the blood, 'tis mine, and the mother of it is my Gayne, my sister when I was sent away."

His passion was high. "The best care, Maer. Your kind owe me that, at least. I will not have my sister threatened. Not her life."

"I pledge it, sire, on my own life."

Artur looked at me and his look was cold.

"Good. You pledge that to me, your life, to your King?" Colder still, his look, and my heart shivered. "Much as I love thee, Maer, I love my sister more. I will kill thee with my own sword, if you fail me, if harm comes to the Lady Morgayne, my sister."

"I don't doubt it, sire, I never doubt that."

The next day, I rode to the Isle of Glas to talk to Nymue. My life at peril if dread came to the Lady? I could not afford that, not for just looking at her magnificent cunt from a doorway, so I needed better insurance. My life is worth more than a look. A lick, at least, or a taste, but not my life for a look.

Still, I could tell Nym Nymue that her choice of blood to serve the Goddess and the Land was good, young Artur having the necessary testicles to do it. Threatening to kill me, his wizard? Truly, Artur knew where the power in the land lay centred - I was a mere bystander, even though I had helped make the boy.

But the Sisters needed to kill foxes and mix the blood of birds together in a pot, and auger their very best. The free will of the boy's blood, and the equally strong, black will of his sister's blood, both in rebellion to the life blood of the Land? Nobody predicted that.

I predicted blood, and a lot of it. As long as none of it was mine.

I proved right, and sooner than I expected. And it was my hands covered in it; I didn't predict that, not at all. As always, half wrong, never half right. I'll learn one day that I can't throw dice, and don't let me near a coin.

Artur summoned Caitlyyn, for she was the best birthing wife known to him, having attended the king and his sister too, and the babes of his younger sisters. It was Caitlyyn, on examining the Lady Morgayne, big with child, who declared the news that the Lady carried two babes inside her. "They hug to each other, I can feel their backs but they sleep a facing."

Morgayne, on hearing she would bear twins, fell silent for twelve long days and shunned all but Caitlyyn and Emmelyne; and I suppose the women spoke best how to manage the birthing, for a babing pair doubled everything that could go bad, including my own life in peril. I contrived to speak to both the serving women at different times, and found some small confidence that they separately told me the same things, and reinforced the best way for the Lady to bear her children.

Twins. I wondered if the Sisters from the Isle of Glas forecast that in their entrails and smoke. An obvious portent, and one hard to miss, I would have thought, but it had never been mentioned. I confess, I was rapidly losing confidence in predictions and prophecies conjured up in a pot, and was increasingly inclined to believe my own eyes and deeds in preference. Keep the black pots for soup and the cooking fire for warmth, and the supernatural prophecies for old priests who count in threes. Perhaps I'm becoming more practical as I get older, depending on myself. One day I might even mend my boots. There's a hole near the toe where water gets in.

Caitlyyn bade young Emmy to collect many flowers and potions, to crush them and rub them into unguents, and I too remembered herbs and liquids and mushrooms that would make dreams and lull pains.

"The birthing won't be easy, Maer, we might need the Lady to be stupefied when her day is upon her."

Morgayne herself was uneasy, and would sit and sit with her hands on her restless belly, a look of dread and uncertainty on her face. "They roil and fight already, Maer. It's as if they hate their closeness and want to be apart." She looked up at me, but I could offer nothing.

So time moved on and the Lady grew pale as her belly grew bigger. Two moons passed, and Caitlyyn came to me one night, and said, "Soon, Maer Maerlyn, it will be soon. The Lady will breach soon."

Artur came, and even he could not calm Morgayne. She looked at him and muttered, "It's your seed, brother, we're cursed by our love."

"What will happen, Maer? I'm afraid for my sister."

"I know it not sire, but will do all I can to keep her well."

"Try, Maerlyn. I cannot hold you to my threat. This is beyond us all, but I beg it, do what you can."

I did.

I did it with dread in my heart and shaking hands, for the love of Morgayne. So intimate with her body, so much more than a touch, I held her in my hands, all blooded and trembling. I tremble still at the telling of it. My pen shudders, and the writing paper tears.

"I'm restless, Emmy. The children within me are sleeping, but I'm restless." Morgayne was turning about the room, the long feathers of her cape brushing the floor. Her belly was big, but even with it huge, she stood tall. She couldn't not be magnificent, the Lady Morgayne. She took her own dread in her hands, I think, and would not let it diminish her.

Artur came, and bid his sister move to his chambers, which were larger and included a private courtyard and a kitchen. "Caitlyyn tells me a woman will circle and circle around a room when the babies

202

push, and might scream and want silence, so best you be here, in the king's place."

Morgayne looked at her brother, but I could not tell all the meanings in that look; how to count them all up? 'Twould be impossible. But tenderness was there, amongst it all; that I could see.

"Little brother, even if these babes are unnatural and wrong, I care it not. Love made them, Artur, and my love carried them these near nine moons. You will be a father soon, brother, and I their mother." Morgayne reached for his cheek, and caressed him there and her touch lingered. "Don't stay, brother, not while I walk and wait."

Artur kissed her full on the lips. "Gayne...?"

"Go, brother. You are king, not hand-maiden."

I wonder what that makes me? I am never king.

"You are tall, Maerlyn." She read my mind. "When I double over in cramps, I can hang my arms from your neck and keep my body stretched." Morgayne looked at me with a wry smile, and I saw that she was darkly fond of me then, because her eyes smiled. "Caitlyyn and Emmy are no use for that, as they are both smaller than me."

"Ah, I see it now, a rack for a Lady, to stretch her bones. Do you manacle me to your wheel, Morgayne, and turn it like a spit on a fire?"

"Would you burn for me, Maer?"

Would you piss on me, to put out the fire, if I did?

"I'd burn Lady, if it would unfreeze your frozen heart."

"Frozen heart, Maer? These last months, I've not been cold, surely. I thought we became friends. It certainly looked like we were friends, you in your alcove, me in my room."

"Ah, yes but we did not touch, just with our eyes." I looked at her straight. "Why was that, Lady?"

She was silent for ten beats of my heart. "Because I could not bear it, Maerlyn. It is a love and a hate between us, Maer. You know it as I do, yet we are strange friends, I think."

"Yeay, Lady, that be true. You torment me and sweeten me, turn and turn about, and I am like a man on a high ledge, always about to fall."

"Yet you're never at my feet, and I keep looking you eye to eye. Why is that, Maer?" Morgayne seemed as puzzled in herself as to her feelings to me, as I was to her.

This time I was silent, and my heart pattered on. "Lady, if you do not know your mind, it is most unlikely that I do. I am hard at thought to put one foot in front of the other, most of the time."

It was my time for a quiet smile, and perhaps I betrayed myself, for she laughed, delighted with something she saw. I didn't know what it was, but then, I don't know most things and make the rest up. Yet people call me wise.

Of a sudden, Morgayne gripped my arm, and winced. "Ah Goddess, it begins. Maerlyn, walk me back to the rooms. I will get Caitlyyn to inspect the babes and their position. I fear them."

Morgayne does not fear, not Morgayne. What children were these that she feared? I looked at her beside me, her arm linked through mine, and I silenced my own dread. She carried enough within her for the both of us.

Morgayne circles and circles, restless, walking. She stops, winces with pain, and walks and walks in restless circles.

I walk beside her and she drags on my neck, arching her back with the pain, and she lets the weight of her body fall. She drags on my neck and I walk beside her.

Morgayne crawls and crawls naked on the ground, her limbs are sheened with sweat, and naked and naked she crawls on the ground.

She screams with the pain, and screams and moans. Birds rise and fly, their wings shuddering, and she moans and screams.

Morgayne is silent, her breath comes in gasps. She grips my arm and her fingers draw blood, and she gasps and gasps but her throat is silent.

She looks at me, looks at me, and begs it to stop. She goes on and on, and the labour won't stop. Her eyes don't see a thing, yet they're black and black with pain. She can't stop.

Morgayne falls to the ground in a swoon.

I call four men to carry the Lady, and they place her on a bed. Caitlyyn comes, and feels the opening to Morgayne's womb, and feels the place of the babes, their limbs, their backs. She feels the beating pulse of Morgayne's heart.

"Maerlyn," Caitlyyn says, "one child will die here, and perhaps the Lady too. One is backwards and blocks the other. I cannot turn the one, else harm the other." She is certain, and tells it. "The Lady is in peril."

Emmelyne comes, and stands by me. "Maer Maerlyn, there is a way. My goats, my nanny goats, when their kids tangle and twist, and climb on each other in the womb. I've cut. My mother showed me how. I've cut the belly, and lifted out the tiny goatlets. I've cut."

I look at the girl. "Does the nanny live, and the little goats too?"

"Aye, sire, I've not lost one yet. I cut, and sew the belly up, just like a bag." Emmelyne is certain, and tells it. "The Lady is in peril, but she carry her babes just like a goat carries her kids and a sheep carries lambs. Cut, sire, and save them."

I think on't, and remember brother Plinius tell of the Roman Caes, born from a mother and cut from her womb. I think on't and my pledge to Artur, who is my friend like a son. And Morgayne, who has become almost a daughter and a lover both. I have no pledge made with her, but I think on't.

I look at Emmelyne again. "Are you sure of your words, tell me no lie. Can she survive?"

"Sire, if the knife is sharp and the cut certain and true, and hands fast into her and counting quick, one, two, three, four and five. Fast, and a certain hand, sire. Mother Caitlyyn to take the babes to clean and swaddle. I to sew, just like my goats." Emmelyne looks at me and says it. "Maer Maerlyn, sire, you must take the knife...."

I do it.

I take the sharpest knife we can find, all bladed on a stone. I command the men to hold the Lady's limbs, even though she lies a swoon, all still; and I count it, to make myself relentless and never stop.

One. And I cut from left to right across the base of Morgayne's belly. She screams and my hands are red in her blood, and I cut. I drop the knife.

Two. With trembling hands I reach inside her flesh for the first babe, and cradle it small and still.

And three, I take the child from Morgayne and Caitlyyn is near and cuts the cord. She takes the babe to clean and swaddle. She whispers, "Tis covered by a caul, sire, a witchling born, and it is a girl, born to her mother." Emmelyne whispers too, and knowledge is born in her, because she knows.

"Clean the veil away, Emmy, quick. Tell no-one of the shrouded child. Quick, pink skin to find on the babe."

Four, and I find the twin child, and Emmelyne passes me a knife for the cord, and five, I pull the squalling thing from its mother and I cannot see its face. "It is a boy, sire, and by the Goddess he wears the king's mark that Uthur wore. It's no mistake, a clear mark."

Six. I reach within Morgayne and no man or woman could be so intimate, I could take her heart in my hands and I'm drenched in her blood. I find the after-births and take them from her, and save them in a jar.

I count quick now, this is too long, and Emmelyne reaches for her needle and her thread, and seven my hands leave the lady's womb alone, and Emmy starts to sew.

I see Morgayne before me and her blood is on my hands, rich red. I hear a cry and echo too, and her children live. I reach down and I do not know it why, I pick up the knife I dropped, and I still don't know why I did it, but I did.

With the sharpest blade against her neck, and Morgayne still dead in her sleep, I don't know why but I did. I cut the hair from Morgayne's head. I cut her hair, never cut by woman nor cut by man, long and black like a raven's wing, cut cut.

I was there.

When the witch Morgayne's belly was torn open and children dragged screaming from her, I, Maerlyn, was there.

Cut from her head, Morgayne's hair is a long black noose around my neck and I wear it still. I'm anointed in her blood, red blood, and she summons me now with her long black rope, tug tug.

The Naming of Children

I was there.

The day a crown was placed on a young queen's head and she sat beside the king, I was there.

de Grance's little daughter Miryamme was almost the ideal bride for Artur the king, and to be his future queen. Almost, that is, but for the complication of Morgayne his sister and two bastard heirs, born in her blood - am I cursed not enough already? My hands pulled the twin babes from Morgayne's womb, and more intimate with a woman I have never been. The Black Morgayne, who makes my ankle itch, scratch scritch; and teased mine eyes with her lush childing body and her darkened cunt.

Two children ripped from her, and Morgayne all oblivious. I saw too much, and she saw nothing, nothing at all.

Emmelyne's eyes were the only other eyes but mine to see the shroud, the caul, all around the girl child, and I bade her wash it away quick and tell no-one. I knew in an instant that it must be our secret alone, the goat maid and the goat; never to tell, but to know. To know is the best kept thing; to use it, ahh, now that is a much better thing. Dilly, dally, wait Maerlyn, wait, even 'till the end of days. The Goddess knew, of course; but I hoped she would hold her tongue and not chatter to her priestesses and predictors about the cursed child.

As for the Sisters, they were not so clever; not spotting the lust the king had for his sister, nor what Morgayne did with it. They didn't see the girl child, either. Entrails might make good sausage filler up beyond the Wall of Hadrian; but to predict the important things, well, the Sisters really needed to think of something else. Like the stars in the sky, perhaps. The twinkling stars might be more convenient, for if one constellation gave an unnecessary or unsatisfactory answer, the sayer of sooths could wait till dawn and there would be a whole new set to choose from. Truth tell, the whole thing with stars is so utterly unpredictable, I could almost believe in them myself. Twinkle, twinkle.

Looking back it all seems rather obvious, but no-one saw it then. Even the mother who carried them both, was she just a portal bag? But Maerlyn, with a tiny bit of knowledge all his own? Useful surely? We shall see. Hush Emmy, tell no-one, tra la!

But I'm wandering. I know why, quite precisely why. I'm meandering because sooner or later Morgayne always wakes, and when she woke that time, she wasn't her usual self.

"The Lady is delirious, Maer. She runs heat on her brow and her body burns." Caitlyyn was concerned and uncertain. "We must wrap her in wet cloth to draw the heat out, and make her drink a coction of wyrm-root to brighten her dreams and slow her heart. It races too quick and I do not like the flutter of it."

I feared for the Lady Morgayne and feared also the king's madness if death came upon her. I remembered Artur's forgiveness of his sword and the pledge of it into mine heart; but thought in his grief his memory might not be so kind. Having only the one heart and keen on it beating on, I vowed for my own life that I would keep dread death from the Lady. My own stupid heart beating for her had nothing to do with it; I fooled myself that much, and fool myself still.

Is that rain, again, on the dry outside, or is it just here in this room, on this page?

We took it in turns, the two birth women and I, to sit by Morgayne so she was never alone. Emmelyne coated the sewn up wound on the cut wide belly with fresh honey from the hive, and she brought a little goatling to suckle at the Lady's breast.

"If she flows her milk, sire, the Lady will heal herself faster, so to feed her own babies. I see it in my sick goats - as soon as the suck begins the nanny forgets to die, for to feed proper her little kidlings. But the Lady, sire, she must be stronger to take two babes on her tit."

Emmelyne found a suckle wife for the two tiny children, a hearty girl from the village with her own toddle near weaned, yet her big fat breasts still a full with milk.

"I'll plump them up," the suckle wife said, "till the Lady be strong enough to cherish her own childs and feed them proper." She took and swaddled up the babies and observed, "Look how the little girl sees about already, the bonny wee thing. She's a lovely one." Her look at the boy was quicker, and she did not lie. "He's an ugly one, certain, with that stain upon his head."

It was true, the boy carried the king's mark clear, that Uthur had worn on his hip and Artur's stain more hidden. But this child was marked with a smear like a bruise on his cheek and brow. Not hid like the king's, but a most definite mark on his face. No doubting the son, there was no doubt at all.

"My son then, Maer, for all the world to see." Artur came and looked upon his children. "His hair, black like his mother's."

"Yeay, sire, the Lady's colour in the boy, and the little girl yours, all fair."

"Aye, Maerlyn; my eyes too, almost."

"Nearly so, Lord, but lighter blue already, I think it." The wee girl looked up at her father, as if to study him hard.

"But she cannot properly see, not yet?"

"No sire. Wait on a month and the babe's look will be proper in her eyes."

Artur reached down and touched his little finger to his daughter's lips, his first kiss, and she but two days old.

"Has my sister seen them yet?"

"No sire. The Lady is still too sick."

"Care for her, Maer. Make her better, I beseech thee."

I beseeched mine own self to do it, and I'll try anything to keep my own heart beating.

"I'll try, Lord."

"I know it, Maer. Your strangest love for my sister, maybe it be enough." His smile was gentle. "May it be enough."

It's all I had, so I gave it to her willingly. Beat, beat. My heart beats blood.

Four days on from the birth, and Morgayne's blood all washed from my hands. Turning them over and over, still seeing it red and running on my wrists; ah woman, your heart was so close to my hands, I've been inside you. Could I know you better?

I was started from my dreamery by the slow warm touch of her fingers on the back of my hand, feeling if I was awake.

"Maerlyn, am I sleeping or do I dream?" Morgayne's voice was low, yet even in her sickness going, it was still enough to lull me still and take me from my senses.

I dared not move, for fear of startling myself. Dare I hope it, Morgayne recovering? Gazing upon her like a daughter now, all caring, my silly lust all gone…. I fooled myself once more; mine own ankle itched and my prod thickened at the sound of her voice and I knew her better, for how else could her spell be so automatic? It was a reflex in me, an instinctive thing, and I think she knew it too.

"Did you save me, heart, my life in your hands?" Her fingers rested on the back of my hand, but I dared not turn it over, for fear she would not hold it. Yet her finger touch, it was so warm, I could not bear it gone. Her fingers drifted away, and I watched them run through the fleece of the little goat as she held it to her breast.

"Is this my child, that lay within me and kicked me so, a little goat?" Morgayne gazed upon the kid, and looked me in the eye, but her eyes were distant and gone and I wondered for her sanity. Had it gone too?

Her focus sharpened. "Why did you cut it, Maerlyn?" Her gaze was impenetrable, and it went straight to the back of my head and pinned me to the wall.

"I had to, Lady, the babes were all backwards and twisted, and would not have birthed, if I did not cut."

"Not my body, Maerlyn." She would not let me go. "My hair, wizard, why did you cut my hair all off, that was never cut before?"

I did not have an answer, for I knew not why I did it.

"I know not, Lady. Morgayne, I know it not, and have no story, no reason." I was all helpless before her. "I cannot tell you the truth, I cannot tell you the lie. Both false; and I do not ask forgiveness, for I know you will not grant it."

"You're right, Maerlyn, I will not grant forgiveness, I will not grant forget."

Morgayne looked at me and laughed. "Tis but hair." And her slow fingers stretched towards me through the air, and it was the slow, dark, mysterious movement I knew so well. My cock hardened and my ankle beat beat with my own blood. "Ah, Maerlyn. Am I better, do you think?"

"Lady, you torment me; so yes, you are recovering."

Morgayne looked at me with her coal black eyes. "But my life, Maerlyn. You saved me. What's the payment for that?"

"I know it not, Lady, I cannot know."

"Must we mint new coin, just a regnum for we two?" She took my hand. "Are we bound together now, Maerlyn, in some strange marriage? A marriage made of blood, my blood?"

I could not answer, for I did not know.

"Bring the braid to me, Maer. I know what to do with it."

I brought Morgayne her own hair, and placed it in her hands. She smiled at me, and it was a peaceful smile, but ahh, was that a tiny glint and was that an eyebrow raised? I knew then she was herself again, laughing in her dark, magnificent glee. She looked at me and asked, "Are you bound to me now, Maerlyn, and me to you, as we live?"

"I think it so, Lady, even if I not planned it." Nor could escape it, even if I wanted to.

"No-one planned it, Maer, none knew it either." Morgayne began to twist and plait her hair, cleverly holding it in the middle of its length, making a rope both ways from that middle. Black it was and a long black rope she made of her hair, all braided from the middle.

Every now and then she looked at me, then down to the rope; and twisted it on some more. Soon it was a good length, as long as my arm, or nearly.

"Take off your jerkin, Maerlyn."

I did, and stood before her, half naked.

"Kneel before me, that I reach your neck."

I did, and Morgayne placed the braided cord of her hair about my neck, and began to plait the ends together so it made a loop, a noose about my neck. She continued to braid the length of her hair and made of it a rope down the front of my chest, down the centre of my gut, till the ends were level with my groin.

"Take off your britches, Maerlyn,"

I did, and stood before her naked.

"Stand before me, that your rod stand before me."

I did, and Morgayne took my prick in her hands, which she never had touched before, and with her long, slow fingers stroked me up full hard. She looked up at me, a standing there, and she smiled and said, "Take your cock and hold it still. I need both hands."

I did, and Morgayne took the dangling ends of her hair and teased it out into little small threads; and with her fingers she pulled and straightened the hair, the greying hair, at the base of my belly, and pulled it up into little small threads. And with her nimble, clever fingers, Morgayne wove together, all plaited and braided, the ends of her hair with the tangle of my cock's nest, and she joined our hair together. All joined together and twisted.

And it's twisted together still. The hair on Morgayne's head is all a silver and a grey now, and mine's a snowy white, but her hair about my neck, it's still that black. If I tip my head-side down and walk on my hands, I'll hang myself from my cock by her hair. I don't want to hang just yet, so I walk with my feet on the ground.

I cut Morgayne's long black hair, and she gave it to me to keep. I'd cut it again if I could, but I don't trust myself with knives, not any more. My fingers shake too much. Her black silken hair is a rope around my neck and I'm bound to her still.

There wasn't a coin, we didn't mint a new reign. I'll need two for my eyes when the boat leaves, and I've no doubt Morgayne will place them there, a strange bride. Or the other one, with her snow white hair.

I'm surprised they get on, in truth, but they do. Perhaps there's only one key to this room, and they take turns watching over me. I

216

never understood it, I never saw them clear. Did they even love me as I loved them, strangely?

Morgayne, the day she wove herself around me fully, celebrated our strange marriage another unexpected way. But I suppose I'd seen her dark eyes on me as we sent Emmelyne to and fro at our lusts bidding, when Morgayne was growing big; so perhaps sweet Emmy not being in the room yet my cock still making a stand by her cheek, the Lady couldn't resist her inclination, nor her desire. Her long fingers reached for me slowly, and my rod beat to her pull through the air.

Simply this, my cocked length in between Morgayne's lips, that normally uttered her croon and curse? I didn't expect it and I don't think she did either. But she did, and it did me and I dare not complain - who'd listen? Her hand was slow and careful as she placed her mind to the task, and she built me up so slow. Morgayne gazed up at me and how could she smile with her mouth so full? But she did, with her eyes and that's the unusual thing; this woman who had glared black filth and broken coal at me before, yet now her eyes were liquid midnight and lustrous black.

She placed her other hand on my gut like a claw, and gripped me with her fingers like she wanted to pierce my flesh, this Morgayne whose belly I'd bled, mine own fingers most intimate there. Her suck was like a communion, dragging up the seed from the back of my spine, and I was a slow spill into her mouth when she urged me forth. I dared hold her head with her hair all shorn off, as Morgayne drank me down, every drop. Cats and cream could be less lascivious, miaow, miaow.

Her licks lipped, my mind front to back like my words, Morgayne confused me so. I couldn't keep up.

"Keep up, heart, it's not so hard, your love for a Lady?" Even then she read my mind and saw the truth affront of me. Yet her hand was so warm as she held the soft droop of my spent flesh in the palm of her hand, and it was the gentlest touch, so unexpected. For the first time in a long time mine ankle didn't itch.

"It won't last, Maer, this frail mood of mine." She knew herself too well, but her warm palm lingered around me, and Morgayne didn't move the cup of her hand away for quite some time, so perhaps it was enough. "I don't know, Maerlyn, how you did it, but I'll never forget that you did."

I never found out if Morgayne meant the cut of her belly or the cut of her hair, and never wanted to ask.

Morgayne summonsed her babes to her arms, and Emmelyne brought up the fair girl child who looked like her father. The Lady showed the child up to her brother, Artur the King, and said to him, "Lilith, I shall call the child Lilith. Kiss your daughter, Artur, that you may know her."

Emmelyne and I looked on and shared us a glance, and our secret know of the child's birth caul was ours alone; waiting, wait. A secret so fine I could taste it.

The suckle wife brought in the ugly boy, and Morgayne looked upon him, her face giving nothing away. "He's not a pretty child, and see how he scowls. Mordant, I name him Mordant. The king's first heir and bastard prince. Look on him Artur, oh my brother, and see your future lying there."

Artur looked down on his son, but did not kiss his brow. Mordant the new prince with his face bruised red, the king's son through the king and his sister's sin. No need to see stars or stare at guts to know the boy child would inevitably do some bad deed or other. What and when was the question. Time would tell, and most like it would pass furious fast.

Morgayne placed her babes one on each breast and they were content, those three. "I shall miss my little goat," she said.

And so the babies were named Lilith and Mordant, a sister and a brother born to a brother and a sister, born to the same mother.

Morgayne dyed her short hair red with vermilion rock, and took upon her shoulders a scarlet cloak, all wrapped around in the memory of her blood, and she became the Red Morgayne.

And the children grew, and in time the blood red witch Morgayne took them down to Tyntangel where she was born and her mother lived, and she reared them there. The children of the Red Morgayne and the children of the king.

The Queen

Little Miryamme was bought to Camlann by her father, de Grance, and fealty made to Artur the king, and a dowry paid too.

Miryamme was thirteen when she first came to court, and met again the man who would make her his queen. Artur was a good man and kind, and he knew the fear in the girl, for he too had been ripped from his mother and his sister too young, and taken far away. So he treated Miryamme like a brother or a father would, as a young girl first coming into her older years, but still so very young.

"Miryamme can wait six years till she be a woman, Maer. I'll not wed her earlier. She must grow to be a woman like any other girl."

As always when he needed wisest counsel, Artur turned to the magickian for advice, for he knew the old man played the fool but wasn't a fool at all. Maerlyn had saved the life of his beloved sister Gayne, so Artur knew his old friend's heart was pure - trapped as it was in the strangest love for the king's sister, just as Artur was trapped in his own love for his sister, his Gayne.

Artur knew too, that he needed his sister's face to fade from his own heart, and place her somewhere unreachable, so time could ease away his pain. Innocent Miryamme didn't deserve a dark shadow over her sweet, young world, so Artur vowed in his own head to try to love her for herself. Time was the thing. Artur's own dowry to the girl was that - a period of innocence where Miryamme's world would be as normal as he could arrange it.

"Is there someone you know, Emmy, who could friend the princess, someone close to her in age?"

Emmelyne remembered her own dreams of the handsome young king, how she would run to her mother, gleefully telling her, "Mother, the king remembers my name and is interested in my goats!"

"Yes sire, my cousin Elayne; she is a year older than the princess, and knows her words and numbers too, and is a sensible girl. Could she be the maid to the princess, but be a friend too? Is that what you ask?"

Emmelyne immediately spotted the advantage in such an arrangement, for if her cousin grew friendly with the princess, she'd stay friendly with the later queen. Emmelyne had learned quickly the importance of a quick ear and a silent tongue in her conspiracies with the Maer Maerlyn and the Lady Morgayne. And she held the future knowledge of the caul over the king's daughter, which only she and the Maerlyn knew, and her own hands washed it away.

So Elayne was announced, and met the princess Miryamme. Over time the girls became affectionate friends, even if Miryamme was a shy girl, and delicate strange in her ways.

"She walks in her dreams, Emmy, and whispers to herself, words after whispering words. But during the day, I don't think she knows she even do it." Elayne paused, remembering something. "She washes her feet, to keep them clean, but doesn't know why she do it."

"Don't wake her, cousin, when she walks; but listen close to her whispers, let's know what she says. We'll talk to Maer Maerlyn. He'll know, and what to tell the king."

And so the world turned beneath Miryamme's feet, and she was surrounded by a conspiracy of strangers who watched her; and in time watched over her, for she was a sweet girl and innocent too, and drew love to her like softness in a kitten's fur draws fluff.

"Miryamme," said Artur one day, "show me your pretty doll, that you hold so close. Her hair is flaxen gold, like yours."

Miryamme shyly smiled at him, her own hair long and tumbling, golden fair in its waves. She stroked the straw hair of her doll, and it was smooth and rubbed from her constant fingers. Emmelyne would take the doll away sometimes and braid new straw to its head, counting those times by the moon.

"See, Artur, my doll is pretty, but she has no eyes, she cannot see."

"Do you want her to see, Miryamme?"

"Oh no. She sees too much if she see."

Artur waited quietly, holding her hand in his. He knew when to be still, this king, and was touched by the girl's simplicity.

Miryamme looked up at him, and her eyes were blue and wide, the palest blue of a high summer sky. A spray of golden freckles fleckered the tops of her cheeks, for Miryamme ran under the summering sun and was a golden child.

Artur glanced up, his eye caught by a movement across the lawn. He flicked his hand, away, away; and Maerlyn paused, then turned away.

"Is that the funny man, Maerlyn, who laughs and plays with his words and his silly songs, hey merry derry?" Miryamme swung her feet under the seat, and didn't change her voice at all. "He sees too much, with his eyes."

She said it so matter of factly, and Artur knew it true. He looked at the girl for a long, long time, sitting beside her on the bench. She looked up at him and smiled her radiant smile, and Artur began to tumble into her eyes.

Miryamme stroked the back of his hand, tracing the pattern of his veins there. After a while Artur grew tired of the repetitive touch and pulled his hand away. But he caught Miryamme's look of sad reproach, and without a fuss, gave his hand back to her. Miryamme didn't irritate him this time, just clutched two of his fingers tightly. Artur didn't see the little smile on her lips as she did so. Nor did he see her finger on her little doll's mouth, sshhh, don't speak.

Miryamme and Artur sat quietly on the bench without another word, the young king puzzling over the girl. After another short while, Miryamme got to her feet, turned to Artur, quickly kissed him on the cheek, and said, "I'm going down to the river now, to count some fishes."

She ran across the courtyard, and Artur followed her with his eyes. She was like a quick fawn in the forest, nervous and fast, her blonde tresses flying away behind her.

He wasn't sure what to do. That wasn't like him. In his practical way, if Artur the king held his hand before his face, he would always count four fingers and a thumb. But Miryamme flickered in his mind, and he never could count quite the same.

A few moments later the magickian, Maerlyn, was by his side.

"I am uncertain about Miryamme, Maer, but I cannot place my hand upon it. She seems fair simple sometimes, with her doll, but there's something else too. I can't grasp it."

"Yeay sire, I see it too. But she's not a simple maid, not like the moon faced boys in the village who sweep leaves with a brush and be happy. Miryamme knows her letters, and I teach her to write with a feather and black ash. She's a clever girl, sire, her eyes are bright and sparkle."

"Aye, 'tis true. But the doll, Maer, and her nervous rushing fingers. What is that?"

"I puzzle it too, sire. Elayne and Emmy, they say she walks in her dreaming sleep, fast asleep but walking."

Artur looked quickly at Maerlyn. "I have seen that." He paused, remembering, realising what Miryamme would have seen; his rut of his sister, her dark nakedness riding his high cock and Miryamme hearing their gasps.

"She walked in her sleep in her father's house. I carried her to her bed. Morgayne my sister sat with the girl till the morning sun rose up." Artur looked at his old friend. "She saw us, Maer, Miryamme saw us." Artur's eyes grew distant, remembering it all, not forgetting.

"Miryamme saw us, my sister and I in our wrongness, she's seen." Artur thought of the girl's doll with no eyes. *Oh no. She sees too much if she see.*

"She knows you too, Maerlyn, when you look at your boots. Best know that, friend, when dealing with the woman soon, when she be queen, even if she be a little girl now." Artur paused, gathering his thoughts, clearing his mind. "No matter. 'Tis done."

He shook his head and got to his feet. "It be what it be, Maer, and we care for Miryamme. She still be my queen, and she herself the innocent one. She must not be punished for my sister and I, Maerlyn. She did nothing but the daughter of a liege prince be."

Artur strode to his duty, and Maerlyn marvelled at the young king's ruthless simplicity. No matter.

Maerlyn sat on the bench a while longer. He remembered when he first saw the little maid Miryamme, at the ceremony of the knife in the rock, hiding behind her father's leg.

What will that do to an innocent head, wondered Maerlyn, seeing all that? Seeing her father and the new king, their big pricks firm, and Artur's seed all spurting on the ground? And the white and black scuttle of Morgayne climbing down from the rock, rubbing her brother's spill on her belly and Maerlyn's own seed smeared to her asshole? And to see Artur and his own sister make the two-backed beast?

Maerlyn's own cock throbbed as it always did whenever he thought of Morgayne, her spell permanently imprinted on his soul, and his ankle itched.

If those visions did that to him, a grown man, what would they do to an innocent girl?

"Come to me Artur, let me touch you, touch you, your softest, softest skin."

Six years had passed since Miryamme first came to Camlann, and now she was a tall and slender girl, almost too thin, nervous like a bird. She wore long gowns, full brocade and lace, all tied about her tiny waist with a velvet band. Miryamme's hair was golden blonde, full waves of it gleaming in the summer sun, long falling down her back.

"Let me touch you, touch you…" There was a distant dream in her voice, as if something echoed in her head.

Miryamme had come to her age six months before, and she and Artur were slowly learning intimacy in slow and gentle ways. Artur was older and knew women, including his sister the Red Morgayne who bore his first children; so he was content to wait for Miryamme to find her way, to discover him in her own time.

Elayne was like a sister to her, and Emmelyne told them both the ways of boys and men. Elayne found the prods and pricks of the guard and watch to her taste, while Emmelyne found her way with more serious men. So Miryamme chattered and listened and knew what to do, and slowly began to wonder about it. Her restless fingers still stroked her doll's hair at night, and she'd dressed the doll in little gowns like her own, and golden straw was the colour of its hair, like her own.

Miryamme's glory of hair was spread across Artur's bare shoulder and in waves upon their pillow. She lay with her head upon his chest, soothed by the strong steady lull of his heart, and her fingers ran silently over his skin. She'd learned through the years to calm her restless touch, to gentle it and flutter it like a butterfly, but she would still dance long moments on Artur's skin, especially when she ran up from the meadow, after dancing hours in the sun.

Miryamme would lie there exhausted, and slowly come back to her senses.

"What have you been doing, Miryamme?" Artur asked.

"Dancing, dancing in the meadow all day," Miryamme replied. "I'm sleepy now, can I sleep?"

And slowly, slowly, all summer long, Artur learned what happened in Miryamme's dreams.

He found she slept best curled in front of him, her back against his belly, her bottom pressed back to his groin. Miryamme was still a virgin queen, *sshhh, not yet, not yet,* but she'd found a way to please her king, while she waited. While she slept, while she dreamed.

Her sleeping drifting walk stopped when Artur was there; but she'd walk again, walk again, when he was gone away. Elayne would guide Miryamme back to her bed, climbing in beside the girl to sooth her, to still her restless hands.

Miryamme delighted in watching Artur stir in the morning, seeing the way he rose out of his sleep. Miryamme was more restless than he ever was, and would often startle awake and quickly look around to assure herself where she was. She'd rest her head on Artur's chest, holding one hand still by gripping it with the other, to stop her nervous flutter. She'd pull a cover back and watch the soft coil of his cock, see how the foreskin covered its head, and watch a tiny pulse beat in the long vein that ran along his resting shaft.

Miryamme watched, and felt a slight shift in the depth of his breathing, and knew he was awake. She didn't say anything, but kept watching the base of Artur's belly, looking for a first movement. He placed his hand on the back of her head, his eyes still closed, but knowing where she lay, what she looked at.

There it was, her slow reward. Miryamme watched spellbound as the coil of Artur's cock slowly thickened and straightened, pulled erect and aroused by the tug of her gaze until his beautiful shaft was hard and straight, the purple red head pushing towards her from its cowl of skin. Miryamme's eyes widened as she saw him thicken, the long veins running along the length of his shaft, and she watched a tiny blue pulse. Later, she would feel that little pulse with her lips, and taste his heat, but now, just her eyes saw his rise.

With a small bite of her teeth on her lip, a subconscious concentration, Miryamme reached down for Artur's shaft and gripped it in her hand, feeling its heat. His chest rose with a quick intake of breath, and his hand tightened its grip on her head. Yes, that touch, touch more.

She watched her own hand as if in a dream, as she explored the length of him, felt the heat of his shaft and the coolness of his tightening balls. Miryamme slid her head down to lie on the base of Artur's belly, and pressed the hot heat of his cock to her cheek.

"I see it, I see it, I feel it, I feel it," she whispered. "It's not yours. Not any more, not any more, it's not yours."

Miryamme placed the tip of her finger over the slit on the cock head and pressed firmly. The cock rose to her pressure. "It's mine, it's mine, I want it, I want it, it's not yours."

She placed her warm mouth over the end of Artur's cock and held it there, not sucking, not licking, just feeling its heat on her lips, her tongue. Artur's hand held Miryamme's head as she began to suck and lick, his fingers gripping as she heated him. Her fingers pressed and squeezed his high balls like a settling cat, over and over. His heartbeat quickened and his breath came faster.

She urged his cock up in her hands, her cheeks sucking inwards with the force of her suck, and she knew Artur was nearing his climax, his cock swelling hotter and the liquid taste of him wetting her tongue. Miryamme's stroke with her hand was long and steady, faster now, pulling him up to his peak. She heard a low moan in the back of his throat, and that was always the sign.

To stop. To grip him hard, stop her suck, stop her stroke. Miryamme felt him quiver, and she quickly pulled his high risen balls down away from his groin, and the pull on his testes pulled Artur back from his spill. He took two deep breaths as she held him firm and still. His cock pumped twice, and his body shuddered with pleasure, but she'd stopped his climax. This time.

"Ah, Miryamme, you stop, yet I don't want you to stop. Wickedness." His voice was affectionate, her wickedness and stillness exactly what he wanted, she'd urge him up again when she was ready.

Miryamme looked at Artur's lean body stretched on the bed, his thickness a beautiful length against his gut, a jewel of fluid beading from the little slit on the head. She lapped her tongue to it, and her lips were the same softness as the plum coloured tip of his cock. Miryamme pushed herself away from his body, sitting up on the bed. She turned to her lord, lying there, and smiled her softest smile.

"Artur, am I to be your queen, to sit by your side on a throne? Am I to be your queen?"

"Yes, my princess, by my side. Why do you ask, do you doubt we will marry?"

"Oh no, I don't doubt it." She smiled, her lovely innocent smile. "The laughing man said it will be." She looked directly at Artur. "The laughing man knows too much, with his eyes."

He does that, thought Artur, he certainly does. Then Artur was distracted.

Miryamme began to stroke Artur once more, and she leaned over him so her small breasts dropped, and he took them into his hands to feel their soft weight. Her golden hair fell like a veil, and hid her. She leaned over him some more so his cock pressed up against her breasts and slid between her little mounds. Her nipples were long and hard, and she pressed the head of his cock to one nub. Her hands stroked, and because he'd come so close before, it was not long before Artur's head tossed restlessly from side to side, and his hand reached down for her hip.

"She mustn't have it, she mustn't, it's mine." Miryamme's words were a soft chant, and she spoke to the same rhythm as the stroke of her hand, pulling him closer to his end, his final surge. "See, on the rock, she crawls upon the rock." Her hand stroked faster and faster.

Artur's eyes were closed, and his mouth opened with his quick breath. Miryamme looked at his silent face as he lay beneath her, and she stroked him, twisting his cock in her hands, her eyes never leaving his face.

"She won't have you, Artur, never again, she won't have you ever again, you're mine." Faster, her voice a whisper still. "I'm not your sister, not your sister." As soon as Miryamme uttered the words 'sister' Artur's cock throbbed, and the long jet of his seed roped across her chest, and Miryamme pulled it all up out of him, pulling up the last surge, and it spread across her breasts.

She held him close against her as his flesh softened. In his guilt Artur moved his hand from Miryamme's thigh and didn't touch her; he couldn't, not after he'd come, thinking of his sister.

Miryamme rubbed her hands in circles on her chest, over her breasts and around her belly, rubbing the hot cream of him into her skin. She had the softest, smoothest skin, her fingers slid and circled, rubbing in his cream, rubbing it all in to her porcelain skin.

When she was done and his spill was all gone, Miryamme lay beside Artur, her head lying on his chest.

"Hold me close, Artur, hold me close."

Artur remembered his vow to Miryamme when she was younger, she's innocent, she's done no wrong, and did as she asked. How could he not?

"It's all right, Artur, it's all right." She looked up at him, and kissed his mouth. "You've known your sister, I saw it with my eyes, with my eyes. But I'll stay your virgin queen, your virgin queen."

Miryamme kissed him again. And again. She loved him. "And every day, your seed will fall on my skin, my skin. It's mine, all mine." Miryamme's skin was soft, so very, very soft, and her fingers rubbed it in circles.

Miryamme stroked his cheek, and smiled her little smile.

Her doll had no eyes. It might see too much, if it had eyes.

A ceremony.

I've always liked a ceremony, especially one where my vanity gives me a leading role, where I can primp myself up in new robes. If I get them made in sufficient quality they can last me several years. The worn bedraggled train of them, after a while, lends a certain learned air, as if I have been hermiting alone in a forest or a wood. Rocks bashed together in a stream more like, with mud from the bank rubbed in. Rub a dub.

Every court requires a circumstance from time to time, and Artur's Camlann had run several years without one. The arrival of his children didn't quite count, due to that event being more of a whisper than a gossip, nobody quite prepared to look the king in the eye. Even I admired my own boots.

And of course, the magnificent Morgayne with her disdain shut even the loosest tongue right up. In the normal course of events that tongue would be mine, but when it came to the Red Morgayne even I knew when to shut my own mouth.

And my neck. I hang for her, every day, by her hair, her silken black hair. It's surprisingly soft, when I touch it.

But the Lady Miryamme, now there's a pretty thing with a gentle smile, but a strangeness behind her eyes. Quite mad I suspected, her poor eyes having seen far too much; and I think she said the same about me. She and Artur reached an understanding of sorts; Miryamme danced in the meadow and walked by the river's edge quite a lot, but at least she didn't fall in. She carried her doll, even then.

"Miryamme is of age, Maer, I need to make the marriage and promise a legitimate heir. The land needs that of me, as my duty to the river and tree. It's why you and Nym Nymue made me, so for the Goddess I do it."

Artur strolled along by my side, casually, and the court could see our business being done; the land in safe hands, his and mine, king and courtier. Artur's hands safe, certainly; mine I was not so sure. I looked at mine hands and didn't know if they held the corn or spilled the corn, whether my fingers were turned up or turned down. I put a hand in my pocket and found a small pebble, and wondered when I'd put it there.

"Yeay sire. But your sister Morgayne, she to invite?"

"Of course she's invite, Maer. She's my sister Gayne, don't ever forget. Besides, she has no animosity to the girl. 'Twas her suggestion first."

"Ah lord, yes, I forget that."

"You forget nothing, wizard, my sister least of all."

His sister least of all.

"Did you forget me, heart, and desert me in my distant castle?" The Red Morgayne, as always, was silent to my side and I never heard her there. My blood thickened immediate, and my damned ankle itched. Would her trance ever leave me? I thought it not, but didn't want it to, either.

"Lady, you did not summons me; I thought it natural that you might, if only to torment and play with me."

"Maerlyn, no." She touched my shoulder. "I'm kinder now, I mothered two little babes through toddle and talk, and they have taught me patience. You think me bad, at your expense? It's not true." Her slow fingers traced through the air, they dragged warm down my arm and my skin prickled; the flesh of a goose would be smoother.

"You should have visited, once at least. Come, make up for it. Walk with me to see the little ones, my bastard prince and princess fair."

I had not thought Morgayne the mothering kind, yet there she stood between her children and caressed them both with her affection, standing with her hands on their shoulders and soft love in her eyes.

Mordant her son and the king's first heir, with his bruised red cheek and red-stained skin, stood black eyed and prideful by his mother's side, silently watching me watch him. I turned away first, for I could see he was his mother's son.

"Is this my father's wit, Mother, who looks at me with his eyes?"

"Be kind, Mordant. Maer Maerlyn's hands were the first ever to touch your skin, when he took you from my belly. I've told you that."

"Show me your hands, nurse, that I know them."

I glanced at his mother. "Your son, then, Lady. A disrespectful sod, you should curb him." I spoke my tongue and Morgayne just smiled.

"The wizard not like me?" Mordant pouted, but it was a prissy pout. This child needed attention, not wanted it.

"Ah, child, you not like yourself, 'tis plain."

Mordant sneered, but a child of seven has limited words, and needs learn new ones fast. He would be a pointless thing, until the day he wasn't. And then his small festering vile would split and spill open, like a pox. A watching thing, this child, to be watched.

By his dark side, little Lilith was her light. 'Twas clear she was her father's daughter, Artur's fairness on her skin, and his eyes, blue as the high sky in summer. She stood a gazing bright, whilst her brother skulked dark beside her.

"Mother Caitlyyn has told me of you, Maer Maerlyn. Verily, show me the hands that held me first, that took me from my mother."

I bent before Lilith and placed myself to her level. She took my gnarled hands into her little ones, and she traced the long lines on my palm with her finger. She held a serious look on her face as she turned my left hand over and ran the same finger over the veins of my blood on the back of my hand. She did the same with my right hand.

"Was I so small, that these hands held me all?" She looked up at Morgayne. "Mother, was I so tiny the Maerlyn's hands held me, like I hold a bird?"

"Yes, Lilith, a tiny thing, squirming like my heart." Morgayne looked at me quick as she said it, and I remembered how I could have grasped it, her heart.

I looked at the girl, and remembered too how she was all covered in her birthing shroud as I pulled her from the womb, how Emmelyne washed it quick away, hush hush. I looked at Lilith, and wondered when her prophecy would fall, when her tell would come.

"These children then, Lord Maerlyn, these the ones we never saw? And their mother too, the king's sister, we never saw her; not her fierce love, anyway."

I turned slowly, hearing a voice I'd not heard for years. Count them, too many. Count them, too long. Even Morgayne, with her preternatural stillness, was stone.

Only Lilith spoke, too young to ever know, but instinctive and quick. "Are you a Sister, Lady, who comes from out of the mist?"

"Yes child, I am a Sister, long sleeping in the Isle of Glas. I was a little daughter too, like you, many years ago. I'm older now."

She laid a formal kiss on Lilith's brow and I wondered if she saw the echo of the caul around the girl, or whether Morgayne's blood hid it from her sight. "I greet you, child. I Nym Nymue be, come to see the king make a queen on his throne."

"Why don't you greet me?" Mordant asked, petulant and jealous of his sister. "I'm a royal prince. I'm important, too."

Nymue gazed down at the boy, as if remembering something from a long time ago. "Yeay, you're a destiny, a prophecy. A prince who returns. But you are ordained, I cannot change you. Yet your sister, she is unknown to me, and I greet her mystery, for I must know it like I know the circles and rocks and the stars above."

"And I, Nym Nymue, am I your mystery too, that you never saw? What does that make me?" Morgayne broke her still silence, a small faint tremor in her voice. The rarest thing, the Lady uncertain?

Nymue turned to face Morgayne, and the two women contemplated each other, still as ice; one little and fine, her hair all white and her gown all white, the other taller and thin, scarlet clad, her blood all red. I took one step back, a rare wisdom for me. I confess it, I'm a genius... two steps further back, and if I was any smarter, I'd run. Or trip over my feet. So I stayed.

"Morgayne, the king's sister; you stayed well hid, I did not see you." Nym Nymue was honest with the younger woman; she did not see. Of course, I can't see one foot in front of the other at the best of times, and trip over them both.

Morgayne laughed, and my ankle beat and her old dark malice was there.

"In plain sight, Nymue, I hid where all could see. If they would but look." Morgayne straightened her back, and was tall above the white priestess. "What use you to the Goddess, Nymue, if you cannot see?"

She went on, her voice low and calm and full of cruel intent, the Red Morgayne. "Yet you say my boy is ordained, a puppet, a thing with no will of his own? What see you on the boy? The Goddess's will, that will act through him all darkness done?"

"I do not know it fully, Sister, he is not clear." But Nymue stood her place, and Morgayne took one step back. "He cannot be put aside, your Mordant. His is destiny. I know that, at least."

Morgayne held Mordant by his shoulder. "See, my son, you are important. If only we knew how."

She turned to Lilith, and looked at her for a long, long time. "Yet you confound them, and are hid, my daughter. Like your mother then, hidden for all the world to see."

Lilith looked up at her mother, the Red Morgayne, her blue eyes wide. "Mother, what does it mean, that I am hidden from the priestess Nym Nymue, who greeted me with a kiss?"

"Nymue does not see you, Lilith, she cannot see your future, and so cannot steer it. That not knowing and not guiding is a torment to her. Mother Nymue's rocks and circles stand still on the land, yet our hearts beat, so who is most alive here?"

"You are right, Morgayne. Your child lives an unseen life. I see her before my eyes, but no shadows stretch away from her. She turn a corner, and she is gone from my sight. A rare thing, your Lilith."

"It sounds to me that you will make your own destiny, Lilith, pleasing no-one but yourself." Morgayne spoke to her daughter, and could have been speaking for herself.

I too looked at the girl, and wondered who she would bind to her will, when she was older and knew what to do with it. A girl child born from a brother and sister's sin, shrouded on the day of her birth, and Morgayne her mother? A powerful thing, and oh so pretty. Oh my word, some man's delight and doom, no doubt about that.

"Oh, look who comes, my father the king." Lilith ran to Artur who picked her up and spun her around, the love in his eyes clear to see. I looked to the Sisters, as they gazed upon the girl and her king, and saw their eyes. Oh look, my boots need mending. A needle, a thread, a seamstress I'll be.

I shall talk to Emmy, I think, and let her know our secret is moving close.

Lilith danced with her father, oblivious of the watching eyes. He kissed her on the lips.

Morgayne came up to one side of me, and her slow fingers trailed down my sleeve. Nymue came to the other side of me, and her hand touched upon my arm.

"Maerlyn..."

"Heart..."

Oh dear, has it just got complicated?

The ceremony itself was simple.

Artur commanded and Artur was obeyed, and even his sister the Lady Morgayne let the girl Miryamme have her day, to be throned beside her king.

Emmelyne braided Miryamme's golden hair in twelve plaited loops, and the princess's head was circled in ancient twists, the wyrm's head eating its tail, curled around and about itself. Emmy braided the little doll too.

Nym Nymue visited the girl, and clad her in an embroidered gown. The importance of the young queen's promise to the land was shown by the shape of a great wave on Miryamme's gown and the dragen rampant and thick. Nymue told the girl her own story of the five great waves and her mortal swim, so Miryamme knew she was chosen, chosen special for the land.

Miryamme walked beside Nym Nymue, the High Priestess of the Goddess, down the long centre of Artur's grand hall, to where the king sat on a carven throne. I, the Maer Maerlyn, stood behind Artur the king and played my part, and the king played his. A court was all made and assembled, and legiances given to the king, and they all played peaceful and their parts too.

Of Miryamme I was no longer sure. I saw that she leaned on Nymue beside her as they walked, and as the princess came closer to the dais I could see that her eyes were part closed as if she might be sleeping.

"Tonight, tonight," I heard her whisper. "I fear it, I fear it. I don't want to. I don't like it."

I looked to Artur as Miryamme came closer, and saw a huge sadness in his eyes as his bride stopped before him, swaying slightly; and I think he knew she was mad, but too late.

But Artur did as he always did. He stood tall, and shook his head the once, no matter. He took the hands of the girl before him, and leaned down to whisper something in her ear, so quiet that only she could hear it. She lifted up her head, and opened her crystal blue eyes so wide and smiled up at him her little smile. Artur turned towards her, placed both his hands on her tiny waist, and steadied her with his own strength, before kneeling before her.

"Miryamme, on this my knee I vow myself to thee. To honour and protect thee, all thy days." He took a breath. "My queen."

Artur stood, and led her to her own throne, there on the dais beside his, and Miryamme sat beside him, and her doll sat beside her too. Nym Nymue stood behind the girl, and placed a simple garland on her head. She too leaned to the girl's ear and whispered something I could not hear. Miryamme looked at the priestess with her big wide eyes, and nodded her head and smiled her little smile. She put her finger to her lips, *sshhh*. Nymue placed a little garland on the doll's head.

I was there.

The day a crown was placed on a young queen's head and she sat beside the king, I was there.

My doll is pretty, and she has no eyes, but still she sees too much.

The Young Prince

"Artur, now I am your queen, will I be different?" Miryamme sat in front of a small table, combing her golden mane of hair, her face reflected in a polished bronze mirror; combing her hair, combing her hair. Her doll sat nearby, its straw hair teased and pulled by Miryamme's nervous fingers, her restless hands.

"What do you mean, Miryamme?" Artur asked. His queen's hands were constantly moving, and she only settled when she slept, curled against his body. His raw strength calmed Miryamme's anxious mind, stopped her worry, stilled her restlessness.

"Will you still anoint my skin with your seed, and make my breasts so soft, so soft? Will the skin of my breasts stay soft?"

Artur looked at his new bride, puzzled at her question.

"Of course, if that is what you want, you can take my spill upon your breasts and your belly, and rub it all in."

"Will I stay your pure queen, ever so pure, never to be sullied or broken?" Miryamme asked her question as if it was the most natural thing in the world for a queen to remain a virgin queen, and never to fuck.

Artur looked upon Miryamme for a very long while, nothing showing on his face, nothing revealed in his eyes. "Miryamme," he said, slowly, "you do know that for babes to be made, you cannot remain a virgin, untouched between your legs?"

"But Artur," she replied, as she picked up her doll and began to caress its straw hair, "you already have two children. You don't need any more." Miryamme went on, and her voice was quite calm as she spoke, "Your sister gave you her womb and you filled it. You don't need mine, it's all mine."

She looked at him with her pretty smile. "But you can look between my legs, if you like it. Just as you looked up at your sister climbing down from the rock on your coronation day."

As she spoke, Miryamme slowly pulled back the hem of her skirt. She turned to face him, her thighs spreading apart, and bared the base of her belly. Miryamme's fingers were already restless, teasing her lips apart.

"See, I'm not like Gayne, I'm not thick and dark like her." She played with herself. "I'm all pretty and light, not dark like your sister."

Despite himself, and the fixing firm realisation that Miryamme was quietly mad and he had driven her so, Artur's eyes remained on the core of her, seeing her fluttering fingers, and seeing the swell of her sex. It wasn't fecund and red rich like his sister's, but covered by fine blonde hair, a fair triangle at the base of her belly, which she revealed to him, her skirts pulled up to her waist.

"Look at me, Artur. Am I not your queen?"

Artur made an instant vow to her, and a vow to himself. He would love his queen for what she was, and keep the core of her innocence pure. Miryamme did not make the things she'd seen, she was blameless before his own corruption, and she could not fight his sister.

"Yes, Miryamme, you are my queen, my virginal queen. Show me. I'll look." Artur leaned back in his own chair, and spread his legs apart to ease his thickening prick.

"Will you always want me, Artur, your queen you cannot have?" Miryamme glanced up at him with the little smile on her face, as she spread apart her lips and played. As she did so she looked across at her doll and whispered, "Sshhh, you have no eyes, you cannot see."

"Yes, I'll always want you, Miryamme, the queen I never can have." Artur spread apart the cloth from around his own thighs, took his cock in his hand, and watched his queen as she played.

Miryamme whimpered as the pleasure climbed within her, and as her power over him grew. "You're mine now, you're always mine. She can't have you, not any more, not anymore." Her fingers dipped and flicked all over her sex. "Just like you can't have me."

Miryamme arched back against the chair, the cloth of her dress all bunched around her waist. She spread her lips wide, and fingered deep into herself. She came, her heel drumming on the floor, and as she came, Miryamme cried out like a distant animal in the night, "Ohhh."

Artur stood, and dropped all the clothes from his body. He walked to his queen, his rod high and hard; and Miryamme looked up at him from behind her drowsy eyes. She reached for Artur's long cock, her fingers still twitching from her pleasure, and took his shaft between the palms of her hands.

With her hands around his cock like a prayer, Miryamme took the head of him into her mouth and began to suck, her eyes rolling back in a dreaming trance, her lips and tongue slow and wet.

Artur reached between Miryamme's legs with one hand, and cupped her hot sex in the press of his palm. He held the heat of her body in the palm of his hand, and she calmed herself onto his hold. The endless twitch of her fingers ended and stopped, and Miryamme began a long, slow stroke, matching her hands to her slowing breath and her gentle suck on his cock.

As she calmed herself, Miryamme roused him with her slow stroke and the hot, wet heat of her mouth. Miryamme slowed edged Artur to his peak. He stood over her, his hands slowly stroking her hair, her long golden hair. She sensed as she always did how close he was, and lifted her head. She smiled up at Artur with her sweetest smile, and her lips were berry red. Miryamme caught the catch in his breath and she changed her stroke just a little, just a tiny little bit.

"Do you want me, Artur, your queen, your beautiful queen?" Miryamme was peaceful now, calm and content, her man in her hands, stroking him, stroking him. "Do you want me, or do you want to fuck your sister?" She said it plain, and knew him so well.

And as he always did when Miryamme invoked his sister, Artur surged a long stream of white cream all upon her breasts, pumping and pumping, threading long streams of his come on her breasts. Miryamme urged up his desperate seed and rubbed it all in, all creamy and hot; she rubbed it in to the flesh of her breasts so she smelt of him.

"All mine, Artur. I call out her name and you answer, but your sacrament is all for me, all mine."

Miryamme smiled her little smile, and took Artur by the hand to their bed, where she lay on her side and pressed herself back against his chest. She took his hands in hers and pressed them against her breasts.

"Am I your queen, Artur, am I your queen?"

" Yes, you're my queen, Miryamme, my lovely queen."

"Hold me then, Artur, that I peacefully sleep. No dreams, I don't want dreams."

Artur held her, and Miryamme slept without dreams.

I was there.

When Lancilet the king's cousin became an invisible prince, and Artur the king turned a blind eye, I was there.

And so the Court was made, Miryamme the young queen safe in her madness and her purity, for who would dare risk the wrath of the king by speaking of these things? Her madness became plain, but she was a gentle girl; and those who knew her heart warmed to it, and loved her too. Folk would sing with her, and Miryamme would dance and make chains of flowers in the meadows down by the river.

I put about that Miryamme was slow to breed child because of a wrongness in her womb; and only Artur and I, Emmelyne and the maid Elayne knew the truth of it, that the wrongness was in Miryamme's head, not between her legs. And the skin of her body was the softest soft, and she plaited the hair on her little doll's head, and remained all virgin pure.

Artur would ride off on occasion to the vale south of Camlann, where the woods would one day be there, and not be there the next; and his sister the Red Morgayne be there too, then not.

And so the court was made, and for a ten of years the land was peaceful, and Artur ruled fair and well. A kingdom came, and it was his. South in Tyntangel, children grew, and the first child on in years was Lancilet, the son of Artur's sister, Claryyne.

The young cousin came up to Camlann and Artur's court in his nineteenth year, blessed by his mother and Ygraine his grandmother. He was a tall and slender boy, dressed all in black and hiding behind his hair like a rock hides behind a water falling, his hair all black and silken. He was slim and graceful, and I watched the village girls watch him, and I saw him watch the stable boys too.

Miryamme saw him, and because Lancilet was the king's cousin, his nephew true, but she called him 'cousin', the queen made him welcome. And soonest, and it was all very quick, Miryamme brushed the hair of her doll, then brushed the hair of the boy.

"Look, Lancilet, I've woven some of your hair with mine, on my doll."

I, of course, know something of rope and tie and weave, and Morgayne's hair around my neck and around my prick told me the bind the queen made was true. 'Twas made by a woman after all, even if a woman delicate mad and that's no lie, but a bind from a woman is a permanent thing.

247

I know it, and I still can't get the knots undone, no matter how hard I try. I suppose I could try harder, but why? One of them would still come along in the night, smile at me and say, "Ohh Maerlyn, heart… Ahh, Maerlyn, my love…."

They tease, the witches, the bitches, yet I love them still; and I think they might love me, in their way. Or perhaps they just pat me on the head. "There, there, Maerlyn… soon, Maerlyn." One for my left ear, one for my right, and me stuck in the middle with both. The wind has dropped, is that my heart I hear, beating soft below the sound of my blood?

I spied also the following eyes the boy Lancilet gave the king, and I saw the soft steadiness there. I knew about lust, so thought it best to keep that little knowledge to myself.

I really must make a chest with secret drawers, to keep my secrets in. My head gets so crowded and I fear I'll open my mouth one day and they'll all fall out. I knotted knots into cloth to remember them all, because I'd run out of fingers to count.

"Is that a new fashion, Maer, your cloak with all its knotted beads?"

The king looked at me, and I looked at my boots. He shook his head and moved on, knowing his secrets were safe. He didn't know what they were, and I'd forgotten, so between us his secrets kept easy.

When I said I kept that knowledge to myself, I meant Emmelyne too.

"Tis useful to know, Emmy, the looks of that boy; keep watch where they fall, and we compare notes, now and then. He favours the king, and would want him, I think."

Emmelyne, of course, remembered her own look she'd given the young king when he asked about her goats and Rednock with his pig, and she was a clever girl.

"Maer Maerlyn, is this news so precious as the knowledge of the king's daughter with her birth shroud?" She whispered to me, her lips close to my ear like a raven on my shoulder.

I pondered a little moment. "No, Emmy, Lilith's caul was never seen by anyone else but you and me. I think we best keep that know behind our own eyes without saying. That is a know worth having. We'll not cash it just yet."

Later, of course, Miryamme looked up at me with her wide open eyes where the sky gets in, and smiled her sweetest smile. "Don't always watch, Maer Maerlyn. Your watching eyes give you away." She stroked on her doll's hair. "You should be like my doll, who has no eyes so cannot see."

Why did I think she was mad? No madder than me, or am I confusing myself with a fool?

Time on, and the queen and boy became inseparable. I suppose Artur had kinging to do, and he rode to the south more often, both to the disappearing vale and Morgayne his sister; and further on to Tyntangel where his children were.

"Miryamme is content with the boy, Maer, and his company does her good." Artur as always was practical, and hid any discontent.

"My cousin Lancilet, I think he gaze at me with his pup's eyes too much, but his longing eyes don't interest me."

Artur looked to the south as he always did when it came to matters of the heart, yet I'm not sure he knew he did it, some automatic thing. He looked away.

"Yeay, I have seen the glance, sire. Young Lancilet hides it well, but it creeps out from under the fall of his hair when he thinks no-one looks."

"So you see it all the time, then Maer, you who never sees a thing because chance it always, you look the other way."

Artur looked at me with his king's wise eyes, and I wondered who taught him so well.

"You taught me well, Maer Maerlyn, for someone who never sees a thing. A compass would spin in your hand, wizard, to change west from north, east from south, and never be still."

Artur smiled at me, his eyes creased in a friendship that had come a long way, from that boy on a ship to the king for a land.

"As may be, sire," I replied. "I can't see it myself, such trickery. If I shoot an arrow, sire, I shoot it true and straight, just like my words, straight and true."

I'm shameless, I don't even convince myself. I've never shot true in my life.

Artur roared with laughter, his hand a slapping me on the back. I don't convince the king, either; but then, I rarely believe myself.

"Sire, you mock me." No, I certainly don't convince myself. I mock myself more often.

"Never change, Maerlyn, never change. I never want the day when your yes means yes, and your no means no."

"Yeay, sire, as you wish."

He walked away, a bounce in his walk, a kinging to do and me to keep it all straight.

A little later (I really must think about minutes one day, and how to count them, one, two, three) I walked down the zig-zag track to the village. Emmelyne had told me, "There's a spying game, sire, that you should know," so I made my way to the watch.

Emmelyne met me at the stable door. She hushed my lips with her finger, and made me shuffle in the straw to quiet my tread.

"Sire, climb to the loft and there's a peeping place, make no noise. Elayne told me how she discovered it, and one day told the queen."

Emmy caught up her skirts and climbed ahead of me, and her lovely bum and dark haired patch were moon round full and all dark between. She glanced down at me and caught my eye gazing at her private place, and Emmy smiled.

"I don't need the Red Lady's permission, sire, to treat you well. If I want prod, will you give it me?"

"Why, Emmy, 'tis long cock making, this scene you bring us to see?"

"Oh, yes, sire, a lusty fuck, you'll see it. 'Tis fun, and most unexpected."

"But the Lady Miryamme, the queen? What she?"

"Ah yes, sire, that's the thing of it. My cousin Elayne did mention it to the queen, and she most wide eyed got, and her fingers all nervous with her doll, and cannot stop herself thinking on't. 'Tis the king's cousin sire, that's who I brought you to see. Lancilet."

Oh my. Emmelyne has been around me too much, she's thinking just like me.

"You'll knot your cloak with secrets, Em, just like mine."

"More cunning, sire. I'll knot the thread of my under skirts, sire, then no-one know my secrets but me."

"Clever girl, Em. I should have thought of that."

"Too late, sire," she grinned. "But hush. See there, another peeping place."

Emmelyne pointed to the other side of the loft, where crept the Lady Miryamme and the maid Elayne, and on their bellies hid in the straw.

Emmy and I stood back, shadows dark around us, and could not be seen. Emmy held her finger to my lips to keep me hush. She tied her skirts high up above her waist, and placed my hand on her bush. Wicked Em, she undid my britches and found me. My other hand found her tit, and the weight of it was satisfyingly full. Her nipple grew long as I twisted it 'tween my finger and my thumb. Emmy pressed back against me, and we waited and we watched.

On the other side of the loft I could see Miryamme and the maid, Elayne, lying side by side in the straw, a peeping down through a crack in the wooden floor. I heard a giggle and a hush.

Below, I saw the young fellow Rednock come in, who had grown of age with Emmelyne and now kept the king's horse. He was a sturdy big fellow, wide shouldered with a chest broad like one of his geldings. He pulled up the cloth of his shirt and threw it over a rail. Curling hair spread on his chest with a dark line down his gut. Emmy's hand clenched my member at the sight of Rednock standing there, and she sighed.

"He's a fine fellow, is he not, sire? I fancy many a wench with a firm thigh and a nice tit would like to wrap themself around him. I'd like him myself, but I've known him too long. He's just like a brother to me."

Rednock was indeed a fine fellow, as he bent his shoulder against a horse, lifting its leg to inspect a hoof and count nails. He whistled happily as he worked, grooming the beast. It was hot, and Rednock's body soon glistened. He started a brushing the horse's mane, and Emmy whispered, "Look, there."

Through the gate to the bay below us, where Rednock brushed down the horse and knotted its mane, I saw the young prince Lancilet come in and greet the king's hand; and I could tell a familiarity was there between them. Big Rednock saw the slender youth, and the grin on his face was wide and hearty. He spoke some words to Lancilet, but I could not hear them, so Emmy and I watched on their silent masquerade, and I wondered at it. I didn't wonder long.

The youth hid behind his falling black hair, and looked sideways at the man. Then he pulled his hair away and said another word, and Emmy pulled on my prick, a whispering, "He's a pretty one, Maer, don't you think? But he not like us girls so much, see where his eyes look."

His eyes might look, but his hand braver be. Lancilet put a hand to Rednock's shoulder, and pushed him back against the horse. The horse shimmied with its hoof, and turned its head to look, then contented itself with its head down a munching hay. The boy trailed his fingers delicate down Rednock's thick arm, making the shape of the big man's muscles, and rousing up another broad grin from the groom.

Lancilet came up closer, touched his fingers to Rednock's chin, and kissed the man's throat. Rednock leaned his self back against the horse's solid flank, and he was equally solid leaning there, with the slim Lancilet pampering him and gently stroking his strong body. Rednock looked down on the boy, and seemed content with it all.

Emmy started a slow pull on my prick, and wriggled her bum soft against me. "Pull on my tit, sire, I beg it of you."

"Need not beg, Em, I'll do it gladly." And I did, Emmy's weighty tit in my palm, and my finger circling around her little hot place, slickening and getting all delightfully wet. She too seemed content at this little play before our eyes, as if put on for us to see.

Across the loft, I spied the Lady Miryamme with her big eyes all wide and her mouth open in a silent O, and I saw her skirts runkled up high to her waist, and Elayne's hand all a moving around between her legs. And I remembered the times when the maid calmed her mistress's twitching and restless hands in her bed, and guessed the girl calmed the queen most cleverly and knew her properly too. Oh, what a summer's day, happy, happy summer.

Down below, Lancilet was on his knees before the other man, who had spread his sturdy thighs wide, and leaned back against the horse. The horse stomped its big front hoof, and bent its head to the hay. Lancilet delved into Rednock's britches, and pulled out a proud, thickening cock. Emmelyne sighed, and wriggled her bum some more, at the sight of that prod.

Lancilet moved his head around, savouring angles and comforting himself to Rednock's cock. Satisfied, Lancilet looked up at the groom, pulling his hair sideways from his face so Rednock could see his mouth and lips as they wettingly went to work. I could see he was a clever boy and skilful too, for Rednock tilted his head back, let out a long moan, a growling big wolf's growl, his eyes all closed in his pleasure. He dropped his big hands to Lancilet's hair, but 'twas clear he didn't need hands to keep the boy's head there. Lancilet sucked hungrily, and took that cock all along his tongue and into his throat. A miracle thing truly, as Rednock's prick was a considerable prize.

My own prick was its own considerable size, and Em cleverly angled her arrangements, sliding herself back on me, leaning forward so both lovely breasts weighted down onto my hands. I thanked the wisdom of the carpenter who built this loft, for a handy rail was there for Em to lean on, and it was all quite structurally sound. We made no loud sound, but a gentle movement started and a faint slick slick of her wet juicy cunt could be heard, so faint. Afar, I heard a rustle of straw, and thought the Lady and her maid were truly enjoying the dumb show too.

Young Lancilet could not have spoke to save himself, his mouth and hands so full. Yet I thought Rednock a trusty man, looking to the boy who pleased him. The boy gazed up at Rednock looking down on him, and went back to his work. Even from up above, I could see Lancilet's eyes were closed, all in a dreamy place

The groom pulled Lancilet's mouth from his prod, and he made the youth stand, pulling Lancilet's slim body tight against his own. He kissed him hard, and Rednock's big hands gripped the young man's ass. Emmy gasped, and was quicker with her hand.

"Go slow, Em," I whispered in her little ear. "I think there is an act two coming, a frolic more to see."

"I think it too, sire. Just the idea of it pleases me, and makes my cunt ache." She looked back at me with a red flame on her throat. "You might be quite older than I, Maer Maerlyn, yet certain you known how to fill it, my aching cunt."

"It pleases me, Em, that I please you, and all a filling up your cunt. But look, Lancilet drops his clothes," I observed; and Em clenched me with her wet dripping puss as she watched.

"Ah sire, see. His bottom is like two moons, round and strange in the sky, pale and white and all a round."

Below us, Lancilet was on his knees, his perfect, lovely ass up high, and his hands all gripping a rail. That carpenter, what a fellow! Lancilet was naked now, as naked as the day he was born. But I don't think his good mother would have quite expected this.

Lancilet's right hand moved to his own slender cock, rubbing it to and fro. He was making small mewling sounds, almost like a kitten, while behind the boy the big Rednock placed a hand on each round buttock, separating them to reveal the tidy pucker of the boy's asshole.

Slipping a spit wet finger from his mouth, Rednock applied his digit to that sweet place and pushed it carefully in. Lancilet bucked like a horse a twitched when a crop lands on its haunch, and I fancied Rednock about to pummel the boy full hard.

Emmy thought so too, and she whispered, "How is he to take that big prick in his ass? It will split him in two, it will." She wriggled wet and quick back against me, rotating her own bum and opening herself up to me. Sweet fuck, her lubricious cunt was the finest dark cleft and I deep in it. Oh Em.

But Rednock fixed the problem of his big thick cock and the youth's narrow channel, for he reached behind for a pot of natural made dubbin that he used to soften a saddle. He took a great glop between the palms of his hands and rubbed it quick, to make it warm and soft; then covered it all on his cock. What was left he fingered deep into Lancilet's tight back hole, popping two fingers in for good measure.

Incomprehensible noises were coming from Lancilet's mouth; the most I could make out was, "Fuck, fuck, fuck," and "now, now, now." Something like that, but I don't think the sense of the words really mattered.

The next big fuck mattered, that was clearly true. Rednock made sure that Lancilet's hands were gripping tight the rail, and his body could go no place. Rednock placed the head of his prick delicate against the young man's hole, and eased himself into the first thumb's length, where he stopped, leaving the boy gasping. Lancilet stroked himself quick to take in the pleasure, or ease the pain perhaps. I saw the great tight muscles of Rednock's strong ass clench, then he drove himself in all the way, 'till the boy's ass was right up against the thick hair of Rednock's groin.

Lancilet let cry a long moan, and Emmy answered, and the other girls too. A brace of barn owls would have made less noise, hoo, hoo.

Rednock grinned, and applied himself to the business of the fuck. The tight muscles of his ass were like thick ropes straining to pull a huge load, and he arched his back and thrust his solid thighs forward and back, and it was a long swathing fuck into Lancilet's tight hole.

'Twas magnificent to watch, to see how the youth thrashed back and called out all sorts of fuck slut words, urging Rednock to take him full hard, full in the ass and oh, sweet fuck, Rednock had his way, fucking Lancilet happy and hard.

All sorts of moans accompanied the two men in their heat. High girlish cries told me Miryamme and Elayne were inspired; and my Em was moaning for a fast fuck now, and I gave her one. Matching my thrusts to the same pulse as Rednock into Lancilet's best place, I fucked my Em and pressed her full breasts heavy and hot in the palms of my hands as I bent over her back. She turned her head back so her mouth could kiss mine, and we kissed, clumsily, for our bodies were every which way but sensible, in our rut.

Down below, I saw Rednock reach under his pinioned boy as he kept pounding in and out of Lancilet's plundered place, and Rednock's forearm went back and forth, back and forth, so I knew the lad's cock was quickly stroked.

I was getting close, and Em was squealing in her pleasure, and I hoped our rhythms were all the same, that we'd all come together; all a caterwauling in the stables, so folk might think it an animal not lust that they heard. Although truth told, I think we mostly be like animals in the barn.

Then Rednock led the final song, as he thrust full hard into Lancilet's body; and of a sudden his pumping stopped and his muscles were still. But his head arched back and his ass full tense, told me his juice jetted deep into Lancilet; then the boy cried out as if he were dead, or about to be, as that creaming pulse brought on his own spurting thrill. His body quivered in his ecstasy, all a shaking and quivering and spunking wet in the hay.

His screaming fuck brought Emmy all on, and she rippled and sighed, and her cunt clenched me so hard I gave up my juice and pumped it to her, three times and another one, two. Ah my, that was good, and I held her tight.

Rednock and Lancilet fell to the floor, still joined like dogs in their middle. Rednock held the boy firm, his big chest against Lancilet's back, and the youth seemed content to be there.

I softened, and reluctantly slid from Em's cunt, and smelled the thick scent of us both. She tidied down her skirts, and turned to me with a smile in her eyes and a laugh on her lips.

"Well, sire, there's an entertainment, sure, for all of us to see. Was a fine thing to watch, was it not?"

"Fine indeed, Em, and good fun; and a fine fuck, you and me. But look, there sneak away the queen and Elayne, both hot and red flushed. You must get Elayne to tell the queen's mood, 'twould be useful to know."

"Ah yes, I see it. A knot on my skirt, is all a secret?"

"Yeay, Emmy, another secret." I could make conspiracies with Emmy, every night. "But whisper it now; look, Lancilet goes."

In the stables below, Rednock tied up his britches and put on his shirt around his back. He kissed Lancilet full on the lips, and said a few words. Lancilet smiled, and hid behind his hair. The other man brushed the hair away from Lancilet's face, and I heard him say, "Don't hide."

Emmy and I stayed still, a tidying up our clothes. We heard a hinge creak shut on a gate, and guessed that Lancilet was gone, and the queen and her maid gone too. Below us, Rednock turned to the patient horse, who had served him well as a wall. He clapped his hand on the horse's rump to make him go forward to drink, then he latched the gate shut to the bay.

"Well, that was a bonny ride, a tight boy what likes a grooming, sure." Rednock spoke his words up loud, as if he meant us to hear. "A good sight, sire?" As he left the stable I thought his whole body grinned. Rednock whistled as he went on about his business, a swagger in his walk; an emptiness in his balls, perhaps, but not for long, I didn't doubt.

I turned to Emmelyne and said, "So much for well kept secrets, Em."

"Yeay sire, we not be much good at peeping."

"Still, we proved the capability of the railing design, didn't we, Em?" That carpenter, what a fellow.

"Didn't you build this stable, Maer, the last summer gone?"

Ah me, so I did! A good design, one of my best.

"Elayne, how be the queen Miryamme, after the afternoon in the stables?"

I was keen to understand the Lady's reaction, knowledge being far better than a guess, and almost as good as making things up completely, in terms of usefulness and influence.

"She be fascinated, sire, and all a wondering at the rut of the men, of her beloved Lancilet and the splendid Rednock."

"She wants the big man, for herself?"

"Oh no, sire. You misunderstand it completely. 'Tis the animal rut up Lancilet's ass that fascinated her the most, and she wants it all herself. She not want the big man, no sire, she wants the slender boy. She wants Lancilet to love her, and take her in her darkest place."

"How do you know this so certain, Elayne? What be the clue?" I didn't doubt the maid's words, but sought the logic of it to support the truth. I could easily make up the lie.

"She whispers it, sire, over and over like she do, and all the while a brushing the doll's hair and pinning up its skirts and touching it, sire. 'I want it, I want it,' she says, all the time, over and over. 'In my bum, in my bum and I stay the virgin queen for Artur, and he always love me, love me, but the prince will love me too, he'll love my little tightness, just like his own, just like his own.'"

Elayne looked up at me, and she mimicked the queen. Naughty girl, so very cheeky, but she did it so real I couldn't stop a grin. Elayne tried a little smile back to be sure; and I smiled and tutted her on the cheek so she knew her naughtiness was safe with me.

But the queen turning to her back hole to be another tight cunt when her usual one was closed up and forbidden in her mind? A curiosity, sure, but I saw the strange sense of it, Miryamme's eyes opened on a high, cloudless day, and her body all a pleasured? A virgin queen no less, but a fuck ass be?

Well, that's a pretty notion, and I liked the idea of it. Many a man's been trapped by a woman's tight ass, and there's nothing wrong with that. I'm partial to a bit of bum myself, when the wind blows right and it's a nice plump rump. Even a prick round the front can be fine, with a boy on a ship coming with vinegar and salt from the islands.

"Encourage her to it, Elayne, whisper it into her ear. Lancilet sleeps on the queen's bed, you've told me that, so it wouldn't be much for Miryamme's hands to find his young prick one day."

I warmed to the idea, and my cock did a little bit too, as I spoke it out loud. I'd argue it a thing of state, an intrigue to know and control,

262

but I suspected myself wanting it for my own curiosity. Still, sow a seed, and people only reap what they water. If the Lady didn't want Lancilet's cock, she wouldn't hold it in her hand, let alone crouch before it, her rump up-turned and her twinkling eye all pretty

Artur the king had matters of state on his mind and defending to do. Men in long boats, with false dragens on their prows made of wood, were beginning to annoy the east. Artur was often away, marching soldiers and horse to the beaches till the foam ran red with blood on the tide, fighting the boats back.

Miryamme looked down from a high tower at Artur circling restlessly at the van of fifty horses, saddled up with the full dragen of Britten bannered and fluttering high. At the sound of a horn he raised his fist into the sky, a salute to his queen; and he rode on fast to the east.

The queen watched as the dust settled, and she watched as the high banners disappeared over the brow of a far off hill. Below, she saw Maer Maerlyn standing motionless, his long cloak trailing all his knotted cords, the folds of the sleeves twisted and wrapped about his body. He too followed the king's cavalry with his eyes. Miryamme saw his shoulders drop, and wondered what burden was on him.

She turned her doll's sightless face to the window. "Maerlyn watches, he always watches, but I hope he won't watch me. I don't like it when he watches." Miryamme whispered her stuttering words, nervously fretting her fingers and turning, turning, turning her restless hands.

Whenever Artur rode away and left her alone, Miryamme's madness crept higher and her walking dreams returned. Elayne and Emmelyne worried, and kept Maerlyn informed.

"The queen walks, sire, her eyes all open but she doesn't see a thing." Elayne explained her duty. "I follow silent and creep on my toes, so she doesn't hear and startle too. Often the Lady will return to her chamber and sleep all night in her bed until the sun rises. She doesn't remember her walking, sire, which I think is a good thing, because then she doesn't fret."

Elayne paused in her telling of the Lady's walking. "But sometimes, sire, she calls out, and the poor soul, she sounds so lost and frightened. 'I want him, I want him, I want him, to hold me in his strong arms and make the dreams all stop.' It breaks my heart in two, sire, when the king is gone and the queen gets so scared."

Emmelyne looked at Maerlyn and said, "I wonder, Maer, if the prince Lancilet might calm her, when the king is gone? He comforts her, I know he does, I've seen them together. Lancilet is a gentle man, and he holds the queen's hands still. She doesn't fuss with him, and might sleep if he calmed her."

"I think you might be right, Em. The queen is a precious thing, and the king would want her peaceful when he's gone, fighting wars."

Maerlyn pondered the suggestion, and thought it wise. Artur, in his usual practical way, had said the very same thing only a week or two previously, before he rode south, alone.

"The kingdom matters more, Maer, than my happiness with the queen. If Lancilet can calm poor Miryamme's restless hands and soften her dreams, then perhaps it's for the best."

Artur had looked at his loyal friend. "Miryamme's madness is not her own making, and I owe her quietness, at least."

So Maerlyn conspired. He enlisted the groom Rednock to promise the young prince a regular pleasure, yet encouraged him to visit the queen, all allowed. Elayne left a door open at night, and lay facing the wall as footsteps crept silently past.

"Lady, are you woke?" Lancilet's voice was a low whisper. Long curtains shifted slowly in a light breeze through the window, and a rising moon was cloud braided and bright.

"Cousin, is that you? Quietly, quietly, don't make a sound. Little mice creep, they creep so lightly, their tiny feet on the floor. Oh Lancilet, is that you, is it you?"

"Hush, Lady, don't worry. Let me look after your hair, let me brush it."

Lancilet sat behind Miryamme on her bed, and took up her brush, rhythmically combing it through her hair. As he did so, her fingers that so nervously clutched at the sheet became still, and she took in a long, shuddering breath. Lancilet brushed her hair some more, and he laid his hand over hers.

After a moment, their fingers entwined, and after another moment, Miryamme turned her head to his, and they kissed. It was a slow gentle kiss, but before long she turned her body some more, and

265

wriggled up closer to him, and the kiss became hungrier, her tongue darting, tasting his lips.

Lancilet's arms wrapped around Miryamme's delicate body, and she was fragile like a flower whose seeds blow away on a breeze. Lancilet was not as strong and solid as Artur, but he was there. Miryamme began her restless stroke of Lancilet's skin, but he held her hands firmly, and calmed her.

"Miryamme, my Lady, what do you desire, what is your wish?"

"Do you want me, want me, Lancilet? Oh, you can't take me, take me; not where I save myself for my king, not there." She pushed back away from Lancilet on her bed, and her eyes grew big and wide. "Oh, Lancilet, Lancilet, if I kneel before you, will you want my other place, my other place?"

She looked over her shoulder at the youth, and made it so sweet, so every day, to offer her sweet bottom to him.

"You've taken Rednock's big thing inside yourself, I saw you, I saw you. I saw you scream and beg, you wanted him so much, so much."

Miryamme looked at the man on her bed, and saw how his cheeks were flushed. She bent down and brushed her hand against his rising cock. "I want it, I want it. She shall not have it, not this lovely boy. She won't. His filthy sister. He doesn't want me, doesn't want me."

She turned to Lancilet and said, as if it were just a bird flying by, or the morning rain hiding the hills, "He just wants to fuck his sister. It's all he wants to do. But I'm his virgin queen, he can't have me." She smiled her beautiful smile. "Oh Lancilet. Can we play?"

Miryamme undid the buttons on her shift and it fell away from her body, revealing her little high breasts and her pale skin.

"Come touch, Lancilet, come close. See how the skin of my breasts is so soft, so very, very soft? My king spills his seed all over my breasts and I rub it all in and I smell of him. But he only does it when I call for his sister. He doesn't do it for me, not for me. No, not me, ohh no, not me." She caught herself, and made herself stop.

Miryamme held Lancilet's head to her breast, stroking his long silken hair like a cat purrs to be stroked, and his hair fell soft like gentle rain on her skin. Lancilet touched the shallow valley between her breasts with his lips, breathing her in. He tasted her with his tongue, wanting to find a trace of the king, but all he found was her faint perfume, a delicate taste left like pollen from a wandering bee.

"Take of your clothes, Lancilet, let me see. I'll kiss you too, lovely Lancilet."

As her arousal grew, and as the prince took off his clothes to show her his slim body, Miryamme's eyes grew big but her breath grew slow, and she fell into a calm place where her restless mind rested, her nervous flutter stilled, and her torment slowed and stopped.

Lancilet took her in his arms and they held each other, gently, softly, lying side by side on the bed. Miryamme closed her eyes and found a quiet place.

Lancilet was gentle with her, and she was still in his arms, her frantic mind calm for a moment, her nervous fingers quiet, holding his. Miryamme's arousal grew, and she rolled on to her belly, offering up her slim haunches to his eyes. She kneeled before Lancilet, as she had seen him kneel before Rednock the groom.

"Do you like it cousin, my cunny all pretty and fair? Come kiss it and taste it with your tongue."

Miryamme pushed herself back, opening her legs and revealing the glistening folds and lips of her sex. Lancilet licked her sweet cunt, placing his hot mouth over her centre. She pushed back against him with a low moan. He sucked her lips into his mouth and Miryamme sighed, a long shuddering sigh. "More, oh more, sweet Lancilet."

She reached back between her legs with two fingers, pulling the folds back from her clit, stroking herself with her own special pace, building up her arousal. "Ooo yes, ooo, more, yes, more."

Lancilet took her sticky wet fingers into his mouth, sucking on them, biting little nibbles on her flesh. Pulling back, Miryamme swirled her fingers to her clit again. "Hmmm, uunh, uunh, more, more."

As she pushed back against Lancilet's mouth, Miryamme widened the spread of her legs, and as she did so the enticing star of her anus was exposed. Lancilet licked across the tight pucker, and Miryamme gasped. The sound encouraged him, and Lancilet licked again, followed by a quick point of his tongue, thrusting in. Miryamme moaned with slow pleasure, and Lancilet pressed once more, forcing the tip of his tongue into her body. She arched back against him, wanting the sensation deeper, inside her, sweeter and full.

"No man has been there, no man." Miryamme's voice was a whisper. "But Elayne has, my naughty Elayne has. She knows. My saucy maid, she's kissed my bum. She's a good girl, she's kissed me and licked me, and stuck her finger in."

She looked back at Lancilet with her sweet smile.

"Lancilet, will you put your lovely thing into my bum? I might scream if I like it, just like you do with the groom, with his giant rod all hidden inside."

Lancilet's cock bounced high at Miryamme's words, whether from the promise of the groom or the promise of her ass, it didn't matter. The high scent of her lust was upon him, and the soft slick of her fingers between her lips all nice.

Lancilet looked around, and there on a shelf was a pot full of oil, a candle wick floating in it, guttering and flickering in the slow air. He wet his fingers to put out the wick, and swirled the oil to spread the heat. Dipping his fingers into the pot, Lancilet slicked his cock with the oil. The moonlight glistened and warm drops dripped onto Miryamme's thighs.

Feeling the liquid drops on her skin, Miryamme thought it like the warm spill of Artur's juice on her, but for once Morgayne was far, far away; and the queen was comforted. "It's like he always loves me, loves me, my skin all lovely and soft."

She gripped a pillow in her two hands, and braced herself like Lancilet did in the stables, making herself ready for his cock.

Lancilet poured a little oil onto the hot gasp of her ass-hole and circled it around, gently penetrating her bottom, slowly pulling back.

Miryamme sighed, pushing up onto his fingers; spreading herself wider, ready for the slow entry of his length.

"Mmmm," she crooned, and Lancilet placed the tip of his cock against her hot centre, waiting as the muscle slowly opened up to his tease. "Ohh, it hurts, it hurts… keep it in, keep it in… ohh, it doesn't hurt anymore." Miryamme let her body relax, accepting the hot fill inside her, letting Lancilet slide in to her depths. He pulled back, and placed another finger of oil where his shaft entered her body, pushing forward again, easing in.

"Ahh ahh," she gasped, as a sudden stab of pain shocked her, and Miryamme locked against him, holding the pain inside herself for a moment before she relaxed. "Ooo yes, that's right, that's…"

Lancilet silenced her with a long, aching thrust, as suddenly all resistance was gone; and he filled her as she'd never been filled before. A long, keening moan came from deep in Miryamme's throat, as all the pain she'd kept bottled up, all the loss she'd never found, found release in this fuck, this deep cleft into the depths of her. She never knew she was so deep. Miryamme opened herself up and let Lancilet take her. So deep.

Miryamme pushed back against the slim cock shafting into her centre, and Lancilet found a steady rhythm, answering every aching moan from the queen with a quick grunt of his own, swathing long slides into her depths. He bent over her back, resting his weight on one hand on the bed, cupping a breast with the other, embracing Miryamme as he filled her tight hole.

An urgency for each other began, the slide of his cock into her passage was faster now, the oil heating from the friction and the heat of their flesh. His cock pistoned in, then pulled out. Miryamme's fingers flickered over her tight little bud as Lancilet fucked her. With a cry, like some night bird far off, her orgasm peaked, and she fell forward, dragging Lancilet down upon her back, his prick deep inside her, gripped by her tightness, her grasp.

With her body all still, but her tight place gripping him and pulling him in, Lancilet thrust into Miryamme. His rhythm was his own now, a deep, hot pressure from the base of his spine coiling into the tightening sac of his balls, urging his cock deeper, deeper, deeper into her ass. With a loud, keening cry of his own, like an answering bird to her calling, Lancilet made one final thrust and his juice exploded inside her.

Miryamme turned her face to his, wide wonder in her eyes. She smiled her little smile, and for once in her fractured life, Miryamme was peaceful and filled.

"Can I have a little bit more, sweet Lancilet, on another day, another lovely day?"

Hey nonny nonny, our little plan worked.

"My Lady sleeps quiet, Maer Maerlyn." Elayne sat with Emmy and me, a magick and his maids, reporting back on the passings in the night, all in the Lady's chamber. "She and the prince Lancilet, they do rut, sire; and all of their sounds make my own finger busy, it's a happy sound."

271

Elayne's eyes were near as wide as the queen's when she said it, and the flush on her neck so sweet. I glanced across at Em, and she all nicely red too. My old prick hardened at the thought of it all. Em saw the shuffle, and opened her mouth just a little. She didn't say a word, didn't need to, not Emmy.

"She's stopped walking, sire, all in her sleep," Elayne went on. "The prince curls behind her, and the queen all happy and warm. She's quiet, sire. Even her doll sits quiet, the queen rarely picks it up."

So the dilly dolly doesn't even look? 'Twas a better thing even than I thought.

When Artur the king returned with foreign blood in his eyes and on his skin, I told him his queen rested pretty, and his cousin worth his keep.

"The boy make happy my queen, Maer? When I cannot?"

Artur sat quietly, pondering this little thing, all a wondering, no doubt. He looked up at me, his eyes mournful and sad, the heavy weight of his campaign a weighing him down. After a moment, he shook his head, and his eyes narrowed.

"For the best, then, Maer. Sounds 'tis best for Miryamme, my queen." He got to his feet. "No matter, what's done needs to be done." Artur turned away from me, to his kinging business.

"Knot another string to your cloak, Maer Maerlyn, and that Emmelyne, tell her to knot her underskirts too."

He laughed, as he saw my puzzled look. "What, you thought I never knew what you two do? Ah Maerlyn, I do my teacher proud!"

Who taught this man? This king knows my secrets better than any woman does.

"Come, Maerlyn, my good friend, come eat with me. We need a quiet time."

Artur looked at me with a distant look in his eyes.

"I feel a storm coming, Maer, I feel a storm. I know it in my bones."

And he looked to the south as he said it, and there was a greyness in his eyes, as he gazed long away to the south.

I was there.

When Lancilet the king's cousin became an invisible prince, and Artur the king turned a blind eye, I was there.

The Well-worn Path

"Walk on, go through."

The young woman spurred her horse into the water, fording the river where a well defined track ran along both banks in opposite directions, clearly marking a safe place to cross. The water came up to the horse's chest and the surge of it splashed up and over the woman's clothes; a light shift clinging to her belly and to her breasts, lush and full.

The horse held its head high; the woman held hers higher, tall and proud, commanding the horse with her own strength and grace; a proud woman on a high horse.

Her father had given her the stallion five years before, on her fifteenth birthday.

"Ride like the wind, Lilith, never fall."

"I'll never fall, Father. You'll ride beside me, always beside me."

Lilith rode as fast as the wind, her blonde hair flying, her cheeks red flushed, the daughter of the king. Breathless and excited, she would jump down from the horse and throw herself into her father's arms, reaching up to kiss him on the lips.

"Artur, don't indulge her. Let her fall. She'll learn faster that way."

Morgayne watched her daughter, knowing the girl was just like she was, could never be taught; but would learn far too much all by herself, and with her father's natural born skill.

Lilith learned to control the steed, eighteen hands high, effortlessly, and never fell.

Standing close to his mother, Lilith's brother Mordant glowered. He could manage horses too, but it was always his will against theirs, and they fought him. He favoured his mother, was dark like her darkness, and stood watching. Lilith moved always in light; Mordant was always in shadow, hiding the blaze on his face.

"Walk on, go through."

She bent to the horse's neck, whispering in its ear. They reached the far bank, and she urged her mount fast up the incline, away from the river. At the top of the slope she wheeled around, looking back towards Tyntangel, far to the south by the sea. She looked on her distant home for a long while, before turning to the north. I'm coming, she thought, are you ready?

The horse and its rider were the only moving things to be seen on the high bank of the river, the grassland smooth to the next ridge. Paths where the small creatures ran criss-crossed the valley, losing themselves amongst rivulets and curling around clustered trees. The air was still, late summer warm. High above, a goshawk circled.

Lilith pulled up the horse, and took off the light cloth of her shift, tugging it up over her head, baring her full breasts, golden brown. She rode uncovered whenever she could, loving the fresh wind on her skin, the rising heat in her breasts. Her skin was tanned, with a faint fine hair on her arms like gold shimmered dust. She twisted the long mane of her hair like a skein of wool her grandmother taught her, tying it with two cords to prevent it tangling in the galloping wind.

She spurred the horse on, and stood glorious tall on the stirrups with her arms outstretched, opening her body to the sky. She rode like this for twenty breaths, her lungs aching as she sucked in air to cool her throbbing heart. She screamed, ripping up sound from her gut, a primal shriek of a woman so alive, a raw thrill from deep in her throat. *I'm coming, are you ready for me!*

The horse slowed, whinnied, and shook its big head, settling to a high trot. Lilith lowered herself to the saddle, her cunt awake and wet, soul fucked arousal heavy in her breasts, her hard brown nipples so tight. She was all rhythmic motion with lust in her gut and a hungry clamour in her head. The king's daughter, coming to claim her crown.

Lilith cooled, reigning in her passion but knowing the strength of it and what she wanted. She was her mother's daughter, too, and Morgayne had taught her cauldron and hex, stone and tree. The Goddess ran in her blood, and Lilith knew it.

Lilith and her horse walked on the well-worn path, heading north to the heart of Artur's country. She followed the map her father had given her, drawn from his memory and marked out in days; the distance each day a good rider could travel.

"You might need a day or two longer, Lilith. The map marks my days."

"I might need a day or two shorter, Father. The map doesn't show all the ways, not the ones my mother taught me."

Morgayne looked on, amused, seeing their daughter challenge her father with her different paths, her secret ways.

Artur glanced across at his sister, a steady gaze in his eyes and a wry smile, as if to say, Look at this creature we have made, she's taken the best of us and makes us both better.

Mordant looked on, then turned away.

Lilith rode north at a steady pace. Seven days on she came to the southern edge of a wide low water, a maze of marshes and the high encroaching sea. The place was crossed by a number of ancient paths, stretching out across the bog and the hundred waters, made of timber plank, cut rushes and cord, packed tight enough to bear her horse's weight. She dismounted and wrapped a cloak around herself, for a slow drizzling rain crept in and the horizon came down around her, holding the land close and the sky closer.

"Well, my friend," Lilith said to the horse, "this will be a dull, wet day for a walk. Let's on."

At first she led the stallion by its halter. Their passage across the marsh was slow, dictated by the animal's ability to make its way over the uneven surface of the track. He grew uneasy, surrounded by so much water, his eyes wide and ears laid back. She walked beside him now, calming the beast with a low sing-song croon, her hand on its neck.

The main path was clear to see, the grass underfoot pressed low with many travellers' feet, and they made slow, steady progress. After a time, they rested on a small raised island, covered with short grass for the horse and small standing stones for Lilith's back. She pondered how many times her father might have rested in this place, making his way south to his sister and his children; making his way north to his kingdom and the demands of men.

As she rested, a strange hush came over the place. The croak and cry of marsh birds fell silent. Her horse whinnied and stamped a hoof twice.

"Hush now, be still." Lilith's voice was a low command, and her senses heightened in the preternatural silence. She stood as still as the stone she had leaned against, straining her eyes and ears in the mist. Alerted by a soft splash, as if someone had kicked a small pebble into the water, not far off, Lilith opened wide her senses and heard the beating of her horse's heart, deep inside its chest. She calmed her own heart and slowed her breath, whispering, "Walk by, don't see."

A small cloaked figure emerged from the mist, about twenty arm lengths away. It seemed to glide across the grass, its cloak long, down to its feet. Lilith could not make out any features, the face was hidden within a deep hood. The figure kept on and passed them by, the only sound a soft swish of the cloak's hem as it brushed along the ground.

Curious, Lilith waited a moment, then followed. The path the lone traveller took departed the main path at near ninety degrees, and Lilith began to walk west, slowly following. She maintained the same distance between herself and the silent walker, keeping her eyes on the glimmer ahead, her hand gripping the rein of her horse behind. She did not creep but followed openly, unable to quiet the horse's plod. But the beast made little sound, the grass on this track longer, less worn.

The figure ahead gave no sign of her presence, and moved steadily on. Lilith saw the marks of small feet light on the ground, bent stalks of grass slowly straightening from the lightness of the gliding weight. The walker ahead was smaller than Lilith, who shortened her pace so she wouldn't catch up.

The little procession continued, and the ground solidified beneath their feet. The marsh world with its water splash and a hover of wind fell behind. Ahead of them, Lilith became aware of a steady low sound, and guessed they were nearing the sea.

The misting rain stopped, and as they walked on the cloud lifted. Cresting a rise, Lilith turned and looked back, where the silent world of the marshy lake was hidden in a wide bank of mist. The path they had trodden trailed back into the grey veil and was lost.

Ahead of them, Lilith saw the path leading down towards a line of dunes, and beyond them the sea, grey distant to the horizon, a wide plain of flat sand, the water far off. Lilith had heard her father speak of the huge tides where the sea pressed up between his land and the wilderness of Wales. She guessed she was seeing the broad estuary where the Sevyrn ran wide to the endless Atlant.

She observed the figure in front of her climb a high dune and look out to the sea. The sea-watcher pulled back the hood from her head, and Lilith saw a white coil of hair and a delicate, pale face; a woman older than she, and smaller. Yet somehow the woman seemed taller than she stood, a strength in her stance that belied her small frame.

Lilith didn't move, didn't speak, and stood close to her horse, its hot life pulsating under the calm of her hand resting on its neck. She stood a stone's long throw from the woman on the dune.

The woman turned her gaze back towards Lilith and the horse, and Lilith saw a puzzlement on her face, as if she were seeing them for the first time.

"Horse, what you? I felt a big life walk behind me through the marsh, following along like lost." The woman stretched out her hand towards the horse. She clicked her tongue, "Tch, tch," and the horse stepped towards her, its head low and ears back, nervous but compelled.

Lilith stood very still, barely breathing, watching this strange greeting.

The stallion went up to the woman and nuzzled her shoulder with its nose. Lilith watched how the woman took up the hanging rein, turned the leather over in her hands, and saw how she looked at the saddle, and the panniers strapped with Lilith's load.

"What you, boy, out here alone? You're fine bred, sure, a noble horse, a big grey thing. What manner of man left you wander here, all a by yourself?"

Lilith was perplexed. Could this woman not see her, even though she stood clear on the path, her shadow stretched dark behind her on the ground? She remembered her whisper, when first the figure appeared in the mist. Walk by, don't see, but didn't think her hex so strong. She stepped forward, and the sudden movement must have broken the trancing air, for the woman started, taking a step backward in her surprise.

"Who are you, girl, who hides in plain sight? What nobility, who rides this fine horse?"

Lilith walked towards the other woman, her hands held out before her, palms upwards, showing no weapons, no tricks, no lies. The woman's gaze as she approached was intense, questions flickering all unasked, Lilith's mystery a clear surprise.

"I am Lilith, daughter of the king, daughter of the Red Morgayne. Who are you, sightless Mother, who questions me, yet cannot see me?"

Hearing Lilith's reply, the older woman went absolutely still, her eyes suddenly blank and gone, her breath a quick gasp. Slowly she returned, taking a shuddering breath.

"By the Goddess, how could I see?" She talked to herself as much as replying to Lilith. "I could not see your mother, Morgayne; and you their daughter… has it been that long already? Is it nearly time?"

The woman slowed her rushing words. "I remember you now, a poppet, and your brother. I foretold your brother, but never saw you to tell. How old now, Lilith?"

"Twenty years, Mother. But you, you know me. I do not remember you."

"Nym Nymue, child; who cannot see."

Nymue turned away from Lilith. "By the Goddess, I turn away and the girl is gone, I cannot see her, I cannot remember her. Yet when I turn back, there she is."

She reached out to touch Lilith's hand. "No ghost, but you might be."

Lilith let Nymue puzzle around her, but didn't speak. She had heard tell of the High Priestess, Nym Nymue, and knew this woman before her was a powerful manifestation of the Goddess, serving the land, despite her small size. Lilith also knew there was no love lost, no love found, between Nymue and her mother, so held her voice, silenced every question she had.

"Come, Lilith, come sit with me. I'll tell you why I'm here, why there's a well-worn path to this place."

Nymue told her of the five tumbling waves, for this was where she nearly drowned, and her hair turned white. She told Lilith of her long prenticeship of stone and maze, wing and wood, and some of the magick made with Maer Maerlyn's help.

She told Lilith how she made Scalibet and placed the knife in the rock, and how Artur took it from the rock and was made king.

But Nymue didn't tell Lilith how she and Maerlyn tricked Gorloys' men and made them see faces, so Uthur could bed Ygraine and Artur make. No, she didn't tell Lilith that.

Nymue crept around the edge of her fear. She saw the girl making her way strong already, and saw the king's blood in her. The king's blood, twice; once through her father, twice through her mother. Nymue sucked in her dread, and faced her fear.

"Lilith, is there love in you?"

Lilith looked at the woman in front of her, and knew they were equal service for the Goddess. Two peas from a pod, could be; yet look - pride and fear, curiosity and dread. Nymue's eyes gave everything away, yet revealed nothing, nothing.

Lilith felt a little prickle of fear on the back of her neck, an itch. Was she destined too, to walk her own way, no-one knowing?

"A strange question, Lady. Why you ask it?"

"I see the future streaming back, Lilith, so much predicted. So much true. Yet your mother, the Black Morgayne, I never predicted her. Nor her love for her brother, your father, simple and true. They both confounded me. Their love blinded me."

She looked into Lilith's eyes, and held them tight with the force of her gaze.

"Your parents, Lilith. Their simple love confounded me. I could not see it, did not know it. They unravelled me." She reached out to touch Lilith's cheek, and the tenderness of her touch was like a mother's touch, full of wonder.

"I see your brother, Lilith. I tell his future, and see treachery and vengeance there."

Nymue drew a simple circle in the sand. "But when I turn my head away from you, you're gone, utterly hidden." She looked at the girl. "I can't see you at all, Lilith. I don't know what you do.

It was a confession.

For Lilith, a revelation.

"So you hope, Nymue, as only a woman can hope, that whatever I do, I do it with love in my heart?

"It's all I can do, yes. Hope the pure love that made you, makes your own love better than theirs, even stronger."

Lilith pondered the Lady's words, and thought of the love in her life. She smiled, and Nymue's heart leapt.

"Love. Do you have it, Lady, in your eyes?"

Nymue thought of the tall, gangling man, and her eyes creased, and she too smiled. Lilith's heart leapt.

So the two women forgot they were destined, and talked about other things.

In the morning, when they woke, back against back lying next to the fire, they each looked towards different horizons. They both looked forward, they both looked back, and this pivot became a spiral. Time stopped, time started.

As Nym Nymue made her way back into the mist, following her well-worn path leading to the Isle of Glas, she turned back to see Lilith astride her mount, the morning sun glowing on her naked torso, her golden skin glowing with life. Nymue raised a hand, farewell; then turned away and the girl was gone from her sight. As she walked down the path, Nymue realised Lilith had never answered her question, Is there love in you? No matter. Not knowing her destiny made her free.

Lilith sat astride her tall horse, watching the proud little woman walk down the path into the mist. She looked to the grass to the north, and saw no path to follow. Lilith kicked in her spurs, and the stallion surged forward.

I'm coming. Are you ready for me, my father?

Lilith in the Valley

Several days on from the meeting in the marsh and hearing Nymue's story, Lilith came upon the end of a valley unlike any other she'd seen before. The sides of it were steep, trees growing close together, but without the usual gaps and clear spaces where paths ran, where animals made their way and hunters followed. There were no hunters here.

The valley was still and quiet, with no sign of habitation, no sign of life. A single thin track, barely visible, ran alongside a little stream, no wider than a long step or a short jump. The stream was clear, swiftly flowing, circling eddies and whirlpools flickering and flashing under the bright sun. Coloured pebbles and rocks lay just below the water's surface, making tiny rapids, little waterfalls.

She bent down, splashing cool water on her face. The water in the stream was cool, refreshing, so she stripped off her chemise and bared her breasts as she loved to do. She bent low to the water, grazing her nipples with the cool flow, and laughed with delight as her nipples puckered tight, pulling up an ache from inside her chest. On a whim, she quickly stripped herself naked and lay in the stream, letting its rippling flow swirl around her body.

She lay there for a moment, her feet facing downstream, the water cascading over her head, her breasts, her body, cooling herself after the morning's long ride. With a slow curiosity she held the weight of her full breasts in her palms, savouring the flesh, enjoying the sensation of her fingers rolling the tight nubs of her nipples. Aware of the rushing force of the stream, she smiled to herself, then rolled onto her front, letting the fullness of her breasts hang down. The water raised goose bumps on her flesh.

Suddenly, she spun around so she was facing downstream, and she crouched and opened her legs so the rippling push and flow of the water caressed her opening core, with her legs spread wide. She opened herself to the water's caress and delighted in its ebb and flow, tingling in her belly with a low, heavy ache.

"Ohh, tumbling stream, you've got a hundred tiny hands! Mmmm, that's a sweet tingle."

She laughed at her silliness, delighting in the water's buffeting batter on her body. She touched herself, opening her lips to the watery play, and wriggled her body to direct the flow against her sex.

After a long while, she stood up in the stream, then stepped to the bank, brushing droplets from her body, brushing water down her legs. Bundling her clothes up and carelessly stuffing them into one of the carry bags tied to the saddle, Lilith stood gloriously naked.

She led her horse down the path, and was soon dry in the warm sun. Lilith walked on, in no hurry, enjoying the gentle tickle of a soft breeze on her skin, the glow of heat from the high sun. Behind her, she felt the gentle power of her steed, its big life beating steady in its chest. Every now and then she felt a warm stickiness between her legs, a high arousal, just from being alive.

Tonight, Lilith knew, when she stopped and wrapped herself in a blanket under the moon, she would take the slim dildo she'd made from rare ivory, and fuck herself with it, fast. She'd writhe and moan, finding her high pleasure, after being sexually alive all day.

Her pleasure slowly built inside her, growing heavy in her belly, swaying heavy in her breasts, the muscles of her thighs tight from her long ride, the muscles of her ass firm from her long walk.

She walked on down the valley, waiting for the evening, her whole body thrumming alive. Lilith's senses heightened, and she felt an animal lust, some instinctive thing in her being. She might not wait until evening.

The valley curved and widened, the stream now a body length from bank to bank, and deeper. The path was no wider though, so Lilith guessed few people came here. The place was quiet, just the hum of wind in high branches and the deeper burble of the brook.

Lilith stopped. Ahead of her there was a wide clearing, the trees surrounding the space cut down. Up from the stream, on a small rise, she saw a small cottage, stone walled and thatched. It looked well kept, the thatch still pale in the sun. The path ahead of her curved up to its door, and she saw the same path curve off to the north.

"That's curious," she said, and perhaps the horse listened. "Both paths meet at the door."

She looked around, but could see no sign of occupation. The two paths were lightly covered with short grass, but Lilith could not tell if feet last passed the day before, or a week before, or a month.

"Come on, let's see."

Lilith turned to her horse, and it did not seem afraid, even in this uncertain place. Trusting its animal instincts, she stepped forward, slowly walking to the door. As she approached the building, she felt a sweet heaviness in the base of her belly, and her nipples thickened as if cold, even though the air was warm. Her heart beat a little faster, and she instinctively touched her horse's neck, to feel its hot heat and animal flesh.

"Ah, I see it."

The reason for the thick sex magick in the air became clear. Carved on the door, near its full height, was a Na Gig, a full carven image of a woman's sex. The slit of it was obvious, and the lips all rubbed and smooth. Lilith ran her fingers down the length of the portal cunt, and her whole body throbbed.

"Sweet goodness, there's power here. Someone's made this, and grown it powerful too."

She looked down, and there on the door stone was an offering and a lock, a rush from the stream below, wrapped with twists of hair, blond and red. She knew that to gain entry here, she too would need to make an offering. Given her heightened arousal all day, Lilith thought that an easy thing; standing hot naked before the door already, she'd brought herself here.

She looked down at her gold burnished torso and thought it offering enough. She trailed a finger down her thigh, realising her full naked walk had exposed the flesh of her legs to a touch from the sun, and her skin was hotter there.

Lilith turned back to her horse, and led it to a wooden stall in the lee of the house. A rider here, regularly, she thought, seeing good straw and a wooden pail for water. She unsaddled the horse, placing her packs and panniers on a stone shelf, then spent a good time currying down the animal, brushing away its sweat and dust, until she gleamed with her own sweat from the effort.

Lilith let the bridle fall. "Go graze, my friend," she said softly, knowing the beast had sense and would return to the quiet safety of this place. The horse whinnied and shook its big head. She watched with joy as he galloped once in a single big circuit around the cottage, as if to close them in and keep them safe.

"Now me," Lilith whispered, making her way back down to the brook, where she found three stone steps down into a hollowed out bathing place. She walked into the water, and it surrounded her. She submerged her whole body and washed away the dust and sweat, rubbing her limbs, squeezing water through her hair, cleansing herself.

After a long, languid moment, she climbed back out of the water and walked dripping towards the cottage. Reaching the flagstone in front of the door, she reverently bent down and picked up the totem, touching it to her lips, then held it between her breasts. She placed her palm against the door and with a gentle push it opened, swinging silently on greased iron hinges. As she touched the wood, Lilith felt a deep throb of energy in her belly, warm and full. Her breasts felt heavy, her nipples tight. She cupped her breasts in her hands, and offered them up to the Na Gig, a lustful holy mother, a sister, a daughter too, an old crone and a virgin child.

"Accept this my body, let me in."

Her voice was clear and steady, seeking entry to this sacred place, offering the one thing that was hers to give. Her body, pure as water, as bright as the sun, cleansed by the stream outside. She stepped inside.

It was a small room, lit by two small window openings either side of the door. Lilith saw simple benches below each window, an open hearth with a black hanging pot, and a central table, wood carved and smooth. Around the wall, at regular intervals, were a series of rush holders, empty now. Below each holder was a dark pool of dropped pitch and ash, from their burning.

She stood quietly at the door, letting her eyes adjust to the low light, letting her senses adjust to traces of sensation, a lingering something in the air. She took in a deep breath, inhaling some languid scent, a faint perfume. There was something familiar to Lilith in the room, but she couldn't quite catch it, some flittering thing. Goose bumps thrilled down her arms, and her breasts felt heavy, pushing tight ice into her nipples from deep within her chest. Her cunt bloomed, and she felt a pulse deep within herself.

Outside, she heard a slow clop of hooves as the horse returned to its shelter. A soft wind brushed across the grass behind her, a susurrus of sound. Lilith placed the totem from the threshold on a shelf by the door, and stepped into the building. She pulled the door to behind her, the wooden handle worn smooth. She felt a familiar touch from the wood, as if her mother's fingers lingered there.

Lilith's heart thumped low, as she realised what this place was.

"Mother, Father, is this where you come?"

There was no reply, but her vision grew sharp. Between her legs Lilith was wet, a sweet intensity of sensation aching within her, curling around the base of her body, pulsing with her heart beat. Her slow lust, which been building all day, was a settling thing on her soul. She shivered, and ran her hands languidly over her body, feeling her curves, her small waist. "Ohh," she sighed, in love with herself and wanting more, her own limbs tangled in his.

"Ohh, Father, is this where you find her?"

"Mother?"

Lilith took slow steps, one by one, around the table, running her fingers along the smooth wood where her parents' hands had touched and their breath fell. She walked towards the inner door to the next room, her arms and legs prickling, her slow conjure building.

Outside, a shimmy of ripples flickered across the pool and the tall reeds quivered. The sun sank low, and a blaze of colour glowed pink and lilac as dusk settled. Small creatures moved, wary.

She pushed open the door, her heart beating faster. Sweet fuck, their lingering lust reached the back of her throat like smoke, and she tasted them like she'd kissed her mother's cheek and kissed her father's lips, so many times before.

She'd never tasted them like this before, never so sweet.

Standing in the room, in the chamber where high magick was conjured and spun by her parents, Lilith could taste and smell the beloved love that made her, and the beloved corruption that made her brother.

She understood how their two twinned lives had twisted around each other and grown; curling together in their mother's womb, until the wizard held her tiny body, pulling Lilith into the light, and her brother, Mordant, to hide in the shadows.

She fell backwards onto the bed, their bed, where her parents came with their forbidden love, their lust for each other, two children from the same womb. Lilith had shared a womb, but she had no interest in Mordant her brother. No, her beloved man was the High King, and she his daughter would sit beside him, to be the next queen.

Lilith had heard tell of Miryamme the Queen, her father's bride, with her feeble head and her empty womb; but the kingdom had no need for another heir. She, Lilith, was the eldest child, lifted first from Morgayne her mother's body by the mage, the fool, Maerlyn.

She knew Maerlyn was no fool. She'd watched him and her mother too, and knew in her bones there was a strange love between them. She could not fathom it, but saw it turning on a long look here and a secret smile there.

So her mother the Red Morgayne, a betraying witch, loyal to herself first, all dark and hidden (and what loyalty to the thin man?), but still the object of Artur's lust. Lilith remembered Nymue's question, Is there love in you? Hers was that pure love as only a daughter could love. Morgayne could slake Artur's lust, but Lilith would calm him with her daughter's love, and be fierce for him, too.

She pushed herself further up the bed until her head rested on pillows, where her parents kissed. Lilith lay back, her body still warm from the sun, her flesh clean and sweet from the stream. She closed her eyes, and her other senses sharpened, the scrape of her fingers loud on the sheet, the scent of her sex faint and lingering; or was that memory?

She gave herself up to the thickening air, the swirl of sex magick that permeated the room, the walls, the very light that streamed from high windows, the conjuring there of her parents; she could smell it. A child born of this would be powerful indeed, and Lilith remembered how her words alone hid her from Nym Nymue.

She knew then she was destiny, unseen, the fate of kings in her hands. Imagine, then, her deeds!

Lilith smiled as she caressed herself, bringing her own sex magick into the heady mix in the room, mingling with the shades of Artur and Morgayne as the air remembered them. She sighed, and thought she felt a touch; but it was her own hand on her breast, its palm pressing hard against her nipple. She moaned and thought she felt a kiss, but it was her own fingers spreading her lips apart and fluttering deep into her sliding wetness.

As her passion rose the sky outside darkened and a gentle rain began. Lilith's voice cried out like a bird's and the wind rose, swirling through the high trees, making tiny waves upon the pool, shaking leaves that twisted and fell to the ground. Animals scurried, and the horse in its shelter stamped a single hoof.

Lilith came and the thunder cracked, and the rain came beating down.

Far south, Morgayne looked up and a tiny smile creased her mouth and eyes.

"What is it, Mother?" Mordant asked, but didn't expect to be told.

Far north, Artur looked up and said, "A storm's coming, Maer."

"Best be sheltered, sire," Maerlyn replied, tumbling dice from a cup.

"It's too late for that, Maer, too late."

To the east, Nymue looked up. Is she this strong, already? I'll never see her now.

To the west, the sea shuddered ceaselessly against the land, rising and falling like breath.

The King's Daughter

I was there.

When the king's daughter, Lilith, rode beside him on a high horse and blood be spilled, I was there.

Conjures begin slowly, they always do. The one of which I tell started with a little shower of rain on a clear day. Or am I getting mixed up with the weather outside? I rolled the dice and forgot to count, clank, clink. "Best be sheltered, sire."

"It's too late for that, Maer, too late." Artur's eyes were distant to the south, and my guts twisted, expecting then to see Morgayne and her slow hands in a matter of days. I knew that look, that longing look. I had it too, but called it my stupidity. Who did I think I was? She the Red Morgayne, with her blood on my hands, scrub, scrub; and her black hair hanging me still, round my neck.

The rain continued continuous, out of season and unusual, but I thought little of it. I knew Nym Nymue controlled mist and fog and the occasional pond, but the last I knew, she was content in Glas. So the rain continued on, 'twas three dull days to my count.

The king was slow and listless, wondering ways to surprise the heathens with their ships, and calling armies to his side. Lot came down from Orkens with his sturdy boys, the sons of Morgayse the king's half sister: Gawaine, Gaheris and Gareth. More red hair than was acceptable or predictable, but the pretty maids from the village didn't seem to mind. They rode on big horses, and made a lot of noise. Good fighters though, all could swing a sword.

The rain thickened, and from the south it came until the third day it was thick grey cloud down low, driving hard against the skin.

I heard a call from the guard on the zig-zag path. "What horse there, walks on alone? Look there, on the path."

I went curious to the palisade, and sure enough, emerging from the driving rain, there walked a slow horse, a big grey. Artur beside me started. "I know that horse. 'Tis Lilith's that she's ridden since fifteen years. Why here?"

The rain bedraggled the creature, yet on it came.

"Groom, go to the horse, bring it to me." Artur called for Rednock, his best man of horse, a whisperer; could calm any beast. But the beast needed calming not. I saw Rednock go to it, to take up its halter, but I saw him step quickly back, a look of fear on his face.

He looked up, and called to the king. "The horse, sire, 'tis ridden, but I see the rider not." Rednock was uncertain. "I'll not touch it, lord."

And as he spoke and stepped away, I heard a high laugh, full of glee, and the hair on my neck rose quick. I knew that laugh.

I glanced to Artur, and his face was split with a broad smile, full quick and bright. He stepped forward, his arms all wide, and he laughed too.

"Girl, what you? Come down from your horse, sprite, come kiss your father! Keep one for Maerlyn too, on his cheek."

And sure there, like a shadow or a shade, I saw a cloak lifted strange from the back of the saddle where it was rolled, and it was pulled up and took on a human shape. As it fell around Lilith's shoulders, for it was no other but she who rode before us, I glimpsed the hiding of her naked flesh as it coalesced and shimmered, and I saw how it was done, her conjuring spell.

Full naked on the horse she rode, but tranced men's eyes that they could not see until she wished it, then covered herself with cloth, her travelling cloak, and her body hid but her shape revealed.

I was full astonished, knowing what power it took to conjure up a hide like that. I remembered the night when Nymue meddled her greatest art, with me beside all rutting and hard, and she fooled the eyes of Gorloys' men; Uthur to pass by and fuck the fair Ygraine. And the granddaughter now could do it? As easy as riding a horse? By the Goddess, Nymue never spoke of this. I wondered if she knew.

Artur reached up his arms to take Lilith by the waist, and lifted her down from the horse, his arms all inside the cloak and a wrapping her body all round. His eyes fair shone as Lilith kissed his lips.

"Father, I've come, and it was a long ride. Do you love me still?" Lilith's eyes were bright, and her smile so full of delight, teasing him, her father.

She turned to me. "Maer! Show me your hands, that touched me first, and cradled my little body like a bird." And she turned my hands all over, and touched them with a kiss. These old hands. I turned them over and looked at them too, and wondered why they shook.

Artur escorted Lilith through to his dwelling, his arm protectively about her shoulder, although I didn't think she needed much protection. Warmth, maybe, after riding through the rain; and sure enough I saw smoke spiral upward through the thatched roof a short while on.

I wandered away to find Emmelyne, thinking it sensible to set upon a spying if we could, knowing Lilith's birth shroud a secret still between the two of us.

"She's got a power to her, Em," I said, explaining what it took to hide from men the way she had. "And she commands the king, I see it. His slow mood, all gone tonight. She cheers him."

"The Lady pleases the king, Maer?"

"His daughter, Em. Think not on it, not that."

Emmelyne looked at me a long moment, then said, "Her mother's daughter, too, Maer; don't forget it."

An unlikely thing, to forget Morgayne, nor her daughter.

"I think, Em, I shall ride to Glas on the morrow, to speak with Nym Nymue and find out what she knows."

"Nothing, Maer. If Lilith be not before my eyes, and I don't blink, I see nothing of the girl. I know her not, and her futures past, never known."

Nymue told me of her encounter with Lilith in the marshes and on the dunes, and I sat, astonished. "You say, Nymue, you saw her horse, but not Lilith, yet the sun shone bright?"

"Yeay, Maer. She shone brighter and blinded my eyes, till she moved and I saw her shadow and shade."

"Just as in the rain. She rode, and blinded ten men's eyes, even her father's first. But he knew, in an instant, when she laughed." I gazed upon Nymue, and she looked up at me. "Her laugh, Nym, she loves him fierce and teases. He craves it, our king."

"Ha," Nymue burst out. "Is there love in you? I asked her that, but she answered it not. Fierce, you say?"

"There would not be a snake, Nym, could slither between them. They each would die for the other, I think it."

"Is't pure then, their kiss?"

"I dread it not, Nym, their kiss."

Nymue sat and pondered long. "Yet Morgayne her mother, I didn't see her, either. And that love was pure, too; a sister's love for her brother."

An ember cracked and flew from the fire. We sat, Nym Nymue and I, and watched it dull to black. She looked at me again.

"I wonder if we were clever, Maerlyn, long ago. Or fools, both of us fools."

I returned to Camlann, and found Artur preparing another march to the east with a small but ruthless band, to intercept and turn back the men in boats, and declare Britten his own, protected under the dragen's high banner.

"They're like scum on waves, Maer, blown up on a storm, but they've no stronghold yet. We'll spill their blood and break their heads, and send them back to the sea. Filth with untrue gods, they dare to sully our Goddess's land." His wrath was slow and measured, but a new fervour coloured his face, blackened his eyes, made distant his gaze.

His kingdom had been threatened for many years, but there was a new spirit in him now, Artur King, that I'd not seen for a long while. The cause of it stood beside him, Lilith his daughter, standing tall, dressed in long leather, a cross-bow slung across her back, her hair tied in long twists like the skin of golden snakes. She was going to ride with her father as his reconnoitre and spy, all eager to depart.

"By my blood, Father, I'll bind us, and we'll ride the high hills together."

Lilith took a sharp blade from a scabbard at her waist, and she put her naked arm against the hard muscle of his arm. With a single, quick and spiral cut she bound two lines of blood, hers and his, in a twist from wrist to shoulder, cut around their arms five times, and bound them both together.

She dipped her fingers in their blood and marked Artur's cheeks with vertical stripes, and he did the same with hers.

"Come, Father, we ride for the east. Command it."

As the cavalcade disappeared over a hill, I looked up and saw the frail Miryamme looking down from a small window. I made a knot on my cloak, to go on the morrow to calm her. Poor child, I had so many knots on my cloak.

I resolved to see Rednock too, something had reminded me about stables. Of course, so many horses; dobbin, dobbin, and all I could ride was a donkey.

I was there.

When the king's daughter, Lilith, rode beside Artur on a high horse and blood be spilled, I was there.

First Battle

Two weeks on, the troop of horse and men and Lilith their spy camped on a high ridge. Off in the distance lay the grey surge of the sea, heaving slowly in from the north and east. Marshes and fens laced the land before them, four rivers flowing down to the northern sea.

Artur had sent on ahead his two swiftest men, to ride along the coast where the bogs and marshes spread long miles, and bade them light beacons if they saw sails. There, far off, glowed an orange light, a dull bounce from the base of the clouds.

"They come," said Artur, "with their long ships and high sails. We wait until they beach and camp, and we'll wake them from their sleep, slit their throats. No mercy, none."

He spoke to his men. "Eat and sleep now, be ready. They'll come with the dawn, I feel it."

He turned to Lilith. "Come, daughter of mine, we'll hide amongst them."

Artur and Lilith rode away from the camp, down a winding track towards the grey shingled beach. They rode slowly, Lilith's big grey stallion shoulder to shoulder with Artur's horse. The horses nickered and pranced, restless and tense like their riders. Both the king and his daughter, the man and the woman, scanned the path from side to side, their eyes sharp.

"There," said Artur, pointing. "There, it will suffice for hiding."

They rode off the path a small distance, and dismounted by a small copse. Beyond it, a muddy bog lay dark and thick; beyond that, a clear space of long grass and rushes edged a small stream running down to the beach. They led the two horses into the copse, where they were hidden from any watcher's sight. Artur lifted down their travelling packs, and Lilith set a long tether for the horses.

From their packs they each pulled wide brown cloaks the colour of earth, and they set about lacing reeds and grasses through the coarse weave, until each cloak, when laid on the ground, disappeared as if it was never there.

"'Tis good," said Artur. "The ground will crawl amongst them, and rise up with sharp knives."

"Tis better," replied Lilith, "for our bodies to be covered in mud, and their dogs sleep on until they die."

Artur looked upon his daughter and saw her face, and knew it ruthless and unforgiving, driven by the Goddess and her own fierce passion. An enemy of hers would suffer, with no forgiveness given.

"Come, Father, undress and crawl with me in muddy waters, and we be as rocks and stone and pass unseen on dark paths."

Lilith took her father's hand and placed it on her breast, over her heart.

"Feel it beat, Father, feel my heart beat, and know it's yours, my heart."

"Ah, Lilith, my love, my sweetest girl; kiss your father and show me."

They kissed, and it was a slow passion between them, burning from a thousand days and a thousand days before, searing their souls together like twisting smoke from a fire. As they undressed each other, their limbs twisted and coiled around the other's body like snakes caressing on a darkened path.

Standing naked under the high moon, Artur held his daughter's taut body hard against his chest, one hand holding the breast over her heart, the other cupping the mound of her sex, his own sex rigid against her spine, hot and hard.

Lilith arched her head back, offering her throat to his mouth, then turned and took his mouth with hers. Her kiss was deep and long, her tongue slow with his. With her hot left hand, her favoured hand, she reached between them and placed his thick heat against her belly, and pressed herself there.

"Ah, Father, I feel your burning love, all mine…"

And she slid down his body, her hands with fingers splayed wide, running down his back to the tight muscled cheeks of his ass. She gripped him, and pulled his body to hers, and lowered her mouth to his high standing prick. Lilith took her father the king into her mouth, looking up at him with her eyes drowsy closing, sucking him slowly as he stood on the ground of his country, his land.

Artur held his daughter's head gently in his hands, and she reached up between his legs and cradled his balls, high and tight in his pleasure. Lilith eased her mouth from his long cock, and smiled. "Slowly, Father, no rush; do it slowly." And with practised hands she pulled the high sac of his eggs down away from his body and slowed him, and made him rise again.

She did it like that three times, urging him up as he stood, until she knew his moment was coming. She released his cock from her mouth and stood, holding him tight against her belly once more, his flesh hot against hers, her long fingers down around his balls again. This time, when she kissed him, she didn't tug his balls down, but urged his seed up, urging him up, kissing him hard in her passion, stroking his long cock, up, faster and faster, her tongue deep in his mouth.

Lilith ground her firm, full breasts against his chest, swaying from side to side to rub her nipples against his flesh, arousing herself against her father's body. She stroked him fast, her palm wet from his early juice, bringing him up to his peak.

"Ah, my father, do you love me?"

And with her final stroke of his cock, Artur the king shot his seed in long spurts over Lilith's belly, her fingers squeezing and pulling the juice from his body, rubbing it up all over her breasts.

"Oh my father, mine, all mine."

And she lowered her head and licked it all from his skin, and all the time his fingers gently held Lilith's head.

After a long moment with Artur's cock losing its swell, he dropped to his knees and held his daughter close, her smiling lips still salty with the taste of his seed. They held each other's cheeks, and Lilith gazed steadily into his eyes. He didn't waver, there was no doubt his love for her was true.

"Come, Father, let us swim in this bog, and coat ourselves in water and mud, that dry on our skin and hide the smell of us from pestilent dogs. Then we go near to the beach in our cloaks, we hide and wait." She too was practical, accepting that their physical love for each other was an essential part of their relationship with the land and the high magick it took to defend it. Artur would say, "No matter," but Lilith knew everything mattered, every drop, every sigh.

Holding each other's hand, they entered into the bog which was warm from the day's high sun, and covered themselves in the mud, head to foot. Once covered, they returned to their little camp site and armed themselves with sharp knives, hung from simple belts about their waists. Other than light leather boots, also laced with grass, rushes and mud, they remained naked under the gillied cloaks. The mud dried on them like a second skin.

Lilith cast a silencing spell on the horses, "Hush now, be slow and unseen," before proceeding side by side with Artur down the track. Once near the beach, they ranged back and forth for a hundred heart beats, until they found an old fire site and knew where the infidels landed from their boats.

They separated, and took up places each side of the central fire site, about thirty yards apart. Falling to the ground and lying still, they became nothing more than jetsam thrown high on the beach at high tide, two flat shapes hidden upon the ground. Both looked out to sea, and they waited, silently.

Sometime later Lilith heard the low sound of running water against the timber hull of a gliding boat, and the rattle of sail and rope against a mast. She looked out from under the edge of her cloak and saw three ships in a diagonal line astern, their wind filled sails bright under the moonlight. She uttered the low cry of a curlew disturbed at night, and from back on the land she heard a single answering call; and she knew Artur's men lay hidden.

"They come, father," she whispered. "We'll turn them back burning to the sea. Hush now, my beloved," and she tranced the nearby stones to make them slide like water, not grate like rock. An eerie silence fell upon the beach, broken only by the rattle of wind in the ships' sails as they closed upon the land.

The silence was broken by the grind of the first prow as it drove up onto the beach, with the other two following in quick succession. The ships' timbers groaned with their sudden stop, and there was a low thud as a supply barrel broke loose and rolled in the belly of one of the vessels. Someone cursed, and the next sound heard was the jump of men down onto the pebbled beach.

Artur and Lilith remained hidden and still, as the enemy set up their camp and lit fires in a row along the shore. The low sounds of commands and orders could be heard, together with the shuffling sound of feet as the invaders moved to and fro across the shore, bringing supplies up from their ships.

Slowly, another lull fell across the place as the small army settled, waiting for dawn before moving inland.

The king and his daughter remained hidden and silent, yet right in the centre of the main camp, quietly waiting.

Time passed, and from the east came the first flush of dawn, with a faint movement of air, low to the ground. A curlew called, and was echoed along the beach and in the dunes by more soft calls.

"Now," Artur the king whispered.

"Now," Lilith the king's daughter whispered too.

"Now, now, now," whispered the command through their hidden troops. "Now!"

Silently, Lilith and Artur shed their cloaks and rose to their feet like ghosts rising from the ground, their sharp knives in their hands. Their proud, naked bodies were dark shadows, covered in the cracking mud. Artur's strong muscled back and his broad shoulders rippled with strength, and Lilith's sensuous curves were tight with lithe muscle. They moved silently amongst the sleeping enemy, searching for where the invading captain lay, to wake him first before letting him sleep forever.

"There," whispered Lilith, pointing. A tent was rigged just beyond one of the fires lit on the beach. In front it, each leaning against a post, sat two guards, nodding at their duty, drowsy from the fire's heat.

Artur pointed to the right, nodding to Lilith, yours. He moved stealthily to the left and circled behind the post, tilting back the man's head as he did so. With one swift movement of his knife, he slit the man's throat and lay his body down. Lilith repeated the sinuous movement, and she too sliced her victim's throat from right to left and lay the second body down.

They entered the tent, side by side; then Artur knelt by the captain's head, his knife poised just above his throat. Lilith stood tall over the man's body, her feet on either side of his torso. She kicked him awake, and he startled, jerking his head up, his eyes widening in shock and slow understanding. Artur held the knife firm, and the tip of its blade drew blood.

"Look on the sex of a woman before you die, filth," whispered Lilith. "See a woman you'll never know, before you see your own heaven. Count yourself blessed that I grant you this, 'tis a special man that sees." And she stood above the captain as he died, her hand caressing her breast.

The rest of the slaughter was quick and efficient, Artur's men moving quickly to and fro on the beach. Artur saved the six youngest men, and commanded they be tied to the mast of one ship. The bodies of the dead invaders were placed aboard the other two ships in long rows between the benches. The dead ships' sails were set, and then the boats were torched alight and pushed out to sea. The wind caught their sails and eventually, so did the burning flame, blazing up high as the ships moved upon the slow rolling waves, out to the long northern sea.

Artur stood naked before the six tied men, with Lilith his daughter beside him.

"Look upon us, I, Artur king of this land, and Lilith my daughter. Look upon us, and take word back to your king, tell him who murdered you and set his bodies burning on the sea. A naked king and his daughter, and a small band of men, slaughtering your army in the night. You are not men, you are mice."

"And we'll do it again," said Lilith. "And again. Fear us, and remember what happened, this dawn."

And they set the sails on the ship, and sent the youngest men back to the sea as a warning.

Artur and Lilith stood side by side as the dawn broke and the sun rose in the east, their mud cracked skin traced with rivers of the invader's blood. They stood motionless, watching the high top of the mast disappear, their long shadows streaming behind them. Finally they turned and made their way up the beach to the slain commander's camp.

"Make food from their leavings, men, and we make way to Camlann before noon. The fastest man, message on."

Artur surveyed the beach and the spilled blood there, black on the shingle and rock. "I fear they will come again, these won't be the last. They'll want your body as vengeance, Lilith, even as they want my land."

"They can try, Father, they'll not have either, while I breathe."

"Come, Daughter, we find clean water and undo this stain."

They collected their gillie cloaks and made their way back to the copse where their horses stood. Lilith untethered them, laying her cheek against the pulse in their necks and feeling the throb of their lives. She remembered Nymue's words, *I thought I felt a big life walk behind me*, and knew that, like that fierce little woman before her, she was in her destiny's days.

She looked to the man beside her, her father, covered in the mud of his land and the blood of foreign men, and her own heart throbbed, and she felt a weight in her belly, heavy and low. She walked ahead of him along the track, knowing the sway of her hips would entice him, the proud tilt of her head arouse him, her long legs encourage him on.

With the rein of her horse in one hand, she reached back with her other hand, her favoured hand, and beckoned for him.

Walking behind, a distance behind, Artur's prick thickened and began to fill, and his blood was hot for her. The muddied sheath cracked and broke, and by the time they reached a water's edge, his cock was high and proud, his man's flesh rising from the clay.

Lilith turned to Artur and smiled. "Come, Father, let us find clear water."

She lead her father into a sheltered pond under willows dropping to the water's edge. The slow flow of the cool stream washed away the mud and the blood from their flesh, flowing away from them like smoke on a clear day. A curious trout came, scenting the blood, and Lilith caught it quick with her bare hands. She took it to the shore, and slid her knife through its belly and cleaned its guts in the water, its flesh a vibrant pink.

"I wonder what Nymue would make of that? " she laughed, "Those guts flowing away in water."

"She favoured birds, I think. According to Maer Maerlyn, so I've heard."

"Ah, dear Maerlyn, whose hands first touched me. What is it, Father, between Maerlyn and my mother? You see it, surely, just as you see me?"

"My Gayne, my sister? My sister, your mother? Maerlyn?" Artur looked upon his daughter, standing by him in the water. "It is the land, it seems, that demands close blood, witchery and magick. I don't dwell on it, for it seems I can't command it. And I can't say no."

He looked at her, and his eyes softened. "I can't say no."

Lilith looked right back at him, her father, and smiled. "Father, you're dirt with mud and guts still, let me clean you proper." She took him by the hand. "Come deeper, let me drown you in deep water, where the fishes dance and swim."

They went where the pool was deeper, and washed each other clean. Lilith scrubbed the mud from his flesh and washed his body all over, and he did the same for her, his big hands gentle on her flesh. Once cleansed, she wrapped her legs around his waist in the water and clung to him, feeling the flesh of his cock soft against her core, for the water was cold and he was shrunk.

"You're small, Father, don't I tease you enough?"

"Your breasts are tight hard, Lilith, I think you tease yourself."

"It's just the water, it's oh so cold!" Lilith's eyes sparkled as she played with him, kissing him on the mouth and tasting his lips, like hers.

The sun rose higher, sparkling on the water's surface, and dragon-flies scattered and dropped. They played in the water, stretching their bodies to ease the ache of the long night away, and slowly, their arousal came back upon them. They came out from the water and lay on a soft blanket, soaking up the heat from the sun on their bodies as they lay quiet, facing each other.

Lilith pressed the golden brown of her breasts and belly against him, and Artur was paler, for he did not ride naked like she did, high on her horse. He gazed into her blue eyes, blue like his, like the wide sky, and traced the soft curve of her cheek. "Ah Lilith, my love, what us, king and daughter? What us?"

"Don't think it, Father, not now. Set aside kingdoms, set aside stone. Am I not enough for you here, after the battle is won?"

She took his long cock in her hands, and shifted her body just so. She raised one leg around his hip, and made him slip inside her, all the while holding his face in her hands. "Ahh, sweet Father, all mine."

And there by the water under the heating sun, Artur loved her, his passionate daughter, held close.

The Hidden Face

I was there.

When Elayne the hand-maiden was made queen for a night, I was there.

As always, there's a long and circuitous set of excitements before any event I tell. One of these days I'll learn to tell a story quick, and make it flow fast like clear water in a stream. But where's the fun in that, all over before it begins and nothing to guess, nothing to remember, nothing to forget? Catch me quick, hoolah, hoolay! I'd rather take all day.

It was simple, this: Lilith first queen of the land more true, by Artur's side as his spy, his hide, her slaughter more bloody than poor Miryamme could ever know. She, poor girl, with her eyes of innocent blue and the straw doll by her side, she could not match the fierce love Lilith gave her father, but stayed sweet innocence, his virgin queen.

Artur still needed his little queen though, and after battle 'twas always the same. He would go to Miryamme's chamber, and whisper sweet words in her ear, and the poor creature would sleep so deep, her little back curled against the king's belly, her skin so smooth it glowed under the silver moon. I could unknot a string, and Emmy and Elayne sleep too, not chasing the poor lamb with her frightened bleat every night.

"Her innocence reminds me, Maer, why I fight the scum from the east." Sworn to de Grance, more like.

Lancilet the prince was accommodated for his care of the queen, for Rednock would take the king's big red horse and Lilith's grey, and break up a sweat huge and hot and his muscles all bulging, curry them down with a brush. Young Lancilet would creep by with a pail and a cloth, and wash the big man down like his own beast, and service the groom with his mouth or his ass, depending on the groom's inclination and how far the horses had run.

The queen didn't always dally and watch, but Emmelyne and Elayne did regularly look. "You said to keep an eye on the prince, Maer, and report all proper and full." Emmy winked, and lifted up her skirts.

"I did, Em," I replied; and found my own need to check the carpenter's work remained solid and straight in the loft. It did, straight and solid into Emmy's helpful wet cunt, while she made sure the balustrade held firm, holding on. That carpenter fellow must have been careless, his work so often needing a check.

In truth, one of my best designs, that stable. Very good sight lines, even if I say so myself.

And Lilith, what she? She would regularly to my chamber come. "Tell me of Nym Nymue, Maer, and Morgayne my mother." She'd look at me with her father's eyes, and insist I tell her destinies and histories, so she could see how the land's women circled around her father and held him safe and made him king. "He's my father, Maer, no woman loves him more."

Truth tell, I believed her. But her birth caul all hidden: I always remembered her tiny baby body covered in it, which Emmy washed away, and I wondered what it meant. I knew Nym Nymue couldn't see Lilith when she turned away, which struck me odd. Surely a portent or two, a spark from a fire or guts from a stoat, something at least, to tell Lilith's truth? She'd look at me with her deep, clear eyes, and tell me where the waters ran.

So the court was made, and prospered a little, and the land settled into a winter. Artur heard tell from merchants and captains that his last message, the six young men sent back in their ship, had impressed the heathen king and made him pause. My ears, better at skulking between the lines, heard tell that they really feared what dragen women would do; and by all accounts, once the whispering was finished, Lilith the new queen was as tall as ten men, grown naked from the rock.

"Their stupid imaginations do you no harm, rumours of giants walking the land. Gogmagog and his bride." I grinned at the king, my friend. "I never knew you were so tall, sire. You hide your height well. You look no taller to me than an average man."

"Seems true, Maer, a useful ploy." Artur looked across at Lilith his daughter who sat making arrows. "But they'll be back, those boatmen. There'll be more blood to wash from our hands, it's not over for us yet."

"There are always deep rivers, father, to cleanse ourselves of blood," said Lilith. "We need to prepare ourselves, train more men, be not afraid."

"I'm not afraid, Lilith, just wary. Weary too, but I hide it."

Ah me, the look in Lilith's eye when he said it.

Lilith made bring an inkster with his woad all black and blue, and made him tattoo a curling twine of a snake on her naked body and that of her father, and it was cleverly made, that encirclement. For when they held themselves just so, and pressed tight hard against each other with their naked arms all around, the body of the snake was one continuous coil around them, made as of one joined creature. And so Artur and his daughter made it clear, and peril to those who doubted, that these two were king and queen for the land, joined in blood and lust and fury, coiled snakes on a dark path.

And Lilith made sweet with Miryamme her father's bride, and kept the simple queen, if not a friend, more like an injured bird that cannot fly. I walked the palisade with Artur by my side and looked down on the meadow by the river, and saw the two women like a mother and a child, Lilith caring for the little queen as if she were her own child, calling to her, "Come, my mother, come dance with me, dancing, dancing, we'll ride a fine horse."

Artur looked upon them both and said to me, "The girl takes my curse and weakens it, Maer. See how she laughs and smiles with the queen."

"It's a natural love, sire, a protective thing."

Artur glanced at me. "Seems like it's many do care for my queen, my helpless creature. I thank them for their kindness."

"She's a sweet thing, sire, but not practical for the land's queen. Your own blood daughter, Lilith, she will bleed for this land, this kingdom. You died tomorrow, sire, she could wear your crown. Men would follow her."

Artur held my gaze, long and hard. "She the first born, Maer, you swear it?"

"By these hands, sire, these very hands you see in front of you." I held my hands out for him to see. "Emmelyne is my witness, she swaddled the girl babe whilst I birthed the whelp."

"The whelp? My son, Maer, and marked king." Artur pointed out the fact of it, as if it was the weather, a dull day.

"I tell it true, lord, I warm not to Mordant your son; nor him me." It was rare I looked Artur straight, but this time I did. "Nym Nymue sees treachery in him, sire, when she trances. She cannot pierce the veil, but his shade blackens her backwards sight."

"And you say she cannot see Lilith, even in clear light?"

"She can see the one but not the other streaming back, that's true. Nymue is afraid of it, not seeing Lilith. Her eyes can't see your daughter straight."

Artur looked down at his arms and the twisted ink upon them, slowly turning his hands over. He looked at me, a stillness in his eyes. "I trust her with my life, Maer."

"I think she take it in both hands, sire."

"Like your hands, Maer, when she was born? A life?"

319

"Yeay. Her life is powerful born, any fool can see that."

Artur laughed. "You see it, Maer?"

"Not I, sire. I'm blind."

"As a bat, my friend?"

"Three bats, a mole, and an earthworm or two. In a dark cave, and my eyes all closed."

"Go from me, Maerlyn. Your words make no sense, yet still I listen."

"I'm gone, sire, as you bid it."

"Do you forbid it, Mother?"

"I do, Mordant. You are not their king, and you shall not command. The garrison are my men, and answer only to me." Morgayne's voice was calm and low. "If you want troops to command, you go north to your father. Prove yourself there."

She was unforgiving, but knew her son was weak inside, cruel but unformed. She watched him react to her words, saw his hurt pride, but she refused to coddle the prince.

"He loves Lilith more, Mother, he doesn't love me."

"Lilith loves her father, Mordant. You only love yourself, and oft times that I doubt. Even a mother finds you hard, without grace. Find grace, my son, and be seen by your father. He sees what you are, not what you think you are."

"Do you love me, Mother?"

"Don't test me, boy."

"You're cruel, Mother."

"I know it, my son. It is my way, I won't change it, just because you hurt. You must mend your own wounds, Mordant. I cannot do it for you."

Morgayne rubbed her own belly where the thin red scar of her children's birth still itched, and smiled at the memory of the mad magickian, who had held his hands so very, very close to her heart.

"Do you mock me, Mother, with your smile?"

She turned her slow eyes towards him, gazing through her son, seeing so far past his eyes that Mordant turned to see who was behind him. Morgayne turned her eyes away as if she couldn't bear his presence any more.

"No, I do not, my son. You mock yourself enough, you don't need another to do it." She smiled at him with a sadness in her eyes. "Take the best horse, and three of the men, and my banner. Ride north for the Red Morgayne. I give you that."

As Mordant turned to leave her chamber, she stretched out a slow hand through the air in his direction. "Remember your blood, my son. You have the blood of kings in your veins. Give fealty as prince, and love your father better, however hard that be. Remember your blood."

Mordant feared blood. He feared the shedding of it, and the pain that went with cuts and falls, so he was timid, even as he was cruel to those around him. He carried the blood bruise on his face and was marked, and couldn't hide it.

He couldn't compare. The men at Tyntangel knew Artur and his firm command, yet mocked the son whenever he turned away, which was often. And when word drifted south of Lilith, how she rode by the king's side and bled in battle with her father, the brother and son were scorned.

So Mordant rode north with three reluctant men.

Oh my, the king's son, that odious boy, that embarrassment for his mother; Mordant has crept to Camlann expecting fealty. The king's son wanting allegiance, just because he was born? Not here, not now, not this court.

His sister Lilith rode forth to meet him, tall and proud on her horse, and Mordant crept in beside her. Could two children of the king be more unalike? Morgayne surely carried them nine moons in separate pods, and my own hands fooled as I held them first.

"Oh brother," I heard Lilith say, "do you come here to fight? Artur your father needs men to fight, can you do it?" And I heard the scorn in her voice, even her own brother despised.

"Leave him be, Lilith," said her father, and held his arms out for his only son, the prince. "Welcome to your father's place, Mordant my son. Come, we eat, and strategy share."

I looked at the king, and marvelled how he said it, refusing his son his pretences; yet I saw his stoic eye and remembered earlier words.

"It must be done, Maer. The boy is so unformed, yet thinks himself king without a crown. I not like his cowardly ways, made all cruel to compensate, but I have to try. He's blood."

"He needs to spill blood, father, break heathen heads from bodies." Lilith turned her head towards Artur, her pale blue eyes steady and straight, and she said it true. "He should be cunning and cruel, the way he tortured animals when he was small; but I can't see it."

"I fear you're right, Lilith, he will find some excuse not to ride."

Artur got slowly to his feet, and made his way to see Mordant in his chamber at the end of the keep. Later, I saw him return to his own sleeping chamber, and Lilith went to him there.

I should not worry at it like a tooth, but I do.

Artur was right. His coward son complained of loose guts before the next ride, some slimed shit in the river, which luckily washed away quick.

The king and a troop, Lilith in the middle of it, went east to follow a rumour.

I went down to the village where dogs were better company than the cur Mordant; but even there I saw him skulking, down by the forge where Rednock beat out shoes for the horses.

Lancilet was in the blacksmith's place, and had found a new skill, joining a hundred tiny loops of beaten metal into an armoured shirt, full flexible it was, and proof against arrows. I watched Mordant slide up to his cousin and drop the rings to the ground, a stupid sneer on his face just because he did it. Lancilet bent to pick the metal loops up, not even saying a word. I saw Mordant studying his cousin, and thought nothing good would come of it.

Mordant turned away and left the stable, but stumbled his toe on an anvil, crying out loud in pain.

"He cannot make an exit, let alone an entrance proper," Rednock commented, his voice as dry as the hay he fed his horses; so even the loyal servant saw the stained prince for a fool.

The filth in Mordant's eyes as he limped away, and the red flush on his face, brighter than the king's mark on his cheek, flagged a warning to me. I made true to myself to be wary, and hastened to Emmelyne to aid my watch.

"He will skulk, Em, and want mischief against the king and his, I'm sure of it."

Sure true, the next days I saw Mordant charm the poor silly queen, his cowardice finding the easiest place to corrupt.

"We cannot warn her, Em, she won't understand. See how he hides his face from her eyes not to fright her? At least the scum from their boats carry swords and are honest in their treachery. Watch close, and warn me."

I spoke to Rednock too, and suggested he not joy the prince Lancilet, for fear what Mordant would say against him and the sweet dark boy if he found them, skulking and digging and twisting his malice in like a knife.

A week on, and the king still away, the filth found it: Miryamme the queen and her dalliance with Lancilet in the night and in the lady's anterior chamber.

Elayne told Emmelyne what the young couple did, how the queen protected her curious virginity while the king was away, and how one night she spied Mordant spying too.

"Mordant knows it, Maer, that the queen's cunt lies empty and unused and she has no need of it, her proof the king's daughter on her horse, and now the king's son in the court."

"He will use this knowledge quick against the king, I have no doubt of it. We must plan against Mordant, or he'll spill secrets that the king wants not spilled, and the queen's innocence corrupted too."

I pondered on it, and scuffed my boots in the dirt and tied five knots, thinking of a better skulk. But I could not do it, I could not think what to do. Being a fool in a hat with a bell, jingle jingle, I can plot against fools, but I cannot plot against malice. Malice runs quieter and makes no noise, so I cannot hear it coming; and it's upon me even before it starts.

"She wants it, Lancilet, I know she wants it. A man's fuck in her quim, proper and deep. She craves it, longs for it every night. She'll beg. She'd beg me, but cannot, because Artur the king is my father, which makes her almost my mother."

Mordant sidled along beside Lancilet his cousin, whispering in the older youth's ear, whispering lies and deceit.

"Her little cunt, Lancilet, she wants it filled. I know you plunder her tighter place, but her empty cunt! You must fill it, full." He stretched the lie. "The king can't do it, he's old and his cock is feeble, but she begs it. Fill it, fuck it, fill her wanting puss."

Mordant slithered on with his message, pulling Lancilet's mind away from the gentle truth of his love for Miryamme the lonely queen, until the cousin believed he could make children where the king could not. Mordant smiled behind his own hand and pressed home the lie.

"She wants a proper fucking, Lancilet, by a man with a cock full hard. The king is all a soft, feeble man, he can't rise. He's weak and limp, and has called me up to Camlann to make me king in his stead. He's told me, Mordant, his full trusted son - I'm dying, he's said. You'll inherit my crown, he's said. Mordant king, in my right place on the throne.

"But first, his queen. Go to her, Lancilet, she loves you, she'll let you do it."

Mordant watched Lancilet closely as he spoke, and saw a flicker of suspicion in his eyes. "She's told me so herself." He pressed home the deceit. "She tells me, Lancilet, because I'm the king's son, full trusted with the truth. Artur wants you, for the queen's fuck."

Mordant was so tied up in his plot for Lancilet to deflower the queen, that he was careless where he plotted. Elayne the queen's maid overhead Mordant snivelling his lies to Lancilet, and heard the plan. She spoke to Emmelyne, who in turn went to Maerlyn and they pondered a trap to expose Mordant's intent and reveal his treachery to the king and the innocent queen.

"But how not to damage Lancilet? For he is a good man and has the queen's heart, and is a better son in truth to the king than his own son."

"I know it, Em, and am thinking of ways." Maerlyn sat pondering, weaving threads in his mind, how to set another's plan in train and continue it better suited to his own path.

Maerlyn knew that a man's seed, when conjured with, was meant to be; and he knew from Nymue's trances that Mordant's way must run. He could dabble with it, but never fully stop a fate. A man be born from a fuck, or a woman, and dread him who try to stop it.

Maerlyn turned to Emmelyne. "Elayne, how tall she be, standing next to the queen?" His voice sunk to a whisper. "She know the queen's voice, could she take it?"

Emmelyne knew the power of words once spoken, and knotted her kerchief, five knots. She listened close to Maerlyn's words and learned his plan, and learned of another love-child born many years before, and Nymue's magick then.

"Maer, you can guide the man, but how the woman's magick make? Nym Nymue made it with you then, but who now can change a face so quick?"

"You have to talk to Lilith, Em, sister to sister. She loves the king and would protect the maiden queen, yet does not love her brother. She has her mother's magick and would surely do it."

The importance of Maerlyn's words fell full force on Emmelyne. "Is this the price of Lilith's shroud, Maer, that only you and I know?"

"It is a part of it, I think, but only a little one. Know it, Emmy, but don't reveal it when you speak." Maerlyn sat still, his eyes distant. "This family's not done yet, I feel it in my bones and my body aches. There's a thunder coming, Em, a storm."

"And Elayne, what her?"

"She's a good girl, Em, and loves the queen. She'll not mind the prince inside her belly, either. Is she ripe, her moon high?"

"Like cows for milk, she regular be. Three nights to thread the needle, if the land wants another squalling babe."

"It seems Em, whenever I get involved, the Goddess wants it."

"Keep away from my quim then, Maer," said Emmelyne with a wink. "When this is done, my bottom's tight, all ready."

The rain started slowly, squalling showers breaking over the valleys, veils of rain shifting quick against the light. The villagers and the fort's garrison hustled animals and children in under cover, and the first runnels of water trickled down paths and over stone. Dust settled, and the horses, returned from Artur's eastern troop, ran loose in meadows by the river, until Rednock and his men brought them home.

Artur called Maerlyn, and told him of more scouting boats from across the northern sea. Scared men had been captured on the shore and bound in ropes, and left with Lilith until they talked then willingly died, rewarded with her smile and her parted thighs. She cleansed herself in the deepest river, and washed their blood away.

Mordant sat in the king's parly and listened, but held his tongue. He did not see his sister, but she watched him and saw his sideways look.

The next night the rain had settled in, clouds low and grey, dulling a dull moon, and paths ran with mud. Maerlyn and the king met in long strategy, maps were drawn and loyal horses counted. The kingdom prepared for war.

Mordant wrapped a dark cloak around Lancilet's shoulders, and the two crept swiftly past the flickering lights of Artur's parly room, tarred rushes burning on the walls and a log fire crackling. Mordant felt a trickle of cold rain slide down his neck and over his chest and he shivered with the chill touch of it. But his words were smooth as honey as he reassured Lancilet that the queen would be alone, the cousin's cock the purpose of this night.

Mordant had brewed a coction, lacing it with forgetful flowers, dulling herbs and the skin of mushrooms from the forest, and fed it to Lancilet to fuddle his thoughts yet tighten his loins.

"You're nervous, Lancilet, no need to be, drink this. It's a rutting potion I learned from my mother, and drank it myself before fucking the village girls south at Tyntangel."

More lies, but Mordant didn't know when to stop. His fates were running on now, and he was caught in the midst of them, like a spider devouring its web.

A swirl of rain rushed hard against the wall and Lancilet paused, catching his balance with a hand against the stone. In his britches, he felt a different thickening, and knew it was the drugged drink acting upon him.

"I feel strange, cousin," he murmured to Mordant, "the light is shimmering bright."

"Don't fear it, Lancilet. It's the drink, it brings a strong courage, and a tightening of the balls."

He touched Lancilet's brow and felt a slight sweat, and knew that the potion was creeping into the other man's brain. His hand wandered lower to Lancilet's thickening cock, not for his pleasure because he had none, but to be sure of it for his plan. The prince's cock rose, and Mordant stroked it hard, carefully teasing Lancilet up while whispering quiet words into his ear.

"She'll want this prod, dear Lancilet. She'll sigh and take it into her mouth, oh yes, and her fingers will play in her cunt and touch your lips and she'll moan."

His voice was cold and remorseless, driving the lustful vision deep into Lancilet's mind.

"Don't be slow, Lancilet, place the queen on her back and spread her legs apart. You'll see her lovely quim, she wants it full and fiercely fucked. Do it, Lancilet my sweet, fuck her up full, and when I'm king you can have the queen's cunt whenever you want it. I've no need for it."

Lancilet could think of nothing but his cock and its tight strain, the drugs were upon him. He brushed Mordant's hand away, and pulled his britches down his legs so his cock rose hard and high against his belly. He wrapped the cloak around himself and crept along the wall, using his fingers for guidance along the joints between the stones. The fast rain swirled around, blinding his eyes with streaming drops. He wiped his eyes clear, and stepped over the familiar threshold to Miryamme's rooms. The walls shimmered and swirled, circling with crystalline light.

"Go now, I'll wait." He heard Mordant's low whisper and a cold laugh, and he was alone in the room. He knew the antechamber well, the small entry room with its cooking fire and a corridor beyond, past Elayne's bed-chamber to Miryamme's room.

Usually he would hear Miryamme's low whisper calling to him with her stutter, "Lancilet, Lancilet, is that you, is that you?" He brushed the water from his eyes, and could hear nothing but the low rush of the rain outside. He shook his head to clear it, and heard a soft sound from the room ahead.

"Lancilet, Lancilet, is it you? Come to me quick, sweet boy."

Miryamme's voice was soft, quickly spoken. He dropped the cloak from his shoulders and reached for the strings that tied his jerkin close. Pulling the cloth away from his body, Lancilet brushed his own nipples and they were tight and hard, tiny points on his flesh, the touch causing his prick to throb.

"Quick, see me."

Miryamme's voice was urgent. He glanced aside to Elayne's room, and saw a huddled shape under her blankets; the sleeping maid waiting on her queen. He went on to the queen's chamber, eager now for her fresh, smooth body, and the delectable quim he had tasted so many times before but entry always denied. A rush of rain blew against the window shutters, and he startled with the sound of it.

There on the bed, in the dim light from the window, lay the slender body of the queen, her head thrown back into the shadows, naked before him. Lancilet quickly moved forward, his cock aching for her, aching for his own desire. Mordant's ceaseless drip of words tormented his mind and made him see nothing but the woman's spread wide legs, but he never heard her silence or thought it strange. He fell upon her, and was welcomed by strong arms, but didn't remember the queen's frailty and didn't think it strange.

With a moan Lancilet gripped her legs and spread them wide, and placed the tip of his engorged cock between the lips of the queen's cunt where he'd always been denied. He didn't think it curious when her hand came down to guide him, and she gripped his ass and pulled him into her with a low hiss, "Yesss."

She pushed up against him with hot delight, bucking her hips up to his, her lips feverish on his mouth in a hungry kiss. "Oh sire, oh prince, please take me, take me, unhh…" She embraced him hard, wrapping her arms around him, pulling him fierce inside her, then turned her head away. "Don't look, don't see. I'm not…."

Suddenly the rain stopped, and the only sound was the slick of their bodies against each other and their fast breath, as Lancilet arched his back with a sudden thrust and surged his seed up into her, his orgasm ripping through his body in pulses before collapsing onto her slender body. With a high cry, she too came, her body shaking against his, "Mmmm, unhh… yesss, mine, this night."

There was a sudden crash of a door flung open, followed by the sound of feet running. Mordant's voice cried out, "Artur, my father, you are betrayed, your queen taken by her cousin, fucked in your place. Her innocence broken, oh my father!"

"What's this, Mordant? You speak filth. My queen would not give her prize to any man but me, and she sleeps. What you? Why bring me here, scurrying in the night?"

"Look father. Lancilet and the queen, there on the bed, she's still wrapped her legs around him like a slut. The king's queen, a slut."

"There's no queen here, Mordant. It's Lancilet, sure, but he favours the maid Elayne; yet they lie on the queen's bed, 'tis odd."

Lancilet pushed back and fell away from the maid, astonished that it was indeed Elayne in his arms and in the queen's bed.

"How is it Elayne? Mordant promised me it was the queen wanted me for her quim, her virgin fuck to take." He shook his head, confused, the staring pupils of his eyes wide, revealing his drugged ecstasy.

"Lancilet, prince, you bed the lady's maid. Miryamme the queen sleeps in my chamber, quietly in my bed. Emmelyne is with her, calming her there. Why did you think her here, and willing for you?" Artur looked down on the youth and touched him gently on the shoulder. "You look to be tranced. Who has done this, my prince?"

"Mordant, sire. He promised it, saying you wanted it, because you're old and feeble too."

Artur looked askance at the youth, and covered Elayne with a quilt. She gratefully wrapped it around herself and was about to slip away, when Artur held a finger to his lips."Sssh, Elayne, you're innocent here, I think."

"Mordant you say, brought you here saying the queen would be in her chamber, then rushed to find me?"

Lancilet nodded, "Yeay, he brought me here, and I heard the queen's voice and saw her face."

"Did he now? Mordant did that, and you say you saw my queen?" Artur spoke as calmly as ever he did, when riding into battle or admiring a young goat-herd's flock.

He turned to his son. "It seems, child, that you plot as well as you command. There are quicker minds than yours, this night." He paused, and watched the red bloom rise on Mordant's face.

"You would stain my queen with your rage, you would fool the prince Lancilet with your lies, you would bring me here in the falling rain to see faces?"

He was like a still pond with no ripples, and Mordant finally understood quiet anger, quiet rage, his father turned against him forever. "What else would you do, my son, to prove yourself a man?"

Well. That's the proof of it, made clear in a puddle. Mordant content to plot against his father and use a gentle boy to do it, and willing to sully the queen's fragile mind along with it.

"Ban him, father. He'll not fight for you, my gutless brother. Send him from this place." Lilith was ruthless and her eyes as cold as the winter sky. "We need to fight, father, and need men to do it, not sprawling, crawling things. Mordant is no brother to me. If he was a flea in a comb I'd crush it."

I saw Mordant quiver before his sister's wrath, his hand shaking against his leg. He gripped it with his other hand, trying to stop the shake.

Artur stood facing the fire, and didn't look back at his son. A huge, ragged breath escaped him, and I saw his shoulders slump. He took another breath, and looked up towards the roof.

"This night, I go to my queen. Lilith, my daughter, we ride tomorrow side by side.

"Mordant, be not here in the morn. I care not where you go. I banish you, my only son. Go!

"'Tis done, these deeds, and what's done cannot be undone. I curse this day."

I was there.

When Elayne the hand-maiden was made queen for a night, I was there.

To War

Artur returned to his sleeping chamber and bade Emmelyne leave.
"I'll care for her now," he said, sitting on the bed and taking the hand
of Miryamme his queen.

"Don't leave me, don't leave me. I don't want to be left alone. Is
my doll looking, with no eyes, no eyes?"

"Sshhh, my queen," Artur calmed her, gently stroking her long
golden hair. "Let me undress, and I'll warm you. You can hear my
heart beat."

"Your heart beat, beat. Don't let it stop."

Miryamme looked up at Artur, her eyes wide. Her hand clutched
his. She sighed, a long shuddering sigh, then her breath settled and
she relaxed her grip. She smiled her radiant smile and reached her
arms out to him. Perhaps she sensed his tension, something beyond
her own fears, for when he got into the bed her arms went around
him, and he slept.

Miryamme held his head against her shoulder and brushed back
the hair from his cheek.

"He's mine tonight, you'll not have him," she whispered, and
whispered it to his sister and his daughter, but couldn't deny them the
power of their love. She resigned herself, finally, to sharing her man
with the women who drove him, who gave him strength. She was
small and afraid and loved him too, but didn't know the power that
gave her.

In the morning she woke to a hard heat against her back and Artur's breath slow and steady by her ear, so she knew he still slept with his cock made hard by the morning's turn. She wriggled her bottom back against him, spreading wider her cheeks to feel his shaft against her hot core. She moved slowly, not wanting to wake him yet, but needing to feel his powerful body wrapping her in his arms.

She whispered to herself, "Safe, safe in my man's arms. He's strong and warm, doll, and when no-one's here, he's mine. Don't look."

In the dim morning light she could see the shape of her doll on the shelf by the bed. She sighed, stretched, and carefully reached between her legs to place the shaft of Artur's cock against her sex, snuggling further back against him. Closing her thighs tight, she gripped his long shaft, pressing her own wetness slick along the heat. "Hmmm..." Miryamme moaned a low moan and closed her eyes.

She ran the palms of her hands up to her breasts and rubbed over her hard nipples, sending jolts down to her clitoris, "Oohh, that's lovely, my queen," as if she was some disembodied thing looking at herself, pale and small, slowly moving. The doll sat looking, but had no eyes.

Miryamme caressed herself, every now and then running her hand down her belly to her sex, fluttering light fingers over her nub and around the wetting head of Artur's prick. His breath caught and she stopped. A little smile spread on her face and she moved again. She smelt her own scent and Artur's rising musk. She licked her lips and began to move down the bed, slowly turning and pushing Artur onto his back. His breath caught again, but she'd learned to move so slowly that she didn't wake him, not yet.

She pulled the bed-covers back, exposing his chest and gut and his beautiful prick, straight and hard, all hers. She reached behind herself, finding another cloak on the bed and pulling it up around her body for warmth, then lay her head on Artur's belly, gazing at her prize. She placed one hand on his chest, sensing his breathing as she looked at him. Hers now, not dreaming, waking; hers.

Silent now, like a cat turns a corner, like a leaf falls on water, Miryamme moved down the bed to enclose the plum-coloured head of Artur's cock in her mouth. She held the heat of her mouth still upon him and took the stiff shaft in her hand. She felt a twitch and rewarded him with a slow swirl of her tongue and a tormenting long stroke of her hand. She shifted slightly to better accommodate his length, then lay there, the only movement the rise and shuddering fall of his breath, the pulse of her blood and the slow suck of her mouth.

As if in a trance she lay, Miryamme the queen, and suckled her man deep and slow. Artur slowly woke from three dreams and his queen was there in one of them. He opened his eyes to know where he was, then closed them again. He placed his hand on Miryamme's head and ran his fingers through her hair. She purred with slow pleasure and started to stroke back and forth, back and forth.

Artur ran his other hand down over her side to Miryamme's taut little ass. She moaned on his cock and moved her leg up so he could find her hot, virgin core and the tightness of her other place. He wet his finger with her slick and placed it against her tightest hole, but didn't push it in. She eased her body down instead and took his finger in her own time. Her eyes rolled back and she was impaled both ends, with a gentle hand on her head, a straight finger in her depths and a long cock between her lips.

Miryamme sucked on Artur's cock, her hands cupping his balls which were tight up against his body, and as she suckled she stroked. She felt his fingers comb through her hair as she twisted a hand around his shaft, and heard a low moan when she pressed his tight sacs up. She began to stroke faster, taking his cock to the back of her throat.

She heard a long sigh from her man and knew he was close, waking hard in the morning with a woman's mouth around his prick and a hot hand gripping him.

"Ahh, you make me, my gentle queen," and with three soft pulses he spilled his seed into her mouth and she swallowed it down. With a small shudder of her own, Miryamme came too.

"Don't look, doll, don't look," she whispered to herself. "His juice all mine, all mine, all swallowed down. It's mine. Not theirs, not theirs." She giggled. "All swallowed down, his cream, and I'm just like a cat, a naughty little cat."

They lay still for many minutes, his softening cock wet against Miryamme's cheek. She reached out onto the bed and found his hand, lacing her fingers through his. Nothing moved, and the air was still around them.

Suddenly, Miryamme sat up and looked down on her man, her king. "Be careful, my love, there's bad blood stirring, I can feel it."

She looked around the room, a momentary glimpse of sanity in her eyes. "I don't like him, your son who is never my son. He pretended to like me, but I saw his eyes, his eyes. Be careful, my king, I don't like your blood. He lies."

And just as quickly, she smiled her radiant smile and her lucidity vanished. Miryamme rested her head upon Artur's shoulder and felt his slow steady heart.

"Beat, beat," she whispered. "Beat, beat."

I was there.

When Artur the king made a fire and blood ceremony with his sister and daughter, to conjure strength for battle, then rode on to war, I was there.

Morgayne rode up from Tyntangel with fifty men from her command, arriving on a dark night when the moon was low and the rooks moaned and croaked, or was it the trees they nested in? She summonsed the news of her son and wasn't surprised.

"A foul child in truth, I've no care for him. He sucked on my tit like a fox and now he skulks away like one. Which direction?"

"East, lady, last seen riding east."

"East then circle back, he'll return this way, I'm sure."

She looked at me with her slow moving eyes and that treacherous smile on her lips, waiting for me to trip over something. "But you, heart? How you?"

A stupid stumbling man, I tripped on my own words and mine own feet every time I saw her, and my chest itched, her noose around my neck coiled tight. I would not cut myself free, even if I was a walking hanging man.

"Astonishingly well, lady, considering…"

"Considering what, heart? Not my presence, surely not?"

I wasn't at all sure, but then, with Morgayne I was rarely sure of anything except the way my ankle twinges still when it's cold. Ah look, snow's falling, scratch, scritch. Softly, softly, falling snow, softly, softly.

She laughed, a low sound that might have been a sigh, it might have been a growl; or was that me, howling at the moon and scratching at the door to get in? Then, of a sudden, her mood shifted quick.

"These boats, they come more often?"

"Regular, lady, dropping men and supplies. 'Tis a slow invasion. They build up camps, all obvious, about ten miles in from the shore. They march on the fosse ways, straight on, and cluster there. Yet leaderless all. There is no banner risen; none seen yet, anyway."

"Their king not come then, all a standing on his boat?"

"Not yet, lady. 'Tis curious strange, but he waits."

"He's coward filth, Mother. I would slit his throat, if I found it."

Morgayne turned at the voice of her daughter. "Ah, Lilith. No sweetness then, no honey?"

"Never, Mother. Not these men in their boats, all coming to take our land. My father's land, your brother's kingdom. We fight them with all the power the Goddess gives us. We fight the filth, wherever it be."

Morgayne studied her daughter, recognising the high passion in her veins and marvelling at the way she controlled it. She saw her own strength and guile in the young woman's eyes, together with the naked courage of Artur, Lilith's father, Morgayne's brother, lover both.

"What hex you summon, to assist?"

"Water and rain, Mother; we bathe in water before battle and coil around us the mud and the snake. We become rock and earth, and rise amidst them." Fury glittered in Lilith's eyes, and from the other side of the room I saw it.

"And Nym Nymue, what does she to assist? The high priestess, what is she in all this?"

I saw Morgayne's fast intelligence gathering up the records of rune and rock, to better know what magick to set behind Artur in his next fight.

"She does not see me, Mother, I'm hid from her eyes."

And Lilith told her mother the story she'd told me, following the white woman through the marsh and down to Nymue's shore and the lady's blindness there, the big horse sensed but Lilith not.

Morgayne sat, not moving and silent, until the tale was told, all done, Lilith's future all hid but Mordant all known. Betrayal known, but not the man betrayed.

"What make you of this, Maer? Nymue not knowing of the girl, unable to see my daughter in her smoke and behind her mirrors, yet servant of the Goddess too?"

"'Tis true. I have seen Nym Nymue and talked upon it. Nym is scared, she cannot see Lilith unless she look with clear eyes in bright sun and never turn away." I paused. "She cannot see Lilith's future, streaming back. Your daughter is hidden."

Morgayne remained still, her eyes closed and her fingers a slow weave through the air, all a trancing herself, all still.

"Lilith's like me then. Nymue didn't see me, either, yet look what we made, despite her." She whispered as if to herself, deep in thought. She opened her dark eyes and looked with pride upon Lilith. "My daughter, unpredicted and unpredictable. Like me, by the Goddess, Nymue did not see me. What power does this give you, daughter mine, that you can move unseen?"

And I remembered Lilith's caul, all washed away by Emmelyne's hands, and I shivered. It was involuntary, a cold chill and mine ankle ached.

Morgayne felt it too, she knew me too well. "Heart, what is it, that walks over your grave whilst you lie in it, asleeping?"

"It's nothing, lady, just cold and mine ankle does itch."

Her slow eyes refused my lie, and her eyebrow she raised and she laughed her low laugh. "Maer, don't fool it. You know something, I can tell. Don't hide."

"Yeay, Maerlyn, don't hide from us." Lilith stood and came toward me, her half snakes writhing naked as she coiled before me,

343

her long braided hair falling to her waist. "You took me from my mother's belly and your hands were the first to hold me, to hold my tiny hands."

She placed those hands upon my cheeks and looked at me straight, her father's still blue eyes before me. "Tell us, Maerlyn, what it is you know, don't hide it."

"True, Maer." Morgayne's low voice was in my ear, her hand upon my arm. "It's the end of days, I feel it. If there's some truth we do not know, tell us now. We might need it."

So I told the tale of Lilith's birth, quick, no lies. I could no longer trade the secret and didn't know what to do with it, so I gave it to women who did. Lilith's caul, now told.

"'Tis no wonder you are so well hid, my daughter, if you were born shrouded and the knowledge kept secret all these years." Morgayne turned to me. "Cunning true, Maer, I grant you that. Well kept indeed, but given up sensible now."

"Come, Lilith. We must decide what to do with this truth, how to use it."

Artur instructed that great pyres be made on the tops of the highest hills, far to the east and the west, the north and the south, and the highest pyre of all he constructed at Camlann, full three men high. It was constructed of dry tree branches coated with pitch and tar, so when it was lit, it would flame to the top of the sky and summon the king's allegiances and sovereign armies, and call men to the reign in its peril.

The fires from the east would warn of massed ships sailing from over the northern sea. Riders on fast horses would report from spies and creeping men to provide intelligence and warnings of armies on the move. And when the Camlann fire was lit, the king would ride to war.

A great timber stage was built an arrow's flight from the pyre, with a great wooden pole in the centre of it, plunging deep into a cavern where a spring gushed warm water, bubbling and steaming from the rock. Morgayne the Red knew this place, blessed by the Goddess, just as Nym Nymue, years before, found a like place to crown the king.

Back then, Morgayne crawled like a spider down the rock and caused Artur to spill his seed on the land, which shook and trembled as the dragen crawled upon it. She took my seed too, and was less generous with it, or more, depending on my memory, depending on my mood.

But now, this was no dragen summoned by five waves breaking, this threat was from the minds of men, far worse.

Winter deepened, and Artur waited.

I played too many games of gammon and always lost my dice, shaken in a cup. "Two ones again, heart, two ones?" Ha. She smiled at me, her favourite fool. But at least she looked and found the spilled dice on the floor. I really should not drop them, but these crooked fingers....

Far to the east, the first fire was lit, and the next and the next, and still Artur waited.

Finally, word came.

"Bring the man food, get him warm before he tell." Artur commanded, and Emmelyne ran to the kitchen. "Get his horse to Rednock, to curry it down and quick."

Lancilet smiled, and left to do the king's bidding, the horse's bridle in his hand.

Artur summonsed round his best parly, his best captains, to hear the rider's tale. Lot sat by the window, old now but still sensible, and his three sons the king's best commanders. de Grance was there from Breton, arriving on his ship with a kiss for his daughter and a truce for Morgayne.

Morgayne sat in the nook next the fire, all cloaked, her slow hands all still as she listened. Lilith her daughter paced restlessly like a cat with five kittens, and wanted to ride straight away. Why I was there no-one told me, or if they did, I didn't listen. I don't hear myself dribble at the best of times, so why start now? Miaow, miaow, little kitten.

The rider's message was simple. Fifty ships, more or less, three thousand men to the shore. Walking men, no horses.

"Ha, swift pickings," exclaimed Gawaine. "We'll ride down on them from the hills, no quarter."

Lilith touched the edge of her knife blade with her thumb and I saw blood, drop drip.

"Yet you not like this, lord. At the van of the second army... I dare not say it, lord."

Artur sat in his tall chair, legs stretched before the fire, his hand idly stroking a hound's head. He didn't turn, his voice didn't rise. "Just say it, tell it true, don't hide."

Drip, drop.

"At the van, sire, followed by a guard."

Drop, drip.

Artur's hand stroked the dog's head.

Drip.

"Your son, sire. Mordant, he rides with them."

Drop.

I've never heard a silence so loud. Even Krachoa was a whisper compared to this.

Drip.

Drop.

I've always said, if you're going to do a ceremony, do it proper, worth doing. Powerful things, ceremonies, for stirring up the blood and rising up the fight in men. Even now, writing this down so no-one but me can forget it, 'twas worth doing.

In the evening, the sun glimmering down and throwing a red glow on distant trees, preparations were made on the platform. Leather straps nailed to the post, to tie a man there and connect him to the earth below, all bubbling hot and steaming.

I made unto the beacon, the pyre, a run of black-powder all running along the ground to the tar drenched base of the stack. The Chinee emperor had shown me the powder and taught me how to make it, those many years ago when the dragen waked, but I could never see a use for it, 'cept pretty flames and shooting stars. But here, 'twould save a man a run with a burning branch.

Lot and de Grance, as Artur's most trusted men, took him to a tent and made him ready.

Emmelyne went with Morgayne and Elayne went with Lilith.

'Twas a ceremonial thing, so I polished my beads and knotted a string or two, and remembered a few of my lines. Serious now, I'll tell it.

Artur walked slowly across the crisp white snow, de Grance at his side and Lot too, and between them he walked. Cloaked in a long trailing fur made of wolf and stag, he walked tall to the base of the platform, then turned and gazed at the troops before him. Like him, they were all bare headed, standing in rows a hundred wide and five men deep, as silent as the snow they stood upon. Their breath showed in the air, silent and steady.

They looked on their king and commander as he mounted the steps and walked to the centre of the platform. At each corner, braziers were lit, flickering red and orange upon the snow, casting moving shadows on the faces of the men and all upon the ground.

Artur kneeled before the symbolic tree, bowing his head, reaching out to it. The land's wood stood straight and tall above his head, and

Artur touched it with his fingertips, bringing them to his lips in a kiss. Gog Magog would be so tall. I'll carve him in the grass some day, a ways away from here.

The king stood and the cloak dropped down to his feet, revealing his fine naked body, oiled and shining gold. The flames flickered on the tight, strong muscles taut on his back, and in the flickering light the half snakes shifted and writhed, coiling around restless. The thick hang of his cock rested against his thigh. The air shimmered and turned in the flame. With a crack, an ember shot from the brazier and hissed itself black in the snow.

de Grance wrapped leather straps about Artur's wrists and stretched the king's arms over his head, strapping him to the pole. He was king, bound to the tree that grew from the land, and would defend it. His body glistened, and he was king.

His sister came, dressed in black, her black feathered cloak gliding stark across the snow. She moved between each of the rows of men, looking steadily into their eyes, seeking loyalty, seeing who blinked. No man flinched, none faltered, even though they dreaded her, the Red Morgayne with her long red hair, a blood drenched woman who remembered men who blinked.

She nodded, and the energy from five-hundred wanting men flowed into her, spiralling up her spine, surging up into her blood. Morgayne stretched her arms above her head and her body quivered with the sex magick streaming, streaming, conjuring up blood from the rock and the earth. Her cloak too dropped away and she was naked, gaunt and tall, her body pale and lean under the flickering light.

She circled slowly around the platform, her arms a slow weaving dance, and Artur's cock began to thicken and move. Morgayne climbed the steps and came closer, four shadows crossing and dancing at her feet. His cock thickened and she reached her slow hand out to his body, reaching for his flesh, then darting away. She circled around him, weaving her conjure, making her spell. The power of five-hundred men surged through Morgayne the king's sister, and the king drew it In from her, their breath streaming together. The king's rod grew stronger, straining for her, her touch, her dream, her song.

"Gayne!" And for a moment she was just his sister, and he remembered running through the castle, the rustle of straw. "I'm here, Artur, it's me."

Morgayne knelt before the king and took his phallus in her two hands, pressing it up against his gut. She looked up to his face, his head drawn back in slow pleasure, his eyes closed. His quickening breath plumed in the cold air. She reached one hand up to his throat and dragged her long nails down over his chest, scratching over his nipples. Artur's gut tightened as her hand drifted down between his legs to cup his high balls.

She lowered her mouth to Artur's plum-coloured head and sucked him between her lips. Her throat moved as she swallowed, and she settled onto his cock, her hand a wondrous slowness as she made him rise and pulled a long strength up his spine. A stream of energy enveloped them both, and she conjured sex magick into his blood. Out amongst the ranks of men a virgin cried out as he came, and it was his first time.

Morgayne smiled as she heard the cry and worked Artur's cock some more, spiralling energy upward, concentrating on her task. Her hand slid between her own legs as she crouched before him and pulled slick wetness out from her core. Her brother the king thrust into her throat and she took him full in, a slow fuck to rise the magick up. Another man cried out, and her eyes blinked closed. And the flames flickered round and the smoke from the braziers spiralled lazily up to the sky.

She eased off from his cock and straightened herself before him, pressing her long thin body against his, offering her mouth with his taste to his lips. Artur tasted the dark tang of his cock, and his sister fucked into his mouth with her tongue. "Oh my brother, take this from me, and never forget."

He kissed her hard, his body swinging from his tied wrists, and she pressed her body against his and held him. Morgayne pressed the hot length of his shaft against her belly which had carried their children, their destiny, seen and unseen, all made. "Sweet fuck, we made them and cannot make them unmade." She eased her body away from his and backed away from him, a last longing look in her eyes. "Sweet brother, I'll not forget."

Morgayne's long fingers trailed through the air, slowly moving, and the air shimmered between them. His rod strained thick and hard against his gut and the tip glistened, catching a flicker of light. "Gayne, I remember...."

A low susurrus of rain fell upon the snow, light as feathers falling, a gentle hushing sound.

"Mother," Lilith whispered, as she passed by the older woman descending from the stair.

"Daughter," Morgayne whispered back. "Go to your father the king, with your love as strong as mine. We made you and cannot unmake. Remember, the goddess can't see you, just as she couldn't see me." She caressed her daughter's cheek. "But look what we made!"

Lilith climbed the stair, her hiding cloak stained with mud and leaves, clay and branches, all to hide in plain sight; here she was.

"Father, I'll ride beside you on a tall horse and hide in the earth; but first, a kiss."

She reached up from within her tangled cloak to caress his face, kissing him slowly on the lips, a daughter's kiss so many times done before, but never so slowly as this. She savoured him, tasting back the mingled taste of her mother on his tongue, her father on his lips.

"We'll ride together, my father, our horses galloping on the wind; we'll swim in cool rivers, you and me, my love."

Lilith took a step back, and for a moment she was just a woman, he was just a man; not king nor queen of the land, not fighting for a thought.

"My love," he replied. "We're ready."

She took a further step back, raising her arms above her head, her hiding cloak falling away to reveal her graceful curves, oiled like his, all golden. Her tawny blonde hair, all braided and twisted, fell wild around her body. Her inked black snakes coiled and moved around her limbs in the flickering light of the flames. Someone gasped, a man who'd not seen her close like this before, and the rain fell softly down.

Lilith went to the four sides of the platform in turn and stood still for a moment so the men could see her, tall and proud, her full breasts swaying and her nipples thick and tight. Some of these men had seen her rise from the ground and fight, and knew she had her father's courage and his passion. They would be lead by this woman to war, follow willingly and maybe die for her. Her naked splendour was their reward. The rain glistened on her skin.

She bathed in a lust thickened gaze from the men, before turning back to Artur, still suspended by the straps on his wrists. She pressed his cock, still hard from Morgayne's suck, between her belly and his, pushing up against him. She wrapped a leg around his thigh and placed his shaft against her sex, and was wet for him. She kissed him again and adored him, her father, the king.

Lilith reached for the knife in the sheath on her thigh, its blade honed sharp. She reached up and cut his bonds, and his arms went around her, all joining up the snakes in a single coil seething round them both. The flames flickered and shadows swayed, and their skin writhed and turned. The snakes turned and crawled on their skin.

353

She took the knife and ran its sharp blade over their flesh, cutting a fine trail of blood on their arms, and the snakes drank dark blood.

They held each other close for a long moment, not saying a word, wrapped in each other's bleeding arms, before going to war.

Artur strode to the front of the platform and stood tall, his king's hard cock proving his prowess, filled with energy conjured up by his women.

"Men," he shouted, his voice firm and strong. "We ride!

"Lilith, summon my armies. We move out, this night."

Lilith took a branch from the nearest brazier, its flame burning bright, and she took it to the black trail of fire-powder leading to the pyre. The first part of the powder lit, burning with a bright blue flame which shot up high, before running through the snow to the base of the huge stack of wood and tar. The flaming thread disappeared into the centre of the pile, and a moment later there was a loud explosion, as a great mound of the powder caught fire and burned.

Within the space of twenty heart-beats, the base of the pyre began to burn fiercely, the tar and pitch spitting and crackling as the fuel caught alight and flames shot higher. The heat quickly became intense, melting the snow and forcing the men to move back, shielding their faces from the furnace.

The fire quickly spread through the whole pyre, flames shooting high to the sky as the dry wood was consumed. Before long, on distant hills and high places to the west, the north and south, more fires were light, sending the message to Artur's waiting armies that the wait was over, every preparation done, it was time to march.

The king and Lilith descended from the stage and made their way to their horses, to lead their troops to war.

I was there.

When Artur the king made a fire and blood ceremony with his sister and daughter, to conjure strength for battle, then rode on to war, I was there.

The Loyal Soldier

Ulgrif had become separated from his troop during the last skirmish, when the defenders swept down the high sides of the valley, dividing the landsmen from each other; too quick on their horses, a slaughter too easy. He had crawled away, pressing his hand hard against the wound on his shoulder. Elricka might be impressed with the scar, if he made it back, if he lived. Pain throbbed fiercely, and Ulgrif felt himself drifting to the edge of sleep and back. He crawled towards a clear stream, thinking to bathe and clean his torn flesh.

He propped himself against a tree close to the brook and looked down onto the site of the skirmish. He counted nine bodies and the dark mass of a downed horse - so one of the defenders at least, walked, or was dead.

He tried to make sense of their strategy, but could see none. Nine days walk from the boats, carrying food just to eat it, walking into the heart of defenders land? Bring the enemy to the coast and kill them there; but to go to them? It made no sense. Ulgrif could count, he had that skill from back home: another five days, another five dead? This was no invasion, this was madness, a waiting death. He grinned a rictus grin; Valhal would need many carts to bring the warriors home to rest if they kept on like this. But he was alive! To keep it that way, he had no other plan.

Grimacing with pain, Ulgrif pulled the leather jerkin away from his wound. He unravelled the cords from the sleeve and inspected the gash, still bleeding. It seemed a clean cut, and he thanked a good man in a forge, making clean blades that cut well. He ran his finger down the rough iron blade of his own sword, more like an axe than a knife, and thought, "Ha, I will mangle, not cut. Some man will hurt more, today, than me." It was a small satisfaction.

He eased himself out of his clothing, bundling it at the base of the tree's trunk where the leaf litter was soft and the ground dry. He crawled towards the stream and fell into it, gasping with the shock of the cold water. The cold throbbed into his wounded shoulder, but it was a different kind of pain and slowly numbed the gash, leaving just his heartbeat pulsing steadily. Ulgrif carefully washed the cut clean, wincing from time to time. He watched his blood stream and furl into the water, and washed himself clean.

Thankful for the relief, Ulgrif lay there, his body submerged with just his head showing, resting on a rock. He closed his eyes, and felt the soft pull of the running water over his skin. After a moment, he felt tiny drops splashing on his face. Opening his eyes, he saw they were splashes of a light rain hitting the surface of the stream, playing the water up over his skin. He sat up, and felt a shadow from the sun. He looked up.

"What you, in a clear stream, yet you stream it with your blood?"

She spoke in his language. Her voice was light, not mocking but curious. She stood over him, her long braided hair a dirty blonde down to her waist. Her arms were bare, with dark tattoos coiling and spiralling on her skin, shimmering with movement and shadows. Her whole body was hidden in a long cloak, made dirty with mud and twigs and leaves weaved through it. She was tall and imperious, looking down on him with a slight smile in her eyes.

Ulgrif remembered rumours of the giant woman who rose in slaughter from the ground, rising from the dirt and rock, killing uncountable men. Was this her, was he dead?

"I bleed, lady, and clean the cut." He gestured to the valley below. "Wounded down there, by attack." He took a gamble and spoke it. "By your men, lady, I think it true."

There was a long pause as she too looked down into the valley. "Yes. My men. How many?"

"Maybe two hands, lady." Ulgrif showed her his ten fingers, with his palms towards her, no weapons hid. She nodded, and gave a small smile at the wisdom of his gesture, no weapons hidden and naked in a stream.

"You took down a horse. Did you kill it?"

"Not I, lady, but its rider has gone. He lives, I hope."

"You hope he lives? What manner of man are you, that you hope your enemy lives, to kill you tomorrow?"

"A simple fighter, lady, not wanting this." He looked around. "But loyal, lady, to my command." Ulgrif thought this woman would see lies before they were told, and truth was the easier story to keep true.

"Loyalty. Now there's a thing." The woman spoke as if to herself. "Loyal, you say? To die for?"

"Probably, lady," Ulgrif replied. "If you kill for it."

She laughed, a cold bitterness in her throat. "Oh no, I not kill loyal so quick. Treachery and betrayal, I might kill slow."

She leaned down towards Ulgrif, offering him her hand. "But you. Come, let's wrap this wound. I have food, and will share it with a loyal man."

"Starve a thief, lady?"

"Oh yes, till they rot."

Ulgrif got to his feet and stepped towards her, water trailing down his naked limbs, bright red blood from the wound still streaming.

"Stay there," she commanded, and went to a big grey horse tethered a short distance away. She unstrapped a travelling bag and placed it on the ground. She extracted a blanket. "Wrap in this for warmth, and show me your arm.

"Ah, the water cleans it well, fresh from the high hills; and washes away blood. Your shoulder will heal, you'll live to carry a sword again."

The woman tore a strip of white cloth from a roll and bandaged Ulgrif's shoulder, her fingers quick and sure. She seemed regardless of his nakedness under the blanket, but her care was intimate and her touch gentle. Ulgrif responded to her closeness, his cock thickening.

"A sword again, lady? You release me to fight this other man of yours, on a second day?"

"What use you to me otherwise? I release you, or kill you." She was matter of fact about her choices. "And I promised you food, so killing you makes no sense, does it not? Besides, if my horseless man is to kill you tomorrow, I need to keep you alive." She smiled, showing him no malice.

"You bargain strange, lady, and playful too. You let me eat and live, even though I be your enemy and wander in your land."

"Ah, but you are a loyal man, and a queen values loyalty."

"A queen? Is it true, then, what they say? You are that queen?"

"I know not what your men say, not all; but yes, I am Lilith, that queen. Tell me, soldier, do you have a name, that might remember Lilith?"

"Lady, I am Ulgrif, and will remember you this day. If I live, that is."

"Ulgrif, you say? Shall we eat, soldier Ulgrif? You can tell me about this army of yours, while we eat."

She reached for the travelling bag and found bread and cuts of meat, sliced from a pig on a spit. Berries too, that stained their lips, and Lilith wiped away a drop from his chin as he talked.

Ulgrif told her of the pretender king who came to the beach with promises. Lilith gave nothing away as she listened, just an occasional prompt, as if it were a trivial thing.

"I saw him once, lady, with a red bruise on his face that he tried to keep all hid. I did not trust him, he always looked beside a man, never looked him in the eye. My captains thought him a foolish boy, but he promised a quick way to Artur the king, so they follow."

"They follow him but mock. Is that what you say?"

"True, lady, they mock him, this would-be king. Do you know him, lady?"

"I've heard tell of him, this prince, but he is a stranger to me. No matter."

Lilith talked about other things, and the night dropped down.

"I will not light a fire, we'll stay hid." She clicked her tongue and heard a soft whinny in reply.

"Your horse, lady, won't he be seen behind the wood?"

"You see him, Ulgrif, my horse?"

He peered back to where the horse was tethered, but could see nothing there. He squinted his eyes for better focus and thought he saw a shadow, heard a hoof stamp, but he could not see a horse. The light rain continued to fall.

Lilith stood and dropped her hiding cloak. "Come, move aside your crooked shoulder, let me share the blanket. We'll sleep warm tonight, soldier, I promise."

She undid the ties and straps of her bodice and let it drop, revealing her full breasts, narrow waist and the muscled ridges of her torso. She bent to loosen her leggings, pulling them down her thighs and over her soft leather boots, then eased the boots from her feet. She was swift and methodical, neatly folding the garments before placing them in her kit bag, which she drew close and made into a pillow.

Ulgrif saw the coiling tattoo of the snakes on her skin and the thin white scars circling her arms and body, and thought the queen had made blood promises, weaving powerful bindings around herself. He wondered if she claimed his company as a queen seeking loyalty, or a woman seeking pleasure.

"Your shoulder, Ulgrif. Is it a hurting still? We be careful of it."

She gently pushed him back to the ground and straddled him, her sex resting against his shaft, her thighs against his hips. She looked down on him and he held her gaze, not looking away. Lilith took the blanket and wrapped it around her shoulders, reaching back to make sure his legs were covered, keeping him warm. She bent forward to kiss him, and slid her sex along his. She was wet for him already, but slow and gentle too.

She raised her body up and reached between her legs to take his shaft, placing his cock head to her entrance. She eased him in without a sound, without a word. Her eyes held his as she slid down around him, slowly taking his heat into her body. She closed her eyes with pleasure.

"Ahh, soldier, 'tis a nice thickness you have there, for my cunt."

She began to move on his shaft, leaning forward to place her hands on his chest. Ulgrif reached up and took a breast in his good hand, pressing the firm flesh up against her body. He never took his eyes off hers. She sighed, and they slowly began to fuck.

Lilith placed her weight over his body at first, her hands upon his chest so she could rise and fall easily on his shaft, finding the best place where her clitoris urged hard on the base of his gut, where the wet of her spreading core sank down. Then, when he filled her, she straightened her back and took him harder, clenching her cunt around him like a fist, grinding down so he couldn't move, he couldn't thrust. Lilith gripped him, made him hers, her silent black eyes daring him to look away.

He matched her and didn't look away, his hand gripping her breast, twisting her flesh; then pulling and tugging on her nipple, trying to get her to drop forward again to his mouth. But she wouldn't be bent. Lilith rode him like she rode her horse and arched her back, her breast escaping his grasp. She took her own breasts into her hands and stretched her throat, looking up with closed eyes to the branches above. She shuddered, a cord thickening on her neck, and a low cry like a distant bird escaped her throat.

"Still, don't move, I'll...."

Lilith gripped a breast with one hand and with the other splayed the top of her sex, frigging herself to her pleasure with her fingers. As she came she let cry a high scream like a hawk. Goose-bumps shivered Ulgrif's arms. He dared not move, and felt her spasms on his cock as her orgasm rocked over her. All the while he looked up at Lilith, and when she finally looked down at him he saw a wonderful softness in her eyes, half-swooning, a woman taking her pleasure.

He was a man still hard, but hers for her bidding. Sitting over him, her body still tight, her muscles still taut, Lilith's eyes widened, as if for the first time she realised there was a heat deep inside her, another fuck, a man with hot blood in his veins.

Just a woman now, Lilith leaned forward to kiss him, to cradle his head in her hands. With his good arm Ulgrif embraced her, and again they began to move. Slowly this time, her wet cunt sliding on his length, they found a rhythm. They breathed into each other, and the rich aroma of her arousal rose up. She placed her arm under his neck, turning her body slightly so she wouldn't bump his shoulder, and traced patterns on his cheeks and jaw with her fingertip, her eyes wide open with a wonder, as if it was a first time.

She smiled, and Ulgrif melted, she was so tender.

"No queen then, lady, tonight?"

She laughed. "No queen, just a woman with her man, keeping warm."

Ulgrif smiled, he was still hers but didn't mind that; and slow became fast, and many heartbeats later he exploded his pleasure deep inside her, and she took hers again with a cry, resting her head on his shoulder after she came. They rolled onto their sides, Ulgrif still inside her, held close.

A short while later the gentle rain stopped, and Lilith and her soldier slept, battle worn and tired, but no fight between them, just a waiting place.

In the morning, they ate. When done, Lilith went to her horse, but before mounting she returned to him. She stood before him, face to face, and looked into his eyes. "Take this token, soldier, it give you free pass." She gave him a coin, her profile on its face.

"Go down to the valley, place all the bodies together. Make a burying place under rocks for the men and make a fire for the horse." She was queen now, commanding, and he a loyal man. "Go north when you're done, Ulgrif, then east to the sea. Your battle here is done, not death."

"You, lady? Where you?"

"West, soldier. My battle is yet to come, but I feel it, riding beside me." She turned from him and mounted her horse. "Remember Lilith, a good soldier's woman."

Ulgrif watched her as she rode slowly down the valley, her horse picking its careful way on the stony path. She didn't look back, but Ulgrif didn't expect her to. She rode out of sight, and a short while later the loyal soldier made his own way to the valley floor and found flat ground for a burying place.

A day later, Ulgrif struck north, leaving a high cairn to mark the skirmish and its dead. As he walked, he turned the coin in his pocket, feeling the outline of his queen's head under his fingers.

The Mist on the Lake

A dusting of light snow covered the tracks and pathways leading to a high, clear place. Artur had set a large camp on the heights of Badon and fed a thousand men. To the west and south lay his kingdom's heart, and he swore this heart would never be taken.

His armies had slowly drawn the invaders west, taking advantage of the long walk from their boats by harassing the men who scouted ahead. Artur's horses would thunder down from the peaks and ridges, slaughter the small bands of men and disappear like ghosts. Rumours of spirits abounded, and of Lilith the queen riding alone, her spying eyes hidden in rocks and trees, rising up.

She brought intelligence of the pretender prince, her brother Mordant. "They follow him, Father, but trust him not, your traitor son." She spat, and spoke no more of him, her sibling filth.

Artur waited, and his men waited too, all ready. Once again, the eastern sky flickered and glowed with the signal fires, lit quicker now and burning every night. Slowly, Artur put together a map of the attack and planned his defences, and a great encirclement.

"'Twill end soon, Lilith, and we shall be remembered, in victory or in loss."

"Never loss, Father, never a loss."

Artur looked upon his daughter and saw her burning heart still fierce, where his was tired but smouldering still.

"It will be what it be, Lilith. We can do no more than that." He looked up from the map drawn on vellum. "Come, let's go to the look, to see their approach down the valley."

They went to a high ridge to the north-east of the camp where they looked out over a long valley, a small river running along its spine, and a well-ridden path. Artur knew the way well, as it was one of the main roads east, one his men regularly travelled. Lilith knew the high ridges better, and rode where the ancient walkers walked.

"Look there," she said, pointing to the head of the valley. The morning light cast long shadows, and in the far distance a mass of small shapes could be seen moving slowly, their blackness in lines before them on the stark snow.

"They come upon us, on a new day, as the sun rises."

Artur was silent, studying the deployment and pondering how to break it. As the light brightened and cleared the distant mist, he saw how a single figure rode ahead on a horse, followed by a group of perhaps a dozen walking men, fifty paces back. Beyond them were the untidy ranks of men, impossible to count yet, but walking on. The army approached in silence, still too far off for any sound to carry, but advancing down the valley at a steady pace.

"I shall ride quick along the ridge, Father, to see to the end of them."

"Out of arrows' throw, Lilith, stay on the heights."

"I am your Lilith. You think I ever be seen when I not want?"

He laughed. "I forget your ways, my love. Of course, not seen."

She looked at him and teased. "You forget, my aged father? I shall make you a cosseting rug and sit you by the fire with Maerlyn and his dice, and bring you hot mead and bread."

She was affectionate, eyes bright with her love for him. She kissed him on the lips, and walked back to the camp for her horse.

Artur studied the valley longer, and from the huddled shape of him, knew that the single rider was his son, Mordant, come to claim his pretender's crown. "It's not yours to have," he said to himself, and he too went back to the camp.

"Rednock, my horse. I ride to parley."

By mid-morning all was clear. The mass of the heathen invaders filled the valley, perhaps two thousand, perhaps somewhat less. Halted now, small fires could be seen burning amongst the troops for food and warmth. Up on Badon Mount, Artur's army likewise sat waiting for command, and the men counted the opposite numbers of men. Peace would be better.

A horn called, and Artur rode slowly down from the lookout and made for the valley below. He was clad in his regal cloak of wolf and stag, Scalibet his blade sheathed at his waist. He rode in clear sight, his head held high. The only sound was the clop of his horse's hooves as they broke the thin snow and left a trail behind him. The ranks of men were silent on both sides. Eagles flew above the ridges and rabbits ran, but other than the birds and their prey, all was still.

Artur rode on until he found a clear space with crisp white snow all around him, where he stopped. The freeze of his breath could be

368

seen in the air, slow and steady. His horse's breath was like a plume, and it too was steady and slow.

Mordant spurred on his own horse and rode to the clear space, his horse prancing, its hooves high. He circled around Artur twice at a distance, as if to impress or to gather courage, the watchers could not tell. His frozen breath came quick, and the horse was skittish. It reared onto its back legs once, and Mordant struggled to control it, nearly falling.

Artur remained motionless the while, not even turning his head.

The commanders of the invading men, amused at Mordant's pretences, studied the king before them. They leaned their heads together in whispers, and made their measure of him.

Mordant finally controlled his horse and rode to face Artur, the plumes of his breath still quick. The slush beneath him was shuffled and brown, all messy. Beneath Artur's horse the snow was crisp and white, the long trail leading back to the heart of his land measured out by the even pace of his horse, in sure and steady steps.

They spoke, but were too far away to be heard. Mordant could be seen gesturing wildly in supplication or anger, the watchers could not say.

Artur touched the pommel of Scalibet still sheathed and shook his head. He spurred his horse and turned his back on his son. He slowly rode back the way he came, following his own trail in the snow, a solitary figure alone in the valley. The watching men were silent, the huddled command stood still, and waited for Mordant to respond.

Mordant circled the clear space once, before pulling up his horse. He unslung a bow from his side and reached behind his shoulder for an arrow from the quiver, stringing it quickly. He raised the bow and took aim at Artur's back.

"Artur, turn now and face me," he cried out, but his voice quivered and cracked. "I be king in your place!"

But Artur did not turn. He rode straight on.

Mordant circled his horse once more, then raised and lowered the bow at his father's back, as if undecided. Finally he stopped and took deliberate aim. "Father, stop!" he cried out.

Artur did not stop, he simply rode on.

The arrow, when it flew, flew fast, and hit Artur's back high up, piercing a lung. He lurched forward but did not fall, coughing red blood which spattered bright onto the stark white snow. Some of the men later swore they saw him spur his big horse on, for it lurched forward into a gallop and he did not fall.

High above the valley, from the ridge, there was a single high scream of agony like a calling hawk, a chilling shriek. A far thunder of hooves was heard a moment later as Lilith followed her father, riding like the wind to be with him, just like she rode as a child.

Down in the valley, the soldiers of the invading army let loose a low hiss and turned their backs on Mordant. Their commanders turned too, and their captain shouted, "Retreat!

"Betraying scum, false prince. We will not follow a mouse who'll shoot a man's back, and that man his father. We are gone from this place."

Mordant circled, uncertain, then he too followed Artur, trailing the red blood on the stark white snow.

Mordant reached the top of a ridge, still following the red trail of blood and the marks of the horse ahead of him. He looked down a long grassed slope to a wide lake below, its far shore veiled in mist, unseeable. Part way down the slope he could see a spreading patch of bright red blood against the snow and Artur's body still and bleeding, sprawled beside a stream. His horse stood by, its big head down low, nuzzling the fallen man.

The princeling dismounted and approached his father, tentative now, afraid of the blood.

"What have I done, Father?" He spoke the words low, fearing an answer.

Arthur coughed, spitting more blood. "You missed my heart, foolish boy. Couldn't you even do that?"

He mocked his son. Mordant saw no forgiveness in his father's eyes and knew himself cursed till the end of his days.

"You never loved me, Father. I was always alone. It was always Lilith, never me."

"Don't pity yourself, boy. You made your choices, Lilith hers." He coughed again, and moaned with pain.

Mordant saw the arrow remained in his father's body, its shaft snapped in the fall from the horse. "What can I do?"

"Redeem yourself, boy? Return my sword to its maker." Artur choked, and spat blood once more. "Take Scalibet to the lake and cast it to the waters."

He struggled to release the sword from its sheath, but finally did so, grunting with pain.

Mordant took it, turning it over in its hands, seeing the carefully crafted blade, the inlaid jewels on the haft. I could still be king, with this sword. He looked down on his father, and was not redeemed. "I will take the sword, Father, and cast it to the waters."

He walked off, going down to the water's edge where he stood for a long while before hiding the sword under bushes. He would collect it later, after Artur had died, go to Camlann and be crowned rightful king.

He returned to his father. 'Tis done. I went to the water's edge and threw Scalibet to the centre of the lake."

"What did you see?" Arthur's voice was fading now, but he wanted an answer.

"Nothing, Father. Just ripples, where the sword hit the water and sank."

"Nothing?" Artur looked up to his son. "You lie, Mordant. You did not throw the sword." He racked his body with a shuddering breath, full of pain. "Go back. Throw the sword, and tell me that you did."

So Mordant returned to the water's edge and stood there, considering his father's request and his own ambition. Again he disobeyed.

"Nothing, Father. A wide spread of ripples, nothing more."

"You kill me, Mordant, and you lie once and that is enough; yet you lie twice and wonder why I don't trust my own son?" Artur looked at him, and Mordant saw sadness in those grey eyes, and finally understood redemption.

"I am sorry, Father. I will do what you want of me."

He returned once more to the lake, and as he did so a thin veil of rain began to fall, clamping down distance and reducing it to grey. Mordant recovered the sword Scalibet from the bushes where he hid it, and proceeded right to the edge of the lake.

He could not guess what Artur expected him to see, for his father had given him no clues. But he finally understood this third time he must cast the sword away, and with it his ambition and his future, and be cursed for striking his father down.

So he swung the weapon about his head three times and released it towards the centre of the lake, right into the middle of the darkest mist. As soon as the sword left his hands the mist parted, and from it gliding quick came a boat, moving fast upon the water, no sail and no oars, but fast moving on the water. In the centre of the boat stood Nymue, come to take her dagger back, that she had made so long ago. She raised her hand and caught Scalibet, and held it high.

In a strong voice she cried out, "Who so carries this sword, shall be the rightful king of Britten, and shall be the future king. Hail Artur, King."

She pointed at Mordant, "Go, bring the king down to the lake and place him in the boat. Hasten, boy, before he dies."

Shaking in fear from what he'd seen, Mordant stumbled back to where Artur lay. The king's breathing was shallow now, barely raising his chest, but he gasped, "What did you see?"

"A boat, Father, and the lady of the lake who caught the sword."

"Ah, your truth at last, my son, you tell the truth." Artur's head fell back, and his breath became more shallow than before, gasping in the cold air, death rattling in his throat.

A squall of rain blew over them, and fierce ripples spread upon the stream. Suddenly, rising up from the fast flowing water, her body sheened blue from the cold, stood Lilith, tall and proud and the water streaming from her limbs, hatred in her eyes.

"What have you done, scum my brother, killed a man?" She rose before him, full naked in her fury. "Killed my father before my eyes? You will die slowly for this, brother, I swear it. I will kill you myself, full slowly, and you'll plead me to make it quick.

"Take up our father's body, brother mine unbeloved," she said, venom in her voice, dark fury in her eyes. "Carry him down to the boat, lay him to rest." She stood before Mordant. "I'll kill you then, don't doubt it." She took a step forward, ice shards streaming from her body. "Filth. Do it!"

Mordant feared his sister's wrath more than his father's blood, and obeyed her. He knelt before his father's still body, lifting him into his arms. He struggled to his feet with the weight of his father's death, and staggered down towards the shore. Lilith followed, tears frozen ice on her cheeks, her body blue and black and her snakes

374

coiled all around. She walked after her stumbling brother, and saw his quivering back.

By the shore the boat lay close, Nymue at its stern, by the steering oar.

"Place the king in the boat, Mordant. I take him now, to Avelynn where he will rest." Nymue paused, then spoke again to Mordant. "I saw part of this streaming back: the blood on the snow. But I never knew it was Artur that you killed, I never knew it was this."

Nymue beckoned to Lilith. "Come, girl, I see you now. But I'll turn and you'll go. I cannot see what you do."

Lilith came forward into the water, grief in her eyes but her pride not broken. She bent over her father's body in the boat, and for the last time, coiled the snakes on her arms with his. She closed his eyes of the brightest blue and kissed him on the lips.

"Sleep well, my father. I'll ride on the wind beside you, never fall."

Lilith's blue eyes were sightless through her tears, which dropped on his cheeks like rain, like blood. She kissed him again on the lips and on his closed eyes.

"Take my father, Nym Nymue, and wash him in clear water. Take him to sleep in a safe place."

"Your wish, Lilith, is mine to be done."

Lilith stepped back from the boat and it immediately began to glide and turn on the water, smooth ripples streaming backwards. It silently moved into the mist and was gone.

The only sound was a soft lap of waves on the shore, rushes brushing together, and the harsh sound of Mordant's ragged breathing.

Lilith turned to her brother, her hand hidden behind her back. "Come, brother, let's talk." She stepped forward out of the water and walked up to him, her nakedness a deliberate provocation.

"What, brother, dare you not look? I know the weight of your eyes upon me, I always felt your look, always knew you were there, a hiding in the dark, following me."

She went closer to him. "Come, sweet brother mine, you always wanted a kiss."

She tenderly reached for the blaze on his cheek, the king's mark made there, raging dark. "Oh my brother, I slept with you nine months, was it never enough?"

Mordant startled back, dread in his eyes, all colour drained from his face but the blaze. Lilith stepped right up to him, her breasts against his chest, and put her arm around him, her grim strength holding him close.

"Oh, my brother, taste my lips." She kissed him hard on the lips, her tongue thrusting between them, fucking into his mouth. "My lips, brother, taste my lips. Taste this."

And with her other hand she plunged her killing knife deep into Mordant's belly, upwards to pierce his lungs, downwards to rupture his gut, left and right to spill his flesh and blood all steaming on the ground.

Mordant's eyes opened wide with adrenalin shock, and he looked down in wonder at what his sister had done. His guts fell to the white snow, staining it pink and red and brown in a spreading circle around him. He fell to his knees for a moment and looked up at Lilith in disbelief. "What..."

Lilith stepped back as Mordant's body fell forward into its own filth, looking down on him as she might look at a gutted fish by a fisherman's basket. She prodded at him with her foot to make sure. She knelt and made one swift cut, then weighted his body with stones, and it sank slow swaying to the bottom of the lake.

She washed herself clean in the cold water, and called her horse down to her. She tied the bridle of her father's horse to the pommel of her saddle, and so too the bridle of her brother's horse to her father's saddle. She sheathed her sharp knife and dressed herself in her hiding cloak.

Lilith rode to Camlann, three horses all in a line.

Mordant looked down from a high pole with his sightless eyes and saw nothing at all.

Epilogue - The Old Crooked Tree

I am here.

I was old before this story began, I am ancient now at its end, but if I don't tell it, who will?

As it turns out, priests and pretenders, sycophants and Welshmen, they'll all have a go. They queue at the door.

But no-one can forget truth as easily as me and make lies up to compensate, painting pretty tales on parchment pages with the edges curled up. It's the rain makes them do it, or the tears. I can never tell which is which, they all seem to drop, especially when the wind blows this old crooked tree and the shutters at the windows bang open, snap shut, rattle rattle, drip drop.

Well.

Lilith came back to Camlann with her brother's head on a pole, and I surmised that circumstances might have been better. She told me, tears ravaging her beautiful face, of Mordant's final betrayal of their father, my beloved friend, with his blood spilled red on the snow.

I washed my hands for hours, knowing I'd birthed the sod, and it was only when Lilith took my hands in hers and said, "But Maerlyn, you held me too with those hands," that I stopped.

Nymue came and said, "I took him to Avelynn and laid him to rest in a cave, still sleeping."

She wouldn't tell us where he was hid, of course, even though Lilith asked.

"It would break your heart trying to get there, girl, you mustn't know."

The girl didn't really want to know, but I think she walked the shores of many lakes and walked many high hills, a looking.

I knew better than to ask, but I suspect Nymue told Morgayne his sister, and between them they sealed the cave up.

Sweet Miryamme never properly understood what happened to Artur, the poor child, so we took her to the Isle of Glas in a wagon, and gave her to the Mothers to care. Later, when she was older and her golden hair turned grey, I found that the Sisters of Ursula were good women of Christ and an acceptable version of that foolishness, and the dear little queen went to their house with her doll and her lovely blue eyes. She was calmer by then and wasn't frightened so much, and only walked in her sleep once a year.

Young Lancilet, he too grew grey after many years gone mad in a forest, wandering about like a lunatic when the moon rises - which I do so very much better - and in time he found his way to Miryamme's window at her nunnery and they let him in. I don't know if he ever fitted the little queen's front passage, but a back door is almost the same, if you close your eyes and use imagination, and your hands around the front.

Well, well.

Young Elayne got the biggest belly from her rut with Lancilet, all confused by faces and his dreams of Miryamme, and stories told by the spineless fool. She counted nine months, and almost to the minute, popped out a boy, whom she named Galahad.

He was a bright and inquisitive lad, given to ponies early on. When he was an appropriate age he went a wandering, searching for quails. Or grails. I never could hear it clearly.

His tale might be worth a tell, along with fishers and virgins all vestal, if only I could bear talking about Christian chapels and chalices. Something about thorns, too, or is it roses? Some plant which popped up by a spring down Glaston way, grow, grow. I'll talk to Brother Joseph, he might remember some of it, and if he doesn't, I can make up all of the rest.

Emmelyne and Rednock converted the stables into a drinking house, and hung a sign with horses' heads upon it. Emmy remembered my birthdays regularly and indulged me in them pleasantly - that might be why I'm older than I look. So many birthdays in one year, I quite forget to count them.

But then the other two came back and said, "Don't encourage him, Em, we'll look after him now."

Well, well, well.

They did, and they do.

It's a big oak they've got me in, hollowed out and all high up, and oh what a view! There's Nymue to the left of me with her long white hair, and Morgayne to the right, all grey now, but still she moves so

380

slow, her fingers on my arm all teasing. My ankle only itches on cold nights, but it's snowing outside. It's a gentle rub, to remind me.

They've made a curious truce, these two, as if the making of Artur was a necessary thing to go so wrong, but the Goddess made them do what they did, and who were they, but to try?

I'm in the middle between them, and don't want to be anywhere else.

Sometimes Lilith comes to visit, and when she does, I try not to look into her eyes. Because when she looks at me I see her father's eyes all blue, and it all comes thundering back. And I remember every moment, everything, and my old heart creaks and one day might break.

Ah there, see, it rains outside, and I can't see any more, because I weep.

I am here, and cannot forget.

About the Author

A.A. Cain is an author of erotic tales living somewhere in suburban Australia. His work has been described as, "almost poetic; stories told by a crackling fire on a cold winter night, with a smooth whiskey in hand, listeners curled at your feet."

Cain's stories move from the floating world of city cafés and fashionable galleries, with contemporary men and women finding pleasure in familiar places, through to mysterious, mythical worlds populated with angels and astronauts, mermaids and men, and always, dark, seductive women.